W9-BLN-804

"24 has changed the face of television—one hour, one minute, one second at a time. . . . A masterpiece."

—AMERICAN FILM INSTITUTE

....

At the thrilling and devastating conclusion of 24 season 8, federal agent Jack Bauer is framed and declared a fugitive of the United States.

Four years later, the ticking clock starts again as Jack Bauer resurfaces—in London.

Now, find out what happened after the clock wound down four years ago.

24
DEADLINE

JAMES SWALLOW

A TOM DOHERTY ASSOCIATES BOOK • NEW YORK

NOTE: If you purchased this book without a cover, you should be aware that this book is stolen property. It was reported as "unsold and destroyed" to the publisher, and neither the author nor the publisher has received any payment for this "stripped book."

This is a work of fiction. All of the characters, organizations, and events portrayed in this novel are either products of the author's imagination or are used fictitiously.

24: DEADLINE

24 TM & © 2014 Twentieth Century Fox Film Corporation. All Rights Reserved.

A Forge Book
Published by Tom Doherty Associates, LLC
175 Fifth Avenue
New York, NY 10010

www.tor-forge.com

Forge® is a registered trademark of Tom Doherty Associates, LLC.

ISBN 978-0-7653-7791-3

Forge books may be purchased for educational, business, or promotional use. For information on bulk purchases, please contact the Macmillan Corporate and Premium Sales Department at 1-800-221-7945, extension 5442, or write to specialmarkets@macmillan.com.

First Edition: August 2014
First Mass Market Edition: August 2015

Printed in the United States of America

0 9 8 7 6 5 4 3 2 1

ACKNOWLEDGMENTS

Thanks to Melissa Frain, Amy Saxon, and Marco Palmieri at Tor Books for giving me the opportunity to tell this lost story from Jack Bauer's turbulent narrative; to Joshua Izzo and Katie Caswell at Fox for their timely assistance; to Evan Katz and Manny Coto for sparing me some time from their busy schedule writing *24: Live Another Day* to answer my questions; Roberto Suro, and the dedicated fans at the *24 Wiki* and *24 Spoilers* for some invaluable research data; also, not forgetting a tip of the hat to my old mate Keith Topping for leading the charge with *A Day in the Life,* and m'colleagues Dayton Ward and David Mack, because they both get how cool this is. And finally, to my very own femme fatale: the lovely Mandy Mills, who is always there for me when the clock is running.

24: DEADLINE

PROLOGUE

He was barely through the door when they came at him.

Two men, one from either side, bolting out from behind the cover of the supply containers and storage racks. In the dimness of the basement, he couldn't make out much detail, just an impression of muscle mass and speed before the blows were raining down on him.

A hard strike from a stubby baton cracked over his forearm and the force of it set his nerves alight. He dropped his gun, the weapon falling from his numbed fingers, and grunted with the pain. His other arm came up to parry a haymaker punch from the second assailant.

Turning in place before either man could lay their hands on him again, he leaned in with a follow-through from the parry and planted his elbow in the chest of the man coming from the left. He felt a rib snap under the impact and heard the assailant gasp in agony.

The room was lit by an industrial lamp, stark white light spilling out from behind an oval cage, casting the space around them with deep shadows. It was more than enough for him to fight with.

Keeping up the momentum, he let the man with the busted rib stagger back and pressed his attack on the one with the baton, who swung it up high for a second blow. Turning his emptied hand into a talon, he shot forward and grabbed at the first attacker's throat, hitting hard enough to blow the breath out of the man's chest. Stumbling, the two of them fell into the pool of light from the overhead bulb, and he kept up the pressure, punching over and over—short, stabbing strikes that landed in the softer tissues of the man's throat.

He was aware of movement behind him. The one with the cracked rib was coming back into the fray, and he turned to put up a defense—but he was slow. *Too slow*.

All the fatigue of the past hours, all the endless strain, it was blunting his edge, and little by little, it robbed him of the precious seconds he needed.

Too slow. The other assailant kicked him hard in the back of the knee and his leg folded underneath him with a jolt of pain. He stumbled and went down toward the dusty concrete floor, palms smacking the ground as he arrested his fall.

He heard someone else call out, but the words were muffled and indistinct, the sound distorted through a fog left behind by the punches he'd taken to the head. Only the tone was clear—a command, sharp and hard. Someone angry about him, somebody who wanted him dealt with in short order.

A tiny flash of blue lightning glittered in the hand of one of the men, and before he could deflect it, the metal contacts of a Taser pressed into his chest and the device discharged.

Thousands of volts of electricity surged through his flesh and he howled. His muscles locked rigid, and for long, agonizing seconds it felt as if he had been dipped in fire. Then he was on his back, shivering with the aftershock. He smelled the faint odors of burnt cotton and seared meat.

They dragged him up by his elbows and dumped him in a careworn plastic chair. He lay there like a puppet with its strings severed, panting, trying to gather himself.

The man he had hit in the throat eyed him murderously, wheezing and coughing out blood, rubbing at his neck. The other assailant stooped to gather up his pistol from where it had fallen, moving with exaggerated slowness thanks to his new injury.

He became aware of others in the room. A larger, tanned man with a boxer's craggy face and thinning white hair stood at the edge of the shadows, hands crossed in front of him with the long shape of a silenced pistol in his grip. Another figure—this one less distinct—was farther out from the pool of light, framed by the glow of a cell phone display. A woman, he realized, the cold blue of the telephone screen casting the planes of her face like an ice sculpture.

"Secure him," said the big man, gesturing with the gun. The two thugs came in and used zip-ties to tether his wrists to the arms of the plastic chair.

He shifted slightly in the seat, thinking about angles of attack. It came to him automatically, instinctively. He began to build a plan about getting the man's pistol, evaluating who was the greatest threat in the room, deciding which of them he would kill first.

"It amazes me you are still alive." The big man spoke directly to him for the first time. There was a distinctive Eastern European accent beneath the words; Georgian, most likely. "You should be dead a dozen times over."

He gave a weary nod. "It's been said." Carefully, he tested the play in the zip-ties. There was a small degree of freedom there, but not much.

"No longer," said the Georgian. "Today, the clock runs out for you." He cocked his head, examining his new prisoner as if considering a puzzle of some kind. "I know all about you. You have made so very many enemies, my friend. I wonder how many men will sleep sounder tonight, after this is done?"

He said nothing, waiting for the right moment.

The other man went on, disappointed that he hadn't gotten the response he wanted. "Yes. It will be a sort of kindness, I think. Look at you. Like a war dog, long in the tooth and too far off your leash to be controlled. Your own people want you dead! I do them a favor."

"So *do* it," he growled. "And be on your way."

The big man glanced at one of others, who produced a cell phone of his own and held it up, framing the two of them with the device's tiny camera.

The gun rose and dull light glittered off the black barrel of the silencer. "Jack Bauer . . ." The Georgian said the name like it was a curse, and his finger tightened on the trigger. "Your time is up."

24 HOURS EARLIER

01

Chet Reagan emerged from the staff room, pulling the top of his scrubs straight and working to stifle a yawn. As he crossed to the front desk, he noted that the waiting room was unusually empty for a weekday. Typically, the evening shift was when things started to get busy at the clinic. People coming off a hard workday would filter into the drop-in medical center, maybe looking for an excuse not to have to go back in the office tomorrow—those, or the folks who couldn't get time off to make a doctor's appointment in the a.m.

Not tonight, though. He saw a couple of people waiting their turn, East Village trendy types rather than the usual locals who lived in the clinic's Lower East Side neighborhood. They looked a little out of their element, and he amused himself wondering what they had wrong with them. A little STD action, maybe? Something they didn't want their regular doctor to know about? He suppressed a grin. The clinic got a lot of that sort of trade.

As he approached the desk, he saw Lindee on duty and he couldn't help but scowl as she made a face and tapped her wristwatch with a long, manicured finger. Chet's gaze flicked up to the TV screen on the waiting room wall, forever tuned to CNB's main news feed, and he saw the time stamp in the corner. *Five o'clock.* That was the time his shift started and that was the time he was here. Sure, he knew full well that their supervisor liked the medical technicians to be in ten, even twenty minutes early, but Chet wasn't about to spend any more of his day at the clinic than he had to. They didn't pay him enough to go above and beyond.

"What?" he asked Lindee. "I'm not late."

"Not early, either," she retorted. "You're lucky there's not a rush on. Could be, though, any second. Did you get the text?" Her eyes narrowed, her dark, oval face tightening in an expression of annoyance.

"No." His phone battery had died the night before and he had neglected to recharge it. "Look, I got in on time, didn't I? No thanks to the cops, though. Damn police are all over the place today . . ."

"The text message," Lindee insisted. "City Hall put all the hospitals and clinics on alert . . ." She trailed off. "Have you, like, been in a cave for the last day? Haven't you seen the news?"

"No," he repeated. "What, did someone famous die?" Chet scowled. One of the most inconvenient things about living and working in Manhattan was that it was also home to foreign dignitaries, embassies and the United Nations—and whenever they were in town in force, every ordinary New Yorker had to deal with the disruption their presence caused. Chet recalled something he had seen in the papers about a big political deal going on with people from one of those Arab countries, but he was disinterested in the details. "I never watch the news," he said. "It's a damn cartoon, is what it is."

Lindee rolled her eyes. She'd had this conversation with Reagan more than once before and long since grown tired of it. Instead, she picked up the remote control for the TV and aimed it at the screen, thumbing the volume control. "Well, you might wanna pay attention to this part."

Chet looked back at the screen as the voice of CNB's anchorwoman grew louder. Over the shoulder of the blond-haired announcer were inset images of the UN building and then a roll of footage showing President Allison Taylor standing before a lectern. "I never voted for her." Chet sniffed.

"*. . . as circumstances continue to be fluid,*" the anchor was saying. "*What CNB can confirm at this time is that President Taylor, in a shock announcement to the world press, has walked out of the peace treaty talks between the United States, the Russian Federation and the Islamic Republic of Kamistan. The president spoke of a conspiracy behind the treaty and of criminal activity that she herself has played a role in. The White House has promised that a full formal statement is imminent, but on a day where rumors abound regarding possible terrorist activity in New York City, a day that has also seen the assassination of IRK leader Omar Hassan on American soil, we can only guess at what revelations the next hours will bring.*"

"Huh," said Chet, taking it in. "So a politician lied about something. What a surprise."

Lindee glared at him. "Don't you get it? This is a big deal! People will get angry . . . People could get hurt!"

But Chet was already walking away. "This is the kinda crap that happens when we mess around with other countries. Wouldn't be anything if those Kami-whatever guys stayed at home, yeah?" He gathered up a clipboard and threaded his way down the corridor toward the examination rooms at the rear of the building. The first job he was going to do this shift was the inventory for rooms ten and eleven—and if he took his time about it, Chet knew he'd be able to stay off his supervisor's radar for at least a couple of hours.

He was two steps into examination room ten when he realized the light switch wasn't working. Chet flipped it up and down twice and grimaced, but in the next second his shoe crunched on a piece of broken glass and he realized that the fluorescent tube overhead had been deliberately smashed. Cold air touched his face and he saw the wired-glass window across the room was open, letting in the breeze.

Lit only by the fading day, the room was all shades of gloomy, and Chet's heart leapt into his mouth as he belatedly sensed the presence of someone else in there with him.

A man in a torn, slate-colored sweatshirt emerged from behind a privacy curtain near the examination bed, and in one hand he held the metallic shape of a gun.

Chet's gut tightened and he felt a cold sweat break out on his neck. "Oh shit." He threw up his hands. "Hey. Hey, wait. Don't shoot me, okay? I . . . I have a family. Just . . . Look, take whatever you want, okay? I won't stop you." They had warned him about this kind of thing when he took the job at the clinic. Strung-out junkies or street criminals looking to make a fast buck by robbing walk-in clinics of painkillers or whatever drugs they could sell.

"Lock the door," said the man with the gun.

"What?"

"Lock it." The second time he spoke, Chet found himself obeying without hesitation. Hands shaking, he turned the latch and then retreated into a corner, eyes darting around the room in search of some means of escape. There was only the open window, and the gunman was between him and it.

The guy looked like he had been in an argument with a Mack truck and come off worse. He sported cuts on his forehead and chin, and through tears in the sweatshirt Chet could see other wounds and contusions of varying seriousness.

"You're going to help me," said the gunman. He eyed the technician's name badge. "*Chet*. I need to clean up. I need fresh dressings. Medicine."

"Are you going to kill me?" Questions fell from Chet's lips before he was even aware of them forming in his thoughts. "That thing on the news, is that you? Are you . . . a terrorist?"

"No." The gunman let the barrel of the pistol drop until it was aimed at a point somewhere near Chet's right kneecap. "But what I am is a very good shot. And I will cripple you if you try anything stupid, understand?"

"Yes." It was the most emphatic answer Chet had ever given for anything.

"Good." The man switched on a bedside lamp before picking up a scalpel and using it to slice open the sweat-shirt, shrugging it off to reveal his bare chest beneath.

Chet's breath caught in his throat as he glimpsed the patchwork of scars across the gunman's torso. He knew the healed pucker marks of bullet wounds when he saw them, and the severe lines of stabbings and old knife cuts. But there were other blemishes there, things he couldn't even begin to guess at. The man's flesh was a map of violence done and violence survived. The most recent was a field dressing over a grazing gunshot, and the cloth patch taped over the wound was black-brown and soaked through. Gingerly, Chet peeled the old bandage away and set to work applying a new one.

• • •

Jack Bauer watched as the technician did as he was told. The man's hands were shaking, but that was to be expected.

"You said you've got a family." The man tensed when Jack spoke.

"Yes?" he said, his voice thick with fear.

"Tell me about them."

Chet swallowed hard. "A . . . A son. Petey. He's six. Wife. Jane."

"Here, in New York?"

"Right. Yes."

Jack weighed the stolen Sig Sauer pistol in his hand. "You should take them out of town for a few days. Get away." He couldn't stop himself from seeing Kim's face in his mind's eye, his daughter smiling up at him and promising him that things were going to be better for them. At this moment, Jack wanted that to be true more than anything in the world.

But fate had a habit of getting in the way of what Jack Bauer wanted, of dragging him into one bloody mess after another. He looked at the man before him, this ordinary guy with his ordinary job and his ordinary life, and for a split second Jack *hated* him for it.

Chet must have seen that flash of fury in his eyes, because he backed away, the color draining from his face. "Wh-what?"

Jack shook off the moment. "Keep working." The impulse had faded as quickly as it had come, but the burn of it lingered. On some level, Jack resented the fact that whatever chance at a normal life he might have had was long gone. He could feel the weight of it all pressing down on him, not just the hours of fighting and running and battling to stay alive, but the ache in his soul. The consequence of all the choices he had made and the things he had done.

Once upon a time he had been a soldier for his nation, for an ideal that he believed was right and good. Somewhere along the line, that loyalty had blurred and slipped away. He turned his gaze inward and found a question waiting there: *What are you going to fight for now, Jack?*

"I have family," he said in a low mutter. "They're all I have."

"Are they . . . here?"

Jack didn't answer. Anything he said to this man would eventually end up in the hands of the people who were hunting him. "I'm getting out," he said after a moment. "Far from here. *Hong Kong.*" It was the first place he thought of, and a good enough lie to leave behind him.

Chet paused, the bandage over the gunshot wound replaced and the other cuts dressed as well as they could be. He turned, pointing toward one of the medicine cabinets. "Look, I can . . ."

"No need." Jack slipped off the examination bed and snaked his hands around the medical technician's neck before he could stop him. Drawing his grip tight, he pulled Chet into a sleeper hold and regarded the man as he gasped and struggled. "Don't fight it."

In a couple of seconds, the technician went limp and Jack settled him gently to the floor. He pulled Chet's keys from the loop on his belt and plundered the cabinets for doses of antibiotics and painkillers. The other man was narrower across the chest than Jack, but the shirt he wore beneath the scrubs was a passable fit. He helped himself to what little cash the other man had on him and slipped away, back through the window he had used to gain access.

Outside, clouds were drawing in and the sun had already dropped out of sight below the tenement buildings that ranged down the avenue.

A block away, he found an aging Toyota with a corroded door lock, and five minutes later he was heading west, hiding in plain sight among the lines of rush-hour traffic.

Jack caught sight of himself in the rearview mirror and those familiar green eyes looked back at him, a memory lurking there. The recall of a promise made; the only promise he still had to keep, the only one he had left.

"I'll see you soon, Kim," he said to the air.

• • •

The elevator doors opened to deposit Special Agent Thomas Hadley on the twenty-third floor of the Jacob K. Javits Building, and he walked out into a kind of controlled chaos. The atmosphere in the Federal Bureau of Investigation's New York field office was strung tight, and he licked his lips unconsciously, almost as if he could taste the urgency in the air. Hadley signed in and was still clipping his ID pass to his jacket pocket when he almost collided with Mike Dwyer, a supervisory agent and his direct superior.

"Tom, good," said Dwyer, pulling him aside. "You're here." In his late forties and stocky with it, Dwyer was a stark contrast to Hadley's trim athlete's build—pale and sandy-haired where the younger man was tawny-skinned and shaven-headed.

Hadley nodded, taking in the sight of a dozen other agents moving back and forth, each intent on urgent tasks he could only guess at. "All hands on deck, huh?"

Dwyer nodded. "And then some."

"I got time to get a cup of coffee?"

"No." The other agent jerked his thumb at a glassed-in office across the room. "ASAC left orders to send you straight in when you got here. He finds out I even let you take your coat off before you talk to him, and my balls will be in a sling."

Hadley's eyes widened. On the long drive in from upstate, he'd gotten piecemeal fragments of what was going on in New York from news radio stations, but nothing concrete. "That bad?"

"Whatever you've heard," Dwyer said, walking away, "it's worse."

Hadley's lip curled and he made his way across the office, catching glimpses of other agents working video feeds or barking into telephones. He'd hoped that the rumors about a terror attack in the city were just hysteria, some overreaction from people who had half the truth and an overactive imagination. But being in the room now told him that wasn't the case.

As he approached the office of Assistant Special Agent-in-Charge Rod O'Leary, he saw the big Irishman was on a call, a handset clamped to his ear. O'Leary caught sight of Hadley through the glass and beckoned him in with a terse jerk of the hand.

"It helps exactly no one if you drag your damn heels," the ASAC was saying. "You want the FBI to do something we can actually call *assistance,* I suggest you get the people at Homeland Security to kindly pull their heads outta their asses." O'Leary nodded as a tinny voice on the other end of the line replied in the affirmative. "Uh-huh. Right. Do that. Call me back when you get it." He dropped the phone back into its cradle and blew out a breath.

"Sir," began Hadley. "You wanted to see me?"

"Close the door, Tom, and sit down."

Hadley dropped into a chair across the cluttered desk from his boss and watched as the other man gathered his thoughts. O'Leary was uncompromising, he was often crass, but he was direct and that was something that Thomas Hadley could deal with. However, in the months since he had been assigned to the NYC office, he had never really felt that the ASAC had been willing to give him the time of day. He wondered what had changed.

"Long story short . . ." O'Leary launched into an explanation before Hadley could ask any questions. "In the past twenty-four hours we've had the head of a foreign government get kidnapped and murdered on our turf by his own people."

"Omar Hassan," said Hadley, with a nod.

"What's *not* public knowledge is that Hassan's killers

had a dirty bomb they were gonna blow right here in New York. Or that apparently, there may be elements inside the Russian government who were involved in making it happen."

Hadley's throat went dry. "That . . . That's confirmed?"

"No, it's not damn well confirmed." O'Leary snapped, his annoyance flaring. "We have the mother of all international incidents unfolding right before our eyes on top of a mess that could have made nine-eleven look like a sideshow. FBI, Homeland, Secret Service, NYPD, everyone is right in the thick of this and we're not even on the same page. Counter Terrorist Unit got their asses handed to them, something about an attack on their systems, so they're out of the game. . . ." He sighed. "And if that isn't enough, it looks like the president is going to take a career nosedive before the day is out."

"Okay . . ." Hadley's mind was racing as he tried to process it all. "So, what's my tasking on this?"

"We'll get to that." O'Leary's manner shifted. "Something else first. I've got some bad news." He paused. "I have to tell you that Jason Pillar was shot dead a little over an hour ago. I'm sorry, I know he was a friend of yours."

"What?" Without conscious thought, Hadley's hand strayed to the spot just above his clavicle, where beneath his shirt there was a tattoo in gothic script that read *Semper Fidelis; Always Faithful,* the motto of the United States Marine Corps.

"I know Pillar was your commanding officer in the Gulf, that you two were tight. I wanted you to hear it from me first."

"Thank you, sir . . ." Hadley fell silent for a moment. The truth was, his time in the Marines had not been a good one, and if not for Pillar it could have been much worse. When Hadley and the Corps had finally parted ways—and on less than cordial terms—it was his former commander who had helped Tom find his way to a career in law enforcement and eventually here to the FBI. The man had said he saw something in him.

Pillar himself had gone on to bigger and better things, first at the Defense Intelligence Agency and later as executive assistant to former President Charles Logan, and the two of them had kept in close contact over the years. Hadley knew that there were some in the New York field office—including O'Leary—who believed that Pillar had helped to gloss over the things in Hadley's past that might have been an impediment to his advancement.

All that was *true,* of course, but Hadley would never admit it. And now his friend and ally was gone.

"Details are sketchy," O'Leary was saying. "The shooting took place inside the United Nations building. Charles Logan was there with him and he's in critical condition from a gunshot wound. The Secret Service are playing it close to their chest, they're not telling us anything. Nothing has been released about any suspects. But the word is, Logan may not make it through the night."

"Is this connected to the Hassan killing and the bomb plot?"

"We can't rule that out." O'Leary leaned forward. "But right now, I need you to focus on a new assignment. I've got people coming in from all over, and on top of everything else we have a priority-one order straight from the deputy director." He grabbed a sheaf of papers and handed them to the agent. "You're going to put together a pursuit team to track down and arrest this man."

"Jack Bauer," Hadley read the name off the file in front of him. "I've heard of this guy. If half of what they say about him is true, he's a menace . . ."

O'Leary scowled. "Where he goes, trouble follows. We lost one of our own last night too, a former agent named Renee Walker. She was part of that whole thing with

Starkwood a while back, but she left the bureau afterward . . . Bauer had something to do with that. I'm willing to bet he's caught up in her death."

"That's what this is about?" Hadley held up the file.
"We want him for Walker's murder?"

"We want him because there's a warrant on his head
for acts of treason and conspiracy against the United
States, and for the murder of a bunch of Russian nationals. All this crap with the IRK, the peace treaty . . ."
O'Leary gestured at the air. "He's wired into it. But we're
not going to know exactly how until he's in an interrogation room. Your friend Pillar was using CTU to ac-
tively chase him, but he gave them the slip."

Hadley's eyes widened. "So Bauer is connected to the
shooting at the UN?"

"It's possible. We don't know for sure. He had no love
for Logan, that's a given. But right now, we're operating
on assumptions and circumstance. That has to change.
We're pretty certain Bauer is still in the city, but so far I
haven't had the manpower to go chasing after him. That's
your job now."

Hadley gave a grave nod, his gaze hardening. "Understood. I'll finish what Pillar . . . what was started."

The ASAC studied him carefully. "Look, Tom . . . I'm
gonna level with you. We've never seen eye to eye, you
and me. I think your methods are questionable. But right
now, I have a manhunt to prosecute on top of a citywide
terror alert, and by virtue of being the wrong man in the
wrong place, you're the guy who's gonna do that for me.
Now, you take whatever it is that's gonna motivate you
and you get this job done. I don't want to see or hear
from you again until Bauer is in cuffs. Is that clear?"

"Crystal, sir."

"Dwyer's got you some people on this. Dell, Markinson, Kilner, couple of others if you need backup. Get up

to speed and brief them." The phone rang and the ASAC snatched it back up, dismissing Hadley with a wave of the hand.

He stepped out of the room and back into the main office, thinking it through. He studied the file image of Bauer's face, trying to read something of a man he had never met.

Hadley's hands drew into fists. If Bauer *was* connected to Pillar's death, he owed it to his former commander to bring him in, and it occurred to the agent that this could also be an opportunity to finally put to rest whatever mistrust had been dogging him since he came to New York. And if that meant he had to use some of those "questionable" methods O'Leary didn't like . . . That wasn't a problem for him.

• • •

Across Manhattan, a few miles to the north in a stone-fronted town house off East Ninety-First Street, another former soldier was considering the same face, and the same objective.

Arkady Bazin had been a boy when he had ridden to war during the invasion of Afghanistan, a youth below the age of enlistment who had stolen his elder brother's birth certificate and used it to pass himself off as old enough to fight. Back then, he had been blinded by a kind of patriotic fervor that seemed quaint to him now, but even decades later, Bazin's love for Mother Russia had not faded. It had transformed into a kind of dogged, ruthless inertia—as if he were a weapon that had been set loose to roll on and on, crushing the enemies of his people.

And there was never a shortage of those. In those first days of fire and blood as a young soldier, Bazin had learned a fundamental truth. War had no end; it was only the battlefields and the faces the enemy wore that changed.

He put down the file in his hand and his lips thinned. Through the arched window behind him, lines of bright light were moving around, casting colorless streaks over the walls and the ceiling of the conference room where he sat. There were television vans parked out there, a line of them sitting bumper-to-bumper with their broadcast dishes deployed and their interchangeable location reporters all prattling away into handheld microphones. The lights fell from camera lamps, capturing the white, blue and red of the flag fluttering over the entrance of the Consulate General of the Russian Federation.

Surrounding the TV crews were American police, grumbling and sour-faced at their duties, and inside the perimeter of the black iron railings that ringed the consulate building there was another rank of watchers. They were armed with Skorpion submachine guns and Makarov pistols hidden under bulky jackets, careful to make sure that the locals did not see them. The SBP—Russia's presidential security service—were here in force to protect President Yuri Suvarov on his international visit, but the events of the past few hours had changed the tempo of that activity from a discreet projection of power to the manner of an occupying military force.

Inside the consulate, the SBP had posted guards on every level. Bazin had glimpsed them in the situation room, in terse communication with the crew of Suvarov's jet out on the tarmac at John F. Kennedy International. He frowned at the thought. Had the decision been his to make, Bazin would have sent his president directly to the airport and had him airborne by now, out of harm's way and off foreign soil.

Truth be told, if it had been his decision, he would have never allowed Suvarov to come to America in the first place, to talk with the rulers of this country and all the others as if they were some kind of *equals*. The very idea made his lip curl into a sneer.

Years of covert operations in and around the United States had instilled in him a deep distrust of this nation and its people. As an officer of the Sluzhba Vneshney Razvedki, the Russian Federation's external intelligence agency, Bazin's exposure to America had largely been in dealings with the traitors, the greedy and the venal among the country's populace. What always kept him focused was the knowledge that his work was a vital kind of corrosive, forever eating away at the imagined superiority of his homeland's old foe.

Some days he tired of it, but he knew he could not step down. The West could not be allowed to win, not even for a moment. They had to be opposed, to the very grave if needed.

Bazin found it difficult to consider the Americans as real people, not in the same way he thought of his fellow Russians. They were inferior, with their self-obsession and their shallow, materialistic manners—and what frightened him the most was the possibility that this pattern of behavior was creeping across the ocean to infect *his* people.

He wanted to see that end, and it seemed like Yuri Suvarov was a man who thought the same. Some small part of Bazin hoped he might actually get to meet the president; certainly they were both under the same roof at this moment. This was a man who understood that the Great Soviet Bear had not perished, only hibernated. Suvarov was the kind of leader who could rekindle the old unity the Russian states had once enjoyed in the day of the Communist era, if only given the chance. He liked to think that Suvarov would see in him a kindred spirit, someone who recalled and revered the day when their nation was a force to be reckoned with in global politics.

But no. Bazin dismissed the thought as fanciful, un-professional. It was right that President Suvarov would never know his face or his name. Bazin saw himself as a loyal son of the Motherland, and it was enough that Suvarov would only know that there were weapons at his disposal which could be brought to bear to show Russia's might to her foes.

He looked down at the file photo again. This man, this Jack Bauer, was just such an enemy. The data on him had been gleaned from spies embedded in the Central Intelligence Agency and allies in the Chinese government, a patchwork of half-truths and hearsay that crafted an image of who Bauer was, of what he was capable of doing. A policeman, a soldier, a spy, an assassin . . . Bauer had been all of these things, but now he was only *a target*.

The sneer returned to Bazin's face. This ex-CIA killer was the perfect exemplar of why he did what he did. They were nearly the same age, with little more than half a year between their birthdates, and perhaps on the surface the two of them might have seemed like the same kind of man. But such a comparison would have sent Bazin into a fury. Bauer's file revealed the truth of him; he was so very *American*, with every mission he had prosecuted spawned from some arrogant sense that his nation had the right to impose its will on the world. Bauer was a rogue, his bloody career at best barely clothed in tissue-thin justifications from his government, at worst the works of a psychopath with no code, no loyalty to anything but his own warped sense of right and wrong. They had never met, but on some level Bazin already reviled this man. He despised the cancerous capitalist system that could create a person like Jack Bauer.

There was a knock at the door, and Bazin looked up as a woman entered. She had the haughty poise of a Mus-covite society girl, but he knew from experience that her outward manner was just a smokescreen. While Galina

Ziminova was younger than him, and at times a little too liberal in her ways for his tastes, Bazin appreciated that the other SVR agent was an accomplished killer and a true patriot . . . even if the "new" Russia she came from was not the one that had been mother and protector to him.

"The team are here, sir," she said.

He nodded. "Bring them in."

Ziminova returned the gesture, and paused as she caught sight of Bauer's picture. "Is that him?"

"Someone you might pass on the street and think as unremarkable," Bazin replied. "And yet this man is marked for death by our highest authority."

02

"We have a clear and direct mandate," Hadley told the others. "A federal warrant for the arrest of Jack Bauer has been issued, and we're going to bring him down."

The other agents in the briefing room exchanged glances. To his left, sitting side by side, Special Agents Kari Dell and Helen Markinson looked as if they had been cut from the same cloth; both trim and austere in their looks, both dressed in a near-identical black pantsuit, at first glance all that differentiated them were their hairstyles. Dell's short bob was henna-red where Markinson's black hair reached to just above her shoulders, and the pair of them watched Hadley give his briefing with hawkish intensity. Scuttlebutt around the field office was that the two women had come up together at Quantico and they made a formidable team. Only a week earlier it had been their work that cracked the Anselmo case wide open. Hadley could work with that kind of skill set. He needed aggressive, proactive people on his team if he was to succeed.

"A fella like that isn't going to come quietly," Markinson ventured, a little of her native Boston drawl coming through.

Dell nodded. "He may not leave us with a lot of options, when the moment comes."

"We'll burn that bridge when we come to it," Hadley replied, and he heard the man to his right draw a sharp breath. He glanced at the other agent, waiting for him to voice what was on his mind.

Jorge Kilner had the kind of open, honest face that looked better suited to a high school quarterback than an FBI agent, but right now his expression was one of deep concern. His hands knitted before him and he shifted uncomfortably in his chair. "This man . . ." He paused, framing his words. "He's not a criminal."

Dell tapped the warrant document on the conference table. "Beg to differ."

Kilner shook his head and went on. "Look, you only need to read his file to know, Bauer is a former Counter Terrorist Unit operative. He's been called upon to do a lot of things by this country, the kind of stuff that would give the rest of us nightmares. We owe him more than just treating the guy like some two-bit crook to be run down and thrown in a cage."

"What we owe Jack Bauer is due process and his one phone call," Hadley snapped. "That's if he's smart enough to put his hands up when we come calling."

The other agent's lips thinned. "Agent Hadley, I knew Bauer and Renee Walker. I don't believe for one second he's responsible for her death."

"Right . . . You were at the office in Washington, DC, during the White House attack." Hadley gave Kilner a level look. "That's good. We can use your insight into the man. But that's all it's going to be. If you think you're going to show undue sympathy to a wanted fugitive, I'll ask Special Agent Dwyer to reassign you."

"No, sir," Kilner insisted. "If someone's going to put the cuffs on Bauer, I want to be the one to do it. To make sure it's done right."

"So where do we start?" asked Markinson. "There's a BOLO alert with Bauer's face on it all across the Eastern Seaboard, and the NYPD have dropped a net over Manhattan because of this whole Kamistani thing. Are we still operating on the assumption that he's within the city limits?"

"Right now, we are." Hadley crossed to the conference room's window and looked out across Federal Plaza. "As Agent Kilner reminded us, our fugitive is ex-CTU, before that Delta Force and CIA. He's trained for urban operations, he knows our methods and our capabilities. He also knows that if he doesn't get out of New York within the next couple of hours, he's as good as caught. We have a small window of opportunity here, people, and it's closing by the second." He turned back and nodded toward the other agents. "We've got monitoring set up on every known contact Bauer has in this city, eyes on airports, train stations, ferry terminals, bridges and tunnels. He's gonna stick his head up, and we're going to be there when he does. Each of you is to coordinate search sectors with tactical command. If you get a scent of him, don't hesitate. Drop the hammer." Hadley aimed a finger at the door. "Get to work."

Dell, Markinson and the other agents got to their feet and filed out, but Hadley put a hand on Kilner's shoulder before he could leave.

"Is there a problem?" said the other man.

"You tell me," Hadley demanded. "When it comes down to the line and you have to draw on Bauer, are you going to follow through?"

"If I have to—"

"*If?*" Hadley prodded him in the chest. "Be realistic, Jorge. You really think a guy like him is going to give you the choice? Markinson is right. Bauer's the *shoot-first* type."

Kilner eyed him. "With respect . . . maybe it's not *me* who should be thinking about his motivation."

Hadley hesitated on the edge of a retort, then reeled it back in. "Your honesty is appreciated. In the meantime, I want you out on the street. Bauer's running on empty, so he's going to need money and gear. He was staying at the Hotel Chelsea on the West Side. Get out there and check in on the location, just in case."

"In case of what? The Evidence Response Team have already looked the place over."

"Still," Hadley insisted, pushing past him to walk away. "Go check in. That's an order."

• • •

As the traffic crawled along Second Avenue past Stuyvesant Square, Jack shrank deeper into the threadbare hoodie he had found on the backseat of the stolen Toyota. Rush hour was always a pain in the ass, but New York City's grid of streets conspired to make it a special kind of hell. Lines of cars and vans inched forward in fits and starts, and drivers leaned on their horns within a heartbeat if someone failed to go with the flow. He watched a pair of cab drivers in the lane alongside moving in lockstep, conducting a raucous argument back and forth out of their open windows. Now and then, a police siren would pulse out a whoop of noise, and in the rearview, Jack saw blue-and-white cruisers forcing their way through the gridlock, sometimes mounting the sidewalk in order to slip past.

The metallic rattle of a helicopter passed overhead and he resisted the urge to peer out and take a look. It would only take a single frame for a mobile camera or static monitor to capture his image and flag it. Jack had stopped to rub a dash of black grime on his cheeks before getting in the car, a broken asymmetrical line that looked accidental but would actually be enough to slow down any facial recognition software that did catch sight of him. It was a stopgap measure, though, and it wouldn't work against a human observer.

His fingers drummed on the steering wheel. He felt *exposed*, pinned in place inside the steel box of the car. Even now, his hunters could be vectoring in on this location. Snipers in the buildings across the street, gunmen in the vehicles trailing him. Every person out there was a potential threat, every window a place for a shooter to fire from.

Jack became aware that the two cabbies had fallen silent, their voices replaced by the mutter of a radio. Other cars around him were doing the same, turning up the volume, rolling down their windows so everyone could hear. He leaned forward and snapped on the Toyota's dashboard radio, and the same voice was there on every station he found.

Allison Taylor, the first female president of the United States, was addressing her nation in a live broadcast. "*My fellow Americans,*" she began. "*It is with a heavy heart that I must speak to you this evening. A situation has arisen that I cannot, in all good conscience, allow to progress any further. At this hour, I am formally resigning my position as your president and stepping down from my post as commander-in-chief. I am passing that grave responsibility to my vice president and trusted friend, Mitchell Heyworth.*"

Jack listened to her voice, imagining Taylor as she stood there before the lectern, her words issuing out across a room full of stunned, silent reporters. He tried to make sense of his own feelings toward the woman. His anger at her actions was still raw and harsh, and it was hard to separate it from the churn of emotion that seethed in the wake of Renee's death.

That Jack respected the office of the president was without question—it was ingrained in him, and on some level, he would always be the good soldier—but he also knew full well the terrible responsibilities it demanded from those who held that lofty post. Jack thought of David Palmer, a man of strong character and high ideals who had struggled to execute his terms in the Oval Office with honor and courage, and of his brother Wayne who had done his best to follow David's example. Others, like Noah Daniels and James Prescott, had been driven to make dangerous choices and pay for their consequences. Today, Allison Taylor would learn that price as well.

"When I leave this room I will remand myself to the attorney general for questioning," she was saying. *"A grave conspiracy has been at work over the last day, and to my shame I must acknowledge that I did not do enough to bring it to light when the opportunity was presented to me. I ask for your forgiveness and your understanding at this time, and I promise you all that there will be a swift, just and above all, transparent resolution to these difficult hours. Thank you."*

The room exploded with questions as the assembled reporters clamored to be the first to challenge Taylor's words. Jack's eyes narrowed and he turned the radio volume back down, processing what he had heard.

She had kept her word to him, her commitment to exposing the plot to disrupt the Kamistan peace treaty and power games behind it. Perhaps he had been wrong about her.

What happened next in the corridors of the United Nations, the White House, the Kremlin and the IRK Parliament would be the business of statesmen and policy makers. Maybe it would mean nations turning against nations, heightened tensions and daggers drawn . . . Right now, all that seemed a very distant thing, a long way removed from Jack's world.

President Taylor's honesty had rung the death knell for her political career and opened her up to the threat of arrest and incarceration. More than that, any possibility that her administration might have protected Jack and his friends had evaporated. His colleagues at CTU, people like Chloe O'Brien, Arlo Glass, Cole Ortiz and all the others, they too would now find themselves at the sharp end. It angered him that they might face prison sentences for daring to do the right thing in impossible circumstances. He felt powerless to help them, just as he had been powerless to save Renee's life as she bled out from a sniper's bullet.

A bleak mood settled on him, a yawning dark hollow opening up in his chest. So many people had been taken from him, so much of his life ripped away in fire and blood. And now, here he was once again, on the edge of an abyss. Forsaken and alone, his liberty measured by the ticks of the clock.

For a moment, Jack allowed himself to wonder what might happen if he were just to open the car door and step out into the street, hands above his head. What would Jack Bauer's fate be?

Forces of his own nation were hunting him, and so were the agents of his enemies. There was a butcher's bill with his name on it, and it would be a race between the American government and the covert operatives of the Russian Federation to find him first. Both wanted to make him pay for the laws he had broken and the lives he had ended. Jack knew that neither one would give any quarter when they came to take him. The best he could hope for was life in some nameless prison off the grid; the worst, a bullet in the back of the head and his body dumped in the river.

He rejected the thought. *No*, he told himself, *I made a promise to my daughter. I won't let her down. I'll see her again. One last time.*

On some level he knew that the smarter choice, the practical and expedient option would be to cut loose and disappear right now, this very second. Jack knew a dozen ways he could become a ghost and rebuild a new life for himself in some other place.

But that felt like a betrayal. Kim was all the family he had left, the last bright star in his life's dark sky. He thought about never seeing her again, and something inside him twisted like a knife of ice.

Even if nothing else was clear to him, the vow he had made to Kim was unbreakable. His daughter, her husband, Stephen, and Jack's beautiful grandchild, Teri . . . All of them were at risk as long as he was still around. He had vanished before, and he would do it again, just drop off the radar and disappear. But first he would keep his promise and say his good-byes. Nobody would be allowed to prevent that. *Nobody.*

"Hey, pallie!" Jack snapped out of his reverie with a start, the sound of a blaring car horn bringing him back to the moment. He looked up and saw one of the cabbies leaning out of his window to shout at him. The taxi driver stabbed a finger at the road ahead and the growing gap where the traffic had finally started to shift. "Where you going, man?" he demanded.

"Home," replied Jack.

• • •

"These orders come directly from President Suvarov," said Bazin, and he paused to allow that statement to bed in. Ziminova said nothing, but he could see that the three other men in the room were all on the cusp of saying something. He made an accepting motion with his hand. "Speak up. I have little tolerance for those who stay silent out of fear of challenge."

Predictably, Yolkin was the first to give voice. "Suvarov

authorized this personally?" Thin and wiry, Yolkin had cold blue eyes and spoke in a flat monotone that droned around the room. "Today?"

"Less than an hour ago. The killing of an American citizen, yes." Bazin nodded. "Was I unclear?"

"Not just a citizen." Mager was the next to speak up. He was perhaps the most *average* of men that Bazin had ever known, so nondescript that you could lose him in a crowd and a moment later struggle to recall his face. "A highly trained soldier. A federal agent."

"*Former* federal agent," corrected Ziminova. "He is a wanted man now. Their law enforcement agencies have been mobilized to arrest and detain him."

"Why not let them do so?" Ekel finally decided to offer his question from the depths of the cockpit leather chair where he slouched, one hand forever toying with a length of his oily black hair. "Would it not be easier to let Bauer find his way to a prison and then pay some murderer to smother him in his cell?" He held up his hands. "We would stay clean in the matter."

Yolkin grunted in a vague approximation of a chuckle. "This is not about staying clean, pretty boy. This is about sending a message."

Bazin nodded. "As usual, Yolkin cuts to the meat of it. Yes. The motivation for this directive is retribution, pure and simple. President Suvarov is angry at this Bauer. It seems he was directly responsible for derailing certain operational plans, and beyond that, the man also had the temerity to think he could strike directly at members of the Russian government."

"Out of revenge," Mager noted. "That idiot Tokarev shot Bauer's woman."

"Tokarev was made to pay for that," said Ziminova. "He was sliced open, like a pig."

"He wasn't the only one," Bazin added, his jaw hardening as he thought of the other murders.

Ziminova went on, picking up the thread of her commander's briefing. "Bauer is also responsible for the deaths of Minister Mikhail Novakovich and his protection detail. Eight men in total."

Bazin had personally known three of those men. He had trained them in counter-terror tactics, back in the days when the SVR had still been the KGB, and the American had seen them all to their graves. It was one more reason for him to be leading this operation, for a settling of that score. He leaned forward in his chair. "Make no mistake. This is a question of *respect*. A question of offense made and reparation to be paid. President Suvarov himself would have been in Bauer's sights had circumstances played out differently. The American cannot be allowed to live after committing these acts."

"That would be weakness." Yolkin nodded. "It would make Suvarov appear foolish if he does nothing."

"That ship has sailed," muttered Ekel.

Bazin shot him a look. "What do you mean by that?"

Ekel colored slightly, then straightened. When he spoke again, he lowered his voice, as if he were afraid that Suvarov might hear him from wherever he was in the consulate building. "It is just . . . They are saying that the telephone lines are burning up between here and Moscow. The prime minister and his cabinet have called an emergency meeting of the Federal Assembly. There is talk that the president will be said to be involved in the Hassan assassination . . ." Ekel hesitated. "Suvarov will not find a warm welcome waiting for him at home."

They had all heard the rumor, and it irritated Bazin that others were discussing it as if it were already fact. He drew himself up and fixed Ekel with a hard gaze. "The prime minister and his friends in the Duma . . . Those men are *politicians,* my friend. But Yuri Suvarov is a *leader.* We follow the orders of the latter, not the former. What does or does not occur when he next sets foot on Russian soil is not your concern. We have been given an order by our commander-in-chief and it will be obeyed. We have been tasked to find and terminate an enemy of the Motherland. Unless that order is countermanded, we will proceed in that intent." He got to his feet and the rest of the team did the same.

As his second-in-command, Ziminova issued the next set of orders. "We will proceed to a staging area to pick up weapons and equipment. From there, we will break into teams and commence the operation. You will coordinate directly with our operator here in the consulate via encrypted communication."

The three men nodded and walked out, leaving Bazin to stand at the end of the long, high table. He pulled a smartphone from his pocket and began to tap out a text message.

Ziminova watched him from the doorway. "Sir," she began. "I know it goes without saying, but we must operate with the utmost care from this point onward. If any of our assets are exposed as we track down Bauer, the fallout could be considerable."

"You are afraid to give the world more reasons to hate us?" Bazin sniffed. "We are Russian. That has never mattered to us. But do not be concerned. I am going to call in a local contractor to assist."

"Is that wise?"

He continued to work at the tiny touchpad. "She has worked for us before. I have every confidence."

The woman hesitated. "Sir. Ekel made a salient, if clumsy point. President Suvarov wants Bauer dead not for political reasons, but for personal ones. This is about revenge. His motive is no different from the American's, when he killed Pavel Tokarev."

Bazin eyed her. "You have read Bauer's file."

"Just the high points."

"And there are so many of those. Even from the incomplete picture we have of this man, one thing is abundantly clear. Jack Bauer is a tenacious, single-minded enemy. Against odds, against reason, Bauer has shown he has no mercy for those he believes have wronged him. That list now has Yuri Suvarov's name on it. Others who have found themselves there are already dead." He shook his head. "The man is too dangerous to be allowed to roam free. Even his own masters have conceded that. You were brought up on a farm collective, Galina. Tell me, what did you do with a dog gone too wild to come to heel?"

Her eyes narrowed. "I put it down."

"Just so." Bazin's phone beeped as an acknowledgment flashed up on the screen, and he smiled thinly. "Ah. And so we begin."

03

Jack ditched the battered Toyota near Eighth Avenue and pulled up the grey hoodie over his head, hunching forward to alter his body language. It would be dark soon, and while nightfall might make it easier for him to get lost among the city's population, he couldn't allow himself to drop his guard, not even for a second.

Fatigue made it hard, though. A deep, heavy weariness had settled in his bones and he could feel it slowing him down. How long had he been pushing himself over the past twenty-four hours? Even with his training, Jack couldn't go on and on without the effects making themselves known. *Four days,* they had told him in Delta Force. A fit man of good health with food and water could make it past the seventy-two-hour mark and still keep his wits about him. He wondered how that number changed when you added in variables—such as recovering from being shot less than two hours earlier, or forced on the run.

But it wasn't staying awake and on his feet that concerned Jack. It was keeping his mind focused. Fatigue was acidic, and it ate away at judgment and clarity. If he didn't watch himself, Jack could be in danger of making the wrong choices at the wrong moment, and that would get him killed. It wasn't enough for Jack to just react to the events unfolding around him. He needed to become proactive. He needed a plan.

He couldn't rely on Chloe or CTU; he couldn't go back to the well with his old resources like Jim Ricker and his former CIA contacts. Everyone who might have been willing to help him was either being watched, shut down, under arrest or dead. He was alone, with no backup, no hardware and nowhere to go. He glanced up briefly, imagining a great noose tightening around him. He shook off the grim image and moved on.

Jack took a deep breath and crossed over the avenue toward the corner of West Twenty-Third Street, moving with the other pedestrians at a steady, unhurried pace. Ahead of him, he caught sight of the Hotel Chelsea's familiar frontage, the redbrick and black iron balconies of the old Victorian Gothic building ranging up toward the darkening sky. He liked the place; it had been Kim's husband who arranged an apartment for him there, calling in a favor with a relative to get him somewhere to live while he was in town. A New York landmark since the nineteenth century, the Chelsea had been home to a laundry list of famous creatives—actors and musicians, writers and painters. His namesake Jack Kerouac had written *On the Road* there, and he remembered the first time he had entered the building, feeling something of the history soaked into the walls. It was a million miles away from the places where Jack Bauer had lived his life, the places he had called home.

The police cruiser parked across the street from the Chelsea's front entrance was clearly visible from a good distance away, and he could make out two cops in the front seat, talking animatedly, occasionally scanning their surroundings for some sign of him. Jack walked on, shifting his course to pass by the doors to the lobby. He angled his head to see if there was a second watcher inside, but saw nothing. It didn't matter. He wasn't going to risk anything as foolish as walking in the front.

A few hundred yards away there was a plain glass door that led into a stack of offices squeezed in between a pair of restaurants, and he slipped into it and out of the line of sight. Throwing a quick look over his shoulder, Jack broke into a jog and threaded down a narrow corridor until he came to a window that opened out onto a court-yard in the center of the block. The first day he had arrived at the Hotel Chelsea, force of habit had taken him out the back of the building to scout for alternative methods of access, and the window was part of a route Jack had plotted in his mind's eye. In his experience, it was always better to have an escape plan and not need it than to need an escape plan and not have it.

Being a building of historic note meant that the Chelsea retained a lot of 1940's era window fittings, making its security easy for Jack to defeat. In a few moments, he gained access to a service room on the second floor and from there he took the back stairs, pausing at each landing to make sure he wasn't being followed.

The apartment door was crosshatched with strips of yellow hazard tape shot through with text that warned POLICE LINE—DO NOT CROSS. Carefully, he ducked low to avoid disturbing them and unlocked the door as silently as he could.

He caught the telltale smell of chemicals inside the entrance hall, the residue of fingerprint aerosols and luminol spray for blood detection. There were black marks around light switches and on surfaces where an evidence team had pulled prints from just about everything. In the apartment proper, it looked as if a careful tornado had moved though the rooms. Every cupboard was ajar, every drawer hanging open like a slack mouth. Jack saw his clothes in a loose heap on the bed, and the suitcases he had packed for his flight back to Los Angeles lay empty on the floor. As he expected, they had taken his laptop computer—not that there would be anything on there for the police or the FBI to use against him—and run a fine-tooth comb over everything else.

When he entered the bathroom, he knew immediately that the investigators had found the go-bag he stashed there. A tile was missing from the hung ceiling over his head, and he peeked up into the darkness within, seeing nothing but dust and cobwebs. Like the escape route, the go-bag was another habitual tic that helped Jack Bauer sleep better at night; a small, waterproof drawstring sack containing a first-aid kit, a survival knife, cash and a few fake IDs. In the event that it all went to hell, it was the one thing he could grab and go. Jack nodded at his reflection in the bathroom mirror. He expected this. The FBI investigators knew the kind of man he was, and they would have known to look for the bag.

And so when they found it, they probably wouldn't have looked for the *second* emergency stash that Jack had hidden inside the smoke hood of the cooker in the kitchen. It was still there, a small bundle of dollars and Euros in high-denomination notes, along with a Canadian passport in the name of John Barrett, an emergency identity that was known in covert ops circles as a "snap cover."

Back in the bedroom, he discarded the clothes he had been wearing and found fresh ones. Like most of his wardrobe, Jack's taste in colors strayed toward the darker tones, a conscious intent to blend in and stay inconspicuous. Packing light and quick, he found a black gym bag and threw in another change of gear.

He picked up a jacket and there was a woman's fleece lying underneath it. He didn't need to touch it to know that it had belonged to Renee.

Seeing it there triggered a flood of memory that he tried and failed to stem. To do the things that his nation had asked of him, to be the man that he was, Jack Bauer had learned to compartmentalize himself. Even as he walked into this building, Jack placed his memories of Renee Walker behind a wall and sealed them away.

Or so he thought. In a heartbeat, it all came crashing back, and he sagged, dropping onto the unkempt bed. His head snapped up and his gaze found the bullet hole in the window, tagged with an evidence marker. A single round fired from across the street by Pavel Tokarev had impacted there, finding its target within.

Suddenly Jack was reliving it. The sound of the breaking glass and the crash as Renee's body fell. The weight of her in his arms as he gathered her up and raced through the hotel corridors. Her pale face, the life in her eyes fading away as he watched, the terrible sense of helplessness as he knew in that moment he would lose her.

Anger and sorrow boiled up inside him. They pressed at his throat, a scream of raw fury pushing to be released. It took every ounce of Jack's iron self-control not to give in to that need. Instead, he took the rage and held on to it, used it to burn away the exhaustion. He made it into his fuel, into the drive that got him back to his feet.

At the door, Jack closed his eyes and let himself think about Renee Walker one last time, before he turned his back and walked away.

• • •

Kilner parked the black Ford Fusion close to the curb and approached the police unit, leading with his badge. "See anything?" he asked the uniformed cops inside.

Both officers shook their heads. "No sign from here," said one of them. Taped to the dash in front of them was Jack Bauer's be-on-the-lookout bulletin, and Kilner's lips thinned as he studied it.

"Hey, level with us," said the other policeman. "Is this guy really dumb enough to come back here? I mean, there's so many cops on the street right now, every perp in the city is taking a powder."

"He's not dumb," Kilner told them, and frowned.

But maybe I am, thought the agent as he walked back to his car and dropped into the seat. *Should have kept my mouth shut in the briefing.* It was clear to him that Special Agent Hadley was gunning for Bauer, and by daring to express doubts about the man's guilt, Kilner had already put himself on the outs with the other agent before the manhunt had even begun. Why else had Hadley ordered Kilner to take a car out to the hotel if not to get rid of him?

He drummed his fingers on the dash and thought about crossing the street to go check on the apartment upstairs. Would Hadley give him a hard time for doing that? Kilner felt conflicted about the whole damn thing.

Instead, he reached into the Ford's glove compartment and found a pair of short-frame binoculars there. Turning in his seat, he raised them and scanned the windows of the Hotel Chelsea, counting up the floors and across, searching for Bauer's apartment. After a moment, he found it, catching sight of the broken window. He wondered about what had gone on up there. The preliminary scene-of-crime report talked about a rifle bullet that had been dug out of the wall, most likely the same round that had cut through Renee Walker and mortally wounded her.

Kilner shook his head. It was no way to die, and even as he knew that Jack Bauer had broken the law in his quest to take revenge for Walker's killing, he couldn't help but wonder if he would have done any different in the same circumstances.

That was still at the front of his thoughts when he saw

what looked like the edge of a shadow moving inside the sealed apartment.

. . .

Jack considered the money and the Barrett passport. It wasn't enough. He needed more hardware if he was going to make his flight from the city a reality. He had no gun, no communications, no vehicle.

Mulling it over, Jack considered that he was being presented with two options. The first had the lowest level of immediate risk, but it would take time and the clock was against him. He could sneak back out of the hotel and start walking, find a way off Manhattan and if his luck held, be lost in back-roads country by late tomorrow. But to do that ran the risk of being recognized at every turn. The NYPD had his face, and it wouldn't be long before the FBI decided to tell the world he was a hunted man, and then there were whatever hostile resources the Russians were mobilizing against him.

The second option was extremely risky, it was high impact and it relied on striking fast before his pursuers could solidify their grip on the city.

In the end, he reflected, *it's not really a choice at all.*

He edged to the window in the apartment's living room and dropped low, looking carefully over the ledge to see down into the street. A black car had joined the NYPD cruiser across from the Hotel Chelsea's entrance, and Jack didn't need to see the bumper to know that it would have federal plates.

He stood up. Across the room was a bookshelf full of volumes about cookery and travel guides belonging to the apartment's owner. The books had been removed one by one and given a cursory search, then piled in a heap back on the shelf. A colorful city guide to Montreal was among them, and Jack walked slowly across the room to get it. He made sure that he passed in front of two windows as he did so, before snatching up the book and bending its spine back against itself.

The evidence team from the FBI had gone through everything, including the books, but theirs had been a cursory evaluation done under pressure of time, and not truly thorough. Hardly surprising, given the chaos that had affected the city over the past few hours. Another team would probably come back to conduct a deeper sweep in the next day or so, but by then it would be too late.

Jack peeled away a loose section of the cardstock cover and used his fingernails to pinch the end of a tiny micro-SIM card lodged there, the same kind of memory card used in millions of commercial cell phones. The little sliver of dark plastic was smaller than the tip of his thumb, but it contained a stock of information that, if anything, was worth more than the bundle of cash he had secreted elsewhere. Quadruple encrypted for his personal use, courtesy of Chloe O'Brian's partner Morris, the data card was Jack's equivalent of a "black book." Now all he needed was something that could read it.

He glanced back toward the window, then down at the MTM Blackhawk watch on his wrist. Jack estimated that he had around ten minutes before his guests were going to arrive. He pulled the cord to drop the blinds and walked back toward the front door.

• • •

Kilner blinked as the man in the dark jacket appeared and disappeared in the window of the apartment. His throat went dry.

"He's there. He's *actually* there." Kilner had to say it out loud in order to fix the thought in his mind. Somehow, Bauer had slipped past the cops and made his way back to the apartment. The agent's mind raced. It was either the most foolish or the most calculated move the man could have made. Did he think that no one would ever look for him here? Or had Bauer come back to get something that the evidence techs had missed?

It didn't matter. Kilner stabbed the speed-dial tab on his phone and Hadley picked up on the second ring. "*What?*" he demanded.

"I have eyes on Bauer," Kilner blurted. "He's at the Hotel Chelsea, right now!"

"*You're certain it's our man?*"

"I just looked right at him." He licked his lips. "Sir, we've got a chance to end this now, before it goes any further . . . If I get up there, I can—"

Hadley shut him down with a snarl. "*Hell, no. You've got your orders, Agent Kilner. Maintain your position and watch the exits. If Bauer leaves the building, follow but do not engage, you hear me?*"

He nodded, deflating. "Yes, sir."

Kilner heard Hadley calling out to someone else, scrambling to move. "*I'm heading to you right now. A tactical team has been mobilized. Listen to me, you remain on station, let the team do their thing. Do not get in the way.*"

"What . . ." Kilner hesitated. "What are their rules of engagement?"

"*Bauer is a lethal threat,*" Hadley replied firmly. "*The tac team has orders not to take any chances with him.*"

Kilner's blood ran cold as he realized that he had just signed Jack Bauer's death warrant.

• • •

Exactly twelve minutes had elapsed before the FBI tactical team arrived. *Sloppy,* thought Jack. *I could have been out of here in half that time.*

With his ear pressed to the door, he could hear the scrape of boots on the landing floor, the faint whispers of the armed men as they arranged themselves before making a dynamic entry. Jack retreated slowly toward the kitchen, activating a cook cycle on the microwave oven before moving on to the bedroom area.

In his mind's eye, he pictured what the six-man team was doing. They would be lining up along the wall outside the apartment, weapons at the ready and safeties off. A point man armed with one of the big Remington 870 shotguns the bureau favored would take aim at the lock mechanism and on a three-count, blow a hole as big as a child's head in the thick wooden door.

He counted with them, and there was a deafening boom as the shotgun discharged. A single 12-gauge breaching round blasted a projectile made of powdered steel and wax into the front door's dead bolt mechanism, instantly obliterating it. A second agent kicked open the ruined door and tossed an M84 stun grenade into the apartment; the flash bang released a shock of light and sound that made the windows shake in the confined space.

• • •

The assault proper began. In pairs, the FBI agents streamed through the doorway with their weapons pulled tight to their armored vests. With the exception of the shotgunner, the other five men carried Heckler & Koch MP5/10 submachine guns, and they had been cleared to use them if they saw fit. Hadley's standing orders had been given the green light by District. Bauer was to be considered armed and extremely dangerous.

To the left, the apartment was open plan, the living area stretching all the way to the far wall, the space broken up by low tables, bookshelves and other furniture.

Three of the six agents fanned out in that direction, the man with the Remington the last to enter, pumping the slide to chamber a fresh round as he did so. To the right was a kitchen area and a door leading to a narrow balcony, and beyond that a short hall down to the bedroom and the bathroom. One man moved into the kitchen, the other two proceeded down the hallway.

The bedroom door was already open. "Jack Bauer!" shouted the agent who entered first. "Show yourself, now!" He stepped aside as his teammate came up with him, and moved into the bathroom. The second man spun in the other direction, finding a large walk-in closet in the corner of the room.

With the MP5/10 aimed chest-high, the second agent reached to pull open the louvered door of the closet. His gloved fingers were on the brass handle when the doors splintered. Jack burst through the thin wooden slats and struck the FBI agent in the face with the flat of a cast-iron skillet he'd snatched from the kitchen.

The agent's head snapped back, the unexpected impact bouncing his skull off the inside of his helmet. His nose shattered and blood streamed from his nostrils. Dazed, the agent sagged to the floor and struggled to remain conscious.

Jack didn't stop to make sure the first man was out of action. If he didn't act with speed, it wouldn't matter one way or another. Dropping the skillet, he bolted across the room and met the other agent as the first man was coming back out of the bathroom, calling, "Clear!"

"Not exactly," Jack retorted, and landed a crippling punch in the agent's throat. The man's cry for help was choked off and Jack shoved him back into the bathroom, using one hand to push aside the MP5/10. He had the momentum and he used it to slam the agent's head down against the toilet cistern, then kicked at his opponent's legs to rob him of what little balance he still had. Clad in body armor, a helmet rig and tactical vest, the FBI agent moved slower than Jack, and in the confined space of the apartment's bathroom that small edge was all that Bauer needed.

He tripped the man into a fall that sent his head ringing off the rim of the sink and the agent fell limp, collapsing into a heap.

In the same second, the small can of deodorant Jack had stuck inside the kitchen's microwave oven reached a point of critical combustion, and with a flat concussive chug, the oven door blew off its hinges. A ball of orange fire puffed out, immediately setting off the smoke alarm.

The agent in the kitchen reeled, catching the heat of the improvised explosive across his back. He swore, falling against the balcony door, and scrambled to bring his submachine gun around to bear.

One after another, a half-dozen small black cylinders came flying out of the bedroom, clattering off the walls and the wooden flooring. Jack tossed flash bangs and smoke grenades he had pulled from the belts of the other agents, and then threw himself aside as they went off in a staccato ripple of thunder.

A dense white fog filled the apartment, taking visibility down to almost nothing. Jack heard the other agents calling out, cursing and shouting for help.

Pulling a discarded T-shirt across his face as a makeshift mask, Jack surged forward, and the man in the kitchen stumbled into him as he tried to feel his way back into the room. Along with the grenades, Bauer had snatched a pistol-shaped X2 Taser from the agents he had neutralized, and he used it to quietly put the other man down.

In the smoke, the other three agents were calling out to one another. "What the hell?" said one voice, high and tight with tension. "You see anything?"

"We need to fall back," said another.

A pair of green targeting lasers snapped on, threading through the haze. "Stay focused. Find this guy!"

Jack kept low, and out of the smoke came a figure clad in blue and black, sweeping the muzzle of his weapon back and forth. The stolen X2 still had another charge in it, so Jack pivoted and jammed it into the ribs of the agent.

The stun gun buzzed like a hornet in a tin can, and the agent screamed. His hand twitched and he unwittingly fired off a burst from his weapon, a cluster of 10mm rounds ripping into the plaster of the ceiling. Jack let him fall and moved toward one of the other voices.

He heard a crash as the agent carrying the shotgun collided with a freestanding lamp, glass crunching underfoot. Jack repeated the same attack he had used on the man in the bathroom and came in low, aiming a lethal kick down at the point where he guessed his knee would be.

His aim was good. Bone cracked and the shotgunner folded, howling in agony. Jack silenced him with a second and then a third blow, before sweeping up the Remington and moving after the last man.

The final member of the tactical team was retreating back toward the vague outline of the ruined doorway when the muzzle of the shotgun was suddenly pressing into his throat. He froze.

"Put your weapon down," said Jack. "Drop the gun belt too. Do it now."

The agent did as he was told. "Easy, Bauer . . ." he began. "What do you think you're doing, man? You gonna kill me? You're just making this worse."

"No one here is dead," Jack shot back, and then with a savage jerk he cracked the agent across the face with the butt of the Remington, knocking him out.

He spun the gun around and fired toward the windows of the apartment, blowing out the blinds and the glass with each shot. Immediately, the smoke began to vent into the evening air. He dropped into a crouch and ran a professional eye over the unconscious FBI agent's gear.

A tinny voice issued out of the radio clipped to the agent's shoulder. "*This is Kilner, tac team report! Report! Does anyone copy this message, over?*"

Jack snatched up the radio handset and stuffed it in a jacket pocket, and then with quick, spare motions, he stripped the downed agents of all the gear he was going to need and stuffed it into his gym bag.

04

Agent Kilner stared at the radio handset, his throat dry. "I repeat, does anyone copy my transmission?"

Only static answered him. The two NYPD cops had emerged from their car after the sounds of the grenade detonations, and now they stood, guns drawn, staring up at the streamers of white smoke billowing out of the shattered apartment windows. Kilner heard one of them calling it in, and the other shot him a look. "We're gonna check the entrance, you stay put!"

Both men sprinted across Twenty-Third Street, veering around stalled cabs and other traffic that had slowed to take a look at the unfolding confusion. Kilner discarded the tactical radio and pulled his cell phone, hitting the redial key. "Agent Hadley, where are you?"

Hadley's voice had the echoing timbre of someone on a speakerphone. *"I'm three blocks away, damn traffic is a pain in the ass in this city. What's wrong?"*

"I've lost contact with the SWAT team! The unit commander insisted on going in straightaway, he didn't want to wait for you to get here."

Kilner could hear sirens in the background of the call, and seconds later the same sound reached him. Hadley swore under his breath. "*I warned them not to underestimate Bauer.*"

Without warning, the Ford rocked as someone wrenched open one of the rear doors and dropped into the seat behind him.

"Good advice," said a voice that was all gravel and hard edges. An FBI-issue Springfield M1911A1 semiautomatic pressed into the back of Kilner's neck and a hand snaked forward to snatch the phone from him, cutting off the call.

The agent tried to turn and the pistol dug hard into his skin. "Wait, no . . ."

"Kilner, right? From DC?" said Jack. "I remember you." He gave him another prod with the gun. "Drive."

"Did you kill those men up there?"

Jack snorted quietly. "They'll survive. Now get this thing moving. I'm not gonna ask you again."

"Okay . . ." Kilner put the Ford into gear and pulled out into traffic.

"Step on it," Jack insisted. "Don't stop for anything."

Kilner moved the car into the middle lane and started heading west, in the direction of the Hudson River. "Where are we going?"

"Just drive." Out of the corner of his eye, Kilner saw the other man lever off the back of the cell phone he had taken and pull the SIM card and battery, temporarily rendering the built-in tracking device useless.

"Bauer . . . *Jack.*" Kilner swallowed and tried to keep his voice even. "There's still time to end this. Give me the weapon, let me take you in. We can work this all out."

"You think so?" Jack shifted a bag on the backseat and leaned closer. "I go in, I'm going to disappear. I know how this works. Either my own side drops me down a deep, dark hole or the SVR gets to me first."

"SVR?" Kilner repeated. "The Russians can't move on

you . . ." He caught up with his own words. "At least, not legally."

"Now you're catching on . . ." Jack's tone shifted as Kilner took his foot off the gas. They were coming up to the crossing with Eighth Avenue and the traffic signals were against them. "I said don't stop!"

Kilner was about to answer, but a flash of headlights in his side mirror caught his eyes. A glossy black Ford Expedition SUV was coming up fast behind them, and he glimpsed a familiar face behind the wheel—Markinson. In the passenger seat was Hadley, a pistol in his hand and a phone at his ear.

Suddenly, hidden strobes flashed blue and red from behind the Expedition's grille and the SUV crowded in on the smaller sedan.

Jack pushed forward and grabbed Kilner's knee with his free hand, clamping it like a vise. He forced Kilner's leg down on the accelerator and the Fusion's engine snarled as it leapt forward.

The agent gripped the steering wheel tightly and snaked the car through the lines of traffic crossing the junction, a storm of blaring horns and shouted curses following them as they hurtled across and down the next block. The speedometer ticked up and up as Jack continued to force him to accelerate.

Hadley's SUV was still coming, the larger vehicle losing precious seconds as it slewed to avoid a bus.

Jack pointed the Springfield back toward the Fusion's rear window and fired off two rounds. The first turned the clear glass into an opaque, frosted mess; the second blew out the window and gave him a clear line of sight toward the pursuing Expedition. He aimed carefully and loosed off another shot, this one blinding one of the SUV's glaring headlights.

Agent Hadley was already up and leaning out of the passenger side window, a weapon in his hand. He returned fire, putting shots into the sedan's trunk. Then the SUV put on a surge of power and closed the distance as the Ninth Avenue intersection came up at the end of the block.

Ahead of them, a pair of water trucks filled the westbound lanes from one side to the other. Kilner moved to hit the brakes, but Jack had other ideas. At the last moment, he reached forward and yanked the steering wheel to the left, throwing the car across and into the path of oncoming traffic.

"*Shit!*" Kilner veered to avoid a head-on collision with a people-carrier and shot across the intersection. Markinson was still with them, however. The female agent nimbly powered the tall-sided SUV through the same maneuver, rocking it dangerously on its higher suspension as both pursued and pursuer wove back and forth across Twenty-Third Street. "Are you trying to kill us?"

"Turn off at Tenth," Jack demanded. He paused for a second. "You said you have a kid, right?"

"What?" The question seemed to come out of nowhere, but then he remembered. Years earlier when they had first met, Jorge had talked to Bauer back in DC after the FBI had him in lockdown. Just the two of them in the car, talking about what they believed was true, about their families and their jobs. "Yes. A daughter. *Fiona.*" Now it was happening all over again, but the circumstances were markedly different.

"You just do what I tell you and you'll see her again." The next intersection was coming up fast. "Make the turn."

Kilner swallowed. It wasn't like he had a lot of options. As they came up on the junction, he swung around a car rolling along in front of them, and tires screeched as the Fusion left a black streak on the asphalt, the rear end fishtailing into the turn.

More gunfire lanced after them as they bounced onto

Tenth Avenue and raced north. Jack shot back. Kilner guessed he was keeping his aim low, trying to put rounds into the wheels or the engine block of the SUV.

Hadley didn't seem to be extending them the same courtesy, however. A bullet barely missed Bauer and blasted a fist-sized hole in the windshield, and in the moment that followed Kilner heard a grumbling crackle issue out of the tactical radio laying were he had left it on the front passenger seat.

"*Stop the vehicle,*" barked Hadley over the open channel. "*Kilner, are you hearing me? Pull over, man!*"

"That guy the one in charge?" said Jack, as they passed Twenty-Sixth Street and continued on through the encroaching traffic.

Kilner nodded. "Agent Hadley. Yeah. He's got a real hate on for you."

"He can take a number and get in line. I don't even know him."

"He was Pillar's guy . . ."

"Jason Pillar?" Jack scowled. "I'm not responsible for what happened to him." He reached forward and grabbed the radio, squeezing the push-to-talk switch. "Hadley. Back off before someone gets hurt."

• • •

"That's not going to happen, Bauer." Hadley shot a look at Markinson, releasing the transmitter switch so his next words wouldn't be broadcast. "Where does he think he's going?"

"Gotta be making a break for the Lincoln Tunnel," she told him. "All he needs to do is ditch the car halfway and get into the service passages. It's a rat's nest down there, we'd never find him."

Hadley glanced at Dell, who was hunched over a laptop in the backseat. "Converge any units we have on

Thirtieth Street. If he *is* going for the tunnel, he's going to have a nasty surprise."

"Air support is unavailable," she told him. "We have two more cars and another tactical team."

"That'll be enough." He spoke into the radio again. "Last chance, Bauer. Because if I have to blast that vehicle off the street to take you out, I will do it."

"*I have a hostage. I'll kill him if you don't pull back.*"

"No, you won't." Hadley dropped the radio and held out his hand to Dell. "Give me the M4."

• • •

Kilner blinked at the exchange he had just overheard.

"He's right," said Jack. "I won't kill you." Then he pressed the muzzle of the M1911 against Kilner's kneecap. "But I will put a hole in your leg that'll mean you'll never be able to take a walk with your kid again."

"Understood . . ." His hands were sweating and he kneaded the grip of the steering wheel. As they crossed Twenty-Eighth Street Kilner saw a blur of white and blue, and an NYPD patrol car swerved out to meet them.

The two cars slammed into one another, running parallel as they bumped, trading paint and sending flashes of sparks out across the roadway.

Jack acted without hesitation, blowing out the Fusion's side window and the toughened glass of the police car's rear compartment. Kilner heard the familiar *tink* sound of an arming pin being pulled and a faint whiff of sulfur. Jack lobbed a smoke grenade into the backseat of the cruiser and ducked back down.

There was a thudding discharge and white haze filled the cruiser's interior. The police car wavered before it skidded to a halt and the officers inside scrambled out, but the FBI SUV was still coming, and Kilner saw Markinson use the heavier vehicle to shove the stalled cruiser out of its way. The Expedition's moon roof slipped open and Hadley's head and shoulders emerged.

The special agent had decided to trade up from his handgun. Now he was armed with a Colt M4 carbine, a weapon of higher caliber and faster rate of fire. Hadley opened up, putting 7.62mm rounds into the trunk of the Fusion. Kilner felt one of the rear tires blow and the car's traction became mushy. He fought to compensate.

"Guess he meant what he said," Jack muttered, pausing to reload the Springfield. "Gloves off, then." He popped up over the rear seat and fired off a salvo of rapid shots that whined off the hood of the SUV in bright ricochets, others cracking but not penetrating the armored windscreen. Still, it was enough to make Hadley retreat back inside the vehicle for a moment.

"Sooner or later we're gonna run out of road, Jack!" shouted Kilner, as the stress and the fear pressed him into his seat. It was hard to keep the sedan from drifting into the oncoming lane. "What are you doing?"

"Getting out of this city," he retorted. Ahead of them, the intersection with Thirtieth Street was coming up fast. They could both see it, the crossroads capped by a black iron structure like the legs of an oil rig; it was the remains of the old elevated train system, now repurposed as a ribbon of urban parkland. "Make the turn there."

Kilner blinked. "They're never going to let you get into the tunnel, Jack. It'll be a kill-box!"

"I know." He leaned forward again and pointed in the wrong direction as they came up on the intersection. "Go down there."

"It's a one-way street!"

"We're only gonna go one way."

Jack did the same trick as he had before, grabbing the wheel and turning it so that the Fusion spun the opposite way and lurched against the flow of the traffic. Kilner hung on for dear life as they charged straight into the path of other cars and vans, sending them skidding away to mount the sidewalk rather than crash. The agent banged on the horn bar in the middle of the steering wheel, shouting for the other drivers to veer off. They were no more than two or three blocks away from the edge of Manhattan now, and the river beyond. They were quite literally running out of road.

The driver's-side mirror exploded as a shot blasted it apart, and Kilner flinched. The bigger SUV, hemmed in on the smaller street, was still lumbering after them, but once more the turn had allowed the car to extend the distance between them. Racing past the Hudson Yards on the right, Kilner glimpsed the bulky shapes of garbage trucks moving back and forth on the courtyard of the Sanitation Department parking lot. He mashed the accelerator to push the Fusion past the front of one of the big white trucks as it nosed out into the street, and somewhere behind there was a screech of tires as the SUV had to throw on the anchors to avoid plowing into it.

Now they were almost at the junction with the Lincoln Highway and Kilner's heart was pounding in his chest. Hadley had shown he was more than willing to risk the agent's life to get his quarry—and Bauer, a man that Jorge respected, seemed just as determined never to let that happen.

The hot muzzle of the pistol jabbed him in the leg. "Get out," Jack snapped. "Do it now!"

"But we're—"

"*Now!*"

Kilner thought about Fiona and a gunshot that could cripple him, and he snapped off his seat belt and opened the door, even as the car was still rolling at a swift pace. He pushed against the frame of the vehicle and launched himself into the air.

The agent landed hard against the asphalt and he tumbled, bouncing to the curb, the rough roadway ripping at his hands and shredding his jacket. Dazed, he came to a halt against the base of a light pole in time to see the sedan bolt forward again as Jack slipped into the driver's seat and stamped on the accelerator. The car careened over the lanes of busy highway, causing shunts and collisions as other vehicles tried and failed to get out of the way in time.

Kilner pulled himself to his feet, every joint in his body aching like hell. He watched the Ford skid to a halt in a small parking lot on a concrete pier bordering the Hudson River.

It was only then that he realized exactly how Jack Bauer intended to flee the city.

• • •

"Hadley." Jack spoke into the radio handset as he scrambled out of the stalled car. "Don't make this personal."

His words got exactly the response he thought they would. "*Too late for that, Bauer. You're done.*"

He sighed. "Listen to me. Stay out of my way, and I will be gone within twenty-four hours. I'll fall off the face of the world and you will never hear from me again." Jack paused, throwing a glance back across the highway to where the SUV had halted. "But if you come after me . . . you'll regret it."

Hadley's reply was low and loaded with menace. "*I will personally put you down before this day is out, do you hear me? Your only choice will be handcuffs or a body bag.*"

There wasn't anything else to say. Jack tossed the radio and shifted the heavy gym bag on his shoulder, bringing up his pistol as he ran full tilt at the door of a small prefabricated office hut. He came through it like a freight train, shouting at the top of his lungs.

"Hands in the air!"

Inside, the hut was divided into an open reception area and waiting room on one side, and a set of office cubicles on the other. Maps, aeronautical charts and pictures of the city skyline taken from the air decorated the walls. In the reception, two men in dark business suits who had been in the middle of a spirited conversation about the performance of the Mets were shocked into silence by the sudden arrival of a furious armed invader.

A woman screamed as Jack's line of sight swung over her, and she dropped the sheaf of papers she was carrying in fright. At her side, an older man who had the looks of a former wrestler gone to seed scrambled back and away, grabbing for something hidden beneath one of the desks.

The old guy was a veteran, Jack saw it in his eyes, the way he reacted as a trained soldier would, not with panic but with something like defiance. He would be going for a weapon, an alarm, or both.

Jack didn't hesitate. He fired a single .45 ACP round into the face of a large analog clock on the wall behind the older man, blasting it to pieces with a noisy, showy display of force. "Don't be a hero," he said.

"Screw you!" spat the veteran, hesitating.

Jack advanced, pushing through a waist-high gate that allowed access to the office proper. He could hear the deep droning of rotor blades, and out through the windows that looked across the rest of the pier, he could see the shark-shaped aerodynamic bodies of a pair of helicopters.

The heliport at West Thirtieth Street had not only the benefit of being closest to the Hotel Chelsea, but also of being a base for aircraft that Jack was fully rated on. New York had a number of helicopter terminals, but they were all too far away for him to risk making a play for. Hadley's FBI colleagues had bought the fake trail that Jack had laid for them, wrongly assuming that he was making for the Lincoln Tunnel. Now he had to make the opportunity he had created work for him.

"Move!" He jerked the muzzle of the Springfield back toward the door. "Get out, all of you."

"Why?" demanded the old man. "So you can shoot us in the back as we run?" He jabbed a finger toward Jack. "Are you one of them rats who killed that poor ay-rab fella? You bring their war here, did ya?"

I tried to save Omar Hassan's life. He wanted to say it, but the words died in his throat. Instead Jack fired again into the ceiling. "I said *go!*"

It was enough for the businessmen, and they sprinted for the door, the woman following on their heels. The veteran gave Jack a sour, disgusted glare and walked out after them. "You're going to spend the rest of your life dead, son," he told him.

"No doubt," Jack replied, and pushed through a second door on the far side of the hut, spilling out onto the helipad.

The first helo was immobile, the rotors tied down with straps to stop them from catching the wind off the river, but the second—a brown-and-green Bell 206 Long Ranger model—was already running at idle. The blades made lazy sweeps overhead as the pilot ran the engine at low power. Jack guessed he was performing a preflight test of some kind, maybe a check after maintenance on one of the chopper's systems. It also explained how the pilot had missed the noise of the gunshots under the whistling whine of the motor.

The passengers and staff he had forced out into the street would be enough to cause some interference with Hadley and the FBI team coming after him, but Jack guessed he would have only moments before armed federal agents came storming across the helipad toward him.

He ran for the Long Ranger and ripped open the pilot's door with a single sharp motion.

"Hey, what the—?" Before he could finish his sentence, Jack grabbed a handful of the pilot's jacket and wrenched him out of his seat. The man hadn't bothered to secure himself with a belt for a simple engine test, and he went wheeling down to the concrete, the headset over his ears ripped off where the coiled cable caught on the door frame.

The pilot tried to scramble back to his feet and he looked up to find the yawning muzzle of the M1911 pistol aimed at the middle of his forehead. Jack didn't need to shout out a command over the chop of the spinning blades. The transaction was clear, and the man backed off, hands out to his sides, ducking low as the rotor wash buffeted him.

Jack clambered into the helicopter's cockpit and secured the door. The pilot broke into a run, and from the corner of his eye, Jack could see movement back near the office hut. He had no time to waste.

The gun went into the side of his waistband and Jack's hands dropped automatically into the correct positions on the cyclic stick in front of him and the collective lever at his side. His feet found the pedals and he increased the throttle with a twist of his wrist. The thudding tone of the rotors became a chattering snarl as he applied more power to the engine. Jack felt the blades biting into the air and the helicopter immediately became lighter, lifting up off the ground.

Something struck the rear of the Long Ranger with a dull, hollow ring, and Jack glanced to his right, catching sight of the FBI team taking aim, firing. He pressed hard on one of the pedals and the tail of the helicopter slewed around, pointing the buzz saw disc of the rear rotor in their direction. Jack kept on applying more power, deliberately aiming the downwash from the main rotors to swamp his pursuers and disrupt their aim.

As he brought the helicopter around, he caught a

glimpse of Hadley trying to draw a bead on him with his carbine. Jack aimed the Long Ranger's nose toward the coastline of New Jersey on the far side of the Hudson and the aircraft raced away like a loosed arrow. More shots rang against the fuselage, but without result.

Moving low and fast, he skimmed across the surface of the river, taking the shortest possible route from shore to shore until he made landfall again over the suburban streets of Union City.

Jack found the fuel gauge and saw the needle resting at 75 percent reserves. Enough to get him into Maine, maybe across the Canadian border, or perhaps toward Philadelphia and Baltimore if he turned south—and then only if he could avoid contact with any police or Air National Guard units.

It was time to go dark. He switched off his transponder, cutting off any attempt local air traffic controllers might make to find his vector and lead others to him. Then Jack deactivated the Long Ranger's running lights and the cockpit illumination until the only light he had was the soft glow of the instrument panel. The sun had set and the azure sky was darkening to black. As long as he could keep below the radar detection threshold and away from urban centers, escape was possible.

At least until this thing runs out of gas, he thought. *And then what the hell am I going to do?*

He glanced down at the black bag where he had dumped it on the empty seat beside him, thinking about the micro-SIM card he had recovered from the apartment. The FBI would have access to his CTU personnel file, and that would have most of the names and numbers from his "black book." If Hadley was smart, he would already have taps on the most likely subjects and communications traffic analysts watching everyone else. And then there were the Russians, who had deep pock-

ets, a very long reach and a whole different set of intelligence resources.

He couldn't call Kim to alert her about his situation,
or pull in favors from his usual contacts. Finishing what
he had started was going to involve thinking a long way
outside the box. He put the helicopter into a shallow turn
and pointed it in the direction of the vanished sun.

Slowly, it came to Jack that the only person who could
help him was a dead man.

05

The warehouse on the outskirts of Pittsburgh had once stored colossal rolls of paper for transport to printing works and factories all over the country, but now it was an echoing, vacant space. Just one more example of the economic downturn writ large across the city's infrastructure, home now to a colony of tenacious rats and little else.

The homeless and the unlucky knew better than to try and find shelter in the place, however. As much as it stood idle and empty, the warehouse still did business of a sort. It belonged to the deSalvo crime family, and they kept it on the books as a place where they could meet without fear of being overheard by the feds. The fact that it was isolated enough to mean that the odd gunshot wouldn't be noticed was just a bonus.

Charlie Williams drove the silver Chrysler 300 in under the half-open roller doors and brought it to a halt, a short distance from a pair of black Crown Victorias parked under the big skylight. In the rearview mirror he could see Roker in the backseat, shifting uncomfortably, visibly sweating even though it was a chilly evening. The other man pulled at the collar of his shirt and kept shifting his jacket like it was too tight for him.

Relax, he wanted to say. *They're not going to bring you here just to whack you.* But he said nothing. He had learned the hard way that "Big Mike" Roker didn't like it when his employees spoke out of turn—and Charlie Williams was very much a servant of the Roker household, as Big Mike and his wife liked to remind him at every opportunity.

He turned off the engine and felt a spasm of pain from his right hand. He thought about the plastic bottle of Percocet tablets in his jacket pocket and unconsciously licked his lips. Today had been a bad day for the old wound, and he could feel the numbness in his fingers like a creeping rot. The nerve damage there had never fully healed, and he'd tried to make his peace with it. But sometimes even an action as simple as maintaining a firm grip on the steering wheel was difficult. With effort, he pushed away the thought of the temporary relief the pain medication would give him and concentrated on his surroundings.

Ernest deSalvo had four guys standing with him. Scanning the warehouse, Charlie saw the shadow of someone else under one of the support gantries toward the rear of the building. An extra man, a spotter maybe. He suppressed a thin smile. Ernest liked to think he was some kind of little general, talking about his side of the organization like it was a military unit with "point men" and "tactical overwatch" and all that kind of terminology. But the fact was, the man's entire knowledge of warfare and soldiering came from a diet of lurid war documentaries on the History channel.

Roker kicked the back of his seat. "What are you waiting for? Get out there!"

"Right," said Charlie, his lips thinning. He climbed out

and opened the back door so Roker could exit with something approaching poise.

Ernest nodded at one of his guys, and the bodyguard came up and frisked Charlie, before giving Big Mike a cursory pat down.

"Hey," Roker complained. "Not without dinner and a movie first."

That drew a dry snigger from deSalvo. "This one. He's always a joker."

Charlie followed Roker toward the group, but stayed back a few feet. His gaze was instinctively drawn toward the man in the shadows. Big Mike hadn't noticed the sixth guy.

"We, ah, not keeping your boy's attention, Mikey?" said Ernest, gesturing at Charlie.

Roker shot him a look. "What?" he demanded.

Charlie sighed and pointed directly at the hidden man. "Is he looking for rats?"

"Who?" Ernest played dumb.

"*Your* boy, Mr. deSalvo. The one who thinks he's playing ghost over there."

The oily grin on deSalvo's face froze for a second. He didn't like being caught out. Then he laughed and spoke up. "Bobby! Stop screwing around!"

The sixth man sheepishly emerged from the shadows and lit a cigarette, staring daggers at Charlie.

"Eyes like an eagle," Roker noted. "It's why I pay him so much!"

"Not *that* much," Charlie muttered under his breath.

"Yeah." Ernest gave Charlie a hard look. "How's the hand, tough guy?" He sneered. "You still on them pills?"

Roker was glaring at him as he replied. "Good days and bad days." Charlie ran a hand over his closely shaved head and looked away.

But deSalvo had already dismissed him. The conversation went on in exactly the way the driver had imagined it would. Ernest wasn't happy with Roker's performance, and was here to remind him that his continued success, his comfortable home and the nice career he had carved out running his car dealership, all those things existed at the indulgence of the deSalvo organization.

Ernest was smart enough not to speak about specifics, but it was all there in the subtext. Roker's dealership laundered money for the deSalvos, but how it actually worked wasn't something that Charlie Williams was interested in. As a matter of fact, he had made it a point to stay as ignorant of Roker's business dealings as possible. *I'm just the driver,* he would tell himself. *Just his security. Nothing more, nothing less.*

And there were some days when he could almost believe that. The other days—those times when Charlie thought about the man he had been before he washed up in Pittsburgh with no money and no prospects—those were the moments when he hated himself. But the pills helped deaden those feelings, just like they killed the pain in his hand. *For a little while, at least.*

The meeting came to an end and Ernest deSalvo made an off-color joke that everyone felt obligated to laugh at. Roker couldn't wait to get away, and he almost ran back to the Chrysler, not waiting for Charlie to get the door for him. When they were back on the road, he leaned forward from the rear seat and angrily prodded his driver.

"What the hell was all that crap back there? I guessed Bobby was around. You didn't need to say anything!"

That was a lie, and both men knew it. "Just doing my job," Charlie offered, wincing as his hand sent another spasm of pain up his arm. "Ernie likes to be the top dog, sure, but you can't let him think you're a chump." The pain was occupying his thoughts, and the moment the words left his mouth, he knew it had been the wrong thing to say.

"I'm a what now?" Roker exploded with rage. It wasn't surprising, all that frustration and fear at being forced into a face-to-face with deSalvo had nowhere to go, so now it was expressing itself in anger toward Charlie. He swore loudly and jabbed his finger toward the driver's face. "I pay your wages, asshole! I pay you to drive and shut the hell up, understand?"

"I understand, Mr. Roker," he said tonelessly, going through the motions of a conversation they had replayed a dozen times.

"That's right!" Roker retorted. As they drove, Big Mike began picking apart every last detail of the meeting with deSalvo, repeating it and reliving it as if he were having a conversation with himself.

Charlie didn't offer any more insights, he just let Roker talk and talk, and by the time they were turning off the highway toward the dealership, the other man had rearranged the narrative of the meet to make it sound like it was Big Mike who had made it happen, talking himself into believing that he was the key player.

The showroom was a glass-fronted hangar filled with new Chryslers like the 300 and a few classic muscle cars. It reminded Charlie of a gargantuan fish tank, the impression heightened by the cool blue-white lighting inside that showcased the polished bodies and chrome accents of the vehicles. Above the entrance, a large banner announced BIG MIKE'S BIG DEALS! and Charlie reflected that it was as much a mission statement for Roker's life as it was a commercial for his dealership. Mike Roker so desperately wanted to be a big deal, and he was forever angry at the world for making him fall short of that.

Charlie frowned as they pulled to a stop at the rear of the building, where the maintenance bay was open to the evening air.

Roker's wife, Barbara, pushed past two of the mechanics working late and strode out to meet them, and she too appeared to be spoiling for a fight. He remembered something his dad had once told him: *This is the kind of person who'll find an argument in a bouquet of roses.*

For a moment, Barbara Roker's sour expression shifted as he got out of the car, and as she saw the driver her face lit up with a predatory smirk. "Hey Charlie," she purred.

"Mrs. Roker," he replied. The woman had made it clear she was interested in furthering their employer-employee relationship in a way that he wasn't comfortable with, and so far, he'd been able to keep himself at arm's length.

But in the next moment, Barbara's expression shifted back toward irritation as her husband stepped out from the 300. "Where were you?" she demanded.

"Ah, crap." Big Mike deflated, running a hand over his face. "Barb. Yeah. Sorry."

"*Sorry?*" she repeated, her voice rising. "You were supposed to pick me up, you prick! I had to get a cab!"

"Something came up," Roker insisted, faking a smile. "Last second. Ernie deSalvo called me. Needed me to help him out."

He made it sound like the other man had come to him on bended knee, but Barbara saw right through the spin her husband had put on the situation and scowled at him. "Oh yeah? He snaps his fingers and you say, 'How high,' right?" She shook her head. "Mike, when you gonna stand up to that roach? You make me sick."

Roker's false front collapsed and Charlie watched his cheeks color. "Do what? I talk back to him and I get a bullet in the face ten seconds later! Where would you get your cash for your stupid shoe collection then, huh?"

"You know nothing," she shot back. "Men like that? They respect strength." Barbara looked toward Charlie. "You know what I mean, right?"

"Don't ask him!" Roker bellowed. "What the hell does he know?"

Charlie opened his mouth to say something that would let him disengage from the unfolding argument, but there was no need. It was already under way and neither husband nor wife were registering him anymore. He drifted toward the bench where the dealership's two mechanics were loitering.

Frank and Josh were in their twenties, and they seemed to think that working for Roker was an entry-level job into the lucrative world of Pittsburgh's criminal underbelly. Charlie didn't have the heart to tell them how mistaken they were.

"What happened?" asked Frank. He was the bigger of the two, thickset with a body honed by hours on free weights at the local gym.

Charlie shook his head. "Same old, same old."

"Huh." Josh nodded to himself, taking in Charlie's answer as if it was something cryptic. The other mechanic was short and compact, and he radiated a nervous energy. "Hey man, you see the news tonight?" He pointed toward a small portable TV sitting on the workbench.

On the smudged screen there was a reporter from CNB talking over footage from New York. There had been a kidnapping and a murder of a prominent foreign leader, and now something was going on with the president. "What's all this?" he asked.

"President quit, man," Frank said sagely. "You know it's gotta be bad if the prez throws in the towel."

"Damn Russians." Josh offered his opinion. "They did it, you betcha. It's like they wanna go back to the eighties or somethin'. Evil empire and all that crap."

Frank glared at the other mechanic. "What do you know about the eighties, dumbass? Your mom was like a baby back then."

"I saw a movie," Josh said defensively.

"What do you think, Charlie?" said Frank. But the driver wasn't really paying attention. On the TV screen, the news feed was showing video from earlier in the day, figures in blue visibility jackets swarming along a street outside the United Nations building. Large yellow letters designated the agencies they worked for—FBI, NYPD, CTU.

The pain in his hand came again and Charlie walked away without answering. With his good hand he reached up toward the inner jacket pocket containing the bottle of Percocets. His cell phone rang before he could touch it.

The phone's screen gave the caller ID as UNKNOWN, and on an impulse he couldn't quite explain, he touched the tab to accept the call. "Yeah?"

"*Hello, Chase,*" said a rough, low voice on the other end of the line. "*Can you talk?*"

In that second, it was as if the ground opened up beneath him and he plunged into a freezing, bottomless chasm. His balance went away and he had to steady himself against one of the parked cars. Suddenly he was aware of every old wound he had ever suffered, every scar weighing down on him. Out of nowhere, the past he had worked so long to outpace had caught up with him.

He swallowed hard. "Who . . . Who is this?" But he already knew the answer before he heard it.

"*It's Jack. I need your help.*"

He shot a look back at the events being displayed on the television screen, his thoughts racing. "How did you find . . . ?"

"*We can talk about that later.*" There was a pause, and in those brief seconds he could almost hear the sound of his world cracking apart around him. "*You owe me, Chase. And now I'm calling in the marker.*"

"Chase Edmunds is dead," he whispered, catching sight of his own face in the smoked-glass windows of the car. The face of a man who had gone on the run from himself, who had gotten lost from all he had been. *Or so I thought.*

"*So was I*," said the voice on the phone. "*It didn't take.*"

He wondered if it would be hard to just break away and leave it all behind once again. Every time in the past he had thought about doing exactly that, it seemed like an impossible choice to make. But now it felt simple. He had already made the decision, somewhere deep down, maybe months or even years ago. "What do you want, Jack?"

"*Check your messages.*" The line went dead, and a moment later the phone beeped as a text message arrived. An address out on the interstate, past Monroeville; he knew where it was.

"Hey! Hey, listen to me!" Abruptly, he realized that Roker was storming across the garage toward him, his face like thunder. "Talk on the phone on your own dime, shithead!"

He looked at the other man, and it was as if he was seeing him for the first time. He saw every little flaw in Big Mike Roker, saw everything he loathed and detested about this small, venial man. "You're going to wind up dead, you know that?"

"What did you say?!" Roker bellowed. "Are you threatening me? Did deSalvo say something?"

"Mike . . ." he began, climbing into the 300. "I'm done. Take your crappy job and shove it. I quit."

"Hey, that's my car!" Roker came at him as he hit the gas and peeled off into the darkness. "Who the hell do you think you are, Charlie?"

"Not that guy," said Chase Edmunds.

• • •

Jack looked down at the cell phone he had stolen from Agent Kilner, the inner workings of the device exposed where he had used a table knife to open the back and disconnect the tracking chip. Nobody bothered him in the roadside diner's corner booth, the sparse clientele of the twenty-four-hour rest stop intent on their own meals and conversations. There was what appeared to be a cheap plastic security camera in a bubble over the doorway, but it was pointing the wrong way to capture a look at his face.

The diner was one of those faux-authentic 1950s places with a swooping roof and a neon sign out on a pole in the parking lot, all jet-age architecture and old tin signs—but it was too shabby to be considered retro, the fake-wood veneer peeling and the tired seats patched with duct tape. A line of semitrucks concealed Jack from the sight of any passing cars on the highway, and he glanced out of the window as a state police patrol car sped past at a clip, vanishing into the evening as quickly as it had appeared.

Beyond the oasis of light cast by the diner there was darkness, and nothing but fields, woodland and pockets of suburbia for miles around. The waitress who had poured him a generous mug of tarry coffee hadn't remarked on the fact that Jack had walked in from off the road without a vehicle. He wondered if anyone had heard him bringing the Long Ranger down in a clearing a couple of miles back down the turnpike. If luck was on his side, the helicopter wouldn't be found until daylight tomorrow.

The coffee was strong and good, and it helped him focus. He turned the phone over again, taking care not to nudge the SIM card protruding from the memory slot, and erased the record of the call he had just made. For a moment, Jack felt a flash of guilt. He knew from the tone of Chase's voice that his contact had struck like a lightning bolt, coming out of nowhere to disrupt whatever kind of new life his former partner had set up for himself in Pittsburgh.

It gnawed at him, the sense that he could roll in and break open one man's attempt to find a fresh start—but it wasn't like Jack had any other options open to him at this point. His associates, his friends and his family would all be under close observation. To get what he needed, Jack's only hope was to reach out to somebody whom the rest of the world thought was dead and gone.

Jack Bauer and Chase Edmunds had first crossed paths several years earlier, during an incident that had brought CTU's Washington, DC, and Los Angeles branches together. A complex plot to kill thousands of innocents in California had been thwarted largely due to the work of the two agents. Edmunds had transferred to CTU LA soon afterward and the two of them became an effective team. Months later, when the whole Cordilla virus attack blew up and Jack was undercover infiltrating the Salazar cartel, it had been Chase who had his back. But it had not gone well for either man during those deadly hours, and when it was all over things between the two agents had changed forever. Jack had made choices that still weighed heavily on him, and it was Chase who'd paid the price.

He wondered what he was going to say when he saw his old colleague again. At lot had happened since they parted ways, and it was only through some nagging sense of responsibility that Jack had continued to keep tabs on the other man.

How things played out in the next few hours would determine if Jack's escape plan would work, or if he was destined to spend the rest of his life rotting in a federal prison. *Or dead,* he thought, recalling the words of the old veteran at the heliport.

There was a good chance that Jack Bauer would end

up killed before the day was out, and he had to find a way to control those possibilities. He had to narrow the focus, control the situation.

He scrolled through the list of contacts on the data card, tabbing slowly past the names and numbers of friends and enemies alike. His finger hesitated over one particular entry and his eyes narrowed.

The information was old, the sole lead toward someone who had never been remotely close to being an ally. Someone who—on another day, in times gone by—Jack would not have hesitated to kill. But right now, he didn't have that luxury.

He tapped the "call" button and waited for the line to connect. What he was going to do next would be another risk, perhaps the most dangerous one he had taken since his decision to flee New York. But if it worked . . .

The call was answered with the metallic click of an automated voice mail system. He wasted no time with preamble or explanation. "This is Jack Bauer," he began. "I want to talk." He gave the unlisted number of the reprogrammed phone, and cut short the call.

"Top you off, honey?" The waitress came back with a jug of fresh coffee in her hand and Jack gratefully accepted a refill. He ordered a burger and fries, and his stomach growled with the thought of it. All of a sudden, Jack realized it had been a long time since he'd refueled.

He was finishing up his meal as the phone trilled.

"You actually called back," he said. "I figured it was fifty-fifty."

"*It's been a while,*" came the reply. "*You have my attention, Jack.*"

• • •

The staging area provided to the SVR operatives was in the rear of a run-down barbershop in Hell's Kitchen, and the place had an ever-present smell of burnt hair and cleaning fluids.

Out in the front of the salon, a couple of men whose security clearance was too low to know the full details of the mission stood guard, watching the street. Alone in the back room, Ziminova had a ruggedized laptop computer set up on a rickety table and a satellite phone plugged into a charger cradle. She drummed the fingers of one hand on the tabletop, idly leafing through the pages of a months-old issue of *National Geographic* with the other.

Bazin and Ekel had yet to return with their vehicle; the commander had talked about picking up some special items of equipment from a safe house in Harlem, and it was taking longer than they had expected. She scowled at her watch.

Although she hid it well, the SVR agent was wired. Galina Ziminova detested inaction, a fact that was constantly at odds with the career that had chosen her. A key part of the espionage operations she worked involved doing nothing, often waiting for a target to make the next move before sweeping in for a kill or a capture. Yet she couldn't make her peace with the silence and the clock-watching. In a mission like this, that tension grew tenfold. With every moment she sat in this room, Jack Bauer was slipping further and further away.

Ziminova's operational record was exceptional—it was one of the reasons she had been deployed to America to work in Bazin's unit—and she had no desire to see it marred by a failure to capture the renegade CTU agent. But still, she could not shake the nagging sense that the mission they were on was more about assuaging one politician's petty need for reprisal, than it was about protecting her homeland.

She considered Bazin for a moment. She had only been a part of his team for the last six months, and she still did not have the full measure of him. Her commander was of an era when the people of the Soviet Union thought of their leaders as men of destiny, larger-than-life figures who exemplified the eternal character of the Motherland. That seemed old-fashioned to her, as a child of the New Russia. To Ziminova, the men at the top were part of the problem, part of the reason she had decided to serve her nation, so that she might defend it in *spite* of them. The Russia that Galina kept in her heart was one where the *people* were the nation, not the men who ruled them.

She frowned at that and glanced at her watch again. The asset she was here to meet was running late, a habitual trait that his handler at the consulate had warned her of. The man was a very cautious sort, given to overthinking things, and Ziminova could imagine that on a day like today, he was turning circles trying to make certain he was not being followed to the rendezvous. Her lips thinned. Tradecraft could only go so far before it became a waste of time.

A page-turn of the magazine revealed an image of an airliner, and Ziminova's thoughts drifted to a different subject. President Suvarov's jet would be airborne by now, racing away, up on a flight path across the North Atlantic that would take it home as quickly as possible. If the United Nations had wanted to question Suvarov about his part in the day's events, they had lost their chance to do so—at least for now.

Bazin's orders for the team included a directive to update the president's chief of staff on the status of the hunt at regular intervals, but for now there was little to report, only that the FBI did not have Jack Bauer in custody. He was, to use the local vernacular, *in the wind*.

From out of nowhere the satellite phone chirped and Ziminova pulled it from the charging cradle. "Go ahead."

"*I have an update,*" said Yolkin. The other agent was

somewhere outdoors, perhaps up on a roof. Ziminova could hear the wind and the far-off whoop of fire engines in the background. "*Mager has confirmation from his informant in the NYPD that there was an armed pursuit in the Chelsea district. There are reports that a commercial helicopter was hijacked, last sighted over New Jersey.*"

"It was Bauer?"

Yolkin paused. "*That is unclear.*"

"What kind of helicopter?"

There was another pause as Yolkin checked the details. "*A Bell 206 Long Ranger. But whomever the hijacker was, the law enforcement agencies are scrambling to find a lead on them. At this level of activity, it could only be our target.*"

There was a gentle *knock-knock* at the doorway, and Ziminova looked up to see one of the guards peering through the half-open door. He jerked a thumb at the other room.

She nodded, dismissing him, before turning her attention back to the phone. "Don't make assumptions," she continued. "Bazin will want hard facts. I have to go, the asset is here."

Ziminova cut the call and hesitated a moment, taking in what Yolkin had said. The aircraft he spoke of had a range of around 350 to 400 miles with a full fuel load. She wondered where Bauer hoped to go inside that radius, but it was a waste of time to chase vague possibilities. They would find the target with facts, not guesswork. She stood up and strode into the barbershop.

• • •

A man of average height with dark hair and a swarthy complexion was waiting for Ziminova in the middle of the room. The two SVR security men—both silent and thuggish in aspect—stood between him and the doorway back out to the street, and as Ziminova entered, one of them turned the latch to lock them in.

The man—*the asset*—kneaded the collar of his coat and his eyes darted to Ziminova and then to the door. "I came as soon as I could," he told her. "It was difficult for me to get away. I can't be here for long, my absence will be noticed."

She had glanced at the asset's file. His story was a commonplace one in the world of espionage. He had been suborned not by love of an ideology or through blackmail, but by simple avarice. A technical officer working for the East Coast's largest cellular network systems provider, he had been well paid by the Russian state in return for minor acts of industrial espionage. The commercial intelligence that he had leaked allowed the corporate interests that worked hand in hand with the Kremlin to compete on a level footing with foreign companies, even stealing a march on their rivals in some areas.

But that information had only ever been part of the deal. The asset had been cultivated for another reason, and now he would learn of it.

Ziminova gave the man a measuring look and set to work on him. "You are going to provide us with full access to your network's logs," she told him, and the man went pale. "Specifically, an area centered on New York City with a radius of . . ." She paused, thinking about it. "Four hundred fifty miles."

"I . . . I can't."

"You can," she said, as if the refusal was a foolish thing. "We know you can. And it must be done very quickly. We're looking for someone, you understand?"

From a pocket she produced a data stick that had been prepared by a technician at the consulate. On it was a captured sample of Jack Bauer's voice and a dedicated suite of pattern-recognition software.

The asset took the data stick with shaking hands. "You don't understand," he was saying. "This isn't what I agreed to. Industrial secrets are one thing, but this is something else!"

"You will be compensated," she told him. "Do you really want to consider what will happen if you refuse?" Ziminova didn't wait for him to come up with an answer. "We do not have time to find a different option. So, the man I work for will have your wife and children murdered one by one until you do as you have been asked." She kept her tone mild, almost conversational.

"*No . . . !*" The asset blinked, his eyes shimmering. "All right . . . But please, don't hurt them . . ."

"Do as we say and they will be fine." She reached out and put a hand on his shoulder. "We will be waiting."

The operative by the door opened it to let the asset leave, and Ziminova watched the man walk away as if in a daze, disappearing out of sight. She glanced at her watch once again. She had destroyed a person's life here, in less than a minute of conversation.

Ziminova wondered if it would be necessary to make good on the dire threat, and in a distant, detached way she looked for some shred of sympathy for the asset. She did not find it. Instead, she wondered if the asset would be brave enough to raise the alarm. If he did so, the entire operation would be blown.

But then she recalled something Bazin had once told her about those they selected to suborn. *We never choose men strong enough to resist us.*

06

Chase parked the Chrysler in the diner's parking lot with the nose pointing back out on the highway in case he needed to make a quick getaway. It was an instinctive action that came to him automatically, some remnant of his training snapping back into place. He'd allowed some of his skills to atrophy over the last few years, and it was good to know that he hadn't forgotten it all.

Before climbing out of the car, he checked the safety catch on the Ruger pistol in the holster under his jacket, and walked into the rest stop. Scanning the faces of the diners, he zeroed in on a lone figure at the shadowy booth in the rear.

The man Chase had come to see had his back to the wall and he had chosen a place that was both out of the way and within a few feet of the fire exit. It couldn't be anyone else.

Chase gave the waitress a wan smile and slipped into the booth. "Hey." He wanted to open with something else, but now that he was there, looking right into Bauer's steady green eyes, he wasn't sure what to say.

"Thanks for coming," Jack told him, and it seemed like he meant it. The older man looked strung out and exhausted, but there was still that edge of something feral in his gaze. Bauer reminded him of a wolf backed into a corner. "It's good to see you, Chase."

"Haven't been Chase Edmunds for a long time," he replied.

"I know," Jack said with a weary nod. "I saw the death certificate." He paused. "I'm sorry. But you're the only hope I've got right now."

Chase gave a humorless chuckle. "So, the New York thing, huh? You're neck-deep in that? Should have guessed."

"It's complicated."

"It always is." He glanced out of the window, then back. "I got a lot of questions."

"No doubt. Look, we should get on the road—"

Chase held up a hand. "No. Jack, I'm not moving from this spot until you give me some answers. You want my help, you're gonna have to talk to me."

Bauer sank back against the seat. "Fine."

The first question—the one Chase really wanted to ask—stuck in his throat and he pushed past it, taking another tack. "I worked hard to make Chase Edmunds a ghost and Charlie Williams a reality. And yet here you are, as if nothing has happened. How'd you find me, Jack?"

Bauer watched him carefully, and he answered the unspoken question first. "Kim's okay. She's back in LA now, married. I have a granddaughter."

Chase tried and failed to conceal the emotions that statement brought up in him, the surge of regret mixed with genuine relief. It was hard for him to parse his reaction. "That's . . . That's good. I'm happy for her." But both men knew that wasn't the whole truth.

Years ago, back when Kim Bauer had been taken captive during a CTU operation, it had been Chase that rescued her, and in the aftermath the two of them had grown close. For a while, it had been serious between them—but things had changed after the Cordilla virus incident, after what had happened to Chase during the race to neutralize that deadly threat. He reflexively massaged his bad arm.

Jack nodded at the injury. "How is it?"

Chase shot him a look. "You cut off my hand with a fire axe, Jack. You cut it off and they had to sew the damn thing back on again. How do you *think* it is?" He scowled and Bauer said nothing. The fact was, Jack had been forced to do what he did. In the course of the whole situation with the Salazar plot, a vial of deadly virus bacillus had been attached to Chase's arm and it would have discharged and infected countless innocents if not removed.

But that act had forever damaged the bond between the two men, and if Chase was honest with himself, it had sown the seeds of his breakup with Kim into the bargain. After surgery, nerve damage across the severed wrist meant Chase had been unable to requalify for duty at CTU despite all the recovery therapy he had gone through. The job that had been his first, best calling was lost to him, and looking back he could only see it as the top of the slope that had taken him down and down to where he was now. Months later when news reached Kim that her father had apparently been killed, it was the beginning of the end for the couple. Chase had never really believed Bauer was gone, and in a way Kim had hated him for holding on to that belief when all she wanted was to move on with her life. The cruel irony that Chase had been right all along was not lost on him as he sat across the table from Kim's father.

"Chloe," said Jack, returning to the first question. "Chloe O'Brian found you, not me. I asked her to look for you after what happened with the bomb in Valencia."

"Right . . ." Chase nodded to himself.

"Angela . . ." Jack said softly, and the mention of the name of Chase's daughter made his chest tighten. "Was she . . . ?"

"No." Chase placed his hands flat on the table. "Thank god, no. She was in San Diego with my sister when it happened. I . . . sent her away." He remembered the moment as if it were yesterday. It was a few years after he had been invalided out of the Counter Terrorist Unit, and things had not gone well for him. He was in debt, adrift in his own life. Although Chase had tried hard to find something new to challenge him, working for a private security concern, nothing he did seemed to matter as much as CTU had. Without Kim in his life, he just couldn't find a focus, and as Angela grew up it became harder and harder for him to connect with the young girl.

And then a group of terrorists had detonated a low-yield nuclear suitcase bomb in a Santa Clarita warehouse, just miles from where he lived. The blast wiped Valencia off the map and murdered over twelve thousand people in an instant. The effect of that brutality was still being felt today, with a section of Los Angeles County walled off to contain the blast zone, a legacy of human tragedies and an ongoing effort to decontaminate the area that would continue for decades.

On the day it happened, Chase had been drowning his sorrows in a bottle of Jack Daniel's on the far side of LA, and something inside him *snapped*. With perfect clarity, he saw the road ahead of him and he knew it would lead nowhere. He decided to let the world believe that Chase Edmunds had died in the Valencia bombing and begin again. Angela would get his insurance payout and with it a chance at a far better life than any he could have given her.

"You faked your own death," said Jack, guessing at the train of his thoughts. "You used the bombing to slip away and make a fresh start. You did well enough to fool most people."

"But not Chloe, huh?" Chase looked down at his hands. "I shouldn't be surprised." He glanced back at his former partner. "It's not easy, is it, Jack? To let everyone who cares about you believe you're gone."

"No," Jack said quietly, and Chase felt a pang of sorrow for the other man. "Now we both understand the price of that choice."

"I guess so. Didn't exactly work out for me the way I planned it, though. Four years down the line and I'm worse off than I ever was." He smiled regretfully. "Then you fall out of the sky and I come running. What the hell does that say about me?"

"It tells me you haven't changed that much. It tells me you're still loyal to your friends." Jack met his gaze. "And right now, I'm pretty short on those."

"What happened in New York?" Chase asked, and Jack told him.

He talked about the plot to kill the leader of the Islamic Republic of Kamistan, of the bomb threat against Manhattan and finally of the conspiracy he had dragged into the light. There was more, though, Chase could sense it—and when he pressed Jack to explain he saw the other man's eyes go cold and distant.

"They killed someone that I cared about. And now I have a target on my back. The FBI, Russian intelligence . . . It's even money on which of them catches up to me first." He sighed. "I just want one thing, then I'm gone. I want to see my family one last time."

Chase said nothing, and in his mind's eye he saw Angela again. He tried not to think about her too much these days, but when he did the remorse was like razors on his skin. He could very easily understand the raw, human impulse behind his former partner's motive. He nodded. "So you need my help to get to Los Angeles in one piece."

"I can pay you. I have a covert account that no one knows about, not even CTU."

"Parachute money, huh?" Chase shook his head. "No need. You were right when you said you had a marker with me. You saved my life enough times. I owe you."

"Thanks."

He stood up and Jack followed suit. "I know a guy," Chase continued. "Guess you could call him a specialist, kinda. He does contract work for my former employer."

"Former?"

Chase shrugged. "I'll explain on the way."

• • •

But as it turned out, taking their leave wasn't going to be that straightforward. As the two of them came around the side of a semitruck, Chase saw the blue Pontiac parked clumsily behind his stolen Chrysler 300 and the two men perched on the edges of the sedan's silver hood.

Josh and Frank were still wearing their mechanic's overalls underneath dark jackets, and as they approached, Josh peered out at them from under the bill of a grimy baseball cap. "Finally," he muttered, slipping off the car.

Frank advanced, flexing his big hands. "Charlie," he began, shaking his head. "You shouldn't have taken off like that. Mr. Roker, he's real mad about it."

Josh pointed at Jack. "Who's this?" He sniffed the air like he smelled something bad. "He looks like a cop."

Chase let out a sigh. "You followed me."

"Yeah. Saw the car from the highway." Frank shook his head. "Mr. Roker wants it back in one piece."

Jack had become very still. Chase glanced at him and neither man said a word, but they knew each other well enough to read intent. There was a question in Jack's look: *Are you going to handle this?* Chase nodded imperceptibly: *I've got it.*

"Keys! Hand 'em over!" demanded Josh, holding out his hand. To emphasize his point, he let the short crowbar he was hiding up his sleeve drop down into his grip.

Chase studied the two mechanics. "Let me guess," he said. "Roker told you that whichever one of you kicks my ass gets my job, am I right?" That Frank and Josh didn't immediately reply told him he was correct. He shook his head. "Look, guys. You need to find another place to work. Big Mike's gonna get you killed one day. Sooner or later, the deSalvos are gonna run out of uses for him and they'll put him down. You get caught in the cross fire, you really think he'll look out for you?"

Frank hesitated, shifting his weight. "You shouldn't talk about Mr. Roker like that. It's disrespectful."

Chase's tolerance broke. "He's an idiot. Tell him I said that, and that I'm keeping the wheels as my severance pay."

"Wrong answer!" shouted Josh, and he rocked off his heels, bringing up the crowbar as he came in toward Chase. In the same moment, Frank took a clumsy swing at Jack that hit only air.

Chase slipped away from the attack and sent a short, sharp punch right into Josh's face. The mechanic recoiled, but he seemed only slightly dazed. From the corner of his eye, Chase glimpsed Jack put a vicious chopping blow across Frank's throat and follow it through with a left cross. Blood glittered darkly as Frank coughed out thick gobs of spittle.

Josh came at Chase again, this time swinging the crowbar like it was a sword, trying to catch him about the head and shoulders with the hooked end. "You're such a tough guy!" spat the mechanic. "Come at me now, man! Come on!"

Reflexively, Chase tried to grab at the crowbar and

force it away, but he used his bad hand without thinking. He couldn't close the grip in time and the improvised weapon raked over his skin and drew blood. Josh lunged, now jabbing with the point as if he thought he could stab Chase with it. He backed off as Josh kept coming.

Nearby, Jack and Frank were trading blows as the bigger man tried to drag Bauer into a choke hold, failing to get a grip on the other man. Chase heard a sickening crack as Jack shot out a hard kick at Frank's shin and broke bone there. The stocky mechanic gave a strangled moan and fell to one knee.

It was time to end this before someone inside the diner saw them and decided to call the police. Josh's mistake was to overextend with one of his stabbing motions and Chase grabbed the crowbar, this time with his good hand. He yanked it toward him and Josh lost his balance, staggering forward. Chase led him into a head-butt that sent the mechanic down to the ground in a crumpled heap. Still gripping the crowbar, Chase came around in time to watch Jack use an elbow strike to crack Frank in the face and put him in the dirt.

A sliver of white bone was protruding from the leg of Frank's trousers, and he gasped as he clutched at it. Jack helped himself to the mechanic's cell phone and crushed it beneath his boot. He nodded at the broken leg. "That'll heal. You'll be able to walk okay in a couple of years. Ten months if you're motivated."

Chase pointed the crowbar's head at Josh as the other man tried to get back up. "Stay," he said "Be smart for once in your life." He used the point to puncture the Pontiac's tires and then tossed the crowbar into the long grass.

Jack gave him a look as they got into the Chrysler. "Is this Roker guy going to be any more trouble?"

"Nah." Chase shook his head and started the car. "You're carrying enough of that for both of us, right?"

• • •

Jorge Kilner winced as he walked through the field office, the bandage around his right calf pulling tight with each step he took. He had another wrapped over the palm of one hand and a couple of adhesive dressings on a couple of small cuts on his face—all the marks left behind by his brief and dangerous sojourn as Jack Bauer's unwilling driver. Falling from the moving car had ruined his coat and now Kilner wore a raid jacket with the FBI crest on the chest and the initials of the bureau emblazoned on the back. Other agents in similar clothing looked up as he crossed the room, none of them willing to meet his gaze. Everyone had heard about the car chase through Chelsea and the stolen helicopter, despite attempts to keep a lid on the information, and by now Kilner's part in the whole sorry mess had to be an open secret from here to Miami.

He scowled as he made his way toward the conference rooms. Some of the civilians who had been at the heliport were milling in an anxious little knot in a waiting area near the coffee machine, and as Kilner walked by them a man in a business suit sprang to his feet.

"Are you an agent?" he demanded.

Kilner's lips thinned and he said nothing, just pointed at the jacket he was wearing.

The businessman launched into a tirade about how it was unfair to hold him here when he was a very important executive with a major corporation, who had a very important meeting with another major corporation in Baltimore that he was going to miss because of the FBI's "interference."

He looked up as Dell emerged from a side corridor, walking an older man out. "Thank you for your cooperation," she was telling him. "If you'll just wait here, we'll get you a ride home and . . ."

The businessman turned on Agent Dell, immediately dismissing Kilner. "Finally. Look, I need to get out of this place. Can you just assume I saw what these people saw and leave it at that?"

Dell's dark eyes flashed. "Sit down and wait," she retorted, with the kind of tone someone might use on a poorly disciplined dog. "You'll get your turn." She glanced at Kilner. "Still with us?"

"More or less." They walked away, leaving the businessman fuming. "You get anything useful?"

Dell jerked a thumb over her shoulder. "The old guy was in Korea and he offered to come with us to find Bauer. Said he had skills."

"He can take my place. I think Hadley will can me for getting caught up with him."

Markinson called out as they approached the open door to the briefing room. "Could go either way," she offered.

"How so?"

"Soon as we got back here after securing the site, Hadley was dragged into a meeting with Special Agent Dwyer and the ASAC. If you listen real hard, you can hear O'Leary tearing him a new asshole even through the soundproofing." She sipped at a plastic cup of water. "But did you not think of actually *stopping* the car, Agent Kilner?"

"No," he said hotly. "That never occurred to me." He glanced between Markinson and Dell. "I *tried* to bring him in. I really did. But you've seen Bauer's file. He's not exactly the compromising type. He wouldn't listen."

Markinson raised an eyebrow. "So you've changed your mind about shoot-on-sight, then?"

"I never said that."

"Well . . ." Dell perched on the end of the table. "However it happened, we need a new plan, and we need to mail it to two hours ago."

"Anything on his contacts?" Kilner asked.

"No, Bauer's too smart to reach out to any of his known associates on the East Coast." Dell shook her head. "Beyond that? Maybe."

"That woman he worked with at CTU, O'Brian?" began Markinson. "We should bring her in, see what she knows."

Dell shook her head again. "Agent Franks and his team are on her. She's gonna be in cuffs soon enough, but we won't get a look in."

"Huh." Markinson looked Kilner up and down. "So the medics said you're okay? No lasting injuries?"

"Just to my reputation."

"Not only *yours*," said a voice from the doorway. The three of them turned to see Hadley standing there, his expression rigid and cold. "We're all going to share in the blowback from this." None of them had heard him enter.

Hadley advanced into the room, and for a second Kilner thought the man might actually be gearing up to take a swing at him. "It was a hard call," he said. "I stand by what I did."

The lead agent glared at Markinson and Dell. "Give me the room," he demanded, and the two female agents left without a word. Hadley closed the door behind them and rounded on Kilner. "Who the hell do you think you are?"

Given what he knew of the man's reputation, Kilner had expected Hadley to explode with rage, but instead his tone was even and icy. "I already gave my statement while the paramedics were checking me out," he told him. "With all due respect, *read that*. You'll see I had no choice. Bauer had a gun on me the whole time."

"Not all the time," Hadley corrected. "Not when he was shooting up a public street and firing on federal agents."

Kilner's temper flared. "Remind me again what *you* were doing during that high-speed pursuit, *sir*?"

Hadley ignored the jibe. "What did he say to you, Jorge? What did you talk about?"

"He told me he would blow a hole in my leg if I didn't do what he wanted," Kilner retorted. "Apart from that, Bauer wasn't that chatty. Then he forced me out of a moving vehicle."

"You had a chance to stop him and you didn't take it. Explain that to me."

The younger agent shook his head. "You're wrong. I *did* take that chance. I tried to reason with him. Bring him in without any bloodshed. But he wasn't listening."

"Bauer shot first," Hadley insisted.

"After you sent in a tactical unit with all guns blazing."

Hadley eyed him. "You don't get to tell me how to run this operation." He pointed at the cuts and bruises on Kilner's face. "Looking at all that . . . Agent Kilner, given your recent injuries I'm wondering if you should stand down and call it a day."

"No, *sir*," Kilner said defiantly. "I'm on for the duration."

The other man's manner started to slip. "You think he's some kind of hero, don't you? Jack Bauer, the man and the legend? I mean, we've all heard the rumors about him, right? The Palmer assassination, the meltdown scare, the whole Starkwood thing. There's enough covert ops ghost stories about Bauer to fill a damn library." Hadley advanced on him. "But you know what I think? I think Jack Bauer is a relic who belongs in the dark ages. He's some kind of deep-black, dirty-tricks killer. He's the *worst* of us, Kilner. No compunction, no conscience, no right to be roaming free."

"You're wrong," said Kilner. "You don't know what he's had to sacrifice. You don't know him."

"And you do?" Hadley held his gaze. "Jason Pillar, a man who saved my life in the Gulf War and then again when I got home, is dead today because of what Bauer has done! Pillar went after Bauer, and he was killed as a result! That's who he is. That's what he leaves behind wherever he goes!"

Kilner shook his head. "Bauer isn't responsible for Pillar's murder. While I was being debriefed, I heard about a leak from the Secret Service. There's a rumor it may have been Charles Logan who shot Pillar. The man he was working for!"

But Hadley wasn't hearing him. "You want to remain on this detail, fine. But from this point onward you are going to do only what I tell you to, and only when I tell you to do it, is that clear?" He didn't wait for Kilner to reply. "The ASAC has agreed to give me the resources we need to expand the search outside the state of New York. I'm going to bring Jack Bauer down, and you would be advised not to hinder that process any more than you already have. Are we clear?"

Kilner opened his mouth to speak, but before he could utter a word, Agent Dell came back into the room at a run, holding a sheet of printout in her hand.

"We got a hit," she said breathlessly. "The chopper that Bauer hijacked."

"Where?" snapped Hadley.

"Someone found it abandoned in the middle of a field off the Pennsylvania Turnpike, near Greensburg. Called it in to the local sheriff's office."

Hadley snatched the paper from her hand. "We're certain it's the same helo?"

"Bell Long Ranger," Dell said with a nod. "It's gotta be him."

"The Penn Turnpike takes you right into Pittsburgh," offered Kilner, thinking it through. "But Bauer doesn't have any active contacts in that city."

"That we know of," said Hadley. He looked up at Dell, suddenly animated. "Get me a map of that area, and I want to talk to the local law. Tell Markinson to contact the Tactical Aviation Unit, we're going to need an aircraft if we want to get out there."

Dell hesitated. "If he left it in plain sight, he has to know we'd find it."

Hadley agreed. "But not before dawn. We may have caught a break here. Let's not waste it."

The other agent left, and Kilner found himself alone with Hadley again. "He'll be long gone," ventured the younger man. "This may even be a deliberate attempt at misdirection."

Hadley didn't bother to look up at him. "Agent Kilner, you're more than welcome to stay here and keep telling anyone who listens why we'll never catch our fugitive. But within the hour I intend to be wheels-up and on my way to whatever flyspeck airstrip is closest to Greensburg."

07

Chase drove on into the evening, taking them out and away from the interstate and on toward Cedar Creek. The tree line grew dense and the other traffic on the road tailed off. After a while, he started to count down mile markers until they passed the head of an unfinished track peeling off the main road.

Jack shot a glance over his shoulder to make sure no one was following them as the Chrysler bounced off the tarmac and onto the dirt path. The track was barely visible from the road, half-concealed by overgrown bushes that clattered against the flanks of the silver car as it passed deeper into the darkness. "Not an easy place to find," Jack offered.

"Not unless you know where to look." Chase nodded and flicked off the Chrysler's lights, easing off on the gas. "That's deliberate. The guy we're gonna see . . . He doesn't like to draw attention. He doesn't like . . ." Chase paused, thinking about it. "Well. *People,* really. He doesn't like people that much."

"Tell me again why we're out in the middle of nowhere?"

Chase kept his eyes on the path ahead. "I'm taking you

to meet Hector Matlow. Calls himself 'Hex.' He's a bit of a shut-in but he's good at what he does. The deSalvos used him to set up all their cyber-crime stuff, crooked on-line gambling sites and porn hubs, the whole nine yards."

"You mentioned that name before," said Jack. "Local hoods?"

Chase nodded. "Your garden-variety scumbags. Nothing to write home about."

"And the other one, Roker? He's connected to them?" Jack watched the other man, considering him. He couldn't help but wonder how the path of Chase Edmunds's life had pushed him into the orbit of an organized crime family.

"He wishes. Mike Roker is small fry trying to make big. Hex does some work for him too, mostly massaging DMV records to make stolen cars seem kosher."

"Right. So how is this Hex guy going to help me?"

Chase turned the steering wheel as the dirt track opened out into a clearing. "You want to make it to Los Angeles under the radar, he'll have a solution." He brought the car to a halt. "This is it."

Jack pulled a Maglite torch from his bag and stepped out of the vehicle. Keeping one hand close to the pistol in his waistband, he panned the beam of the flashlight around to get his bearings.

They were standing before the remains of an abandoned trailer park. A half-dozen mobile homes stood atop crumbling wooden foundations, all of them dark with rain, dirt and disuse. There were no signs of habitation anywhere, nothing that would indicate the presence of another human being in this place. It looked as if it had been this way for years, perhaps even decades.

He aimed the torch up at the roof of the nearest trailer. There were no visible telephone cables or power lines running from any of the double-wides. It was as if they had been dumped here in two orderly rows and left to slowly rot. A mulch of windblown leaves had gathered at the bases of the trailers.

"Your man lives here?" Jack frowned.

"The thing you have to realize about Hex," said Chase, producing a flashlight of his own, "is that he's what you might call *eccentric*."

"How do you know him?"

"He owes me a favor." The tone of Chase's answer told Jack that was all he was willing to say for the moment, and so he didn't press the issue any further.

Chase took the lead, walking between the dead trailers, counting them off until he reached the fifth one. He pulled at the latch of the door and it came open with a metallic snap. He beckoned Jack and the two men entered.

Inside, the trailer was devoid of all decoration, furniture and fittings except for a waist-high chest refrigerator that Jack caught in the glow of his torch beam. Chase fumbled at the wall and found a light switch. Over their heads, a fluorescent tube flickered on and drenched the interior space with greenish illumination.

Jack cast around. The inside of the trailer had been refitted with heavy gray panels, a second interior wall that showed no features other than the seams where each panel had been bonded to the next. He'd seen this kind of thing before; the trailer had been shielded with the same sort of counter-spectrum materials the US military used to hide forward bases in battle zones from the eyes of drones and satellites.

He squinted past the overhead lamp and saw what appeared to be a camera rig in the far corner. "He's watching us."

"*Listening too,*" came a sharp reply, broadcast from a hidden speaker. "*Charlie, is that you? I told you never to come here without calling first. And I definitely told you not to bring strangers.*"

Chase gave the camera a wave. "Hey, Hex. Yeah, sorry about that. But I had to move quick, y'know? Didn't have the time to call." He nodded to Jack. "This is an old friend of mine. I'll vouch for him. He's got a situation that requires your unique skills."

"That so?"

Jack approached the camera. "I need transportation."

"Right. And what about you, Charlie?"

"Just helping out a friend."

"Are you? Because that dickhead Big Mike has already been on the line to me, trying to get me to track you down. I told him I couldn't help. He swore at me a lot."

Chase gave a faint smile. "Thanks."

"I don't like him. I don't like you, either, but I don't like Roker a lot more."

"So, are we going to deal, here?" said Jack.

There was an overly long pause, and for a moment Jack thought that Hex had decided to dismiss them. But then the voice returned. *"Okay. Take any weapons you got—guns, knives, sharp sticks, whatever—and put them in the ice chest. Your cell phones too."*

Chase opened the refrigerator lid. There was no power going to the chest, but the walls of it were thick enough to trap any outgoing signal. "Hex is a little paranoid," Chase noted, and did as he had been told.

"I heard that," snapped Hex. *"Don't try anything clever. I got two Claymore antipersonnel mines buried in the walls of that trailer. I flick a switch and they'll turn the pair of you into chunky salsa."*

"Is that true?" Jack asked in a low voice.

Chase shrugged. "I wouldn't test him."

Jack frowned and did the same, dropping in his M1911 and Kilner's doctored cellular next to Chase's iPhone and Ruger semiautomatic. The lid slammed shut, and in the same moment a slab of the empty trailer's floor abruptly popped up. As Jack watched, it rose up like an inverted drawbridge, revealing a set of concrete stairs below. The faint odor of cooked food filtered up to them.

"Come on in," called Hex from below. "And no funny stuff."

. . .

The hidden hatch came down on them as they reached the foot of the staircase and Chase heard it seal with the thud of heavy bolts. Looking back up, he could see the door was made of thick cast iron, like something he would have expected to find on a World War II submarine.

Ahead of them, a wide space stretched away. The ceiling was low and lined with industrial lamps, and everywhere he looked Chase could see skeletal metal shelves piled high with every conceivable kind of supplies.

Jack peered closer at one of the racks, heavy with boxes of canned goods and toilet paper. "Did this guy rip off a supermarket?"

Elsewhere, there were cartons of US Army–issue combat rations and gallon drums of purified water alongside steel boxes that contained various types of ammunition, filter pods for gas masks and emergency medical kits. Every available inch of space had been converted for storage. They moved forward, into an open area that was a cross between a teenager's basement apartment and a military bunker. In one corner was a state-of-the-art desktop computer with multiple monitors and a radio setup with an antenna that vanished into the ceiling. Chase realized that the underground space they were in was easily the width of the whole false-front trailer park over their heads.

"Keep your hands where I can see them," said Hex. Of below-average height, Hector Matlow was a little too doughy for the heavy-gauge cargo trousers he was wearing, and the hooded camouflage sweatshirt across his shoulders was dirty and unkempt. Once upon a time, he might have had teak-dark skin but his face had the obvious pallor of someone who didn't see daylight very often. His pug nose wrinkled as he hefted the nickel-plated .38 snub revolver in his right hand. "Don't try anything," he insisted. "And don't touch my stocks. It's not for you."

Chase spread his hands. "We're not here for your MREs, Hex."

Jack moved to one wall where stacks of books lay in orderly rows, above them more shelves containing boxes and boxes of complex war games. A folding table nearby was set up with just such a game in mid-play, an abstract map with a hexagonal grid filled with tiny square counters, each one representing a squad of infantrymen or a tank. "The Battle of Stalingrad, am I right?" asked Jack, meeting Hex's gaze.

That got him a nod. "Couple more turns and I'm gonna win it."

"Who are you playing against?"

Hex's brow furrowed. "*Against?* I don't have any opponents."

"Okay." Jack glanced at Chase and gestured at the stockpile around them. "So I guess your friend here is a prepper."

"Is that what they call it?" Chase had heard of such people, but never come across someone who had embraced the idea as much as Hex clearly had. Forty years ago, someone like Matlow would have been referred to as a "retreater," someone who had abandoned a normal lifestyle in order to disconnect from a society they saw as flawed and ultimately doomed. In more recent times, technology had paradoxically made it easier to do so, provided you had the money and the resources.

"I prefer to think of myself as a *survivor*," Hex told him. "Because that's what I plan on being when the collapse comes."

"That's what you do down here?" said Chase. "I always thought you were . . . I dunno, growing weed or something. You're waiting for the end of the world? How's it going to happen?"

Hex snorted. "Look, man, when the crunch comes, people won't be ready. I will, though. I lived in the city for years, I saw how it is. That's why I sold up, came out here and dropped off the grid. Me, I'm ready for anything. Invasion. Viral pandemic. Financial meltdown. Supervolcano eruption. *Anything*. I just work for you and your pals to keep the motor ticking over, know what I mean?"

"You really believe that?" asked Jack. "That the end is coming?"

The other man nodded emphatically. "Do you watch the news?" He went to a wide-screen TV on the far wall and snapped it on. "How many times has this country taken hits from terrorists, enemy combatants, even our own people? Oh, it's going to all fall apart, man. The only question is *when*." On the screen, a reporter was standing outside the White House as a text ticker along the bottom of the screen scrolled past. Hex shook his head grimly. "Frankly, I'm surprised it hasn't happened already."

The volume was down low, but Chase heard the location reporter talking about President Taylor—no, scratch that, *former President Taylor*—and the shock wave her abrupt resignation had sent through the government. As they watched, the view changed to footage shot earlier that evening, of former Secretary of Defense James Heller arriving with the Taylor administration's Ethan Kanin for what the anchorwoman called "emergency talks."

Chase saw a shadow pass over Jack's face as he saw Heller, but then a moment later it was gone.

"I guess I can't fault your logic," admitted Jack. "So why don't we talk about how I can make a generous contribution to your survival fund?"

• • •

The drab green Ford Econoline van that the SVR team had been issued was leaving Hell's Kitchen when the satellite phone chirped, and Ziminova pulled the handset from the cradle. "Yes?"

"*Let me talk to Arkady,*" said a strange, toneless voice on the other end of the line. It had the genderless neutrality of someone being masked electronically, but still the Russian agent got the instinctual sense that she was speaking to another woman. The display on the phone showed a garbled string of numbers that shifted and changed, indicating that the incoming call was being bounced across multiple voice-over-Internet-protocol servers, effectively rendering it untraceable.

Ziminova glanced across at Bazin. "The contractor," she explained.

He nodded and tapped his ear, indicating for her to switch on the speaker. "This is Bazin," he said to the air. "You have had ample time to consider my offer. Will you accept the contract?"

"*It's an interesting job, I'll give you that.*"

Ziminova frowned. She disliked the idea of bringing an outsider into the loop on this mission, especially a foreigner, even if they were someone with the talents that Bazin so prized.

"Is that a yes?"

"*Jack Bauer . . .*" The dulled, mechanical voice sounded out the name. "*He's a singular target. Many have tried to deal with him before and failed. It'll be a challenge. Not to mention the time pressure.*"

Bazin smiled thinly. "You are looking to increase your fee, is that it? You want 'danger money'?"

"*Thirty percent on top of my usual payment, Arkady. That's my counter.*"

Ziminova's commander didn't hesitate. "Done. It does not matter to me how he is dealt with, only that Bauer is terminated with extreme prejudice. And quickly."

"*What about collateral damage?*"

He shrugged. "I am indifferent to it. The method of execution I leave to you to decide. The only stipulation is that you provide proof after the fact that he is dead."

There was a soft chuckle. "*You want me to send you his head in a box, is that it?*"

"Whatever is most expedient. The man who has ordered this will wish to be certain that the job was done."

"*I can arrange that.*" There was a pause. "*A third of the money now, nonrefundable, the rest when you get the proof. Use the Brightstar Cayman Trust account. You know the codes, same as last time.*"

Bazin nodded. "The transfer will be done within the hour. I will have one of our people forward you all the data we have on Bauer's most recent movements."

"*I have my own resources,*" said the assassin. "*But go ahead.*"

Ziminova raised an eyebrow but said nothing. Bazin nodded again. "Of course, if we find Bauer first, you understand that the deal is off, yes?"

"*Good luck with that.*"

"A pleasure to be working with you again, my dear."

"*Likewise, Arkady. I'll be in touch.*"

The phone went dead and Ziminova cut the line, studying the handset for a moment as if it might give her some clue as to the identity of the mystery "contractor." "Why do we need this person?" she asked. "Surely that money can be spent in better ways?"

"You don't trust mercenaries?" said Bazin.

"Loyalty to money is not loyalty," Ziminova replied. "It is greed. And the greedy can always be manipulated."

"Perhaps," Bazin allowed. "Think of this as . . . an insurance policy. And remember, Bauer is 'a singular target.'

Our friend there may not even live to collect the rest of the bounty on his head."

"President Suvarov approved it?" She failed to keep an edge of faint scorn from her tone.

"It is within my authority," Bazin replied. "You share Ekel's view of the president."

The statement came out of nowhere and caught her off guard. "Sir?"

"Am I wrong?" Bazin pressed the issue, studying her for any reaction.

"I didn't vote for him," she replied, at length.

Bazin laughed without humor, but in the next moment, Ziminova's commander became cold and serious. "He is what our country needs, Galina. That is something beyond politics. It is about strength of intent."

She didn't respond. Ziminova had not risen to her rank by openly stating her opinion at every opportunity.

But Bazin would not let it drop. "Speak freely," he said, and it was an order. "I know you have your doubts."

She framed her words carefully. "When the presidential aircraft touches down, there is a good chance that Yuri Suvarov's authority as Russia's leader will cease at the same moment. I find myself wondering how you will respond to that, sir."

He was silent for a moment, and she wondered if she had gone too far with her words. Then Bazin looked away. "I will do what I have always done. I will do what best serves my country and my people."

"Bauer thinks that way as well."

"Never compare *me* to someone like *him*." Bazin rounded on her, his eyes flashing. "Not unless you wish to earn my annoyance. I am nothing like Bauer, and we are nothing like the Americans." He gestured around at the city passing by outside. "This place . . . these people. They do not deserve to be the victors, in any battle. They have not earned it, as we have. We endure, and for what?

To see this country and its soldiers, men like this Bauer, march about the world as if it is their playground?" He shook his head, as if coming to some sort of understanding. "We find our target and we pay him back for his crimes. In that, there will be a lesson to America . . ."

"What lesson?"

"That Russia is not to be disrespected."

• • •

Jack took a seat on the arm of an overstuffed chair across the game board from Hex, and he toyed with one of the counters. "I need to get to the West Coast within the next day. Los Angeles. And I need to do it without anyone seeing me."

"Tall order." Hex's fingers rattled as he tapped them on the frame of his revolver, thinking through the demand. "So why should I care? I let you in here 'cause I owed Charlie for a thing, but that don't get you anything more."

Without hesitating, Jack reached into his pocket and placed an inch-thick wad of bills on top of the war-game map. "That enough to make you care?"

Hex's eyes widened and he snatched up the cash as if he was afraid Jack would suddenly change his mind. "I don't usually deal in actual physical currency," he added, licking his lips.

"So spend it quick," suggested Chase. "Y'know, before the *crunch* and all."

The money went into an ammo case for safekeeping and then Hex was looking back at Jack, measuring him. "Okay, that's your down payment. So who's after you?"

"Everyone," muttered Chase.

"I need specifics," Hex said, leaning forward. "What is it, local cops or staties? Federal? Or is it the Mob, the triads? Come on! I need to know everyone you've pissed off, even if it's the Rotary Club and the Freemasons. Who wants to punch your ticket?"

"For sake of argument, let's say all of the above," offered Jack. "I can't risk showing my face on a commercial flight. Railroad stations and interstate highways are going to be monitored . . ."

Hex dropped into a chair on castors and wheeled across to the computer terminal. "So you got a BOLO out on you. When did it drop?"

"Three, four hours ago," said Jack. "I'm not sure."

"Let's take a look-see." Hex flipped switches to bring the terminal online, and Jack saw that the machine was connected to an isolated encryption circuit of the same kind they had employed back at CTU. Hex noticed him looking and nodded. "Yeah. See, most of the time I keep my deck cut off from the World Wide Web so I can't be digitally backtracked. I use burst-encoded wireless transmissions . . . There's nothing to connect me to the real world. It's kind of like being in a submarine . . . I only stick up the periscope when I need to look around, then it's back to the bottom again."

"A fake ID and a fast ride isn't going to cut it," Chase said, thinking aloud. "You can't do anything that's going to leave a footprint, Jack. You need to be a ghost."

He nodded, watching Hex perform a quick-and-dirty hack to get him inside the firewalls of the Pennsylvania State Police's primary server. In a few moments, a directory of the day's warrants and all-points bulletins were scrolling down the screen. Jack caught a glimpse of his own face and pointed. "There."

"Hello . . ." Hex tapped an icon and the BOLO dispatch appeared in a new window.

The accompanying still image had been taken from Jack's old CTU identity pass, the rigid and unsmiling face that he saw in the mirror every day.

"Jack Bauer. Wanted for . . . *Holy crap* . . ." Hex trailed off.

"Wanted in connection with the murders of multiple Russian nationals and a former federal agent," Jack read aloud, listing out the crimes that the FBI had announced to the world at large. "Possible terrorist associations. Additional violations include assault with a deadly weapon, obstruction of justice, breaking and entering, grand theft auto, reckless endangerment . . ." He skipped the rest of the list to the last line. "Consider armed and extremely dangerous. Approach with caution."

Hex swallowed hard and he seemed to remember the revolver, which he had put aside on the desk near the keyboard. He eyed it, clearly deliberating about grabbing it. "So . . . You're what, America's Most Wanted?"

"Here and now?" said Chase. "More or less."

"It's worse than you think." Jack looked Hex in the eyes, holding his gaze. "There's a good chance that the Russian intelligence service is also hunting me. Is that a problem for you, *Hector*?"

"Damn right it is! You have to get out of here now!" he insisted. "I don't need the kind of heat you've got on you, man!"

"And we will," Jack said carefully. "As soon as you help us. You understand how serious this is now, right? I want to be gone; you want me gone. So make it happen."

"Okay." Hex's hands clamped together and his fingers knit. He was starting to sweat. "Okay," he repeated. "Lemme think . . . Will they be watching LA? Do they know you're heading west?"

Jack and Chase shared a look. "It's likely."

Hex got up and started to pace in a small circle. "So. Airports, railroad stations and bus terminals are all out of the question." He made a looping motion with his finger, drawing a line in the air. "Driving the back roads could work, but you'd have to take a complex route and that means two, maybe three days travel."

"Can't wait that long." Jack shook his head. "With everything that's happening in New York and all the fall-out from Taylor's resignation, there's a chance for me to slip through the cracks. But that'll be gone by this time tomorrow, at best. By then, I'll have the full attention of every lawman in the nation."

"Plus a long drive means more chance of getting caught," said Chase. "It means changing cars, avoiding witnesses . . ."

"Can't you just go north?" Hex insisted. "Hop the border into Canada, get lost in Canuck country?"

"Not an option," Jack said flatly. "It has to be LA." He looked away, thinking of Kim. "I made a promise."

"You heard him," insisted Chase. "What else is there?"

Hex's face set in a grimace. "Trucks are a possibility, but they'll be checked if the feds are monitoring turn-pikes and toll roads . . . Look, unless you want to steal a jet fighter from the Air Force or dig your way to California, you're boned! Nothing short of an underground railroad is going to . . ." He stopped speaking abruptly, staring out into space.

"What?" Chase pressed.

"You can . . . take a train." Hex's face split in a grin. "Oh yeah. That could work."

"Didn't we just agree that was a no-go?" Jack shook his head. "Train stations will have transit cops on duty and security cameras watching the platforms. That's too big a risk."

Hex dropped back into his seat, shaking his head. "No, no, I'm not talking about *passenger* trains. I mean hop-ping a freight. Riding the rails, old-school." He worked the keyboard, bringing up a map of the USA. "See, the majority of folks think that trucks and planes carry all the cargo around the country these days, but it's the trains that still do the heavy lifting, they've done it for more than a hundred years . . ." He spoke without taking a breath, his fingers a blur over the keyboard, warming to his subject. "When the collapse comes, they're gonna be one of the first connections to break, you get it? When diesel fuel is worth more than gold, those big locos will be left to rust . . ."

The map showed a complex web of overlapping rail lines, networks cross-connecting from East Coast to West Coast, from Canada all the way down to Mexico. Jack looked for and found Pittsburgh, sitting on a nexus of lines spreading to all points of the compass. Hex worked the image, repositioning it to center on an area many miles away, toward the Midwest. A long ribbon of crimson wound across and down from the edge of the Great Lakes, before bending back across the American heartland to form an arcing pathway that terminated at the Port of Los Angeles.

"Union Pacific will get you where you wanna go," Hex announced. "There's a high-speed freight run that originates in Chicago and it doesn't stop until it hits LA, only been up and running for the last couple of years. That's your ride, right there. No waiting, no metal detectors, no cops. Minimal security once it's on the move."

"That'd work," said Chase, "except for the whole *nonstop* part. How exactly are we supposed to get on a freight train moving at sixty, seventy miles an hour?"

Jack studied the map. "Can't be that fast all the way. They'd have to slow down for gradients, curves . . ."

Hex snapped his fingers and pointed at him. "Exactly! And I can give you the closest point where the train will be at the best, lowest speed . . ." The route map lit up with clusters of dots arranged in varying density as a measure of the typical speed of the freight train. After a moment, Hex leaned in to peer at the screen and grinned.

"This looks good. *Yeah*. Here we go. About five miles outside of a small town in the middle of flyover country, a few hours' drive from here." He shot a look at his watch. "Just before dawn tomorrow, the Blue Arrow cargo run from Chicago is going to be passing along this stretch of track. It's gotta slow down here because the rails aren't built for high-speed wagons. That's where you can hop on."

"That's if you don't get ripped to shreds trying," Chase said grimly.

Jack studied the map. "What's the name of the place?"

"Oh, you gotta love this." Hex smirked as he read it off the screen. "The town's called *Deadline*."

08

The night seemed to crowd in on them as the Chrysler sped along the highway, the engine a low and ever-present hum as Chase kept the speed at an even fifty-five. On leaving Hex's bunker, his first instinct had been to dump the car and look for something else, but the clock was against them and the 300 had the benefit of still having plenty of gas in the tank, and a GPS with a back roads route that the hacker had helpfully provided. Before they set off again, Jack and Chase recovered their guns and rendered their cell phones inert. The phones went into the trunk, alongside the car's LoJack antitheft circuit, which had been the first thing Chase had removed after leaving Big Mike's Autos.

Jack was in the backseat, the black gym bag he had carried from the diner on the seat next to him. In the rearview, Chase watched him removing the contents item by item, checking and taking inventory of what was there. He saw police-issue tactical radios, a gear vest with armor plate inserts, banana magazines of 10mm ammunition and the familiar shape of an MP5/10 submachine gun. "Jeez, Jack. What did you do, empty a police armory on your way out of the city?"

"Something like that," Bauer said absently, checking the SMG's action before reloading it. "You got anything else apart from that Ruger you're carrying?"

He nodded and tapped the base of the driver's seat. "Roker always keeps a Remington short-frame under here. Y'know, in case of *complications*."

Jack fished out the silver pump-action shotgun and worked the slide to eject all the cartridges, methodically checking each one before reloading them again. "This should be enough."

"For what?"

"Like you said." The other man stifled a yawn and rubbed his brow. "In case of complications."

"Hex is solid." Chase anticipated the unspoken comment before Jack could voice it. "He's not going to talk to the FBI. You know these survivalist guys, they hate the federal government and everyone in it."

"It's not the bureau I'm worried about." Jack replaced the shotgun and sat back. Patterns of color washed over him as the occasional beam from the headlights of another car traced across the Chrysler. "The Russians . . . They're the wild card. Don't have to adhere to due process or follow protocol. Suvarov's proven that his people are more than capable of anything. If they connect me to you . . . to Charlie Williams . . ."

"They'll eventually figure out Hex is a known associate, yeah," Chase concluded, frowning. "Hadn't really thought that far ahead . . ."

"If he's smart, he'll sell us out the second they come to his door," said Jack. "And by the time that happens, it won't matter. We'll be long gone."

"All the more reason to stay one step ahead." Chase shifted in his seat, guiding the car around a slow-moving semi. A faint tremor went through his bad hand and he tensed, feeling the muscles in his arm go rigid for a moment, pulled taut like steel cables. After a few seconds, the pain ebbed and the spasm went away. Sense memory brought the chalky taste of Percocet tablets to his mouth, immediately associating it with the ache, and he licked dry lips. The plastic pill bottle was still in his jacket pocket, unopened.

He pushed the thought away. "This freight train thing, it's a good call. Along with the false flags Hex laid out, it should work." As part of his payment for finding them a route to California, the hacker had also set up a number of dummy purchases using some of Bauer's less reliable cover identities. Anyone searching for Jack would find a handful of airline and bus tickets to various destinations, every one set out to muddy the waters a little more.

Jack nodded slowly. "We'll see what happens. I always plan for the worst-case scenario."

"That's a little downbeat." Chase tried a wan smile.

"It's experience," said Jack. "So, what was the thing you did for Matlow?" he asked, changing the subject.

Chase sighed. "I kept him out of jail. He . . . got caught up in something that went wrong. Someone was killed. I got him away from it before the deputies got to the scene."

Jack settled into the wide seat, and he seemed to vanish into the shadows back there. "You knew him . . . through Roker?"

"Yeah. For my sins." Unconsciously, Chase's hands tightened on the steering wheel. "After I left Valencia and did my disappearing act, I bounced around for a while. But I was bleeding money." He hadn't wanted to talk about it, but here and now with the steady rush of the road and nothing else ahead of them but silence and blacktop, Chase could feel the burden of those years of bad choices rising up to the surface. "I wound up in Pittsburgh with nothing to my name and a lot of regrets. Work was scarce . . . Well, work that was *legal* was scarce, yeah? The other kind, not so much. So Roker pulled me in. He needed muscle and I needed a job, *any job.*"

Maybe it was because he had finally overcome the inertia in his life and cut loose from Roker and the deSalvos, or maybe it was because Jack Bauer was the one guy in the world who could actually understand what he had been through. "I signed on as security, as his driver, but it turned out to be a lot more than that. Repo work at first, with the emphasis on forceful recovery." He started to talk, and it all began to fall out of him. "See, Roker's got a lot of angles he works and one of them is selling cars to idiots who can't afford them. Once his marks couldn't make the vig, he rolled back the cars and sold them again to the next fool in line. But that action had the attention of the deSalvo syndicate, and they've got his dealership locked in as a way to launder some of their cash flow." He took a long breath. "I just wanted to drive. But with this damn hand, there wasn't a lot I *could* do." Chase said the last words with more heat than he meant to, and what came next seemed to come from nowhere. "When they said you were killed in action, Jack . . . Hell, I didn't believe it for a second, but Kim did. It was like she had been waiting for it, you know? After she lost her mom, it was as if she knew it would be inevitable that you'd follow. I hope . . . I hope she's not in that place anymore, I really do. I mean, you said she's got a kid now, right?" He paused for a moment. "That's good. I wish it could have been different between her and me." His eyes stayed fixed on the dark band of the road ahead. "The thing I regret . . . more than anything . . . is that I messed that up." It came to Chase then, a sudden, sharp insight into his own motivation. *Is this me settling that score? Is the reason I came running to help Jack Bauer because I owe his daughter for letting her down?*

A police car going in the opposite direction rushed

past, but there was no sudden flare of flashing lights, no screech of brakes.

"Look," Chase began again, glancing over his shoulder to look the other man in the eye. "What I mean is . . ."

He halted, the rest of his words left unspoken as he realized he was talking to himself. Bauer's eyes were closed and his breathing was even. The fatigue of the past hours had finally caught up with him.

"Yeah," said Chase, and turned back to the road, heading deeper into the night.

· · ·

The Cessna Citation X made a slow loop of the airfield, and as Kilner looked out of the oval window, the pilot's voice came over the intercom to advise them they were about to land. Kilner fastened his safety belt across his lap as Markinson dropped into the seat next to him. "How far are we from the site?" he asked.

"Thirty minutes away, I reckon," she replied. "Ground transport is already waiting for us down there."

On the other side of the aisle, Hadley looked up from the document folder in his hand and shot her a look. "If these local yokels have touched that helo, there will be hell to pay."

"You expecting to find a note pinned to the dash?" said Kilner.

"I've already heard all that Jack Bauer has to say to me," Hadley replied. The small jet shuddered as it turned in for a final approach, the air brakes deploying to decelerate. "I'm more interested in what he did next."

"The sheriff's department is canvassing the area," offered Dell from across the cabin. "Somebody will have seen him."

"As good as everyone says he is," Hadley said firmly,

"he's not invisible. We just need to keep the pressure up, keep pushing. Bauer will make a mistake, and when he does we'll be there."

There was no hesitation in the man's words, Kilner noticed, not the slightest iota of doubt. Hadley had made the capture of his target into a personal mission. Kilner wondered how far the other agent would go in order to bring it to the conclusion he wanted.

The aircraft's undercarriage hit the runway with a thud and the jets howled as the pilot reversed the thrust to slow them. The airstrip wasn't really rated for something like the twin-engine Citation, more suited to smaller prop planes and lighter aircraft, but Hadley had forced through a temporary waiver from the FBI's aviation unit that essentially allowed him to have the jet put down on anything short of a football field as part of the manhunt for Jack Bauer.

Hadley was out of his chair, gathering up his gear and making for the hatch even as the aircraft was still rolling to a halt before a brightly lit hangar. Kilner peered out of the window again and saw a pair of white-and-green cruisers from the Westmoreland County Police Department parked with an unmarked black SUV. Uniformed officers stood in a loose knot, waiting on the new arrivals.

Contrary to the way things were portrayed in the movies, in the real world the arrival of a posse of federal agents in a local jurisdiction didn't automatically equate to an immediate rivalry and conflict over who was going to be in charge. In Kilner's experience, the opposite was usually the truth. State or county cops with less manpower and typically with operational budgets that were already stretched to the limit would welcome the involvement of the Federal Bureau of Investigation. In the last decade, FBI resources had become increasingly focused on rooting out terrorist threats in addition to their other law enforcement remits, something beyond the reach of smaller police forces. The hunt for Bauer fell squarely in the middle of that category—even if Kilner felt it should be otherwise.

"I'm Sheriff Bray," said the officer waiting for them at the foot of the jet's stairs. He was a portly man with a thinning beard and deep-set eyes, and he nodded to a taller, thinner officer at his right. "This is Deputy Roe."

Hadley gave them a nod and made cursory introductions for Kilner and the others. "I hear you have my helicopter, Sheriff."

Bray nodded, frowning with it, and Kilner immediately got the impression that the man wasn't comfortable with the situation that had been dumped on him. "That's right. Green-and-brown Bell 206 Long Ranger, couple o' bullet holes in the fuselage. Your doing, Special Agent Hadley?".

"Clearly I need some more time on the range to sharpen up my aim," Hadley replied as they walked to the waiting cars. "Who found it?"

"A Mr. Todd Billhight," said Roe, glancing at his notebook. "Chopper's parked in the middle of a field on his land. Said he was out for a smoke, on account of his wife not liking his cigars . . . Saw the thing from across the way, then called it in."

"He didn't hear anything?" asked Dell.

Roe shook his head. "No, ma'am. It's been pretty windy here tonight. Most folks have been indoors."

"I want a copy of Billhight's statement," said Hadley. "Have you searched his property?"

"First thing we did," Bray nodded. "Soon as we realized this was connected to your guy Bauer. But we came up empty. If the subject was there, he didn't stick around."

"The highway is close by," added Roe. "We got units moving in both directions, checking in with local homeowners, looking for stolen cars, whatever."

Bray hesitated as he opened the door of his vehicle. "Look . . . I gotta ask this before we get going here. I read the paper on Bauer and he's clearly some serious son of a bitch. If he's involved with that crap on the news, exactly how much of a danger is he going to present to my men and my constituents? His rap sheet makes it sound like I should be calling in the National Guard, for chrissakes."

"I'm not going to sugarcoat it, Sheriff," said Hadley. "He's a trained killer, pure and simple. A class of fugitive I guarantee you have never come across before."

Kilner watched the expression change on Bray's face and his lips thinned. "But that's why we are here," he broke in, before Hadley could practically hand out a shoot-on-sight order. "To bring him in, cleanly and swiftly." Hadley's eyes flashed at Kilner's interruption, but he let it pass.

"Let's get you out to Todd's place, then," said the sheriff, clearly eager to get things over and done with.

● ● ●

Sleep had never come easy to Jack.

It was almost as if the ability to disengage and drop into true rest had been burned out of him somewhere along the line. Short of using chemical assistance—and there had been times in his life when he had done exactly that—Jack existed in a state where sleep seemed like a kind of little death. When he was out, the world turned on without him, but he had never been one to sit back and let things pass him by. If he could have literally slept with one eye open, he would have. It was hard to come down from the baseline state of alertness that he had learned to maintain back in Delta Force. He found it hard to disengage, and it was worse when he was riding in a plane or a vehicle. It was as if there was a small piece of his animal hindbrain that had been broken, a switch in his head that would forever be jammed in the "on" position. Some part of him wanted to be ready, to be prepared for the moment when action would be needed.

On the rare occasions when sleep—real, honest, deep sleep—did come upon him, it wasn't a welcome experience. It was more like a silent assailant coming at Jack from the shadows, slipping a hand around his throat to drag him away, down and down into the darkness.

In the military, he had learned to snatch moments of rest wherever he could, small snapshots of it that he could grab in between watches or in the lulls before operations. Like an apex predator, he took it in pieces here and there. But going deep, really letting go . . . that was never easy. Sleep meant lowering his guard. It was allowing himself to become lost, to be vulnerable, just for a while.

But it would happen. And then he would bolt awake, skin filmed with a cold sweat, as if he were a drowning man who had broken free of bottomless waters. He remembered finding himself in snarls of bedsheets next to Teri, his fingers curled around the trigger of a gun that wasn't there. She had made those moments easier for Jack, for a time. But then one day his wife was gone, and the peace that her presence next to him had brought went away, and he knew he would never get it back.

In sleep he went to that darker place. A wilderness of shadows, populated by ghosts and memories that refused to stay buried. Things from the here and now would become fluid and melt like hot wax, time would merge. Past and present spinning together.

In sleep, Jack went to every hell he had ever known, and he wondered if it was a kind of penance for each drop of blood he had spilled, each life he had been forced to end.

Sometimes it would be the heat and the sand of Afghanistan, and he would be the younger man, the one still new to it all, not yet so hardened by loss, not tempered by fire. He would walk through those dusty streets and come upon a house, knowing and not knowing all at once what he would find inside; the last seconds of a brother soldier, watching and never being able to stop the brutal act of execution as his friend's head was taken from his neck.

Other times it would be the bloody ruin of what happened in Kosovo during Operation Nightfall. He would be there with Saunders, Kendall, Crenshaw and the others, secure in the knowledge that the man they were there to kill was a war criminal of the most ruthless stripe. And then he would see the perfect mission plan crumble around him, see his men perish in a hail of gunfire, and burn with the guilt of knowing the bomb he planted to kill Victor Drazen had ended the lives of innocents instead. Over and over it would play out, the horror of it embedded in him.

But on the worst nights, he would be in China again. Jack would wake from the dream of freedom to find his world inverted, the reality of it twisting inside out. It would always begin the same way, with his interrogator Cheng Zhi kicking him awake inside that reeking, decrepit cell. Jack spent twenty long and painful months there, stolen away from the world by the Chinese ministry of state security as payback for his part in the death of one of their diplomats. He felt a special kind of fear then, felt it rushing back over him in a cold wave as his mind told him that he had never really left that terrible place, that his memories of being released on the demands of the terrorist Abu Fayed were just a fantasy. And Cheng would study Jack with a pitiless gaze and tell him that no matter how far he went, no matter how long he lived, he could never truly escape the cage they had put him in. Sometimes, impossibly, Teri would be there too, and he would have to watch her die, forced to witness the murder of his wife that in reality, he had come too late to prevent.

So Jack Bauer did not sleep, *not really*. Instead, he skirted the edges of it and tried not to dream.

His eyes were open; he didn't sense the transition from the doze he had fallen into in the back of the Chrysler. The car wasn't moving anymore, the dull hum of the engine silenced. He felt chilly air on his face and he saw that the driver's-side door was hanging open.

"Chase?"

The other man was gone, and as Jack leaned forward to reach for the seat in front of him, the inertia reel on the seat belt across his chest locked tight, jerking him back. He cursed and pulled at the latch, but it was rigid and he couldn't move it. Jack's hand slapped at the pocket in his jacket, feeling for the collapsible multitool he carried there, but he couldn't find it. He was certain he'd had it before they left Hex's hidden compound, and he searched the dim interior of the car in case it had fallen to the floor.

Jack found nothing, and his skin prickled as he realized that the black bag holding all the gear he had brought with him was also missing. Why would Chase have taken it? Where would he go? It made no sense.

A cold, horrible voice in the back of his mind told him his friend had betrayed him just like his former colleague Tony Almeida did, just like all the others Jack had foolishly believed he could trust. He shook his head, forcing the thought away, and looked out through the windshield, still pulling vainly at the immovable seat belt.

He didn't recognize the landscape. The night was a curtain of featureless black and there were no stars. A white glow spilled from the Chrysler's headlights, illuminating flat, dusty ground that faded away beyond the range of the beams. There was another car out there, a dark and blocky shape barely visible behind the dazzling flood of its own high beams.

Jack saw Chase walking toward the other vehicle, dragging the black bag across the ground behind him as if it were too heavy for him to lift. He called out his name, shouting at the top of his lungs, but if the other man heard him, he didn't react. A second figure moved out from behind the other car, and a kernel of doubt grew in Jack's chest.

Had Chase really betrayed him? Had something been done, some drug been slipped to Jack while his guard had been down? He believed that Chase Edmunds was still the man he had always been, even after the trials life had put him through, and Jack could not accept that his former partner would sell him out . . . But was that his greatest mistake? Was his sense of trust so damaged, so corroded that he had misplaced it once again?

Now he was pulling at the belt with all his might, and still it would not budge, still he could not slip out of it. He saw the other person moving to meet Chase in the middle of the spill of light, but they were unrecognizable, only a silhouette backlit by the headlights.

Chase halted, as if he had suddenly seen something, and he let the strap of the bag go, raising his hands. The other person raised a hand too, but there was something silver in it and a crack of thunder sounded.

"*No!*"

As if he had been kicked by a bull, Chase twisted away, an ugly stream of crimson jetting from his face. He crashed to the ground, falling out of sight. His killer turned toward the Chrysler and advanced on it with slow and purposeful steps, the big frame of the silver pistol glittering.

Jack's fury translated to action, and he grabbed the jammed seat belt with both hands, wrapping it around his wrists to gain traction. With a wordless shout of effort, he pulled on the buckle with all his might and the metal tab suddenly shattered, setting him free. He slammed into the passenger door and burst out, scrambling from the car and across broken, drought-cracked earth. He felt dizzy and slow, as if he had been starved of oxygen.

Jack fought to regain his balance and looked back as a shadow fell across him. He saw a woman's face framed with short, black hair, familiar pale skin and a wicked mouth. Once he had found a kind of solace in her arms, before he discovered it was nothing but a lie. Her eyes were cruel and icy. "Jack," she purred. "You can't run. You must know that."

"*Nina* . . ." He breathed. "You can't be here. You're dead. *I shot you!*"

"You did," she agreed, and now blood was pooling across her neck, soaking through the white silk blouse she wore. Nina Myers tapped a finger against her head and smiled. "But you can't kill me *up here,* Jack." The woman who murdered his wife, whose treachery had almost destroyed him, looked down at Jack with cold amusement. "That voice you hear in the back of your mind? That's not Cheng, it's not Drazen or Marwan or any of the others. It's me." She raised the gun and the muzzle yawned like a tunnel mouth. "It's always me."

The pistol discharged with a monstrous crash . . .

• • •

. . . and Jack bolted awake, a chill on his skin.

Light flashed over him from the tractor of a passing truck in the far lane, and he blinked, sucking in a deep breath.

"You all right back there?" From the driver's seat, Chase shot him a glance over his shoulder. "Jack?"

"I'm okay," he lied, grimacing as he adjusted the seat belt where it had tightened over his chest.

"Bad dream?"

He ignored the question. "How long was I out?"

Chase's lip curled. "Don't worry, you didn't miss anything." He nodded as an interchange sign hanging over the highway appeared in the glow of the headlights. "Not far now."

Jack leaned forward and saw text on the marker that read DEADLINE—NEXT EXIT.

09

Deadline was a town that had died twice.

First born as a small hamlet that had accreted around the path of the growing railroad network, named off-handedly by a construction gang foreman with a dry sense of humor, for a time it had been the home to a colony of hardscrabble farmers and strong-willed types who liked the savannah landscape and the open skies. But when the Great Depression came, it struck the township like a hurricane. People lost their jobs, their homes, their livelihoods, and Deadline became a skeletal caricature of a real community. It stayed that way for years, until the shadows of war fell across distant Europe, and from out of nowhere the promise of new purpose brought the town back to life.

Drawn by the countryside and the nearby railroad, in the early 1940s the US Army came to Deadline with big plans. Families who had struggled to farm the unforgiving land for generations were bought out wholesale with generous government dollars. They left their homesteads to start anew closer to the town center in newly built houses. The military moved in armored divisions still fresh from hammering Nazi panzers into scrap metal, and ten thousand soldiers along with them. They named the place Fort Blake and built wide and far.

For the locals, it was a golden age. The town became an engine to serve the needs of the base, with everything from diners and dry cleaners, through to a more illicit economy to cover the baser needs of the troops. Twenty years after the tanks had rolled into town, Deadline was a fully symbiotic entity, its entire existence supported by troops who were now on the front lines of the Cold War. Men and weapons trained and waited for the call to arms, for the lightning-fast deployment against a Soviet army advance that never ever came.

Then one day, the Berlin Wall fell and the enemy Fort Blake had been built to defy went away. Just as politics and the threat of war thousands of miles away had brought the town back from the brink, now the reverse happened. In a matter of years, defense cuts and reductions in force took the soldiers away, mothballed the tanks and slowly choked the life out of Deadline. The base was stripped, shuttered and left to decay. Those who could find the money sold up and followed in the army's boot steps. Those who had no choice but to remain watched their lives crumble, forced to cling to welfare handouts while all around them entire neighborhoods went derelict. Whole streets became silent, echoing to the mournful howl of the freight trains that passed on by and never stopped.

The town dried up and blew away. All that was left was a shabby main drag with a mix of cheap motels, strip clubs and liquor stores that catered to a transient population of truckers on their way to somewhere else.

When the next influx of money and new arrivals came, there was a far darker purpose motivating them.

· · ·

"Nice place," said Chase, as they turned off the approach road and into the town proper. They had passed ranks of shuttered, boarded-up housing on the outskirts, but now they were seeing signs of life. Lurid neon signs and dilapidated storefronts made the whole town seem run-down and unwelcoming. The streets were wide but traffic was light, nothing more than the occasional battered pickup or motorcycle. The slab-sided shapes of big tractor trailers congregated in ill-kept parking lots across from greasy eateries and dingy bars, and the whole area had a decaying feel about it.

Jack gave a grim nod of agreement. He'd seen better-appointed neighborhoods in Third World war zones, and there was something disturbing about seeing a place like this in the heartland of his home country. Unconsciously, he adjusted the position of the M1911 pistol in his waistband and scanned the side streets. "How far are we from the railroad?"

"Close enough," Chase replied. "But we're early. We got plenty of time to kill. So we find somewhere to bed down, lay low and wait out the clock." He nodded toward a brightly lit sign on the far side of the street, a half-mile distant. "Looks like a motel up there. As good a place as any to hole up. They may even have cable TV." The car rolled to a halt at a crossroads as the traffic lights dangling from a wire overhead clicked to red. "I mean, we don't wanna draw any attention, right?"

Jack was going to reply, but a throaty, rumbling growl cut him off and he saw the flash of headlamps behind them as something else approached the intersection. He knew the sound, the powerful engines of big cruiser motorcycles, Harleys, Indians and the like. As a teenager he had ridden the same kind of bikes around Santa Monica, but he had never been able to connect to the nomadic subculture they symbolized.

Six heavy bikes rolled up to halt at the stoplight,

crowding in around the Chrysler like a pack of wolves circling a bison. Jack tensed, letting his hand fall to the butt of his pistol, and he shot a warning look at Chase. The other man nodded, keeping one hand on the steering wheel, and the other within reach of his own weapon.

The motorcycle on the driver's side was a Gilroy Indian Scout with blue-black details and a lot of chrome, obscured somewhat by a layer of road dust. The rider leaned slightly from his saddle and peered at the car. The biker's black leather jacket was thick and patterned with rigid plate inserts, better to protect him in the event of a spill. Jack saw the three-part patch on the man's back— his *colors*. Two curved "rockers" at the top and bottom declared him to be a member of the Night Rangers MC, and in the middle, an oval patch showed a monstrous, wraithlike figure with clawed hands crossed over its chest. The wraith held a huge serrated combat knife in one hand, and an old Western-style Colt Peacemaker six-gun in the other. If the triple patch wasn't enough to convince him that these men were outlaw bikers, Jack also saw the smaller, diamond-shaped sigil on the rider's chest. Inside the patch was a "1%" symbol, indicating that he wasn't part of the so-called 99 percent of law-abiding motorcyclists out on the roads.

The biker turned, removing a butterfly knife from his pocket, opening it with a flourish and using it to pick trail dirt out from under his fingernails. The action was all theater, all calculated menace. He extended his arm and gently tap-tapped the blade on the driver's-side window.

Chase lowered the window an inch. "Evening," he said. "Can I help you with something?"

The biker leaned down to get a better look at who was in the car, and Jack saw a name tag that read BRODUR. Next to it were other symbols, all part of the complex secret heraldry of the outlaw biker community—a skull and bones, an eight ball, a dollar sign. "Nice cage," he

said, looking over the Chrysler. "This year's model . . ."
Brodur seemed lean and angular, with a square face, a
shaved head and five o'clock shadow around his blocky
chin. He made a show of glancing at the car's plates.
"Out from Penn, huh? You gentlemen aren't lost now,
are ya?"

"We're just passing through," Chase replied. "We're
not looking for any trouble."

"'Course not." Brodur's answer was languid as he
toyed with the knife. "Word of advice? Keep on passing,
pal. Folks from out of town can get themselves in a fix
around here if they're not careful."

"I'll keep that in mind," said Chase, as the light flickered over to green.

"You do that." Brodur settled back on his bike and
throttled away, allowing the tip of the butterfly knife to
scratch the paintwork on the car as he passed. The other
riders went with him, revving their motors as they went.

"Son of a . . ." Chase scowled as they drove on. "Like
I said, *nice place*. I guess those boys must have been the
welcome wagon."

Jack shook his head. "No, they were outriders. Fresh
off the highway, same as us. They're just making noise,
showing us who the big dogs are here."

"What makes you so sure?"

"I did an undercover op with an outlaw MC in Los
Angeles. Years ago, before your time, before CTU. I know
how they operate."

"I'll take your word for it." They were approaching the
entrance to the motel, and Jack caught sight of an old
plaster sign in the shape of a cartoon tepee. "Apache
Motel," Chase read aloud. "And they got vacancies. Great.
Not exactly the Hilton, but we can't afford to be choosy."

Jack threw a glance out the back window as they
pulled into the motel forecourt. Another pair of Night
Ranger motorcycles growled past behind them. "Find a

spot for the car where it can't be seen from the road. Like you said, we don't want to draw attention."

• • •

The office door opened and the asset was three steps into the room before he realized that it was already occupied. He reacted with an almost comical level of shock, nearly dropping the papers he was carrying. He glanced back and forth between Ziminova, who stood with her hands folded in front of her by the bookcase, and Bazin, who had taken it upon himself to sit behind the asset's impressively large desk.

"You can't be here!" he blurted.

Bazin opened his hands to take in the room. "And yet . . ."

"No! *No!*" The color drained from the man's face and he took a step forward. Then, as if he suddenly remembered where he was and who he was talking to, his voice dropped into a near-whisper. "You can't just come to my office, you shouldn't be here—"

"*You* contacted *us,*" said Ziminova. "You said you had something."

"I do! I have! But I was going to bring it to you!"

Bazin smiled and shook his head, toying with some of the items on the desk. "You do not get to make that sort of decision."

"It doesn't work this way!" he insisted.

"It works," said the woman, advancing on him, "however we say it works."

What little fight the man had in him ebbed away at that moment and Bazin saw the defeated look in his eyes. "I can't have you seen here. That will cause problems for me."

"We understand," Bazin allowed. "Better than you think, my friend. We're not going to put you in jeopardy, that would be bad for all of us. But as was made clear to you earlier, time is of the essence."

"I . . ." He swallowed hard. "I want some assurances."

Bazin nodded. "You'll have them, of course." He glanced at Ziminova, who continued to watch the asset in the manner of a hawk observing a field mouse.

The asset didn't stop to confirm what those nebulous *assurances* actually were, he just nodded back and seemed to accept that Bazin was telling the truth. It was pitiful, in a way, how simple this man was to manipulate. The reality was Bazin had no intention of keeping his word to the asset past any point at which he was no longer of use. He tapped the brass frame of a family photo on the man's desk, and the action was enough to focus his attention.

He dropped into the seat opposite Bazin and picked up the wireless keyboard of his computer, turning the flat-screen monitor so both of them could see it. "I ran the search protocol she gave me during a gap between our peak traffic and this was the result."

The screen sketched in a wire-frame graphic of the eastern half of the United States, painting clusters of dots up and down the map to indicate the locations of cellular communication towers. Around the cities, they formed dense blobs of light, but in the rural areas they became more thinly spread. The zone in the map was as Bazin had directed it to be, large enough to encompass the maximum range of the civil helicopter Jack Bauer had stolen.

The asset's hands moved over the keyboard, and he pulled the flash memory stick Bazin's subordinate gave him from an inside pocket. Blinking, he slotted it into a port on the side of the keyboard and a pop-up window appeared. He tapped the "enter" key to run the program again, and there was a momentary babble of noise from the speakers on the bottom of the monitor. To anyone listening, it would sound like a garbled radio transmission, all guttural chokes and grunts—but in fact they were listening to a stream of sampled voice elements captured from various sources. The sound was the aural fingerprint of their target, the voice pattern of Jack Bauer broken down into its base elements.

Moscow had paid their friends in Beijing very well for this file, and they had provided it willingly. It seemed the People's Republic of China were also on the long list of those who wished Bauer to be dead and gone.

The program on the flash drive used the network provider's own internal software to parse the thousands of phone conversations that had gone through its servers over the past few hours, sampling and comparing bits of the pattern with the calls that had bounced around the Eastern Seaboard. It wasn't a widely known truth that most cell towers contained a memory buffer that retained details of calls and routings that passed through them, holding on to that information for up to a day before they were purged and reset. Like the National Security Agency's PRISM monitoring software or the covert access channels of the Counter Terrorist Unit, it was a dirty little secret that the Taylor administration had tried very hard to keep out of the public eye.

Of course, what the NSA and CTU were aware of, so was the Russian government. Back home, the SVR had a similar setup in operation to spy on their own people, just like the Chinese did, the British, the French . . . But whereas the American agencies needed legal, authorized presidential mandates to make a search for a certain voice pattern, all Bazin needed was a man of weak character and the threat of bloody murder. It amused him that the Americans had provided him with the tools he would use to track and kill one of their own.

"Here," said the asset, as the program locked on to a splinter of voice traffic. "Bouncing off a cell tower near

Monroeville in Allegheny County, Pennsylvania. About fifteen miles east of Pittsburgh."

"*Hello, Chase.*" The voice was broken and echoey. "*Can you talk?*"

"Is that him?" said Ziminova.

Bazin said nothing, listening to the distorted conversation. "*Who . . . Who is this?*" asked a second voice, a younger man.

"*It's Jack,*" came the reply, and Bazin's smile grew. "*I need your help.*"

"You have your answer," he told the woman. Bazin glanced at the asset and snapped his fingers. "Copy that exchange onto the flash drive, and then erase the cell tower's buffer remotely."

The man licked his lips. "That will take time."

"Just do it," Ziminova insisted, moving to hover over him.

"All right . . ." He set to work, typing furiously. After a moment, he detached the memory stick and handed it to Bazin, unable to stop his hands from trembling.

Ziminova studied the data on the screen. "The cellular telephone where the call originated. You can track it, yes? Isolate other cell towers that it pinged after this call was made?"

"I already looked for that," he managed, pausing. "Whoever you . . . I mean, the person who made that call . . . they made a second call, then a while later a third call came in. Then they deactivated the handset. It went off the grid."

"You have records of these communications too, I take it?"

"No." The asset looked fearful and shook his head. Before Bazin could say more, he spoke quickly. "Please understand! The second and third calls were directed through a BlackPhone encryption application! The buffer couldn't read them!"

Bazin and Ziminova exchanged looks, considering that fact. "What about the recipient of the first call, this man called 'Chase'? You have data on that person's mobile device?"

"Yes. Some." He paused, blinking.

Ziminova studied the man carefully. "He believes we are going to kill him when we are done here. Don't you?"

The asset's eyes shimmered wetly. "Yes," he managed.

"No," Bazin corrected. "At this time, you are far too useful to me to be wasted for no good reason. Unless you are going to *give* me a good reason." He pitched his voice in a careful, conversational tone. "Are you?" he prompted.

"No," said the man, swallowing the word in a shuddering gasp.

"So answer her question."

"The other cell phone belongs to someone called Charles Williams, registered to an address in East Hills, Pittsburgh. He pays his bills on time, every time. He doesn't use it very often." The words flooded out of the man in a rush.

Ziminova drew out her own phone and switched to speaking in Russian. "Sir, I will contact operations at the consulate, give them the name and address, get them to run it. Mager can talk to his informant in the police force, check for any criminal records."

Bazin nodded. "Good. And call Yolkin, have him get to this man's home as fast as possible." She returned his nod and stepped out of the office to leave the two men alone.

The asset broke the silence. "I'm a traitor now," he said, almost to himself.

"You have been that for a quite a while." Bazin went back to English, maintaining his sympathetic tone even as his loathing for the foolish little man grew. "It's too late to have regrets. But don't blame yourself. This is not your fault. We are giving you no choice."

"Is this going to get worse? Is it going to end?"

Bazin allowed some of his distaste to show through as he drew out his Makarov PM pistol and held it down on the surface of the desk. He did it to underline the dynamics of power in their relationship, just to make certain there was no misunderstanding. "Those things are beyond your control," he said. "Never forget that."

• • •

The man at the front desk of the Apache Motel had the kind of paunchy look that made Chase peg him as a linebacker gone to seed. He wore a too-loud bowling shirt over the top of a greasy T-shirt bearing a picture of Dino, the cartoon house pet from *The Flintstones*. Immediately, that was the name that Chase tagged the man with in his thoughts.

Dino measured the two men with a gimlet gaze that didn't change when Jack peeled off a few hundred bucks and paid for two rooms. They were handed brass keys on big wooden fobs that mimicked the tepee shape of the sign outside on the street, the room numbers burned into the surfaces. "Pay-per-view costs extra," he said, his words coming in the thick and scratchy tone of a habitual smoker. "You want it?" When neither man responded, his expression became a leer. "Or the real thing?"

"Just the rooms."

"Enjoy your stay," Dino said robotically, turning back to the magazine on his desk. Chase could tell by the look in his eyes, he was already forgetting about them. And that was fine. They didn't need to make any impression.

The rooms were on the second floor, side by side with grimy windows that looked out onto faded planters full of brown, half-dead grass. The important thing was they could see the car from there, as well as get an angle on the office and the street. The downside was that the flickering glare of a gas station sign directly across the road poured yellowed light in through the windows, and the thin curtains did little to attenuate it.

Both rooms were mirror images of one another, with hard double beds and that kind of faux-wood veneer paneling over everything that hadn't been in style since the age of disco. One room smelled slightly less ripe than the other, so they chose that as the place to bunk, but not before setting up the other as a decoy. Jack and Chase arranged the curtains, the lamps and left the TV on low, all to give any casual passerby the impression that someone was in there. The other they left poorly lit, and between them they quietly moved a wardrobe to block the door from being able to open fully. *Just in case.*

There was a small window in the bathroom with a safety bar across it, probably to prevent anyone from using it as a fast exit rather than paying their bill, but it wasn't hard for them to unscrew it and pop out the frame. Again, *just in case.*

Without talking, they divided up the bedclothes between them and made sleeping arrangements on opposite sides of the room, low down on the floor and away from the actual bed. Chase frowned at the remains of an ancient rusty patch on the dark carpet, which heavy applications of cleanser had never been able to remove. Someone had bled in here, probably from a stab wound. He wondered what he would see around the room if he had a UV lamp, and decided that he was probably better off not knowing.

Jack was at the window, peering through a gap in the musty shades.

"Can you see Dino from there?" asked Chase.

"Who?"

"The desk guy."

"Yeah." Jack paused. "Doesn't look like he's calling us in to anyone."

Chase looked up. "He didn't make us."

"No," agreed Jack, "but that doesn't mean he doesn't have standing orders to tell someone when new people come into town."

"Who is he gonna tell? The local deputy? If there's a cop within a hundred square miles of this burg, it'll be a miracle."

"I'm not thinking about the police." There was another low rumble of motorcycle engines, a throaty growl like a powerful animal.

Chase came to the window and saw more bikes like the ones that had surrounded them, turning wide semicircles on the road as they made for a gaudy, neon-drenched strip club down at the end of the main street. The sign on the roof said the place was called THE CRANKCASE.

"So, if you know something about outlaw motorcycle clubs," he began, "you know something about those Night Ranger guys?"

"Heard the name once or twice," Jack admitted. "But I don't think they were ever on any CTU watch list. That doesn't make them clean, though."

"Just not dirty enough to be a threat to national security," added Chase. "I've seen these types of creeps before, though. They make their way running guns up and down the interstate, that kinda thing."

Jack gave a slow nod. "That'll be part of it. But out here, you can bet they're dealing drugs as well. Crystal meth or oxycodone."

"Oh yeah, *hillbilly heroin*." Chase walked away. "All the more reason to steer clear of them." But Jack didn't step away from the window, not for a while.

Chase sat on the bed, checking his Ruger, and tried not to watch the other man. Better than anyone, he knew how Jack Bauer had fought his own personal demons in a battle with drug addiction, and the hard road he traveled to get free of it. And as he thought of that, Chase wondered if his former partner had been able to keep himself clean in the intervening years. Jack Bauer had the strongest survival impulse of any person Chase Edmunds had ever known, but that had been a long time ago.

Jack seemed to sense his attention and shot him a look. "You must be tired after driving. Go ahead, get some rest. I'll take first watch." He lowered himself into a chair near the door, with Big Mike's Remington across his lap.

As he said it, Chase had to stifle a sudden yawn. "You sure? If you wanna go first, I can deal."

The other man shook his head, and his gaze turned inward. "I don't need to sleep again. Don't like what I see in there."

10

In the history of all the bad choices that Laurel Tenn had ever made, it was starting to look like this was the worst.

The whole sorry business with her rat of an ex-boyfriend Don had been the catalyst, and just knowing that he was out there looking for her was enough to make Laurel want to get out of Indianapolis and never, ever look back. If she'd known what he was into, about the scams he played and the gambling, she never would have hooked up with him. But what was done was done, and in the end the only real choice open to her was to flee.

She had no blood family that she knew of. Her friends—not that they really deserved that name—were mostly Don's friends, and reaching out to any one of them would see her wind up right back where she started. The foster parents left behind after she had cut and run years earlier were out in Oregon, far enough away that they might as well have been on the moon. And she doubted they'd want to see her again.

There was the small matter of money too. With a bag containing what she'd been able to pick up from Don's apartment and the clothes on her back, Laurel had exactly twenty bucks and change to her name. But then she remembered what Trish from the Double Eight bar had told her, about the nice guy from out of town who was recruiting girls to work the kitchens in a casino across the state line. A job and a way out. Two days ago, desperation and panic had made that seem like the smart choice.

But the casino wasn't where the guy had said it was. There was only more road. The elderly bus carrying Laurel and Trish and a handful of others just kept on rolling down the interstate, only stopping now and then to pick up more groups of other folks who seemed just as down on their luck as she was. Not just girls, either. Older people, men and women who could have been Laurel's mom and dad, with nothing in common but the same kind of hard-knock stories. Everyone desperate for a job, struggling to find a way to make a buck when the factories they had worked in had relocated to the Far East or been shut down entirely, when the welfare wasn't enough to pay for food or meds or heat. She heard one man mutter about a promised job as a construction laborer, and it was then that Laurel started to think that all of them had been lied to. There wasn't any casino. There never had been.

But she wasn't really, truly afraid until the sun went down, and they were still driving, and the men on the motorcycles with the black leather and hard eyes came riding into formation with the bus. One of them caught her looking as she peered wide-eyed out of the window, and he grinned back at her. He had a mouth full of chromed teeth and tattoos on his face that looked like claws.

The older guy, the construction worker, he was the first one to say anything about it. He demanded some kind of answer from the driver and the nice-guy recruiter from

Indianapolis. So they pulled onto the shoulder in the middle of nowhere, then they walked him off the bus and beat the shit out of him. Right there in full view of everyone else, pushing him back and forth between the bikers, punching the man bloody until he finally collapsed in a ditch. Laurel couldn't see if he was still breathing.

When the driver got back on, he didn't need to ask if anyone else was going to complain. No one else dared. The recruiter told them that there was good, solid work for every person on the bus, but anyone who thought they could make trouble would go the same way as the older guy. They returned to the road and drove on in silence.

Trish started quietly weeping, at least until the recruiter stalked up the aisle and made her quit that with just a look. Dark-haired and elfin-faced, most people considered her prettier than dishwater-blond Laurel with her farm-girl build, and the other woman was convinced that they had inadvertently signed themselves up with sex traffickers. *But that kind of thing only happens in other countries,* Laurel thought. *Not here.*

The only thing she knew for sure was that with each mile they put behind them, she was getting farther away from any kind of safety.

Then the bus turned off the highway and rattled over a railroad cutting, and Laurel caught sight of a sign for a town called Deadline.

• • •

Chase's breathing became slow and regular, and Jack knew his friend had drifted away into some badly needed sleep. He turned his attention back to the window, scanning the motel parking lot and the street beyond.

In one way, it was strange that the two men had just

picked up where they left off. After the years that had passed between them, after the bad blood and the experiences they had both suffered through, an outsider might think it was hard to fathom. But the reverse was true; Jack and Chase had bonded under fire, and that kind of connection never really went away. Jack didn't count a lot of people as friends, not in the real sense of the word. Chloe O'Brian. Bill Buchanan. Carl Benton. Chase Edmunds was on that very short list too, for what it was worth. Too many of them were gone, and Jack regretted that Chase had almost ended up the same way.

The fact was, it was *easy* to slip back into the old partnership. It was something they were good at, and in their shared time at CTU they had done good work, they had saved a lot of lives.

There was still the one unvoiced doubt, though, still that implicit question that Chase had not yet brought to the surface. Jack admitted that he had used Chloe to keep a weather eye on Chase after he faked his own death—but he had never interfered with the other man's new life until now.

Why? Jack sighed. He didn't have an answer for that. There had been a number of times when he could have reached out to his former partner, but he had never risked it until today.

Because it wasn't of use to you, said Nina's voice from the back of his mind. *And you've always been about making the most expedient choice, haven't you, Jack?*

He scowled and kneaded the grip of the shotgun, silencing the traitorous thought. Jack looked down at his wristwatch, at the steady sweep of the second hand, and he thought about the railroad a few miles distant. It would be hours until the cargo train passed through. Hours for him to sit here and watch the world go by.

Out there in the night somewhere, the FBI fugitive pursuit team and Suvarov's SVR hunter-killers were searching for him, sifting whatever fractions of data and fragmentary leads he might have left behind. If they came, he would be ready, but Jack hoped it wouldn't come to that.

What he wanted was to get through this without firing another shot. To just watch the clock and let the time run out. Jack reached into an inner pocket of his jacket and fished out a small fold of thick paper. He opened it, revealing a careworn photo of his daughter, his son-in-law and their little girl. The three of them smiled back up at him, frozen in that untroubled moment, free of all the darkness that dogged Jack's shadowy life.

By tomorrow afternoon he would be in Los Angeles, and he would see Kim and tell her it all. He owed his daughter that. He couldn't just vanish again, not after last time. Talking to Chase had brought all that back, giving him fresh understanding of exactly what he had left behind the last time his family had believed him missing and presumed dead.

I can't put Kim through that a second time, he told himself. *I won't.* After a moment, he carefully refolded the photo and put it safely away.

Out on the street, movement caught his eye. A battered old Greyhound bus was slowing to a halt across from the motel.

• • •

For Laurel, Deadline was like a horrible flashback to the no-account place she had grown up in, and it loomed large on the other side of the windows as the bus rolled down the main street. It was everything she had spent her life trying to escape from, trying and failing time and again to break free of the pull of a dead-end town, always wanting something better but falling short of the means to get it.

She wondered if it was some kind of payback for all the bad things she had done in her life. Was it karma, in a way? Had a higher power decided that Laurel Tenn was never going to be free, and dragged her back to this?

She shook off the bleak thought as the bus grumbled to a halt in front of a gas station and the recruiter stood up, pointing at them with a stubby wooden baton that had seemingly come from out of nowhere.

"Okay," he barked. The pleasant smile he had worn back in Indianapolis was long gone, and now he was shark-eyed and tired from the journey, his tone clipped and angry. "We're almost there, so listen up. You wanna take a piss, use the restrooms here. You're not gonna go all at once. Women first. Four at a time." He beckoned them, and Laurel got to her feet with Trish and two others. "Nobody screw around."

A cold breeze hit her legs as she stepped onto the gas station forecourt, the thick mix of diesel engine exhaust and gasoline stinging her nostrils. Laurel wiped a hand over her face and pulled her thin jacket tight over her shoulders, daring to look toward the bikers who had escorted them the last few miles. The one with the chrome teeth was laughing loudly at something another man was saying. The other guy, muscular, shaven-headed and hard-faced, had been waiting for them. He studied the bus passengers with an indifferent sneer. She got the sense that he was in charge.

Laurel caught part of their conversation and her blood ran cold. "You pick out one you like?" said the hard-faced man.

"I get a choice?" said Chrome Teeth. "Rydell's getting generous all of a sudden?"

"Always rewards hard work, don't he? Thought you could use some entertainment."

The biker noticed Laurel looking in their direction and

she turned away, moving quickly toward the women's restroom around the side of the gas station proper.

"What is it?" said Trish, her voice still breathy from when she had been crying. "Oh god, what are we going to do?"

Laurel was afraid to look behind her for fear the hard-faced man was following them, and she pushed the other woman into the restroom as quickly as she could. "I think . . . I think you're right," she managed. "They don't want no cooks and cleaners here. The others, I dunno, but us . . ." Laurel trailed off. Her thoughts reeled with horrific possibilities of all the kinds of abuse she could be put to. She stumbled to the sink and held on to it. Her stomach twisted and Laurel felt as if she was going to vomit. Panic built up inside her like a flood, and she could feel it seconds away from breaking free. The fear was like nothing she had ever experienced before. If it got loose, she knew it would consume her.

"I can't go back out there!" Trish whimpered. "Laurel, please don't make me."

"Don't start crying again," she told her, but it was already too late. Tears streamed down the other woman's face and Laurel knew that if she lost control, she would end up the same way, paralyzed by her terror. She grabbed Trish's arm and shoved her into one of the vacant stalls, locking them both inside.

Others came and went, cycling through the restroom as the two young women pressed into the corner of the stall and waited. Just as Laurel had feared, there was no other way out of the cinder block toilets aside from a small skylight in the roof, and that was out of reach, the cracked and dirty glass up there threaded through with wire and nailed shut. The stall stank of pungent industrial cleaner and human waste.

"We have to call the cops," whispered Trish, after long minutes. "I don't got a phone. Did you see one outside?"

"What cops?" Laurel hissed back at her. "You think they'll come running?" She shook her head. "Girl, we've gotta get out of this on our own. Get a car, or something."

"I don't know—" Trish was shocked silent as one of the other stall doors banged.

Outside, Laurel could hear the grumble of the bus engine starting up again. Was it possible they might be missed if they just stayed in here, stayed quiet? For the first time, she started to entertain the possibility of *escape*.

She dropped into a low crouch and peered through the gap under the raised door, ignoring the stronger smell closer to the floor. The other stalls were empty, all the other women who had chosen to use them gone and back on the bus. Laurel opened the latch, and Trish grabbed at her, trying to stop her from turning the handle.

"No, no," she gasped. "No, don't. We'll stay here. Just stay."

"We can't," Laurel shot back. "We're like rats in a trap. Come on, this might be the only chance we get!"

She opened the stall and walked quietly toward the restroom door, straining to listen. Laurel could hear voices, and she recognized Chrome Teeth cursing angrily.

"How the hell should I know?" she heard him snarl. He was coming closer.

Behind her, Trish's hands were flapping at the air in front of her like trapped birds, and Laurel fought down the urge to slap her, to try to knock some sense into the other woman. "He's going to find us," Trish bleated.

Suddenly the door was opening inward and Laurel caught a glimpse of the tattooed biker as he pushed his way into the room. "What the hell are you stupid—"

She didn't give him the chance to finish. Without thinking about it, Laurel launched herself at the door and slammed her full weight into it with unexpected force. The door flicked back on its two-way hinges and cracked the biker in the face, sending him staggering across the asphalt.

Acting on pure animal fight-or-flight reflex, Laurel ran through the open door, aware of Trish hesitating a split second before she came racing out after her.

Laurel broke into a sprint, dashing away between the gas pumps, aiming herself down the main street in the opposite direction from which they had come. "Trish, go!" she called.

She heard a high-pitched shrieking yelp, and risked a glance over her shoulder in time to see Trish losing her balance and tumbling to the ground. Chrome Teeth had recovered swiftly and managed to catch her, grabbing the black ponytail that fell over Trish's shoulders and using it to savagely yank her off her feet. Laurel felt sick inside, hearing the other woman cry out as she collapsed.

Callous, rough laughter sounded behind her. "Get that skank, you asshole!" shouted the biker. Laurel bolted across the mouth of an alleyway and ran for the first building she saw—a glass-fronted convenience store, washed out by the harsh glow of fluorescent lamps.

She stumbled through the door, almost colliding with a spinner rack of comic books, and found the shocked face of an overweight man behind the counter. "You have to help me," she blurted out.

But the man stepped back, raising his hands. "I don't want any trouble," he told her, terrified by her appearance.

The door rattled open behind Laurel, and she turned to see the big, hard-faced man enter, his lips drawn back in a cold smile. He glanced between her and the guy behind the counter, and licked his lips. "You think he's gonna give you a hand, little sister?" She saw his name—Brodur—written on his jacket. "*Naw*. What he's gonna do is turn around right now, ain't ya?"

The other man looked at the floor, and sheepishly turned away, retreating into a back office.

Laurel slipped down one of the aisles, ducking low. She heard Brodur chuckle.

"Come on," he called. "What you even running from, huh? You don't even know. Got skittish and decided to make a break . . . To where? Where you gonna go?" He made a spitting sound. "Shit. We got work here for you people, you get that? You can earn. Who the hell else is offering that, huh? *Answer me!*" The last was a shout, as his tolerance for Laurel's disobedience faded.

When Brodur came around the end of the aisle, he had a butterfly knife in his hand, gripped low and ready to inflict harm. Laurel was armed too, holding a heavy bottle of cheap fortified wine by the neck; she smashed it into his torso, the glass shattering, dousing the biker in sticky fluid and cutting his chest, the skin of his neck. Caught by surprise, he flailed, sweeping wildly through the air with the knife and missing as Laurel ran. Shouting and cursing, she heard him coming after her as she burst back through the door and ran heedlessly across the street.

Ahead of her, Laurel saw a sign like a stylized Indian tent and beyond it, shadows, overgrown bushes and a few parked cars. One of the only useful things her ex-boyfriend had ever taught her was how to hot-wire an ignition. Here and now, that might be the only lifeline she had.

• • •

Jack put down the shotgun and moved closer to the window to get a better angle on what was happening. The arrival of the bus had immediately drawn his interest. It seemed out of place, and the state of the vehicle made him suspicious. He very much doubted that Deadline was on any commercially run route ... So what did this mean?

The bulk of the vehicle blocked off any view of what was happening on the far side, but he glimpsed another group of Night Ranger outriders congregating around the perimeter of the gas station. Figures moved around inside the bus, but he couldn't make out any details.

Breathing silently, Jack strained to listen for any sounds that carried from across the road, but he heard only the occasional snatch of laughter or the mutter of engines, brought to him on the cool night air.

But then there was a sudden flash of motion and he saw a woman bolt out from behind the cover of the bus and sprint into the nearest building. A man chased after her, and Jack recognized him as the biker who had led the pack that stopped at the traffic signal. *Brodur.*

He tensed. The scenario was already playing itself out in his mind's eye. Was he looking at a kidnapping going wrong, human trafficking, or worse? The bus had to be connected to the outlaw MC, but Jack had never heard of one-percenter gangs involved in those kinds of crimes. It wasn't the usual modus operandi for such criminal groups, who typically kept to protection rackets or smuggling low-mass, high-value items like guns and drugs.

Barely a minute had elapsed before the glass door of the convenience store crashed open and the woman came charging out again. She was running like the devil himself was at her heels, and as she dashed across the street, Jack realized she was making a beeline for the shady parking lot of the Apache Motel. Brodur came staggering out after her, following at a more leisurely jog, as if he didn't care to exert himself more than he needed to.

The girl was blond-haired and young, and she desperately looked around as she ran onto the motel forecourt, searching the windows and doors for some kind of escape route.

Jack's breath caught in his throat. For a fraction of a second, he saw Kim's face there instead, his daughter fleeing like she was a panicked animal. Then he blinked and the moment was gone. It wasn't Kim, but the fear on the woman's face was very real. She faltered, almost stumbling, and vanished into the shadows near to where Chase had parked the Chrysler. Brodur walked steadily up the middle of the driveway, past the motel's office without giving it a second look. He had that butterfly knife in his hand and Jack could see his shirt was ripped and discolored from what might have been slashing wounds.

Jack looked back into the room. Chase was out cold, dead to the world. The Remington shotgun was close to hand, but using it would commit Jack to going loud, and that would destroy what little chance remained of them staying undisturbed. He had the M1911 pistol in his waistband, but without a silencer that too would bring everyone running the moment he used it.

Across the street, the bus spat dirty blue smoke from its exhaust and rolled away, continuing on. Brodur's associates stayed behind, milling around as they waited for the other man to return. Jack stood at the window, unmoving. He watched the biker slow to a halt and peer into the deeper shadows, head bobbing like a hunting dog looking for prey.

The girl had nowhere to go. From up here on the second floor, Jack could see that clearly. She had to be hiding behind the Chrysler or the battered F-150 pickup a couple of spaces over, but that concealment was really a trap. Brodur would be on her in a moment and then . . .

And then what, Jack? Nina's voice ghosted through his mind again. *If you go out there, if you get involved, you'll blow this whole thing. Better if you sit back and let it happen.*

He saw the way it would go down. Brodur would take

the girl, and he would not be gentle with her. Jack knew the type, the kind of man that made him sick to share the same gender, who liked to use their fists on women because they believed it made them somehow stronger. The girl— maybe someone else's daughter—would suffer. But eventually, she would go away and so would the biker, and Jack and Chase would remain hidden.

Down in the forecourt, Jack heard Brodur give a low, musical whistle, as if he were calling out to an errant pet.

• • •

Laurel froze when the sound reached her, and she felt her heart thumping in her chest. In her hands she held her jacket, taken off and balled up so she could use it to muffle the crash of glass when she broke the window of the silver car. Now she shrank back, catching the noise of heavy boots crunching on the tarmac as Brodur stalked closer.

She dared to peek around the curve of the fender and saw him sketched in black shadow. Laurel could smell the too-sweet odor of the fortified wine that had splattered over him in the convenience store, and what light there was caught the wicked edge of the knife in his right hand.

"Why do they always gotta run?" he said aloud, asking the question to the air. "Come on, girl. Get out here, take your medicine."

The panic that she had managed to keep in check finally tipped the balance, and Laurel exploded out of cover in a scrambling run, throwing her jacket at Brodur with all her might, trying to distract him.

The biker batted it away with a grunt and then he was on her before she could get any distance, landing a punch that hit her hard in the kidneys. Laurel cried out and fell against the grille of the parked pickup truck, her legs turning to rubber.

"I could have got you work at the 'Case," said Brodur, using his knife to gesture down the street. "Now what's going to happen instead, huh?"

"You're going to step away and lose the blade," said another voice, and Laurel saw a man with haunted eyes emerge from behind the pickup.

Brodur's eyes narrowed. "That silver cage . . . you were in the back." He grimaced. "Get lost, dickweed. You're new in town, so maybe you don't get it. This is MC business."

"Step away and lose the blade," repeated the other man, and there was steel beneath the words. "I won't tell you again."

The biker didn't waste any more time talking; he swung around and went for the man with a guttural snarl.

11

A part of Jack Bauer—the conscious, calculating part of him—went away as the biker thug came barreling toward him. A different aspect of Jack slipped seamlessly to the fore, the part of the former soldier that was all trained aggression and instinctive violence.

Brodur charged like he was an angry bull, and he had the body mass to back it up. The man was densely muscled and quick on his feet, but he had the rough technique of a street brawler, doubtless learned the hard way through dozens of bar fights and roadside dustups. By contrast, Jack's fighting method was all about lethality, and the application of maximum force with minimum hesitation. Neither of them could be considered a defensive combatant.

Brodur led with the butterfly knife, but he was clever with it, slashing at the air to drive Jack onto his back foot but never extending enough to risk overbalancing. Each slice was a miss, but he wasn't aiming to cut him, not yet. The biker was trying to limit his movement, make it so Jack couldn't slip out of his range before he got close enough to pin him down.

Anyone else would have automatically retreated before

the dance of the keen blade, but Jack did the opposite. He closed the gap with Brodur before the biker could change his tack and brought up his forearms to parry the blows, knocking the other man's feints away, breaking the pattern of his assault.

Jack's assailant snarled and spun the knife in his hand, turning a cutting motion into a reversal that would bite into the outside of Jack's forearm and go deep. He wasn't smart enough to avoid telegraphing the move, though, and Jack caught his wrist before he could complete the twist, stopping his advance cold.

Brodur put both hands behind the blade and forced it toward the other man's face. Jack responded in kind, and for a second the two of them were locked against one another, muscles in their arms bunching as they fought with sheer force to direct the blade toward their opponent.

It was hard for Jack to keep his grip steady, and he could feel the inexorable slip of the weapon as he lost ground. Brodur was heavier than him, stronger with it, and pound for pound he had the muscle advantage. Jack could hold him for a few moments, but not indefinitely. Close now, he could see that Brodur's pupils were clearly dilated, and he guessed that the biker was under the influence of something. That could make him unpredictable, irrational, more dangerous.

Even as the thought occurred to Jack, Brodur suddenly jerked forward and butted him in the head. The blow was poorly executed and it hit off the mark. Had it been dead-on, Jack would have been dazed and reeling, open for a follow-up stab that could have opened his throat. As it was, he was only shocked backward a step, losing his block.

Shaking off the pain, Jack saw Brodur wheel around as something flashed at the corner of his vision. It was the woman, enough of her wherewithal recovered that she was making a break for it.

The biker didn't want that. His other arm shot out and he batted her back. The woman took the blow full force in the chest and she spun away, colliding with the flank of the high-sided F-150 pickup.

Jack used the moment of distraction and came at his opponent. Going low and fast, he landed three strong punches along the line of Brodur's ribs. His arm moved like a piston, each hit a brutal one.

Brodur let out a strangled bark of pain and came back at Jack, once again leading with the butterfly knife. But Jack had the measure of the man now, he anticipated the paths of the biker's attacks. Brodur didn't have the training or the skills to mix up his game, he was reliant on might and viciousness. That was Jack's edge, and he played it hard.

The blade came up and across. Jack caught the advance cleanly between the angles of his forearms with a fast counter that broke the bones in the biker's wrist. Brodur bellowed as the butterfly knife dropped to the ground and bounced away, but rather than falter, the pain seemed to stoke his fury even higher.

Whatever was in his system had to be making the busted wrist seem distant and unimportant. Brodur's other hand, a big meaty paw grimy with engine oil, enveloped Jack's face and tightened. The biker was trying to crush his skull, thumb pushing into the orbit of his left eye, fingers compressing the bones of his jaw. Jack lost his balance and fell against the hood of the Chrysler. He was starting to regret his decision not to wake Chase from his deep sleep.

Then in the next second the suffocating hand was gone and Brodur was cursing a blue streak, turning in place, snatching at his back while his ruined hand dangled uselessly at the end of his other arm.

Jack saw the blond woman backing away, horrified by what she had just done. The full four inches of the butterfly knife's stainless steel blade were buried in Brodur's shoulder, through the leather of his jacket and into the meat of him.

The biker found purchase on the handle and he pulled it out with a wet gasp. "You filthy skank," he spat. Letting it drop, Brodur reached for a hidden holster in the small of his back, feeling for it with his uninjured hand. "Playtime's over, bitch!" His fist came back wrapped around a short-frame Smith & Wesson revolver, his thumb drawing back the hammer.

Bolting forward, his vision still blurry, Jack snatched at the discarded blade. It was covered in fresh blood, and it almost slipped out of his fingers, but then he had it firmly in his grip and he was crashing into Brodur before the biker could pull the pistol's trigger.

The woman had the right idea, but not the right target. Jack used one hand to snake around Brodur's throat and yank his head back, and the other—knuckles white around the handle of the butterfly knife—he slammed straight into the biker's chest, feeling the tip of the blade skip off the edge of a rib and go deep. Brodur tried to scream as Jack stabbed him through the heart, but his voice died in his throat, becoming a strangled moan.

The big biker spasmed and his legs gave out, the light in his eyes fading. Jack let Brodur fall to the ground, blood seeping from the new wound in his chest.

"Dead," gasped the woman. "He's dead."

Jack gave a weary nod. "Thanks for the help."

Her face twisted in anger and she spat venomously in Brodur's face. "Good. *Bastard!*" Then the moment passed and she seemed to remember where she was. "Who are you? Are you one of them?" She eyed the revolver where it had fallen and grabbed for it before Jack could react.

"I'm not with him," he said, moderating his breathing. "We have to hide his body. If they come looking for this guy . . ."

"*We?*" she shot back. "I'm not part of this." She looked around desperately. "I have to get out of here . . . I have to . . ." The woman's voice trailed off to nothing. "Oh god. Trish and all the others, they're still on the bus. Oh god oh god . . ."

Jack took a second to make sure that they hadn't drawn any attention. They seemed to be in the clear for the moment, the fight having taken place in a shadowed corner of the motel parking lot out of sight of the main street. He wiped his hands down on Brodur's clothes and then dumped him in the bed of the pickup, dragging a loose tarp across to cover up the corpse.

The woman watched him work, kneading the grip of the gun. "I'm Laurel," she offered, finding her jacket on the ground and gathering it up. She wasn't pointing the gun at him anymore.

"Jack," he replied. "You're not from here."

She gave a derisive snort. "I don't even know where the hell *here* is." She looked out toward the street, and Jack could sense she was weighing her chances.

"You want to run, I won't stop you," he said. "But you've got to know the odds aren't good on your own."

Laurel looked back at him, and disgust crept into her expression. "So you're gonna do what, *look after me?*" Other men had clearly used that line on her before, and with the worst of intentions.

Jack pushed aside how much Laurel reminded him of Kim and shook his head. "You go out there, they'll catch you. They'll make you tell them who killed that creep. And I don't want anyone asking questions about me."

She was quiet for a long moment. Then the revolver went into her jacket pocket and Laurel gave him a measuring look. "You got anything to eat?"

• • •

"Yeah, that's the fella," said the waitress. Her name was Margaret and she seemed distracted, her gaze drifting away every few seconds to the small handful of other customers who still remained in the diner and the county cops who were milling around out in front of the place.

"You're sure about that?" said Kilner, holding up Jack Bauer's ID photo.

"I said yeah, didn't I?" Margaret glanced between Kilner and Hadley. "He was a decent tipper. Look, I don't wanna be rude or nothing, I mean I do my civic duty and all, but you boys are making my customers nervous." She jerked a thumb at the diner's sparse clientele. "Around here, the federal government don't got the best of reputations, if you catch my drift."

"Yes, I'm sure all those welfare dollars your state sucks out of Washington, DC, are a real burden," Hadley replied briskly. "Look, ma'am, I don't have any interest in the local truckers bucking their taxes by using agricultural diesel instead of regular." He jabbed Bauer's picture with a finger. "However good a tipper he was, this man is a wanted killer. Is that clear?"

Kilner watched the color drain from Margaret's face. "*Whoa*. For real?" She blinked. "So the other guy was, what? His victim? His accomplice?"

"The other guy," Hadley repeated. "You got a security camera over there. Where's the recorder it's attached to?"

"Ain't one," she told him, lowering her voice so no one else would hear her say it. "It's just for insurance, y'know? A fake."

Hadley swallowed an angry reply and walked away a few steps. Kilner frowned. "I'd like you to talk with Deputy Roe. We're going to need a full statement from you and a description of the other man you saw here tonight."

"Is he, like, one of them serial murderers?" Margaret seemed to take a kind of glee from asking the question.

Before he could frame any kind of answer, he saw Dell

enter the diner and beckon them over. Kilner followed Hadley, sensing the frustration in the other FBI agent. So far, the helicopter had given them nothing they didn't already know and none of the locals canvassed by Sheriff Bray's deputies had seen hide nor hair of Jack Bauer. The diner was their first real lead, but so far it was proving to be tantalizingly vague.

Bauer had stopped here to eat and made one, maybe two phone calls. Around half an hour later, another man had arrived and they had talked before leaving together. That was the sum total of information that had been gleaned, and Hadley was pulling at the leash like an angry pit bull, becoming more aggravated with each passing hour at the very real possibility that their quarry would leave them behind.

But Dell's expression, her sly grin, made Kilner reevaluate that thought.

"Tell me you've got something that's worth a damn," said Hadley.

"I may well have," she replied, guiding them back out the doors and into the chilly evening air. "Remember when we arrived there was a police cruiser already here? And paramedics too?"

Kilner had to admit, he hadn't registered the latter. "I thought they were here for the canvassing."

"Nope," said Dell. "Local dispatcher got a nine-one-one call around the same time that Todd Billhight phoned in about the helicopter. Turns out a friendly trucker did the good Samaritan act for two chumps who'd taken a beating and got dumped by the highway."

"What does that have to do with our fugitive?" said Hadley.

"Bauer's BOLO was on the dash of the cruiser sent out to give them a once-over. One of said pair of chumps saw it and opened his mouth about it. The deputy took it upon himself to bring them back here."

"Did he now?" Kilner saw the flash of a wintry smile, there and then gone again, on Hadley's lips. "Show me."

In the back of the ambulance were two younger men, and they were very much the worse for wear. One of them, the skinnier of the two, had the beginnings of a nasty black eye and the bigger of them had a leg in a splint and a swollen, reddening throat.

Hadley flashed his badge at the paramedic standing with them, cutting him off as he tried to say something about needing to get to proper medical attention. He held out his ID to the pair and glared at them. "Special Agent Hadley, Federal Bureau of Investigation."

"Oh shit." The shorter one said the words before he was even aware of it.

That earned him a hard look from his friend. "Josh!" he rasped. "Shut up."

Kilner held up the photo of Bauer. "You know this person?" The way the short one reacted, he knew the man did. "Where did you see him?"

"Look," said the man with the busted leg. "I gotta get to a hospital. Can we do this on the way or something?"

Hadley came over and examined the man's injury. He made a face. "That looks nasty. Bauer do that to you?"

"Who?"

"This man," said Kilner, showing the picture again.

"Frank . . ." began Josh, a pleading tone in his voice.

Kilner evaluated the situation; he knew bottom-feeders when he saw them. These two guys were at best wannabe mooks who had the misfortune of crossing paths with Jack Bauer and his mystery companion. Maybe they'd mistakenly tried to roll them, or maybe there was more to it. But instinct told him that Josh and Frank here were little more than collaterals, people caught in the wake of Bauer's escape more than involved in it.

Hadley seemed to come to the same conclusion. "This man is very dangerous. I need to find him and whoever is with him. Now, you can tell me what you know, or I can drag you both into holding for the next ten hours and you can live with however much those breaks and bruises are hurting. Because no one is going to the hospital unless I say so. Clear?"

"That's the guy," Josh blurted. "He got the drop on—"

"*Shut up!*" shouted Frank. "Stop. Talking. *Asshole.*" He winced at pain from his leg. "Okay. Okay. He's right, that guy, what'd you call him, Bauer? He's the one that busted me up."

"Why?" said Dell.

"We were just here for the car," Frank said between gasps. "Like, a repo."

At Hadley's urging, they described a silver Chrysler 300 with Pennsylvania plates, and Dell stepped away to contact the NY office and get the license running through the database.

"Who was the driver?" Kilner demanded. "The man Bauer was meeting?"

"Charlie Williams," said Josh after a moment. "Car didn't belong to him, he took it. That's all," he insisted. "We were gonna get it back."

Frank nodded. "Yeah. So, can we go now?"

Hadley nodded distractedly and strode away to where Bray was talking to one of his men. "Sheriff? I need those two idiots arrested on suspicion of aiding and abetting a known federal fugitive. I want you to lean on them hard, and get me full statements when you're done." He didn't wait for a reply, and started toward the parked SUV.

Bray shot Kilner a surprised look and then called after the other agent. "And just what are you gonna be doing?"

"I have a name and a vehicle. I'm going to find both."

• • •

Chase awoke as a rolling burn spread down his arm along the tracks of his nerves. He gritted his teeth and levered himself up to a sitting position, fingers briefly touching the butt of his Ruger semiautomatic among the pile of his jacket before gripping his scarred wrist. In the semidarkness of the motel room, the web of blemishes and pockmarks around the place where his wrist had been severed were invisible—but Chase knew them intimately, like the streets where he had grown up. Lines of fish-belly-white scarring that would never take on color, never tan in the sun, a reminder that would stay constant for the rest of his life.

"Jack?" he whispered. The seat by the window was empty and Chase frowned. He was alone in the room, listening hard. Had Jack stepped out for some air? That had to be it.

The pain alternated between slow, sullen throbs and random jolts that made his arm twitch. It had been a long time since it had hurt this badly, but then it had been a long time since Chase had used his bad hand to throw punches. A pang of self-loathing settled in on him even before he committed to the act of reaching for the pill bottle. With motions that had become almost reflexive muscle memory, Chase popped the plastic cap and dry-swallowed a single tablet. He kneaded the flesh of his arm, as if by doing so he could work in the effects of the painkiller a little quicker.

Shadows moved by the window. He slipped behind the room's only easy chair and drew the Ruger, taking aim at the door.

The latch clicked and the door opened slowly, until it reached the stop where the cupboard was wedged in the way. "It's me," said Jack, and he slipped into the room. Chase rose, but he kept the gun at hand as he realized the other man wasn't alone.

A woman, her features lost in the dimness. She balked at the sight of the pistol and froze.

"It's okay," Jack told him, and he closed the door, switching on a bedside lamp. "This is Laurel. We're helping her."

Chase gave the woman a look. A little younger than him, she looked strung-out and fearful. Her face was dirty and scratched, as if she had been knocked down.

"You said you had something to eat," she began.

Jack nodded toward a bag on the dresser—inside were snacks, bottles of water and sodas they had looted from a gas station vending machine back along the highway. Laurel helped herself to a 7 Up and a stale sandwich, demolishing it hungrily.

"Waifs and strays now?" Chase said irritably. "What the hell, Jack?"

"This is Chase," Jack told the girl. "He's okay."

"Not right now," he shot back. "Who is this?"

"Laurel," said the girl. "Laurel Tenn." Chase noticed how she had positioned herself close to the door in case she need to make a run for it, and by the way she held her jacket close to her, she had something hidden in its folds. A weapon, most likely.

Jack sighed and went to the sink in the small bathroom cubicle. "Brodur, that biker from before? He was going to kill her." He ran his hands under the taps, and rivulets of red streamed away down the plug hole.

"Not for starters," Laurel added, with a grim look in her eyes.

Chase's lips thinned. "So you got in the way." The blood on Jack's hands was answer enough as to the thug's fate.

"You'd have done the same." Jack returned and took a bottle of water for himself.

No, I wouldn't. Chase wanted to say those words. *I*

wouldn't put us at risk. But then he realized that all the years in the wilderness after leaving Valencia behind hadn't hardened him as much as he wanted to believe they had. It actually made him a little angry to see that he was still that same man, deep down. He hadn't changed, and neither had Jack Bauer. *What kind of idiot does that make me?* He frowned. "This is a complication."

"Hey!" Laurel glared at him, talking around a mouthful of bread. "Don't speak about me like I'm not in the room!"

"You're right," Jack agreed. "But there wasn't a good alternative."

"Never is." Chase sat down on the bed and blew out a breath. "Fine. She stays here until we go. Then she's on her own."

"I'm not the only one in trouble," Laurel insisted. "Trish and the others . . ." She faltered over the name. "Look, you know what these Night Ranger pricks are doing here, right?"

"Human trafficking," said Jack, and Chase's eyes widened.

But the woman was shaking her head. "That's only a part of it. I mean, I heard things . . . I saw things. But you never believe that kinda crap, do you?" She seemed to deflate. "Not until it's too late."

"Since when are biker gangs involved in the people smuggling game? It's not their bag."

Jack gave Laurel an encouraging nod. "Tell him what you told me."

She swallowed the last of the soda. "These guys . . . recruiters . . . they go looking all around for folks who are down on their luck. Not just girls. Workers. A lot of them. They offer good money, short-time jobs, out of state. No tax, cash in hand, all quiet."

"And you believed that?" said Chase. "You had to know it would be something illegal. At *best*."

"I know!" she retorted. "Everyone on that stinking bus knew that! But when you're drowning, you take the first rope you're thrown, right? *Right?*"

He gave a reluctant nod. "No argument there."

Laurel was silent for a long moment before she spoke again. "But then I got cold feet. I wanted to run, Trish and I tried to run, she got caught . . ." The woman took a shuddering breath. "They didn't want me and Trish for just *work*, though. Some, but not us. And the other girls."

"Saw the same pattern in Serbia, years ago," offered Jack. "Trading in human beings. Modern-day slavery."

His words seemed to trip something inside the woman, and Laurel suddenly stood up, her face going pale under the grime on her skin. "I gotta . . . get clean." She almost ran into the bathroom, slamming the door shut behind her.

• • •

Jack walked over to where Laurel's jacket had fallen and picked it up, unfolding it. He pulled out Brodur's revolver, snapped open the chamber to examine the loaded bullets.

"I can see it," Chase said, his voice soft. "Right then, when she talked about her friend."

"See what?" Jack put the pistol back on top of the jacket and turned to look at the other man.

"*Kim*." Chase gestured at his face. "Around the eyes. And the hair. Don't pretend you don't see it too."

Jack's lips thinned. "That's not why I went out after her."

"You sure?"

He gave his former partner an iron-hard glare. "I'm sure. If you think I'd let *anyone* get assaulted and murdered twenty feet from where I was sitting, then you've forgotten a lot about me, Chase."

The other man nodded at the glowing yellow-orange numerals of a digital clock on the bedside table. "If you wanted to kill time, read a book . . ." He sighed. "So what do we do now? Call the FBI? That's not gonna work. And we sure as hell can't take her with us."

"I'm considering the options," said Jack. With exaggerated slowness, he slipped off his jacket and started to remove his shirt. The pain he had experienced in the fight with Brodur was still there, and to his dismay he saw that the bullet wound he had taken during the situation in New York had reopened. "There's a medical kit in my bag. Pass it here."

Chase nodded and found it for him. "Sooner or later, Brodur's playmates are gonna come looking for their buddy. Then what?"

Jack peeled off the used dressing and worked at cleaning up the wound. "How long do we have until the cargo train gets here? Six, seven hours?"

"Something like that."

He nodded to himself. "Plenty of time."

"For what?"

"You know me." Jack gritted his teeth as he rolled out new bandages over his skin. "I like to keep occupied."

12

The argument was loud enough that it could be heard on the stoop of the house, filtering through the ornate door that fronted the expensive colonial-style suburban home. The man halted with his hand reaching for the big brass knocker and listened.

He could hear two distinct voices. A man, all snarls and growling, and a woman, her pitch high and wheedling. The words were lost to him, but the tone was clear. *Husband and wife,* he guessed, *years of resentment seething between them.*

He banged on the door, and after a moment he saw a shape through the frosted glass panels, moving down the hallway toward him. The husband, who didn't even halt his tirade as he walked.

"For crying out loud," he was saying, "can you just shut your mouth for one damn second? I can't hear myself think!" The door opened a few inches on a metal security chain, and the husband's face was revealed. Ruddy complexion, sweaty and irritable. "Yeah?" he demanded. "What do you want?"

Dimitri Yolkin held up a passable fake of an NYPD

detective's badge. "Mr. Roker?" He didn't really need to ask. Yolkin had seen a grinning, larger-than-life-size advertising cutout of "Big Mike" Roker inside the car dealership a short while earlier, after he had broken in to investigate the office there. It had been the next step in his search, after finding nothing of note in the sparse apartment rented to one Charles Williams, nothing worth following up but the paperwork that led to the car showroom. From there, Yolkin had found Roker's home address and now he was here. "I have questions for you."

Roker's deep-set eyes narrowed. "What kinda accent is that? You ain't no Pittsburgh cop, take a hike."

"Who's that out there?" called a shrill voice from the kitchen.

Roker glanced away, starting to close the door. "Shut up, it's nobody—"

Big Mike, Yolkin reflected, wasn't really that big at all. With a quick, hard blow, the SVR operative slammed the heel of his hand against the door with such force that the security chain popped out of its latch. The side of the front door clipped Roker across the cheek and he ducked back, shocked by the sudden flurry of motion.

Yolkin quickly stepped in over the threshold, drawing a silenced CZ 75 semiautomatic. Roker panicked and fled toward the back of the house, almost slipping on the hallway's tiled floor. "Barb!" he shouted. "Oh shit, call the police!"

"What?"

The wife's question gave Yolkin enough time to make it into the kitchen on Roker's heels, and when she saw him she screamed and fumbled for a telephone handset fixed to the wall.

The Czech-made pistol coughed and the phone exploded into hot fragments of plastic and circuit board, eliciting another scream from the woman. "Your husband told you to be quiet," said the Russian, offering the muzzle of the gun to the two Americans. "That is good advice."

The kitchen was large, almost half the size of the entire apartment in Kiev where Yolkin and his family had lived when he was a youth. In the middle was an island table topped by expensive marble and festooned with various electrical cooking gadgets. He pointed at two stools and gestured for Roker and his wife to sit down.

"Did Ernie deSalvo send you?" asked the woman. "Oh, Mike, you stupid shithead, you pissed him off one time too many . . ." Tears began to stream down her face.

For a second, Roker forgot he had a gun aimed at him. "You gotta blame me for everything!"

"I do not know who this 'Ernie' is," Yolkin corrected. He shrugged. "I do not care."

"Then what the hell are you doing here?" Roker shouted.

"Calm down." Yolkin moved to a position where he could see all entrances to the kitchen and keep the happy couple in his sights. "Charles Williams. Where is he?"

"Charlie?" The wife blinked. "You come looking for Charlie? He ain't here!"

"Oh yeah." Roker shifted in his chair and tapped his collar. "I see them tats you got. I get it now. You're with the Russkie Mob, right?" He managed a weak smile, his confidence returning. "He owe you money or something?"

"Something," Yolkin repeated, content to let the American continue with his mistaken assumption. "He works for you."

"Not anymore," Roker spat. "I fired the prick tonight. He stole my damn car!"

"Charlie *quit*," insisted the wife. "Like you coulda stopped him!"

"Why?" said Yolkin, the gun never wavering. "Why did he leave tonight?"

Roker paused, wrong-footed by the question. "I . . . I dunno. He got a call. Talking to some guy. Next thing I know he tells me to go screw myself . . ." The man licked his lips. "Look, buddy, you got a beef with him, that's nothing to do with me. Right now, I don't give a shit about what happens to that son of a bitch."

"Where is Jack Bauer?" Yolkin didn't think that Roker knew the target, but he threw the name out there anyway, just to fish for a reaction. Both husband and wife didn't show any sign of recognition, but he would have to be sure.

"Never heard of him."

He nodded, reached into a different pocket and produced a digital recorder, placing it on the kitchen table, switching it on. "I want you to tell me everything you know about Charles . . . *Charlie* Williams. Begin now." Yolkin gestured with the gun again. "Or I will kill you both."

As it was, the threat was hardly necessary. Roker was almost falling over himself to spill out every last detail he could dredge up about the man. Along with the study of the apartment where Williams lived and its contents, now with Roker's effusive descriptions Yolkin was building a picture of Jack Bauer's apparent accomplice. *Ex-military or former law enforcement,* he suspected. *A comrade-in-arms.* That fit the kind of profile the SVR had on Bauer. He was a man who valued loyalty. In dire straits, he would be more likely to reach out to those he respected rather than those whose silence he could buy.

Around twenty minutes had elapsed by the time Roker ran out of things to tell him. Yolkin got up and nodded. "That is all?"

"That's all," Roker replied. His body language had altered, and now he seemed to be almost conversational with his captor, as if they were on an equal footing. "Listen, buddy, if you see my car while you're looking for this dick, let me know. There'd be a finder's fee."

"You are certain that is all you know about Williams?"

Roker's smile faded. "What the hell did I just say? Yeah! That's all I know."

"You understand I have to be certain. I have to motivate you, in case you are withholding something." Yolkin turned and shot Roker's wife in the thigh.

She shrieked and collapsed to the tiled floor, blood gushing from a ragged wound. Roker dove after her, his face white with shock.

"Keep pressure on the wound," Yolkin instructed calmly. "She will bleed out in a few minutes if you do not do so."

"*Motherfu—!*"

Yolkin silenced him with a look. "Is what you have told me really all that you know? Think carefully."

"Oh god. Barbara, oh no." Roker began to cry. "I'm sorry, I'm so sorry . . ."

"If Williams needed to get away, where would he go? Who would he talk to? If he had to disappear, what would he do?"

"I . . . I don't . . ." Roker hesitated, and Yolkin saw the fractional glimmer of a thought forming in the man's wide, fearful eyes.

"Tell me," he prompted. "She will die if you do not."

"Matlow!" bleated Roker. "Hex Matlow, that pencil neck hacker . . . Charlie knows him. He's a smartass . . . He could, I dunno, help . . ." He looked down at his hands. "There's so much blood. . . ."

There was an expensive smartphone sitting on the kitchen table and Yolkin snatched it up. "This is yours? Matlow's contact information is on here?"

"Y-yes," Roker managed. "Please! *I don't know anything else about Charlie Williams!*" His words became an anguished shout.

The Russian considered the reply for a moment. "I had to make sure. Yes. I have it all." He raised the pistol again.

The next bullet went through Barbara Roker's forehead, killing her instantly. The two shots after that struck Big Mike in the throat and the chest respectively. He would take a little longer to die.

Yolkin switched off the digital recorder and recovered it and the American's smartphone, before he paused to carefully gather up the spent bullet casings from his weapon.

As he walked back to his car, he dialed an encrypted number. "I have something," he said.

• • •

"How d'you wanna play this?" said Chase, as they crossed the parking lot toward the Apache Motel's front office. Then he frowned and shook his head. "Wait. Why am I asking? Your usual approach?"

"What's that?" Laurel was trailing behind them, eyeing every shadow, trying not to show she was afraid.

Jack glanced over his shoulder at her. "You should stay in the room."

"No way," she insisted.

He considered making his suggestion into something more forceful. Having a civilian in the mix could get in the way of what Jack had planned, but then there was something in Laurel's eyes that told him she was no stranger to blood and violence. She didn't seem like the squeamish type . . . and her insight could prove valuable. For now, Jack decided to let her stay close at hand.

He glanced back at Chase. "We need more intel before we make a move."

The other man nodded. "Copy that."

Jack had conducted many interrogations in his time, and been the subject of them more often than he wanted

to recall. They were a game, in their own way, a contest
of willpower—and the sordid truth was that in the end,
everyone broke. No one could hold out indefinitely, not
even someone with Jack's steely self-control. Eventually,
you would falter . . . The only variable in play was how
long you could delay that terrible moment of surrender.
You could never really win; you could only *endure*.

Having too often been on the wrong side, Jack had
gained a unique insight into the power play required to
draw out intel from an unwilling subject. He was good
at it.

If this had been a CTU assignment, Jack would have
planned it down to the very last detail. The target would
be isolated, maybe taken in transit, or more typically, secured from a surveilled location by a snatch-and-grab
team. A specialized mobile unit would be on station to
act as an interview site if needed, that or the target
would be rendered unconscious and taken to a secure
"blind room" at the nearest CTU substation. There, a
hostile interrogation would commence, with a full medical and technical support staff on standby. Every answer
would be scrutinized and sifted for detail, searching out
falsehoods and weaknesses with voice-stress analyzers,
thermal imagers and pulse monitors.

But right here, right now, Jack had none of those
resources to call upon. There was only the hard-won
experience that he and Chase shared.

Years ago, as field agents for CTU Los Angeles, the two
men had developed a working shorthand that bordered
on the uncanny; their rate for mission success had been
among the best that Division had ever seen. Jack had
never really considered himself to be a team player, and
for the longest time he had resisted taking on anyone that
could be considered a "partner." But Chase Edmunds had
quietly impressed him with his skills and his tenacity,
and for a while the younger man had become a trusted

brother-in-arms. They saved each other's lives several times over, and Jack knew the value of having someone to cover his back when the bullets started flying. The people he truly trusted to do that could be counted on the fingers of one hand.

But that had been a long time ago. A lot had changed, not just between the two men, but also in their personal circumstances. Even from a cursory look, Jack could see that Chase had lost something along the way, that some vital spark in him had been put out . . . or was it just that it had been hidden away? At once, he knew that this Chase Edmunds both *was* and *was not* the man he had known years before. Still, he couldn't deny that it felt *right* to be working with him again. This was what they were best at, and it didn't matter if they were under the aegis of the Counter Terrorist Unit or just stepping up to take a stand against something. He didn't need to ask Chase if he felt the same way. He knew it.

"Follow my lead," said Jack, as he pushed open the glass door and entered the narrow reception. Like everything else in the motel, it was decorated in fake-wood veneer, with the added bonus of a few drab Western-style paintings hanging on the walls. A radio was playing a bass-heavy track distorted by cheap speakers and poor reception.

Behind the front desk, the manager bolted upright with a start, dropping the glossy magazine he had been poring over. "Yeah?" He blinked.

Jack leaned across the desk and found a line of switches that controlled the flickering neon lights outside. He flipped the switch that turned on the NO VACANCIES sign and gave the man a level look. "We need a little local information."

"Dino" blinked and glared at Jack, then at Chase, as he entered the office behind him. "What do I look like, a tour guide?" He grimaced and stood up, squaring off.

"You girls wanna have your fun together up there, go ahead. I don't judge. But keep outta my way . . ." He drifted off as Laurel came in, and a leer automatically snapped into place on his face.

The girl indicated Jack and Chase. "I don't think they got that kinda relationship, pal."

Dino's smile melted away. "Triple occupancy, that'll cost you extra."

"Who are you working for?" said Jack, and he pushed through the waist-high door that marked the line between the inner and outer areas of the front office.

"Hey! You don't get to come in here, asshole!" Dino grabbed for the handle of a dented aluminum baseball bat concealed down the side of the desk. "I'll mess you up, you and your pal!"

Jack struck out and punched the man hard in the chest. Wheezing, he staggered toward a door and Jack propelled him back. The door banged open under Dino's weight and he stumbled through. Beyond was a grimy apartment stinking of stale cigarettes, little larger than the motel rooms, with an open kitchen area and a wall dominated by a wide-screen TV. Jack shoved Dino into a threadbare recliner and pulled Brodur's butterfly knife from inside his coat. Dino's eyes widened at the sight of the blade's wicked edge as Jack flicked it open.

"You better answer him." Chase filed in with Laurel, closing the door.

"I'll ask you again," said Jack. "Who are you working for?"

Dino tried to recover some shred of defiance. "Man, screw you!"

Jack held the knife in his fist and pressed the tip of it into Dino's knee joint. The big man cried out and twitched. "Who pays you?" Jack demanded.

"The MC!" Dino grated, shaking, trying to shrink away. "The bikers pay everyone to look the other way, everyone still dumb enough or screwed enough to be stuck here!" He shook his head. "You cops? Rydell's boys will chew you up and spit you out, count on it!"

"Who's Rydell?" said Chase. "He in charge?"

"Top dog. Night Rangers Original is who he is," Dino spat back. He snorted with derision. "Nah, you ain't cops. Lookit, you're clueless! You got no idea where you are or what shit you just stepped in, pal." He attempted to straighten up. "You oughta run while you still can."

"Where's the bus?" said Laurel, her tone sharp and hard. "C'mon, needle-dick! Where the hell are Trish and all the others?"

"Answer her," said Jack.

"I don't have to say nothin' to you," he replied. "You can't touch me. I work for the MC, I'm *protected*. Get it?"

Jack nodded. "Yeah. I get it." Then he put a gloved hand over Dino's mouth and pushed the blade into his knee, deep enough to scrape bone.

The man howled and wept, and Chase smelled the ammonia stink of urine.

"Ah, he pissed himself!" said Laurel, recoiling. "Jeez."

"That'll happen," Chase said with a wan nod.

Dino rocked forward. "Why . . ." He whimpered. "Why you picking on me, man? I'm . . . I'm an American, I got rights. You can't torture me like some . . . bin Laden asshole . . ."

"I know what you are." Jack flipped back Dino's head. "Anyone with a spine would be long gone from here, but not you. You like it, don't you?" He leaned closer. "How does it work? The bikers who want some privacy come over here with the girls?" He nodded toward the office. "You keep the radio up loud so you don't have to listen to them getting smacked around? You clean up for the MC when they get too rough?"

"I don't make the rules!" Dino shot back, gasping for breath. "They're just hookers, man! Just trash!"

"*No*," Laurel spat. "No, we're not!" The woman tried to push her way forward, but Chase blocked her. "Get out of my way," she told him. "Gimme that knife, I'm gonna jam it up his ass!"

"You don't have any friends in this room," Jack said coldly. "The only thing that's going to change the amount of pain you go through is what you tell me right now."

The man sagged, shrinking away from the blood-stained blade. "What . . . do you want? Just keep away from me . . ."

"Where did they take Trish . . . the girls?" said Laurel through gritted teeth.

"The . . . Crankcase." His breathing was labored. "Pretty ones, anyway. Some get sold on sometimes, I dunno. Nothing to do with me. They don't let me in there no more, not after . . ." He trailed off. "Rydell said so."

"It's not just a strip club for horny truckers, it's a brothel," said Chase.

Dino nodded. "S'right . . ."

"What about the rest?" Jack held the knife in front of the man's face. "The workers? What happens to them?"

"Fort Blake. The old army base south of town. They bus 'em out there." He shook his head. "People keep away. Anyone who goes lookin' never comes back." Dino licked his lips. "Okay, I talked. Lemme go."

Chase was about to say how bad an idea that was, but before he could speak Dino made a sudden break for it, lurching forward, up and out of the recliner. He made a ham-fisted grab for Jack, who caught him easily. He cracked him hard across the temple with the metal handle of the butterfly knife. The paunchy man twitched and collapsed back into the chair, robbed of consciousness.

Laurel broke the silence that followed. "You two have done this kind of thing before, haven't you?"

"We've got what we needed," said Jack. "Help me secure him."

• • •

They drove slowly down the main street, passing the
Crankcase on their left. The strip club had once been a
big garage, but that had been a long time ago. In the intervening years, someone had gutted it and walled up the
roller doors, put in a few glass bricks in lieu of windows
and installed more garish neon. A floodlit sign outside
bearing the silhouette of a shapely woman sprawled
across an engine block promised all kinds of special, illicit treats, and by the gathering of motorcycles lined up
on the sidewalk, it was popular. The strains of a loud
Southern rock soundtrack blared out of the entrance
doors as they flapped open to release a worse-for-wear
truck driver nursing a bloody nose.

"Classy," said Chase, watching the man stagger into a
nearby alley. "And real friendly too, I'll bet."

Jack scoped out the design of the building, looking for
other egress locations, gauging escape routes and possible choke points. The Crankcase was a two-story construction, the upper level just about visible in the gaps
between the neon letters that spelled out the name of the
strip club. Gaining entry wouldn't be the hard part, he
reflected. Getting out in one piece would be the challenge.

He turned the Chrysler away and parked it in a side
street across the road. "Back entrance will be guarded,"
Jack said. "Too risky to try that. We'll go in the front way."

"So, we're doing this, then?" Chase replied, his jaw set.
"Do I get a say?"

"I don't know, do you?" Jack checked his pistol.

"You wanna walk into thug central with no plan, no
gear and no backup?"

"I have a plan," Jack replied, pulling back the Springfield's slide to make sure a round was already chambered.
He nodded at the black bag sitting next to Laurel in the

backseat. "I have gear." Then he looked at Chase. "I have backup."

Despite himself, Chase snorted with amusement. "Three people, a bunch of guns and a car is not exactly CTU."

"I haven't been part of that for a long time, Chase. And neither have you."

The other man paused. "Fair point."

Jack turned to look at Laurel. "Still got that revolver?"

"Yeah," she said warily.

"Don't use it unless you have to." He handed her the car keys. "If things go wrong, take this and head for the interstate. Keep driving and don't stop until you reach a city."

"How am I gonna know if things go wrong?"

"Something will catch fire," Chase offered. "Or explode."

"Stay out of sight," Jack told her, and got out of the car.

Chase fell into step with him as they walked back toward the Crankcase. "So. That plan you got?"

"Remember the Memphis thing?"

"Huh." Chase straightened his jacket and the gun hidden beneath it. "Memphis was a screwup from start to finish." It had been the last assignment they had partnered on before the whole undercover operation with the Salazar cartel.

Jack nodded. "Agreed. My thinking is, this time we won't make the same mistakes."

"Just new ones." Chase held out a hand to halt him. "*Jack*. Stop for a second. Are we *really* going to do this? We came to Deadline for a reason, and that reason doesn't get here for hours yet. We start making noise, stirring up the locals, we won't live long enough to make that train." He shook his head. "You're risking a good plan on the fallout from some random act—"

"Get to the point," Jack grated, his patience waning.

Chase took a breath. "You came to me out of the blue, you asked me to help you get back to Kim. I'll do that. *I owe you that*. But this?" He gestured toward the strip club. "It's not on us. If you want, when we get to LA we can get the word out to someone who can deal with it, but not you and me, not right now." The other man's voice dropped to a whisper. "If you need to prove something, this isn't the way to do it."

"Is that what you think?" Jack glared at him, keeping his temper in check. "We haven't seen each other in a long while, Chase, but you know me. Do you think I've changed?"

The younger man answered after a moment. "No."

"Have *you*?"

"You tell me."

"Do you think I could look my daughter in the eye knowing I'd ignored what's going on in this town?" Before Chase could answer, he went on. "Do you think for one second that the FBI and the state police don't know about the Night Rangers? For an MC to keep a whole community under their thumb, that takes money and force. Bribes. Influence. Like I said, I saw the same thing in Serbia when I was with Delta. There was always more to it than just drugs and prostitution. This is no different. So. I'm not going to walk away." He held his gaze. "And I don't think you will, either."

At length, Chase gave a nod. "Okay. We go get Laurel's friends. What then?"

Jack resumed walking. "We turn over some rocks and see what crawls out."

• • •

For someone who liked to consider himself as "off the grid," the speed with which agents of the Russian government discovered his location would have shocked

Hector Matlow to the core. The number of the "dead drop" digital mailbox Matlow had given to Mike Roker was meant to insulate him from a permanent wired connection, but after a few calls the SVR team had been able to marshal technicians from one of their covert cybersecurity installations in Minsk to track the American hacker and find a probable location for him. With the carte blanche President Suvarov had given Bazin's unit in their search for Jack Bauer, they had the resources they needed in short order.

He considered this as the Augusta AW109 swept low over the treetops, running dark so that anyone who spotted the helicopter would have no clue as to its identity. Like Bazin, everyone on board the aircraft wore a set of night-vision goggles, turning the world around them into a lunar landscape in shades of pale green and deep black. He peered at the paper map in his hand and looked up at Ziminova, who sat across the rear compartment from him. She had a plastic case open in front of her, and she was at work assembling the pieces of a weapon: a stubby, wide-mouthed tube, a pistol grip, a wire-frame stock ending in a shoulder pad.

"I would prefer a more nuanced entrance," he told her. "Stealth more than sound and fury."

"What is that phrase the British have?" she said, without looking up. "*Needs must when the devil drives.*"

"There is a risk you will kill him."

Ziminova nodded. "A margin of error. But if the sensor does its work . . ." She trailed off.

On that thought, Bazin turned in his seat to address Ekel, who sat up front in the copilot's position. On his lap he carried an olive drab portable monitor and keyboard setup, trailing wires. The device's screen showed a series of start-up displays as it came on line. The text on the screen and the keyboard was all in Chinese. Bazin tapped him on the shoulder. "You can read that?"

"Of course," Ekel replied. "Who do you think stole it from Shanghai?"

The helicopter was slowing and Bazin looked at the map again. "We're here," he announced to his team. "Get ready."

As the AW109 slowed to a hover over a clearing in the trees, Ekel pointed at the ground. "Sir, if you would?"

"Of course." Checking to make sure he was securely strapped in, Bazin leaned over and pulled on the latch holding the helicopter's side door shut. It slid open on oiled rails, allowing the cold night air to gust into the cabin, buffeting them. Bazin looked down, seeing rectangular shapes arranged in messy rows beneath them. There was no sign of movement.

He picked up the heavy sensor head from where it lay on the floor of the cabin, taking care not to get entangled in the cables that led back from it to ports on the side of Ekel's monitor unit. Bazin could feel power running through the sensor as he aimed it out of the side of the helicopter and down at the ground.

"Working," announced Ekel.

"No other aircraft in the area," reported the pilot. "But that may change at any moment."

"Understood." Bazin craned his neck to look back at Ekel's screen. The display showed an image that resembled waves breaking on a shoreline as viewed from above. Some were disrupted by blemishes, others smooth and regular. The ground-penetrating radar system had originally been built by the Chinese army to detect buried land mines, but in the hands of a trained user, it could seek out anything concealed beneath the earth.

After a moment, Ekel pointed at the screen, to where a particular trace was moving around. "There. Someone is down there, under the trailers. It has to be him."

"You think he's aware of us?" asked Ziminova. She had finished assembling the weapon, a Pallad single-shot

40mm grenade launcher. She broke it open and dropped a high-explosive round into the breech.

"He will be soon." Bazin shot a look out the window. "Ekel, where is our man?"

"Twenty degrees to the right. Moving away now."

"Understood," Ziminova replied, and she raised the gun to her shoulder. She took a second to steady her aim and then fired. The hollow chug of the Pallad's discharge was lost in the sound of the rotor blades.

Bazin watched the shell drop in on the roof of one of the overgrown trailers, and at the last second he flipped up his NVGs to avoid being dazzled by the blast.

The trailer detonated into matchwood, orange fire and black smoke forming a brief inferno that lit up the clearing and the surrounding tree line. In the immediate aftermath, he could see where the grenade had excavated a great scoop of dark earth out from under the smashed trailer. The corner of a hidden construction was now visible, bricks collapsed and a metal frame twisted.

"Another?" offered the woman, rolling a second shell in the palm of her hand.

Bazin shook his head and pulled back the slide on the Skorpion submachine gun strapped to his chest. "No need. We'll go in from here." He signaled the pilot with the flat of his hand. "Drop us off, then wait on station."

Ziminova was out swiftly, leaping to the damp grass before the helicopter's wheels had even touched the ground. Bazin followed at a warier pace, but he was the first to glimpse movement as the aircraft climbed back into the sky, twisting the plume of smoke away in its rotor vortex.

A figure, hobbled and slow, dragged itself out of the wreckage and started to move sluggishly toward the trees. Ziminova fired a burst from her Skorpion, stitching a line through the dirt in front of the survivor that made him recoil and collapse.

Bazin approached, walking through a snowfall of light debris that had been kicked up by the grenade blast, torn pages from books, scraps of tissue paper, fragments of cardboard. He raised an eyebrow as his boot landed on something that strangely resembled an abstract map of Stalingrad. He dismissed it and carried on, dropping into a crouch next to the cowering, smoke-blackened figure.

The man was bleeding from his ears and nostrils, and his eyes were wide with raw panic. Bazin cupped his chin in his hand and turned his head to look directly at him. "Hector Matlow," he said, slowly and carefully enunciating his words. "Good evening. You are going to help me."

Matlow nodded weakly.

13

The inside of the Crankcase was aptly named. Dark and dingy, with a strong odor of smoke and engine oil that lingered in the air, the core of the club was a raised dance stage lined with brass stripper poles. Two women were up there as Jack and Chase entered, both wearing a G-string and nothing else, both gyrating blankly to the harsh background music with dead-eyed, mechanical movements.

It was immediately clear there were two distinct groups of clientele at the Crankcase. The smaller group were the road-weary truckers, who nursed their beers and kept to their side of the club; the other, outnumbering the truck drivers three to one, were a hooting chorus of bikers who cheered on the dancers or argued amongst themselves. Jack glimpsed Night Ranger MC patches with rockers showing county names from all over the Midwest. They congregated at tables surrounding the end of the worn catwalk, and past them on one side of the club interior was a long wooden bar. Behind it prowled a heavily bearded man-mountain in denim who served drinks like each one was an insult to him. Glass broke and someone shouted, a punch was thrown, but it seemed like par for the course.

They were three steps into the place when a biker wearing a jacket identical to the one Jack had seen on Brodur stepped into their path. "And who the hell might you be?" he demanded. Tall and wiry, he had matted black dreadlocks that reached past his shoulders and a scarred chin that jutted out when he talked. He carried a pool cue in one hand, although Jack noted that the nearest table was on the far side of the room. "You ain't familiar to me."

Jack looked the biker up and down. "Where's Rydell?" he asked in a bored tone. "He here?"

"What's it to you?"

The pause before the reply told Jack that this guy didn't know the answer, and he waved him away, walking on. "Forget it. You can't help me. Get lost."

The pool cue came up in a threatening rise. "You don't talk to me like that, asshole."

Chase stepped in, his expression hard and unforgiving. "Don't be stupid, tough guy."

"Where d'you think you are?" snarled the biker. "You got about ten seconds to start showin' some respect, before you get messed up—"

Jack silenced him with a glare. "Is this one of those things where we have to kick the shit out of someone before we get an answer?" He gave Chase a sideways glance and the ghost of a nod.

Chase caught the thin end of the cue in his open hand with a slap of wood on flesh. He shoved the biker back with enough force that the top third of the stick snapped off and he jammed the ragged, splintered end of it into the meat of the man's throat. The volume of rowdy conversation in the rest of the bar dropped off significantly.

Without waiting for the other man to reply, Jack went on. "We're here to see Rydell. Chicago sent us."

"Chicago?" The name of the city made the biker hesitate. "What you doing here? You ain't supposed to be here."

Chase spread his hands, moving the broken cue away. "Says who?"

"Rydell ain't around," said the other man, regaining something of his composure. "Wait up. I'll get Sammy."

"You do that," Jack said to his back, as he pushed away through the crowd toward a door past the line of the stage.

"*Chicago?*" repeated Chase, in a low voice.

Jack nodded. "This MC can't move anything on any scale that'll make money without bumping up against Mob connections. Chicago's the biggest, closest organized crime hub to this place. I figure the Night Rangers would have some kind of a relationship with the families there."

"Good guess. Let's hope they're on friendly terms."

Jack shook his head. "We'll see about that. If I'm off base, we'll know when they come out shooting."

Chase looked around, taking the place in. "Stairs at the back," he said, indicating them with a nod of the head. As he did so, a pair of bikers walked down, laughing harshly. "Probably lead to the cathouse."

"If the women Laurel mentioned are all on site, they'll be kept secured." Jack considered his options. On the surface the Crankcase seemed like a slapdash construction, but someone had thought carefully about how to build in choke points around the exits to stop anyone from making a fast getaway. "We need a better angle."

The dreadlocked biker returned, followed by an older man who was thickset and florid-faced. He walked with a shuffle, and Jack guessed that under his jeans his right leg was a prosthetic.

"Sammy," said Jack, as if he knew the man. "Thank your friend here for the warm welcome."

Sammy squinted at the two new arrivals, then back at his associate. "Sticks don't know when to keep his mouth shut." He scowled. "I know you?"

"My man Charlie," Jack nodded toward Chase. "I'm Joe. And this is what you might call a surprise visit."

"Surprise is right," said the biker Sammy had called Sticks. "Why you even here?"

"We were told to come take a look," Chase offered, picking up the thread of the lie and spinning it out. "There's been talk, y'know?" He gestured around. "About what goes on in Deadline."

"Our people in Chicago, they don't like talk," Jack added. "It makes them nervous."

Sammy's scowl deepened. "This is not a good time. I just got a new load in. We're real busy here. Come back tomorrow."

Jack smiled thinly. "Not gonna happen." He pressed on, keeping up the momentum. "Look. I didn't want to come all the way out here to nowheresville, and I don't want to be here any longer than I have to." He had learned the hard way that keeping an undercover "legend" intact was mostly a matter of confidence. If they could keep Sammy and his friends off-balance and reactive, the bikers would have less time to ask questions that Jack and Chase wouldn't be able to answer. "I'm sure you don't want us getting in your way, either. So let's deal with this and we can all get on with our lives, yeah?"

"Check 'em," ordered Sammy, and Sticks came forward to give Chase a cursory pat down. He obliged, and the biker found his gun in short order.

"Now what are you doing with that?" Sammy said, his eyes narrowing.

Jack opened his jacket to show the M1911 he was carrying. "You think we'd come in this rat hole without some iron?"

Sticks warily performed the same check on Jack, before stepping away. "Unless they got it up their asses, these boys ain't wearing wires."

"Sure, whatever," said Sammy, nodding distractedly. "My office is in back. Come on." He shot Sticks a look. "Keep people out until we get done, okay?"

• • •

"Got it." Sticks watched the two men follow Sammy across the bar and vanish through the door. Belatedly, he realized he was still holding on to the broken pool cue and angrily tossed it into a corner, before marching back to the bar to snatch up a bottle of beer. He drained half the longneck in a deep pull, running the conversation over in his thoughts. *Like we don't have enough crap to deal with.*

First there had been the problems with the red, white and blue out at the base, then some shit with the bus. Nobody seemed to know where the hell Brodur had gotten himself to. *And now this.*

Sammy seemed like he had a line on things, but then Sammy wasn't a rider anymore, and that meant he wasn't part of the MC, not really. Not like Sticks was. Sammy lost that leg under a truck outside of Kansas City, and as a kind of payback for all the good work he had done, Rydell had given him the Crankcase to run. But Sammy had been grounded for years now, and that changed a man. Rydell would want to know about this new wrinkle and Sticks wondered if Sammy would be slow to tell the club president.

He decided to take advantage of the situation, and fished in the pocket of his cut for the battered cell phone that all the MC's top-rank soldiers had to carry. After a couple of rings he was talking to Lance, Rydell's master-at-arms. "*What?*"

"Lemme talk to the big dog," he said.

"*Why would I do that, Sticks?*"

"I'm at the 'Case," he told him. "And we got visitors from outta town."

• • •

Sammy's office was little different from the bar proper, all bare brick walls and hardwood floors. But unlike the other room, the ex-biker had imposed his character on it.

"Like a museum in here," Chase remarked, and that drew a nod from the other man.

"Lotta memories," Sammy admitted. The door slammed shut behind them, cutting down the constant grind of the strip club's music to a dull thudding.

Jack looked around. Every square foot of wall space that could be filled had been. There were framed pictures, many of them depicting men on motorcycles from the 1970s to the present day, others showing groups of GIs against a backdrop of Hueys and rice paddies in some distant part of Southeast Asia. There were pages from newspapers, mostly lurid headlines about the menace of biker gangs, many specifically mentioning the Night Rangers. One wall was dominated by what seemed to be the pelt of a mountain lion, and the other pride of place was split between a black leather jacket bearing the MC's colors and a glass case containing two dissimilar objects.

Jack peered closer. The case held a badly crushed fuel tank from a Harley-Davidson, displayed as if it were a war trophy. Next to it was a grimy, sun-bleached mesh-back trucker's cap. Old, rust-brown bloodstains discolored the bill of the cap.

Sammy smiled bitterly, noting Jack's attention. "First one of those I got real easy. Almost killed me. Second one . . ." He nodded to himself. "Took me a couple of years to track him down." The old biker tapped a big Bowie knife resting on a cradle before him. They sat, and

Sammy leaned across the wooden desk in the middle of the room. Four black-and-white monitor screens in front of him blinked back and forth between images from security cameras dotted around the strip club.

Chase caught Jack's eye and subtly nodded toward the screens. Jack saw shots of the dancers leaving the stage, alternating with back rooms and corridors, private dances and other, more illegal activities going on behind closed doors.

"Rydell is getting sloppy," Jack began, starting with a challenge. "He's drawing attention to this place."

"How's that, exactly?" Sammy's hand stayed close to the knife. "You saying someone's talkin' outside of church?" He shook his head. "Never happen. This place is just a lil' ol' titty bar and we're like family down here, you get it? Brothers for life." He pointed at one of the pictures on the wall, showing a group of Night Rangers standing around a gravestone.

"The girls . . ." Chase nodded toward the monitors. "If your people aren't careful about where they pick them up . . ."

Sammy tapped the desk with a meaty finger. "Don't tell me how to do my job, son. We don't sign on anyone who's gonna be missed. Hell, most of these mooks come willing." He grinned. "Tough economy out there, y'know? Sure, so we don't have a dental plan, but we pay."

"Is that right?" Jack arched an eyebrow.

The other man shrugged. "Enough to keep the bitches on their feet, the chumps hard at work. Not enough for them to go elsewhere." He gave a rough chuckle. "Like there's anywhere else *to* go, anyhow."

"How many girls in the stable?" Jack kept his expression neutral, but inwardly his disgust with Sammy was rising by the moment.

"Plenty." Sammy made a vague, circling motion with his hand. "I lost count."

"That's not true," said Chase. "I'm willing to bet good money you know exactly how many 'dancers' you've got under this roof, and exactly what you're using to keep each and every one of them in line."

Sammy's eyes flashed, but in the next moment he was grinning. "Charlie here's a sharp one, ain't he? Okay, yeah, you got me. I'm kinda like the head cowpoke and this here's my herd." He pointed at the monitors. "I rope 'em. If I need to, I brand 'em."

"You said you had a new load," Jack pressed.

The other man nodded. "Gonna put them on rotation. Gotta keep the brothers interested, y'know? They like some fresh meat now and then. The girls that have been here a while, if they don't earn . . ." He shrugged again. "They get sold on or Lance takes them to the works. I make sure they know that. *Keeps them in line.*" He leered at Chase.

Jack wondered what "the works" referred to, and filed the name away for future reference. "You keep them here, at the club?"

"What, you want a free sample?" Sammy leaned forward. "Why d'you even care about the girl-flesh? That ain't your angle. You know how the deal goes, Chicago gets their cut of the product, all the rest of it is our bag." There was a moment of hesitation in the ex-biker's words, and Jack could see the questions starting to form in his thoughts. Sammy's hand drifted away from the knife and toward the telephone on his desk. "I tell you what, I reckon I've said enough. Rydell's busy, but I'll get Lance down here. You oughta talk to him."

From the corner of his eye, Jack saw Chase rub his thumb across the side of his nose, like he was scratching an itch. To anyone else, the gesture would have seemed casual, random even, but to Jack it was a warning sign—a secret signal from their time working as undercover operatives. *He's made us.*

Jack's hand shot out and grabbed the knife before Sammy could pick up the phone and brought it down hard, the tip spearing through the middle of the man's palm, pinning it to the desk.

• • •

The level of ambient noise inside the Crankcase made it hard for Sticks to hear anything other than one word out of every three, so he shoved his way past the men congregating near the door and out into the night. He nodded at Fang as the other biker passed him in the opposite direction, getting a show of the man's chromed teeth in return.

"You find that bald fool yet?" he hissed, covering his cell phone's pickup with one hand.

Fang gave a languid shrug. "Brodur does what he does, man. Probably got that little blond hottie in the bushes somewhere, gettin' back to nature . . ."

"He needs to keep it in his pants, is what," Sticks retorted. He fell silent as he heard a sharp voice on the other end of the line.

"*This better be good.*" Rydell's tone was deep and harsh.

"Two guys just blew in off the street, boss," he began. "Outta nowhere. Say they're from Chicago, come to take a look-see. Like it's a kinda surprise inspection, or some shit."

"*Are you high?*"

"No!" Sticks insisted, although he had smoked a joint a little earlier. "Boss, no. This is on the level."

"*Ah, Sticks,*" Rydell shot back, "*it most certainly is not on the level, and do you know why?*" He didn't wait for a reply. "*Because I was talking on the phone to our associates in the Windy City no more than three hours ago. And you know how those guinea pricks like to think they're smarter than us farm boys. If they were sending someone down here, they'd be crowing about it."* Rydell paused. *"These guys, they look like cops or feds?"*

"Nuh." Sticks shook his head. "I mean, I guess not. Cops don't have the stones to come sneakin' in here, anyhow." The biker turned his head and spat.

"Well, then we got ourselves a question, don't we?" In the background of the call, Sticks heard a woman cry out and men yelling. Then there was an echoing gunshot, and silence. After a moment, Rydell was back. *"I'm dealing with issues out here, bro. Do me a favor, find out who these two jerks are and put 'em on ice. I'll come deal with it when I got time."*

"You got it."

"Don't screw up," Rydell warned, and cut the call.

• • •

According to FAA regulations, Hadley and his team were supposed to disembark from the Cessna Citation while the jet was being refueled, but the FBI agent had told the airfield coordinator in no uncertain terms that none of them were going anywhere. Through the open hatchway, Kilner could smell the distinctive tang of avgas as a dumpy six-wheel bowser nuzzled at the aircraft's wing, pumping fresh fuel into the tanks. The ground crew hadn't objected. The FBI were footing the bill for all the overtime.

Dell and Markinson leaned over a table in the back of the cabin, studying a highway map of the surrounding states. "So far, this Williams guy is coming up blank," said Dell, running a hand through her hair. "Nothing on the NatCrime database, hasn't had so much as a speeding ticket. If we could get something more, we might be able to figure out where he could be taking Bauer."

"Could be he's just some unlucky stiff Bauer has taken

hostage," offered Markinson. "He's going to force poor Charlie to drive him somewhere, then . . ." She mimed a pistol. "*Pop, pop*. Two in the back of the head."

"That's not Bauer's style." Kilner frowned.

"Oh, right," said Markinson, eyeing him. "I forgot. You're the expert on this guy." She leaned in. "People change, Jorge. Just because you want him to be a good guy in a bad place doesn't make it true."

"You seeing it from Hadley's side now?" he shot back.

The other agent shrugged. "I'm considering all the angles."

"Jack Bauer knows Charlie Williams," said Hadley, approaching them with a sheet of paper in his hand. "That's the only explanation that fits."

The paper was a printout of the results of an identity search on Williams as conducted by the New York office. Kilner took it and skimmed the text, noting the face of the man on a scan of his driver's license. "Says he works for Roker Dealerships Limited, a car sales outlet."

"Pittsburgh cops are looking into it," said Hadley. "But what interests me is this." He tapped the page. "Go back a few years and Charles Williams vanishes. No details before that point. It's like he just washed up one day from out of nowhere."

"So," said Dell, tapping a finger on her lips. "Fake ID, then? New name, new life. Was he one of ours, someone from the Witness Relocation Program?"

Hadley shook his head. "Already checked. WitSec don't know this guy. No, I'm thinking he might be CIA, or someone from Bauer's past. Someone we don't have on our radar."

"Can we get a line to the Counter Terrorist Unit?" Markinson put her hands on her hips. "Those people worked closely with Bauer over the years. We could apply some pressure . . ."

"All divisional CTU operations are currently being

held in abeyance, pending a full investigation into the
Hassan assassination," Hadley replied. "That order came
down directly from Vice President . . ." He paused, cor-
recting himself. "From *President* Heyworth."

"The new guy didn't waste any time," noted Dell.

A chime sounded from the fax printer attached to the
workstation at the front of the jet's cabin and Kilner
moved to it, taking the still-warm pages as they dropped
into the tray. "It's from the Pittsburgh Bureau of Police.
They sent a unit out to Williams's apartment, but it had
already been turned over."

Markinson's eyes narrowed. "Somebody else is looking for this guy too?"

Kilner read on and his frown deepened. "There's more.
A patrol car reported a possible break-in at the Roker
dealership, same thing as at the apartment . . ." When he
pulled out the last page, he stopped.

Hadley snatched it out of his hand and grimaced as he
read it. "They sent another unit to Roker's house, the guy
Williams was supposed to work for. *Preliminary identi-
fication of victims: Roker, Michael and Roker, Barbara.
Husband and wife, owners of the property.* Both dead
from gunshot wounds from close range." He handed the
page back to Kilner. "Okay, now we may be tracking two
killers, not just one."

"You don't know Williams is responsible for that,"
said Kilner, but the words came out flat and without
force.

"Could be this new guy covering his tracks," Dell said,
thinking aloud. "He's got something to hide. Fits the profile."

"What's the timeline here?" Markinson looked back
at the road map. "What are we suggesting? Bauer calls
Williams, Williams murders his boss and wife for who
knows why, meets up with Bauer and hits the road . . .

and finds time to beat up two idiots along the way? It doesn't track."

"The car is registered to the Roker dealership," said Dell. "This is all connecting up. We just have to work out how."

"Jack, what are you doing?" Kilner whispered. With every new piece of information, it was getting harder and harder to give their quarry the benefit of the doubt.

A strident tone sounded through the cabin and Hadley pulled his cell phone. "Go for Special Agent Hadley." He tapped a key so all of them could hear the voice on the other end of the line.

"Tom, it's Mike Dwyer here. I just got off a call from Liberty Crossing. You want to tell me what this is all about?"

Kilner watched the other agent form his response. Liberty Crossing in McClean, Virginia, was the location of the National Counter Terrorism Center, a cross-agency facility staffed with personnel from all the major US law enforcement and security organizations. The FBI was a key stakeholder in the NCTC, providing staff and intelligence to analyze threats to America on a round-the-clock basis, in tandem with the bureau's National Security Branch. As a think tank and predictive tool for threat tracking, the center was at the cutting edge. "I reached out to someone I know there, sir. I thought it could help."

"You went around me. You bypassed this office."

"I was ordered to use all the means at my disposal to catch Bauer. I figured it would be quicker to go directly to my contact at the center rather than waste time going through proper channels."

"You decided it was better to seek forgiveness than to ask permission, is that it?"

"Yes, sir." Hadley didn't flinch. "I take it they found something?"

Dwyer took a moment before he answered. "*They did. A couple of hours ago, a traffic camera captured an image of the car you're looking for, heading westward off a junction from Interstate 70. According to the NCTC, facial recognition has a sixty percent match on the vehicle's passenger. It's Bauer.*"

Hadley turned to Dell and jabbed a finger toward the cockpit. "Get in there and tell the pilot I want us airborne and flying west five minutes ago!" Kilner saw a low smile cross his face as he turned back to the phone. "And the driver, sir? It's the other suspect, Williams?"

"*Not exactly,*" Dwyer replied. "*The driver is a man who is supposed to be dead.*" He paused. "*Take me off speaker.*"

Hadley glanced at the others, then nodded to himself. "Okay." He tapped the phone and raised it to his ear. Kilner watched him move across the cabin and out of the hatch, stepping onto the runway where he could speak without being overheard. "He broke protocol. Dwyer sounds pissed."

"So what?" said Markinson. "None of that will matter after Bauer gets what's coming to him."

• • •

"*Hold for ASAC O'Leary,*" said Dwyer, and there was a click in Hadley's ear as the line switched.

"Sir?" He straightened, waiting for the inevitable tirade.

He didn't have to wait long. "*There's a difference between acting on your own initiative and abusing your authority,*" snarled O'Leary. "*If you thought I'd let you get away with anything because my attention is on this Hassan thing, you're dead wrong.*"

"With all due respect, sir—"

"*Don't ever use that phrase with me, Hadley. You don't*

*respect the chain of command, you never have. I should
have known better than to give you Bauer to chase. Now
I'm starting to regret my decision."*

"I have good leads. We're closing in."

*"Which is the only reason you're not on your way back
to Newark right now."* O'Leary blew out a breath. *"I
guess I shouldn't be surprised you went to your pal Jacobs
at the NCTC. I know all about him. He served under
Jason Pillar in the Marines, just like you did."*

"Sal Jacobs is a good agent."

*"That's debatable. What I know for sure is that Pillar
helped him get that job, just like he helped you get yours.
Let me ask you, Hadley. What did Pillar tell you? That
one day in the future, he'd bring you in to work for him
up on the Hill? You think I don't know that he was setting up his own little network?"*

Hadley frowned. "It doesn't matter now, does it? Pillar's dead."

*"Yes, he is. So do your damn job. Because if Bauer gets
away, you won't have it for much longer."* O'Leary cut
the call.

Behind him, the fuel truck was moving away, and Hadley heard the slow, building whine of the jet's turbines as
they came alive.

14

Sammy released a strangled, agonized sound from the back of his throat that was somewhere between a howl and a sob.

The Bowie knife had gone cleanly through the center of the ex-biker's right hand and a good half-inch into the surface of his wooden desk. Jack expected him to reflexively grab for the blade's handle with his other hand, but Sammy spat curses and clutched at something beneath the frame of the desk.

Chase saw it too. "*Gun!*" He threw himself aside and Jack did the same, as Sammy's fingers grasped the pistol grip of a concealed sawn-off shotgun. Both barrels went at once, even before the weapon had cleared the spring clips holding it to the underside of the desktop. A hollow discharge of buckshot ripped a chunk out of the chair in front of Sammy and blasted apart the glass cabinet containing the dented fuel tank. Jack heard the clatter and whine of pellets ricocheting off the brick walls.

Sammy reeled back, his chair spinning away, trying to keep his balance while one hand was still nailed in place. He came around with the smoking sawn-off, wielding it like a club, battering Jack about the head.

As Chase picked himself up, fresh red streaks across his cheek where he had taken a near-hit, Jack vaulted across the desk and bodychecked Sammy. He hit with such force that he dislodged the knife and Sammy went back, his ruined hand ripped open and gushing blood. Jack placed two hard, sharp punches into the other man's throat. Bone and cartilage cracked, and this time Sammy went all the way down—and stayed there.

"Shit . . ." Chase wiped blood from his face with the back of his hand. "You think they heard that?"

The constant thumping of the strip club's rock soundtrack hadn't lessened in all the time they had been there, but Jack wasn't about to stick around to find out. "So much for undercover," he muttered.

Chase drew his Ruger and moved to the office door. "What now?"

Jack kicked the sawn-off aside and lowered his head to look at the monitor screens. Out in the bar, it seemed like business as usual. He spotted Sticks gesturing animatedly to another Night Ranger outrider, waving a cell phone around. Jack glanced at the other monitors. "Looks like two, maybe three men upstairs. Let's do this quick. We need to move before anyone comes looking for our friend here."

"A diversion is what we need," Chase replied.

"Yeah." In a glass-fronted liquor cabinet near the desk were two bottles of Wild Turkey, and Jack pulled the corks on both, slopping the bourbon all over the piles of papers and across the walls. Sammy had a cigar box on the desk with a gasoline lighter resting on top, and Jack flicked it alight.

"That's not what I meant," said Chase, catching on.

"Get ready." Jack pulled his gun and tossed the lighter back at the desk. The naked flame immediately ignited the spilled alcohol, and a line of bluish flame swept across the wood paneling. The office was top-heavy with flammable items, and it would take only seconds to turn it into a torch. "*Go!*"

He pressed his hand into the small of Chase's back, and the other man slipped out into the corridor leading from the bar. Jack pulled the door shut behind him, trapping the fire inside the room.

The corridor led away toward the back of the strip club, past a stand of out-of-order pay phones and doors that opened on to reeking toilet stalls. A wide wooden staircase rose, and Jack indicated it with a nod. "Take point."

"Got it." Chase moved quickly, holding his pistol down low. In the dingy interior of the club, their weapons wouldn't be seen until it was too late.

Jack chanced a look back over his shoulder and for one brief instant he locked gazes with Sticks on the far side of the barroom.

• • •

"You hear that?" Fang rubbed the claw tattoo on the side of his face, eyes narrowing. "I thought I heard somethin'."

But Sticks was talking, not listening. "Find Marshall and Tyke," he said, raising his voice to be heard above the buzzy shriek of guitars coming over the Crankcase's sound system. He prodded Fang in the chest to underline his point. "And get irons too, 'cause we have ourselves a—"

He stopped dead as he caught sight of movement out behind the now-empty dance stage. At the edge of the harsh glow of the spotlights, he saw the two strangers emerging from Sammy's office. Their movements were quick and furtive, and Sticks immediately feared the worst. If they weren't cops, then they had to be something worse, he guessed. Perhaps they really were from

Chicago, but Mob hitters sent down to Deadline to whack the Night Rangers for some infraction Rydell had made, or maybe guns-for-hire dispatched by any one of a dozen rival MCs. It didn't matter. They had to be dealt with.

On an impulse, Sticks brought up the cell phone he still had in his hand and snapped a couple of shots of the two men. One of them must have caught the flash in the corner of his eye, because he shot a look in the biker's direction before disappearing toward the back of the strip club.

"What're you doing?" Fang spun around to see the two men and he immediately tensed like a dog catching the scent of an intruder. "Whoa, is that them?"

Sticks abandoned his conversation and pushed through the gathered riders and truckers, shoving them out of his way, leaving a wake of angry curses and shouts behind him. Fang kept pace with him, at his side as they reached the mouth of the corridor. "Check on Sammy!" he snapped.

Fang nodded and grabbed the office door's brass handle, turning it before he realized that it was red-hot. "Hey—"

Whatever he was going to say was lost as the door came open with a heavy gust of hot, fiery smoke. Fang reeled away as flames curled like talons, sucked out into the corridor by the pressure change in the air. It had been a long time since the Crankcase's pitiful sprinkler system had been overhauled, and too late it was clear that if it had ever worked, it certainly wasn't working *now*.

Sticks grabbed Fang by the collar of his jacket, hauling him back as the flames bit into the wooden flooring and went searching for anything else that would burn.

Behind him, a shock of panic jolted through the Crankcase's clientele, and chaos erupted as everyone made for the door at once.

• • •

The strip club's fire alarm bleated, but like the unmaintained sprinklers it failed to do the job it was designed for, giving off a muffled squeal that was barely audible among all the other background noise.

Chase ascended the staircase at a pace, holding the Ruger down and to the side. A blond-haired biker was coming up off a stool as he came into view.

"Hey, what's going on down there, izzat smoke?"

He didn't give the guy the chance to think. Chase brought up the pistol and cracked the butt of the gun across the bridge of the biker's nose, smashing it with a single blow. Blood gushed out across his face and he staggered, shaking off the pain. In the next second, the man roared like a bull and charged at Chase with his hands out.

It was an easy assault to deal with, and a part of Chase liked the fact that his old skills were snapping back into place so seamlessly. He dodged the attack and hit the guy low, sending him sprawling down the staircase in a messy tumble. Below them, there was a thud of displaced air as the fire started to take hold.

Jack sidestepped the first guard as he went down and turned at the top of the staircase, aiming down the upper corridor. "Target!" he snapped.

Another Night Ranger, this one a gangly figure in denim with a shock of black hair, came racing toward them clutching a compact Mini Uzi submachine gun. Unlike the other biker, this one didn't hesitate. He mashed the trigger of the SMG and let the recoil jerk his hand up and across, spraying a salvo of 9mm rounds across their path.

Chase threw himself into cover behind a decrepit leather chair, ducking as shots tore the stuffing from the seat back. Despite the gunfire, doors along the corridor were opening as those inside heard the racket. A skinny redhead—one of the women who had been dancing when they arrived—froze on the threshold and shrieked in panic.

Jack didn't flinch at the new line of attack and fired twice with his M1911 pistol. Both rounds hit the biker in center mass and he jerked backward, unloading the rest of the Uzi's magazine into the walls and the ceiling. A stray round from the machine gun caught the redhead between the eyes and she fell back into her room.

Gray smoke was following them up the stairs now, and heat came with it. Jack moved forward on the left, keeping his gun close to his chest, and Chase moved in parallel with him. They kicked in doors, panning across each room with their guns, seeking targets.

Each of the rooms was the same kind of sordid, perfunctory space, set aside for the Crankcase's callous human trade. A parody of a boudoir, all snarls of bedsheets and sex toys laying in a mess. "Everyone out," Jack shouted. "This is your one and only chance! You stay in this place and you'll burn with it!"

His words were enough; women spilled out of the rooms in disarray, desperate to flee the indignities they had been forced to suffer here.

Jack called out to Chase. "Can't go back the way we came in, there has to be another way out."

"I hear that."

"We need to find it, fast." Jack tried a door that didn't open at first, then he raised his foot and kicked squarely at the lock, snapping it out of the frame. He pushed through into a darkened interior and out in the corridor Chase caught the stink of stale sweat and cannabis. He glimpsed a blur of movement and suddenly Jack was pulled off his feet, wrenched aside and out of Chase's line of sight. He heard a girl's high-pitched scream, and the crash of something breaking.

Leading with his Ruger, Chase rushed the room and came upon the other man in the grip of a huge, naked biker easily as big as a sumo wrestler. In the half-dark of the room, Chase made out the biker's tree-trunk-thick arm around Jack's throat, pulling tight to choke the life out of him. "I'm gonna snap your neck, little shit!" he bellowed. Jack struggled, his gun lost in the melee, punching and kicking his assailant to no obvious effect.

Chase didn't hesitate. The training *was* still there. He *was* still good enough to do this. He didn't think about the nerve damage, he didn't dwell on the bottle of painkillers, he just raised the semiautomatic and fired a single shot before the biker could position Jack as a human shield. The bullet went through the big man's left eye and blew out a welter of blood and brain matter over the wall behind him.

Jack pushed away as the biker's corpse dropped like a felled tree. He sucked in a ragged breath. "Thanks."

Chase nodded, finding the girl who had cried out hiding by the bed. "C'mon," he told her. "We're getting you all out of here." He was suddenly breathing hard, the old familiar sting of adrenaline rushing through him.

• • •

Jack coughed out tainted spittle and stooped to scoop up his pistol from where it had fallen. As he bent low, he felt the heat radiating up through the floor from the strip club beneath them. Smoke was gathering along the roof, and it wasn't just the death grip of the biker that was making it hard to breathe.

His plan, such as it was, had passed the point of no return. *Get in. Find the captives. Get them out alive.* Everything else was secondary to those objectives—but if he could destroy this snake pit in the bargain, Jack was ready to call that a win on all counts. These bikers were not the usual kind of trained soldiers that he faced, but that didn't mean he could afford to drop his guard. What outlaws tended to lack in skill they more than made up for with violence and enthusiasm. Momentum would be the key here, he decided. From the moment Jack had been forced to attack Sammy, he had set into motion a chain of events that couldn't be stopped. Thugs like these reacted to threats with the same pack mentality as wolves; bark loud enough at the start and you might force them to back off . . . but give them time to think it over and they would come for you in force.

He strode back out into the corridor and found the victims of the Night Rangers in a loose, fearful cluster. They were all looking to him and Chase for guidance.

"Please tell me you're a policeman," said a petite, dark-haired woman.

"Concerned citizens," Chase corrected, helping the girl from the room as she walked on bare feet across the rough flooring.

"This place is on fire!" said one of the others. "Oh god, those creeps left us in here to die!"

"Not gonna happen," Jack told them. He shot a look at Chase, lowering his voice. "I'll go for the roof, make sure it's clear. There's got to be a fire escape at the back. Get them ready to run. Give me a two count, then follow."

"Copy that," said Chase. "Be right behind you."

Jack sprinted down to the end of the corridor, turning his momentum into shouldering open a push-bar door. He spilled out onto the roof above the entrance of the Crankcase, and immediately a gust of hot, dry air washed over him. Smoke and licks of flame were spilling out the front of the strip club. He heard the crack and pop of bottles behind the bar exploding in the heat, and down where the MC had parked their motorcycles there was a chaotic mess of angry bikers trying to get their precious rides away from the building inferno. That was good; the confusion would work to his advantage, but not for long.

With the flickering, dying neon of the club's illuminated sign between him and the bikers, they couldn't see him moving around up there, but it was obvious that the front of the bar was not a viable escape route. The Crankcase was going to burn to the ground, and nothing would stop that from happening. Jack guessed that like law enforcement in the town of Deadline, whatever had passed for their fire department had long since been abandoned.

He turned around and scrambled up along a raised section of the flat roof, heading toward the back of the building. The heat was radiating up here too, and sweat prickled his chest. Jack blinked to clear his vision and moved low and quick, aiming the pistol into every shadowed corner. He'd been sloppy, letting that big thug get the drop on him. The next time it might cost him his life.

He circled around a skylight, thin streamers of smoke issuing out from the places where the window frames were loose. Inside, the flickering orange glow made it look like a portal into a furnace.

Peering over the edge of the roof, Jack saw a wide yard at the rear of the Crankcase with ten-foot brick walls topped by barbed wire. The only way in or out was a metal gate that opened onto a backstreet, and from his vantage point he caught sight of a heavy steel padlock securing it. Overfilled Dumpsters and heaps of beer crates congregated in one corner, and a black Chevrolet van was parked along the line of the far wall. Three more Night Rangers were out there, two of them arguing about what to do while the third one milled around, anxious and twitchy. Each man was armed with a TEC-9 semiautomatic.

"Screw this," one of them was saying. "I ain't sticking around here!"

"You want Rydell to know you left your post?" snapped the other.

"This ain't the army, pal," came the retort. "I'm not going to stand here and watch this place burn." He started toward the van, but got two steps before his fellow biker stopped him.

Jack assessed his chances, considering and discarding angles of attack one after the other, trying to find the path of least resistance to the objective he wanted. Namely: three dead men and a way out of this place. Everything about the situation was stacked the wrong way for Jack—he was outnumbered and outgunned, low on time and options. If he waited too long, the fire would do the job for the bikers. He had to move, and chance the odds—

Without warning, from behind Jack there was a sudden, violent crash of breaking glass. Seared by the rising heat from the fire, the skylight imploded and collapsed into the flames. It caught him unaware, and he froze.

The noise caught the attention of one of the bikers, who swung up his gun and caught sight of Jack's shadow, framed against the roof by the fire glow. "Hey!" he shouted, pointing.

Jack twisted and brought up his pistol. The biker saw the motion and started shooting before he had aimed, sending wild rounds into the lintel and ricochets across the rooftop. The other men reacted the same way, and in seconds the three of them were chopping at the brickwork as Jack dropped behind an air-conditioning vent.

He shot back, blind firing around the side of the vent box.

"Who the hell is that?" Jack heard one of them say.

"Who the hell cares?" shouted another. "Waste him!"

Going flat on his belly, Jack swarmed across the roof toward the top rungs of an iron escape ladder. Bullets lanced through the air over his head, the drone of their passing perilously close, making him flinch. He rolled onto his back, ejecting the M1911's magazine and slamming a fresh one into the butt of the gun.

It was like lying on a griddle. The fire had its teeth in the building now, and if Jack couldn't get off the roof in the next few moments he never would.

Got to risk it, he told himself. But could he take out three men before one of them got off a kill shot at him? Jack didn't pause to consider the alternative. He could hear a roaring noise getting louder as he rolled to the fire escape. Chase's voice issued out from somewhere behind him as he came out with the escapees in tow. *No time to think about it,* Jack decided. If the roof caved in, they would all perish.

He popped up from behind the edge of the roof and time seemed to slow, becoming fluid. Jack saw the three bikers, each of them training their TEC-9s in his general direction. Two were close together, and they almost had a bead on him. The third was near the gate, taking aim.

He fired. The first bullet hit one man in the chest, a good kill that took down the target immediately. The second shot was discharged so close to the first that the report of the pistol was a single crashing echo. That round punched through the throat of the next biker, dropping him.

But the third man had Jack's range and was firing back even as he swung the muzzle around in the last shooter's direction. Bullets chopped at the roof under Jack's feet and the roaring sound reached its peak.

He saw a bright flare of white headlights on the backstreet, and from out of nowhere a blocky silver shape collided with the metal gate and smashed it off its hinges. Sparks flew as the Chrysler stormed into the yard, slamming the last shooter aside as he bounced off the front fender. The car skidded and crashed into the rear of the building, the front end crumpling.

"Laurel!" Jack vaulted over the ladder and slid down its length. He sprinted to the ruined car as the driver's-side door creaked open. The woman rocked back from the safety airbag that had inflated across her, wiping the powdery discharge it left behind from her face.

"Hey," she managed. "Something caught fire."

"Guess so." Jack helped her from the wreck as more figures came down the fire escape, half-falling, half-running. "Thanks for the help."

"Didn't do it for you." Laurel pushed away from him, still unsteady on her feet as she ran to the dark-haired girl who had spoken to Jack a few minutes before. "Trish!" She embraced her. "Are you hurt?"

"Catch up later." Chase was the last to come down the ladder. "We gotta jet!"

"The van." Jack ran to the vehicle and found the door was already open. He ducked beneath the dashboard, cracking the plastic casing around the starter cylinder, feeling for the connections to hot-wire the starter. Behind him, a side panel slid open and the van lurched as Laurel loaded the women into the back. He twisted the frayed copper ends of two wires together and the engine turned over, grumbling into life.

"I got the gear," Chase shouted, sprinting across from the wrecked Chrysler, dragging Jack's bag behind him. He slammed the door closed as he clambered inside. "Floor it!"

"Hold on." Jack stamped on the accelerator and the black van lurched forward, the rear end skidding as he aimed it through the wrecked gate and out into the darkness.

In the rearview mirror, the Crankcase was wreathed in orange flames, stark against the black sky.

Mission accomplished, Jack told himself. But the fact was, the night's work had only just begun.

• • •

"Oh shit," breathed Sticks, panting as he tried to get his breath back. "Oh shit oh shit oh shit." Outside the burning strip club it was mayhem, as Night Rangers shoved aside the few truckers who had escaped the club with them, wheeling their motorcycles out across the street in a ragged pack. Fights had already broken out over who had started the fire, and in some places brother bikers helped other chapter members stagger away, all of them gasping to get fresh air in their lungs.

"That's . . . that's right," wheezed Fang. He had grabbed a bottle of beer on his way out and now he dropped to his haunches on the road, upending it over his head. He let the cold beer pour over the fresh burns down the side of his face, hissing in pain through gritted teeth.

The roof of the Crankcase gave a strained, crackling moan, and as Sticks watched, the upper floor of the building slowly caved in. Wood splintered and metal twisted, catapulting plumes of red-hot embers up into the night. The big neon sign, now dead and unlit, quivered and began a slow tilt forward. There were still people trying to get away from the club as the sign came apart and collapsed across the front entrance. Sticks saw a handful of bikers and bikes alike vanish under the twisted framework, flames coiling in the displaced air.

"Too slow," Fang offered. "Poor chumps."

"Kansas City charter," Sticks said coldly. "Who's gonna miss 'em?" He shook his head at the destruction before him. "But this . . . oh, man. Rydell is going to bust a nut."

"Those guys. It hadda be them."

Sticks nodded, suddenly remembering the phone he was still clutching in his hand. "You think they're still in there?" The wind carried a faint scream from somewhere inside the burning building, but no one was making any motion to venture back toward it.

"Would *you* be?"

He gave a woeful shake of the head and tapped the speed-dial button. "Lance," he grated, swallowing a cough as the line connected. "We have a big problem."

• • •

Rydell sat in a crouch, holding the big gold-plated Desert Eagle in his hand, waving the muzzle of the .50 caliber pistol around to illustrate his points. "Have I made the situation clear?" he asked the man in front of him.

The man was around the same age as Rydell, probably in his mid-to-late forties. There was only a few years between them, but while the biker was big, broad-shouldered and hard-faced, this guy—this *civilian*—was out of shape and flabby. Rydell sneered. It never ceased to amaze him how so-called stand-up folks like this maggot seemed to think that the world was going to be even with them. After all that this idiot had suffered, losing whatever crappy office cubicle job he had and being reduced to taking a chance on the cash-in-hand gig offered by the MC's recruiters, he still believed that there was such a thing as fair play. That he was somehow *entitled*. Rydell had learned that kind of thing was a fantasy a long time ago. The world was a hateful place, and a man either used it or got used by it. He rolled the Desert Eagle around in his grip, like a gunslinger.

This guy, he had been complaining a lot. About the food, the work, about every damn little thing. Enough that when Rydell had gotten wind of it through one of the brothers minding the works, he had to come see for himself. To set an example.

It was important, Rydell reflected, to make sure that

these chumps understood their place in things. *Cattle gotta be branded,* his daddy had once said.

The flabby guy was trying to talk, but he couldn't manage it. He'd be dead soon. A .50 cal round in the gut would do that to you. Rydell crouched there and watched him bleeding out into the cracked, overgrown asphalt of the old parade ground. "I'm gonna leave you here," he told him. "So the others can see how whiners get dealt with."

He pointed with the gun, toward where the tumbledown barracks stood. There were faces at the windows, all the other civilians, the other *cattle* who might have been listening to the crap this mouthy prick had been spouting. They might have been getting ideas, but that wouldn't go any further, not now.

Rydell stood up. "Don't feel you gotta die quiet." He kicked the man in his wound, making him whimper. "Best for me if you scream and howl some. Sends a message."

Lance was coming his way, jogging across from the ruined blockhouse that had once been the officers' quarters building. A lot of the infrastructure across the derelict Fort Blake army base had been "abandoned in place," as the military liked to call it, and that had worked out just fine for the needs of the Night Rangers MC.

"What now?"

"You need to hear this, prez." Lance held out his cell phone. "Sticks called back."

Rydell didn't like the look on the face of his burly master-at-arms, and he snatched the phone from him, annoyed that he wasn't going to be able to watch the dying man breathe his last. As he raised the handset to his ear, for the first time he noticed something off in the distance toward the town. A plume of smoke, black against black, climbing lazily into the sky.

His anger kindled. "What was the last thing I told you, you dumb asshole?"

"*Boss, no*," said Sticks, and with those words Rydell knew the worst had happened. He gripped the gun tightly, and if the other biker had been standing there before him, he would have become the second person to bleed out here tonight. "*Wasn't my fault, it was those guys—*"

"Where's Brodur? Where's Sammy? I want to talk to them, not you."

"*Brodur . . . don't know where he's at. But Sammy, boss. Sammy's gotta be dead.*" Before Rydell could ask another question, Sticks was spilling it all out. "*The 'Case is all burning up! They set it alight! The guys from Chicago, they hadda be the ones!*"

"They're not from Chicago," Rydell grated. "Idiot. What about the girls?"

"*Not sure. They might have got out with them.*" He paused. "*I gotta picture,*" Sticks insisted. "*On the phone!*"

"Send it." Rydell stabbed the "end call" button angrily and gripped the phone so tightly that the plastic case gave off a popping, cracking sound. A few seconds later, it buzzed and he glared at it.

"Who we looking at?" Lance hovered at his shoulder, trying to peer at the images. They were blurry and off-angle, but by luck more than judgment, Sticks had captured a shot of two men in the Crankcase's back corridor.

"This is what I get when I try to delegate," Rydell growled. For a second, he wanted to smash the phone on the ground and grind it to pieces under his boot heel. He took a breath through his gritted teeth and glared at Lance. "You see them? Find these two and bring them to me."

"They could be anywhere, boss . . ."

Rydell turned and shouted into his face. "*Find them!* There's only three roads in or out of this town! You know how the cops do it, block them off! Whoever those two fools are, they're messing with MC property. That don't get to happen."

Lance nodded and set off at a jog.

Rydell felt something touch his foot and he looked down to see the man he had shot trying to grab at his leg. He brought his boot down and hastened the end of his object lesson.

15

Toward the edge of town, where the landscape began to drop back to wide-open spaces and endless dark horizons, the road threaded past an overgrown steel-and-concrete barn as big as an aircraft hangar. The remnants of colorful signage across it were green with mildew and decay, and weeds coiled around everything.

It had been what modern urban planners would call a "retail park" when they first broke ground in the 1980s—a site for a big-box store surrounded by the flat expanse of a parking lot, where locals and soldiers from the army base alike would have been able to get cheap consumer goods and cheaper groceries. But that never really came to pass, and Deadline's one and only mega-mart suffered a slow, lingering death that eventually left it vacant and empty. In retrospect, it had been the first sign of the town's impending collapse, although no one living there wanted to accept that.

Some of the worst storms of the century had punched holes in the sheet-metal roof during the bitter winters a few years back, and now nobody dared to venture inside the empty shell. The place was shuttered up, each great patch of thick fiberboard across the doors and windows emblazoned with a sun-faded sign warning that the building was unsafe.

Jack drove the van clean through one of them, smashing the way in through the back so anyone passing on the road wouldn't see signs of disruption. He killed the engine and stepped down from the driver's seat, kicking up the thick dust on the floor as he went.

Laurel and the women held their collective breath as he and Chase walked back to the broken doors and listened. Somewhere out in the night, a motorcycle engine throttled up, but it was moving away, fading. After a while, there was only the dull moaning of the wind.

"Clear?" said Chase.

"Clear," agreed Jack. "We lost them, for now."

The other man gave a low whistle and it echoed off the walls. "Whoa. Look at this place. It's like the end of the world in here."

Jack nodded. The glow of the van's headlights illuminated what pieces of the big store's infrastructure were still bolted to the floor. In the distance, the glass-fronted doors of long-dead refrigerator cabinets reflected the beams, and there were rows and rows of empty shelves that had once been heavy with all kinds of products. In the far corner, where the roof had partially fallen in, a cloudy night sky was visible through a great rip in the ceiling. Chase's description was apt; the skeletal remains of the mega-mart could have been the set for some post-apocalyptic horror movie.

"I'll go look for a vantage point," Chase told him, and vanished into the gloom.

Jack walked back to the van, scoping out the floor, measuring it for lines of sight and possible exit routes. Laurel had taken charge and was leading the women to check each other over for injuries, keeping them calm.

His impression of her shifted. She had seemed so vulnerable when he went to her rescue in the motel car park, but now Jack realized that there was more to Laurel than he had seen on the surface. She was afraid but she wasn't letting it rule her. She had risked a lot to rescue her friend, the girl called Trish—and he hadn't forgotten that her brave-but-risky arrival in the car had also kept him alive in the bargain.

"We can't just wait here, can we?" Trish was saying. Her terror was real and palpable, and it was in danger of spreading through the rest of the escapees like a flash flood. "They're gonna come after us!"

"Why did we stop?" said one of the others. "Why can't we keep driving?"

"Not enough gas," Jack offered, nodding at the vehicle. "You'd barely make it five miles out of town before the engine died."

Laurel gave Jack a level look. "Some of these girls have been in that place for months. We have to get them away from here."

"Every drop of fuel in this burg will be under the control of the MC," said Jack. "Can't just gas up and go. We need another plan."

"He's right." An older woman, shivering in the chill, nodded bleakly. She told him her name was Cherry, and that it had been three months since she had come to Deadline, drawn by the same hollow promises that had snared Laurel and the rest. "We can't run away. What about all the others?"

"What others?" said Jack. He looked back at Laurel. "The ones off the bus?"

"Those were just the new arrivals," said Cherry. "I'm talking about the ones they got out at the works." She took in the other women with a sweep of her hand. "More than just us."

"The works." Jack repeated the name. "The guy who ran the strip club, Sammy. He mentioned that."

"That rat!" spat another girl. "Hope he burned alive back there!"

"You won't see him again," Jack assured her. "What was he talking about?"

"The army base, outside of the town," said Cherry. "What used to be Fort Blake, until the government closed it down. Rydell and all the Night Rangers use it like it's their clubhouse. That's where they take the others. Like a prison out there. Like you see in them war movies."

"How many people?" asked Laurel, her face pale.

"A hundred?" Cherry shook her head. "Don't know. I was only there one time. But they got folks living out of shacks, working them like dogs."

"For what?" said Jack.

"For the MC," Cherry insisted. "They're promised pay but all they get is to be slave labor!" She shook her head. "And people outside of Deadline, they don't know about it or they don't care."

"This town, it's a sinkhole," said Laurel. "Pulls in desperate, poor folks, makes them disappear, and the world just rolls on . . ."

Jack remembered something else that Sammy had said, back in the club. *We don't sign on anyone who's gonna be missed.*

He found the woman looking at him intently. "So. Do you have some kind of plan, mister? If we're still here by daylight tomorrow, it won't matter none that you burned down that place. We'll be got."

"They'll take it out on us," said Cherry, with a grim nod.

Jack glanced at his watch. "I won't let that happen. You'll all be safe by dawn. We'll go our separate ways."

"And how *exactly* are we going to do that?" demanded Trish.

"I'm working on it."

Footsteps sounded, and Chase returned, emerging

from the shadows. "Hey, Jack. I found a way up to the roof," he explained. "You can see the road going west from there, but that way is a bust."

"Why?"

"I watched them put a semi across both lanes, jack-knifed it." Chase seemed edgy, and as Jack watched, he absently flexed his right hand, as if it were paining him. "Couldn't see clear without binocs, but there's a bunch of those bikers camped out there. Waiting for us."

Jack's jaw hardened. "Safe bet they've done that on every route out of Deadline."

Chase nodded at Laurel and the others. "They need transport, Jack. Big, fast and right now."

"The bus!" Laurel said suddenly. She turned to Trish. "What happened to the bus that brought us from Indianapolis?"

"It drove on," said the other woman. "I didn't see where to."

"The works," Cherry insisted. "Like I said, new arrivals. That's where they take anyone they don't want as their *entertainment*." She said the last word with venom.

"All roads lead to Rydell," Jack said, almost to himself.

"He's a stone killer," insisted Cherry. "He likes to make it hurt." She fell silent, and Jack found himself wondering what the woman had seen—or worse, *experienced*—that had made the Night Rangers' leader so terrifying to her. "If he turns on you, that's it. Better if you get away without him ever seeing you."

Jack shook his head. "We're way past that."

• • •

The jet's wings returned to level flight and Kilner felt a shudder move down the length of the aircraft from nose to tail as they passed through a pocket of clear-air turbulence. At his side, Agent Dell gripped the armrests of her seat as if she were trying to squeeze blood out of them.

She noticed his attention and grimaced. "I really don't like flying," she admitted. "Probably doesn't help that I worked a bunch of air-crash cases with the NTSB."

"She's a real ray of sunshine," said Markinson, with a smirk. "Isn't that right, Kari?"

"Bite me, Helen," retorted Dell.

Kilner ignored the exchange and looked up at the digital clock mounted on the cabin bulkhead. "If Bauer is smart, he'll already have ditched that car and found another vehicle."

Markinson had a copy of the captured images from the traffic camera in front of her. "Does he look asleep to you?"

"It's this other guy, the driver, I don't get." Dell tapped the picture. "NCTC comes up negative on a facial match for him against criminal records, but then we run it through the federal law enforcement database and out pops the jacket for a dead guy."

"*Presumed* dead," corrected Hadley, without looking up from a sheaf of printouts in front of him. He hadn't spoken since the materials had spooled out of the jet's printer, studying them with an intense, unwavering focus. "Chase Edmunds is not the first person to use a national tragedy as a means to create a new identity. The same thing happened after nine-eleven."

Kilner shot him a look. "So you're certain it's him?"

"Of course it's him." Hadley almost sneered.

"That's a pretty calculating thing to do," said Markinson. "Don't you think? I mean, thousands died when the Valencia nuke went off. What's one more missing person on top of all the others? It's not like anyone could walk into the middle of the blast zone and start checking dental records. Not for a couple of centuries, at least."

"It doesn't matter why Edmunds faked his own death,"

said Hadley. "What matters is that he's aiding and abetting a federal fugitive, and a potential killer. This man was Jack Bauer's partner at CTU Los Angeles, he was in a relationship with Bauer's daughter ... And as a self-made ghost, he's the ideal accomplice." At last, Hadley looked up. "So he can share in the culpability when we catch them."

"A former officer in the DC Metropolitan Police Department," Dell read aloud from another copy of the suspect's file. "Transferred to the SWAT Emergency Response Team ... Later recruited to the Washington and Baltimore office of the Counter Terrorist Unit. Invalided out due to injuries suffered in the line of duty." She shook her head. "As if Bauer wasn't enough to deal with."

"This changes nothing," Hadley insisted. "We knew the target had outside help. Now we have a face, a name. And we can use that."

Markinson was nodding. "According to his records, Edmunds left behind a daughter and a sister in San Diego. If we track them down, apply some pressure ... ?"

"Do it," said Hadley. "Call the ASAC on duty at the San Diego field office, have them pull in the relatives."

Kilner shifted in his seat. "Is that really necessary? Edmunds dropped off the grid years ago. There's nothing to indicate he's reached out in all that time. I doubt his family even knows he's still alive." He paused. "Again, assuming Bauer's wheelman there *is* Chase Edmunds."

Hadley closed the folder in front of him and stared directly at the other man. "Are you going to continue to challenge everything that comes out of my mouth, Agent Kilner? It's becoming tiresome."

The temperature inside the jet's cabin seemed to drop twenty degrees. "I'm just doing my job," Kilner retorted. "Pointing out alternatives. Considering all the possibilities."

"Make sure you stay on the right side of being obstructive," said Hadley. "When this is all over, remember who be making the report to the deputy director." His cell phone rang and he glanced at it. Kilner saw something behind Hadley's expression change and the agent picked up the phone, moving away to the front of the cabin where he could talk without being overheard.

Kilner watched him go. When he turned around, Markinson was staring at him. "Stop poking the bear," she told him. "Or else he'll see you wind up in the cell next to Bauer's."

"Don't you get it? Hadley doesn't want to put Jack Bauer away," Kilner said quietly. "He wants to put him *down*."

• • •

"Talk to me," said Hadley, turning his back on the other agents. "What have you got?"

"*I thought we were going to keep this quiet,*" said Sal Jacobs. The FBI agent was calling back from his desk at the NCTC. "*Now I have people looking over my shoulder, asking me why I ignored procedure!*"

"That's on me," Hadley told him. "You won't take any flack for it, I promise."

"*Easy for you to say.*"

"Remember who we're doing this for, Sal. Jason Pillar was as much a mentor to you as he was to me."

"*I know. I know, we both owed him.*" Jacobs took a breath. "*Look, I coordinated with divisional in Missouri and I asked their tech guys to keep an eye out for anything unusual.*"

Hadley nodded. The route Bauer had been taking when the image was snapped would pass right through the middle of the operational area managed by the FBI's St. Louis field office. "Go on."

"*Projecting Bauer's possible pathways leads to nothing but a bunch of two-horse hick towns and dirt farms. Right now, there's a storm front coming down from Canada, so nothing is going to be flying, which means he's not aiming for an airstrip. He's got to be on the back roads, Tom, off the interstates where he might be seen."*

He nodded again. "I'm with you on that. We'll be pushing right into the edge of that storm in about twenty minutes. How does this connect with St. Louis?"

"Turns out our colleagues in Missouri are up on the phones of an outlaw biker gang running contraband across that whole area. The case is mired in red tape and going nowhere, but they're still monitoring. No permission for voice recording, just meta-data, for all the good that does . . . You know how it is these days. If a crook isn't in bed with Al Qaeda, it's a long way down the priority list . . ."

Hadley's patience was slipping. "Get to the point, Sal."

"Their wiretaps just went crazy. Every phone they're tracking lit up. Someone's stirring up these bikers."

He made an exasperated noise. "And why should I give a damn about what could just be some turf war out in the sticks?"

"The taps caught a photo message. One of these idiots sent it in the clear. Now, by law that means it is inadmissible as evidence but . . ." A smug tone entered the other agent's voice. *"Go ahead. Ask me whose face is in the picture."*

"Bauer?"

"The boys and girls in St. Louis seem to think so."

Hadley felt a rush of adrenaline flood through him. "Where?"

"St. Louis is patching their traffic data through to the plane. You should get it soon." Jacobs was quiet for a moment. *"I think this will square my debt."*

"Not quite," said Hadley. "One more thing. I want all we've got on these bikers. I want to know who's the top kick."

"*Checking . . .*" He heard Jacobs tapping at a keyboard. "*Benjamin Rydell. Multiple counts of assault, attempted murder, in the frame for a bunch more. A real charmer.*"

A risky plan began to form in Hadley's mind, but with O'Leary's warning echoing in his thoughts, Hadley knew he would have to go off-book in order to bring this operation to a close. "Give me the number of the cell phone that St. Louis pulled the picture from."

"*Why?*"

"Just do it, Sal."

• • •

Chase took one of the MP5/10 submachine guns from the gym bag and went back up to the roof, using the weapon's peep sight as a makeshift spotting scope. It wasn't a replacement for a real set of starlight optics, but it was all he had to work with and right now that seemed to be the plan of the moment. Adapt, improvise, move forward. He was no stranger to making it up as he went along, but even so Chase yearned for a proper plan of attack.

A couple of hours ago he was thinking about how he was going to kill time until the cargo train from Chicago rolled through, and now they were in the middle of a crusade against a violent gang of criminal bikers.

He looked around. *Where the hell am I?* he asked himself. *I don't want to die out here in the middle of nowhere.*

The thought cut off as a spasm went through his right hand and suddenly his nerves were alight.

He swore. This was a bad one, the worst seizure he'd had in a while, and he dropped the SMG, sinking to his haunches. Chase's breath came in quick gasps and he felt sweat beading his forehead, despite the chill wind up on the roof of the abandoned store. With a snarl, he forced the hand into a fist and punched it against an air vent, trying to beat back the burn from his agonized nerves with a different sort of pain. It didn't help, and so he had to sit there for what seemed like long minutes, riding out the hurt until finally, mercifully, it began to subside.

As sensation came back to his numbed fingers, he clumsily worked off the top of the pill bottle and tapped a tablet into his mouth, crunching it between his teeth. Chase heard movement behind him and fumbled the bottle away as a shadow came up from the access ladder leading down to the lower floor. "Jack . . ."

The other man nodded and showed him a scrap of paper in his hand. "Tried to get an online geo map of the area on my cell, but there's no signal this side of town. So Cherry drew us one instead, from memory."

Chase managed a brief grin, picking up the SMG from where it had fallen. "Low tech is better than no tech."

Jack showed it to him. "The old army base is here," he said, pointing at the sketch. "We can avoid the road, go cross-country." He paused. "If you think you're ready for it."

Chase hesitated. "If you didn't want me to back you up, you would never have called me tonight. Right?" The words came out more defensively than he had hoped.

"How long have you been taking the pills?" said Jack, after a moment.

His first impulse was to lie about it. That was what he had been doing every time that question came up, lying to Roker or the doctors at the free clinic, or to himself. He eyed Jack. "You know about that, huh? Guess I shouldn't be surprised. I mean, you know about *everything*, right? Can't get the drop on Jack Bauer."

"I've been on the same road, Chase." The other man looked away. "And you know it. I kicked my addiction, but once you've been there, you know the signs."

Chase showed him the pills. "Painkillers. For the nerve damage."

"Are they still working for you?" The question wasn't judgmental, just flat and direct.

"Not as well as I'd like."

He sighed. "I'm sorry."

"*You're* sorry?" Chase fought down a surge of bitterness. "Hell, you only cut off my hand! *I'm* the one who couldn't put myself back together."

"If you tell me you've got it under control," said Jack, "I won't doubt you. But I need to hear you say the words."

It seemed to take Chase forever to find the words. "I can handle it."

"Good." Jack walked to the edge of the roof and looked out. "I've got a couple of bulletproof vests in the bag. We'll take those. Radios too. Laurel and the others can stay here, keep out of sight."

"So we go in, find the rest of the folks the Night Rangers shanghaied, get that bus and get them out."

"Yeah."

Despite himself, Chase smiled a little at the other man's understatement. "Rydell and his guys aren't going to be happy to see us. And we don't know what else we're going to find out there."

"I have an inkling," said Jack. "I'm not leaving Deadline until I'm sure." He turned suddenly to face his former partner. "I know what you're thinking. That we don't have to fight every battle that comes our way. Maybe that's true. But if we don't do this, right here, tonight . . . who the hell will?"

Chase gave a rueful nod and looked at his watch. "Clock's running."

• • •

He was lighting a smoke when he heard the chattering tune, and at length he realized that the sound was coming from Lance's phone, still there in the outer pocket of his jacket where he had dumped it.

The display said CALLER ID BLOCKED and for a second, he considered tossing the device away. The night was shaping up to be problematic enough without one more thing coming down the pipe to damage his calm.

He sucked in a lungful and jabbed at the button. "Who the hell is this?"

"*I want to talk to Benjamin Rydell,*" said a voice he didn't recognize. There was a strange buzzing on the line that made his teeth itch.

"Last folks to call me Benjamin were the nuns at the orphanage, pal, and you ain't one of them."

"*This is Special Agent Thomas Hadley of the Federal Bureau of Investigation. It's my understanding that you have an interest in someone I'm looking for. The man in the picture you were sent?*"

Rydell hesitated, his mind racing. *Was this joker on the level? How had the feds gotten this number? Was he being set up?* "I don't know about any pictures," he said. "I just found this here phone on the sidewalk. I'm hanging up now."

"*That would be a mistake,*" said the voice. "*Then you would miss the opportunity to make a deal that could considerably benefit the Night Rangers MC.*"

He wanted to cut the call, but part of him was interested, enticed. He couldn't help but voice the question. "What kind of deal?"

"*The man in the picture and his accomplice. I want them. Think about what you might like to get in return.*"

Rydell cracked a crooked smile. All of a sudden, his evening was starting to improve.

16

The long grasses surrounding the site of Fort Blake had been left to thicken until they were waist-high. It was more than enough for Jack and Chase to use to conceal their approach, moving low and quick toward the collapsed fences that were all that remained of the old base perimeter.

With hand signals, Jack directed them toward the tumbledown remains of a pillbox set in the ground. A hexagon of brown, crumbling concrete, the old guard post stank of animal urine, but it gave them a shadowed lookout from which they could survey their target.

"I see movement," said Chase. "They got a fire going outside that two-story building to the right."

Jack nodded. He heard the husky rumble as a pair of riders cruised up and down outside the decaying officers' quarters, each trying to drown out the other with the growling revs of the engines on their customized Harleys. Other members of the MC were standing around an oil-drum fire, drinking and joking, staying warm as the cold began to settle in. The chill in the air was turning damp. "Storm's coming," he said quietly. "Could work for us, if we're lucky."

"You know," Chase began, "part of me keeps on wondering where the hell I left my badge." He patted his chest, where a federal shield would have hung over his black bulletproof vest if this had been a lawful operation. "Then I remember we're not cops. Or CTU."

"Concerned citizens," Jack said without turning, calling back to what Chase had told Trish at the strip club.

"I just want to be sure of our rules of engagement. We're not in the Wild West here."

Jack nodded at the men whooping and shouting as the two bikes turned dusty circles on the parade ground. "You sure about that?" He paused. "Rules are the same as they always are. There are targets, and potential targets. It's their choice which way they go out." To underline his point, Jack paused to check the MP5/10 slung across his chest. He flipped the safety catch to single-shot mode. "Just try to hold off on any gunplay until we're inside. The moment one of these creeps wises up to us, they're going to call their playmates to come running."

"Copy that," said Chase. He raised his own SMG and scanned the area through the sight. "I see lights on, on the far side of the parade ground there. More buildings. Smoke coming from a chimney."

Jack didn't answer right away. He felt a vibration against his side, from the pocket where he was carrying his cell phone. Taking care to cover the screen so the glow from the display wouldn't be seen, he bent low over the device and studied it. The text message he had been trying to send from the derelict mega-mart had finally connected and been dispatched; clearly the spotty coverage throughout the town of Deadline extended out this far but no farther. He turned off the phone and slid it back into an inner pocket.

"Got someone coming out of the old officers' quarters," Chase reported, still looking through his gun sight.

"Recognize anyone from the club?"

Chase shook his head. "Nope. But whoever this guy is, he's got pull."

Jack could make out the sounds of someone talking, but not the actual words. Chase seemed to be right. The new arrival's appearance had made the rest of the boisterous bikers fall silent.

• • •

Rydell strode down the cracked steps to where Lance was waiting for him by the oil-drum fire, and the master-at-arms bobbed his head.

"Boss," he said. "I did like you asked. Got the roads outta town sealed up tight, got outriders at each roadblock."

He gave a distracted nod. "Whoever's left, tell them to split up and start searching the town. Every place out there. They find something, nobody makes a move until they talk to me first, right?"

"Right," Lance repeated. "You wanna waste these chumps yourself?"

"Wasting them is the last thing on my mind."

"What?" The other man frowned. "But the 'Case . . . and Sammy. I mean, they shed blood. They hurt the club. They gotta pay for that."

"I want them *alive*," Rydell insisted. "Roughed up . . . ?" He shrugged. "Sure, whatever. But still breathin'. These pukes just became a commodity."

Lance followed Rydell to where his bike—a Dyna Super Glide Custom in black and gunmetal—was parked. Two other men, the club president's "honor guard," fell into step with him. "You going somewhere?" said Lance.

"You wait up here," Rydell told him, dismissing the question. "Keep these guys around, watch the works while I'm gone." He straddled the big hog and kicked the bike's engine into life. "I gotta set something up. Where's Fang at?"

"In town," said Lance, his confusion deepening. He came closer, lowering his voice. "Boss, what kinda . . . commodity? What's that mean?"

Rydell showed him a shark's predatory smile. "It means we're not the only ones who want this prick's head on a spike." He aimed two fingers at his eyes. "Stay frosty." He twisted the throttle and the Super Glide raced away, angling back toward the highway, two more bikes trailing in its noisy wake.

• • •

The Night Rangers hadn't posted many lookouts, and Chase guessed that might be because they had become complacent. The bikers didn't feel threatened in any way here, that was clear as day. They owned the town of Deadline, body and soul, and he imagined that the idea of anyone crossing them never occurred to the outlaw gang. These guys had carved out their own little fiefdom, right in the heartland of the state, ruling the place like a band of medieval marauders.

It was a situation Chase and Jack could use to their advantage. From the tumbledown guard post, they shifted the line of their approach and crossed behind a collapsed wall toward the ill-lit buildings he had spotted earlier. Closing in, Chase could see that the aging wooden shacks were what had once been the barracks for Fort Blake's enlisted men. A couple of them had fallen in, roofs folded up and walls split from storm damage and neglect, but the others all showed signs of occupation.

Each barracks hut was raised off the ground on thick brick supports, and Jack slipped close to the nearest one, pressing himself flat to the outer wall. They were in heavy shadow here, the clear sky that had been above them at sunset now turned cloudy. It was to their advantage—cloud meant no moonlight, less chance of being spotted.

"Hear anything?" Chase whispered.

"Voices," Jack replied, straining to listen through the clapboard wall. "Can't make anything out." He let his MP5/10 drop on its sling and eased himself up to look through a grimy, cracked window. "Cover me."

Turning his head side-on to present the smallest possible profile, Jack peered inside. After a moment, he dropped back down and leaned close to Chase.

"More bikers?"

"No." Jack shook his head. "Prisoners. Dozens in there, crammed into every corner. This has to be the bunkhouse for whatever sweatshop the Night Rangers are running."

"I doubt they're making knockoff sneakers."

"We need to get eyes on," said Jack. He beckoned Chase to follow him and they pushed forward, careful and stealthy.

Slipping around the edge of another barracks shack, Chase spotted an open-sided hangar with a wide, angled tin roof. Beneath it were a couple of nondescript hard-side trucks parked on either side of an old Greyhound bus that was covered in road dust. "Motor pool?" he asked.

Jack nodded and pointed. A group of bikers were standing close by, a couple of them crouching over the fairing of a motorcycle that was missing a fuel tank, the wide-bodied hog surrounded by a halo of parts on a greasy white bedsheet. Each of the Night Rangers was offering conflicting advice about how to best maintain the bike, and the conversation was in danger of turning violent.

They backed off; there was no way past on this side of the barracks without being seen by someone. They would have to find a different approach.

"How are we gonna get the bus?" whispered Chase,

as they paused in the undergrowth between two of the shacks.

"One objective at a time," Jack replied. He pointed toward the far side of the parade ground, toward what had once been bunker-like garages for tanks and armored vehicles. The smoke Chase had seen earlier was issuing out in steady streams from chimneys across the concrete roofs. He thought he could smell the faint tang of ammonia, but it was hard to be sure in the damp air. "We're going in there," said Jack. "Look."

Doors on the front of one of the bunkers had opened, and as Chase watched, a ragged group emerged. Men and women, their faces pale and dirty, came out in a disordered line and set off toward the barracks. Three bikers walked with them, each armed with either a shotgun or a cattle prod. They forced their charges onward with the bored brutality of indifferent prison guards, shouting at anyone who moved too slowly.

Every one of the workers looked like they were fit to drop, and Chase had to wonder how long they had been here. At his side, he felt Jack tense as one of the bikers used the butt of his gun to discipline an older guy who was dragging his feet.

"Shift change," Jack noted. "Here's our chance."

"We can't take out three men at once," Chase noted.

"We're not going to. We play this smart. These idiots aren't paying attention. We're gonna use that." Jack dropped back around the side of the empty shack as the guards reached the door.

Chase threw a look over his shoulder as he moved away. The bikers hustled the workers into one of the barracks buildings before moving on to roust the next "shift." They banged on the walls of the shack with the cattle prods and made threats. No one dared to complain, he noted, and that spoke volumes. These people seemed broken and without hope, resigned to their fate.

Out of sight around the side of the building, Chase watched the new group as they spilled out of the hut, cowering against the threat of violence. He felt Jack tap him on the shoulder and he turned. The other man pressed something into his hands: a heavy, mud-smeared army blanket he had pulled from where it had been left hanging over a broken windowpane. Jack had a similar mantle over his shoulders, turning it into a makeshift poncho.

"Undercover again," said Chase quietly. "Because that worked out so well last time."

"Move," Jack retorted. "Join the back of the group. They're not taking a head count."

Chase nodded and did his best to ignore the dull stink of the blanket, wrapping it around himself. It was big enough to conceal the bulk of the vest and the SMG, but all the same he made sure to hunch forward as much as he could and hold it close to his chest. He kept his head down, eyes to the ground, and shuffled after the rest of the prisoner group.

Jack walked alongside him, holding a hand to his face as if he were nursing a wound. "Be ready. If they make us, we'll have to improvise."

"Same as always."

• • •

Eventually the raised voice faded away to be replaced by a muttering, tearful tone that Ziminova could just about hear over the sound of the rushing river. She rested against a tree, smoking one of the long, poisonous Polish cigarettes that were her single vice, waiting for the questioning to end.

Bazin was a master of improvisational interrogation, it had to be said. Taking the hacker Matlow with them aboard the helicopter, her commander had directed the pilot to take them a few miles north to where a river ran swift and deep through the edge of a wooded area. They parked the aircraft in a clearing and with Ekel's help, Bazin dragged the wounded American to the water's edge and proceed to bring him to the cusp of drowning. He did it over and over, there in the icy, clear river, lit by the beam of a battery lantern in Ekel's hands.

Ziminova didn't watch, but she couldn't avoid listening. First to Matlow's sputtering, angry retorts. Then to the rapid erosion of his annoyance into true fear and abject terror. Finally, to the breaking of him as the cold crept into his bones and threatened hypothermia.

At the end, she heard a frantic, wild splashing and then only the rush of the water over the rocks. She turned and stepped up as Bazin crossed the grass, drying off his big, boxer's hands. Ekel carried his coat for him, following a dutiful step or two behind.

Ziminova didn't bother to ask if Matlow had talked. *Of course he had talked.* That had never been in doubt.

Bazin glanced upward, and she did the same. It was starting to rain, a haze of fine droplets falling down out of a sky thickening with clouds.

"What have we learned?" Ziminova asked.

"Much of use," he replied, glancing toward the pilot aboard the Augusta. Bazin made a spinning motion with one finger and she saw the man nod. He started flipping switches in the cockpit, and the helicopter's rotor blades began a slow, languid turn about their central hub. "Bauer plans to use the railway to reach his family in Los Angeles."

"A train. How European of him."

"Bauer is working with this person Williams, as we suspected. I persuaded Matlow to give up all he knew. He provided the locations where Bauer will embark and disembark."

"I will contact Yolkin and Mager and have them redirect their team."

Bazin released a long, slow breath that turned to vapor in the night air. "This may represent the last chance we have to intercept the man. We must move with speed, but also with care. If we lose Bauer now . . ." He trailed off, then refocused his attention. "While I was at work, did we receive any further communication from the president's staff?"

"No word from Suvarov or his people," she confirmed. "His flight will land in Moscow in a few hours."

"Perhaps by then I will have something in hand to report," Bazin said.

She made a show of looking past her commander. "And Matlow . . . You left him to the river, then?"

Bazin gave a matter-of-fact nod. "Drowning is a tragic end, and he met it without courage." He started toward the helicopter as the engine note grew louder, and Ziminova followed, tossing her cigarette into the fast-flowing water as she went.

• • •

The doors to the base's old vehicle store were inch-thick steel plates on rusted roller wheels, and they complained as they were hauled shut behind the group. The biker with the shotgun, the one who had been so generous with his insults and violent encouragement, jerked a thumb over his shoulder at the benches set up across the floor of the bunker. "Get to work, assholes," he barked. "I'm already sick of lookin' at ya."

"*Damn*," breathed Chase, as he took in the scope of the Night Rangers' operation.

Jack said nothing, but he shared the other man's sentiment. The former tank garages had been stripped down to the bare concrete when the army moved out, leaving nothing but a wide, echoing space with low ceilings and hardened walls that could stop an artillery shell. The MC had repurposed the vehicle bays, bringing in portable generators to run racks of construction lamps and industrial equipment. Metal benches and workstations were arranged in rows, and there were people toiling over them, their features hidden behind used surgical face protectors or the pig snouts of heavy rubber dust masks. Jack saw red-colored metal drums sporting diamond-shaped warning labels, polymer sacks of powder and large fluid tanks, white plastic cubes the size of a compact car. It was hot inside, with a thick fug of chemical discharge in the air that instantly coated the back of his throat. Ammonia, hydrogen, acetone, all mixing to form an unpleasant brew that made him want to back out to the fresh air once again.

The reason behind the weakened, sickly faces of the workers was clear now; this place was a toxic nightmare, filled with any one of a dozen different kinds of lethal compounds. And the end result of it all, the product that "the works" was creating, lay out on drying racks along one wall of the chamber. Steel trays were covered in mounds of what looked like rock candy, irregular milky-white crystals as big as dimes. Some of the workers were cutting them up and weighing out set amounts into small baggies, under the watchful eye of a biker with a baseball bat cocked over one shoulder.

Methamphetamine. It didn't come as a surprise to see that the Night Rangers were dealing the illegal street version of the potent stimulant—it was a common commodity for outlaw biker gangs to traffic in—but the fact that they were manufacturing crystal meth themselves, and on this kind of scale . . . That was out of the ordinary.

"This isn't a meth *lab*," muttered Chase. "This is a meth *factory*."

There had to be thousands of dollars' worth of freshly produced ice right there on the racks, Jack guessed, and that was just what he could see. Instead of cooking up small batches in some trailer park drug den, the MC had set up shop in the ruins of Fort Blake. Suddenly things started to fall into place. Deadline wasn't just a random town where the Night Rangers had decided to plant their flag, it was the nexus of their unlawful enterprises. The enforced prostitution at the strip club and the trafficking in human misery was just a side deal. The drugs were at the rotten heart of it all.

"Hey!" One of the guards saw them hesitating, and shoved Jack in the shoulder. "What the hell you staring at, dumbass? Get to work—"

The biker froze as Jack reacted to the push, his improvised cover slipping before he could stop it. The other man saw the pistol grip of the MP5/10 beneath the tattered blanket and reeled backward, pulling a revolver from his belt.

Jack and Chase reacted instantly, shrugging off their disguises, bringing up the SMGs, safety catches snapping off. Fear rippled through the workers and there were screams. The two of them automatically fell into firing stances, Chase aiming back toward the rear of the garage, Jack aiming forward toward the doors. Still, he hesitated to start shooting.

"Pull that trigger and you're a dead man!" Jack snarled at the biker with the pistol, as his cohorts went for their own guns. "One stray round and this place will be an inferno! You want to take that chance?"

Nobody moved. Jack's warning was no trick, and everyone around them knew it. The process for making crystal meth, something nicknamed the "red, white and blue" method, was highly dangerous thanks to the use of a number of volatile chemicals. Phosphorus, hydrochloric acid and methylamine were all part of the hazardous cocktail. Under the wrong conditions, a poorly controlled meth lab could create poisonous or explosive gasses like phosphine and hydrogen. Worse still was the so-called "Willy Pete," the white phosphorus that could ignite on contact with air and burn with furious heat.

"It's your call," Jack told him.

Slowly, a feral grin rose across the biker's face, and he eased back the hammer on his pistol. His friends did the same, slackening off the triggers of their firearms, reaching instead for other weapons. "I don't know who you think you are, or where the hell you came from . . ." continued the man, and with his other hand he drew out a curved karambit knife, the wicked talon-curl of the blade catching the light as he twirled it around his fingers. "I guess I'll find out when I'm done gutting you."

Jack let his MP5/10 drop to dangle at his side on its bungee cord sling. "Make your play," he said.

• • •

"You're out of line," Kilner heard the pilot saying. "Sir, I know what the orders say, but I can't land there."

"You'll do what I damn well tell you to!" Hadley snapped back. "You've got the location, put this thing on the ground, *now*!"

Markinson and Dell exchanged worried looks, but Kilner wasn't going to wait for an explanation. He moved up the Cessna's cabin, gripping the tops of the seats as he walked to steady himself. The jet had crossed into bad weather an hour after they had gotten back in the sky, and despite all the pilot's entreaties to let him turn around and find another route west, Hadley had refused at every turn. Now it seemed that their disagreement was threatening to spill over into something worse.

"What's going on up here?" Kilner said as he reached the cockpit door.

"This is above your pay grade," Hadley snapped, shooting him a hard look. "Get back there and sit down."

"He wants us to land," said the copilot, holding up a map.

"Why is that a problem?"

"Because there's no damn airstrip there!" said the pilot, his temper flaring. He snatched the map from the copilot and stabbed a finger at what was clearly a long stretch of paved highway. "This is a road, not a runway!" He shook his head. "Special Agent Hadley, I don't know where you're getting your information from, but we can't put down there. End of story."

"You're trained to make an emergency landing on that kind of surface," Hadley shot back. "This aircraft is more than capable of doing it."

Kilner couldn't believe what he was hearing. "Hadley, wait. You can't be serious—"

"I told you to *back off*!" Hadley bellowed. He turned on the pilot and jabbed at the air in front of him. "You listen to me. Land this plane where I told you to. Or I will make certain that both of you will lose your wings, your pension, *your entire careers*! Jack Bauer is the most dangerous man in America and he is down there! We lose him and I will burn you for it. *Believe me*." His words were like thunder, and in that moment not one person on that aircraft doubted that Hadley would make good on his promise. The agent's hand drifted toward his holstered sidearm, and Kilner paled.

But then the pilot gave a sullen nod. "Fine. Get back in the cabin and strap in. I'm doing this under protest. And you can bet your ass I'll be filing the mother of all grievances with divisional command when this is over."

"Just get us on the ground," Hadley snapped, and pushed past Kilner, back toward his seat.

"That'll happen," said the pilot bitterly. "One way or another."

Kilner fell into his chair and pulled his seat belt tight as the jet dropped suddenly. "I know you want Bauer," he said, "but you're risking our lives!"

Hadley's moment of fury had gone as quickly as it had arrived. "I've already risked everything on finding him," he replied, and looked away through the window as the ground came rushing up to meet them.

17

The biker with the curved karambit knife came at Jack, wide-eyed and laughing. In the hard illumination from the industrial flood lamps behind him, he could see that the Night Ranger had been abusing his position on the drug-lab factory floor to help himself to the raw product; his pupils were dark and dilated.

Dealing with an assailant in a chemically altered state always represented another level of risk. Someone on meth could be impulsive and dangerous in random ways that Jack couldn't account for. An ordinary adversary could be counted on to react in a predictable manner that an experienced fighter could measure and counteract. But all bets were off with this guy, who leapt with the knife slashing at the air, lethally focused on nothing more than cutting Jack Bauer as quickly and as violently as possible.

If it had just been the two of them, Jack would have extended his distance, let the biker lose his momentum and waited for the ideal time to strike. That wasn't an option here, though. There was little room to maneuver among all the workbenches and chemical drums, too many civilians at close range who might get in the way or end up as collateral damage. He would have to finish this one fast. The biker had three more friends to back him up, and Jack couldn't expect Chase to handle those odds on his own.

The karambit sang as it described a horizontal arc through the air, level with Jack's throat. He dodged, bending back to let the weapon pass, but he wasn't quite fast enough to miss it entirely. The razor-sharp tip of the blade barely touched the skin over his left cheekbone, but it left a cold touch as it cut the flesh, heat burning in its place a split second later. Jack flinched at the jolt of pain but didn't let it slow him. He saw the biker coming back the other way with a return swipe, hoping to bury the blade in his chest.

Jack's arms caught the biker's and brought them across each other in a motion like a pair of shears snapping closed. The move trapped the biker's arm and cleanly snapped the radius bone halfway along its length, causing inches of it to rip out of his flesh and through the sleeve of his denim shirt.

The attacker released a yowl of agony and he lost his grip on the karambit, his hand opening with the shock of the pain. Even the meth he had smoked a while ago wasn't enough to numb him, and he recoiled.

But not quickly enough. Jack caught the knife as it fell, snatching it before it hit the ground and bounced away. Without conscious thought, he mirrored the attack of his assailant and sent the karambit back to its owner. The tip of the blade pierced the left eye of the biker and Jack pushed it home, sinking it deep like a fishhook.

One down.

The biker tumbled to the floor, but even as he dropped a second man was bearing down on Jack, an enraged roar on his lips. This one was a lot bigger, one of the guards who had been walking around inside the drug factory. If not for the thick ponytail that fell to his shoulders, he could have been the brother to the man-mountain Jack had seen behind the bar at the Crankcase.

He rushed at him, catching Jack before he could side-step out of the way. They collided with a freight train impact and he felt the MP5/10 submachine gun dangling from his shoulder snag on something and become lost. Before Jack could process that, the big Night Ranger had both of his thick, meaty paws around the front straps of his bulletproof vest. Jack felt the world turn around him as the towering thug dragged him off his feet and hauled him around in a fast, dizzying spin.

• • •

Chase ducked and wove, calling on old boxing moves as the rail-thin biker with the crackling cattle prod carved up the air in front of him. The bright, actinic glow of the prod's electric discharge left muddy purple afterimages on Chase's retinas, and he blinked furiously, knowing that all it would take to be beaten was one straight-on connection with the weapon. He had taken a Taser hit in SWAT training half a lifetime ago, a savage jolt through his torso to teach him and his fellow cops how to deal with such an eventuality. It wasn't something he was in any rush to repeat.

He glimpsed a second figure joining the first and now there were two of them coming at him through the blur of motion and crackling electricity. One struck high and the other went low, forcing Chase to stay on the defensive. He tried to keep outside their reach, but he was aware they were backing him deeper into the drug factory, trying to limit his options. Chase let his training take over, dodging, moving, presenting a shifting target. For the bikers, it was like clutching at smoke, but they knew that all they had to do was wear him down. Sooner or later, Chase would plant a foot wrong and they would fall on him, and beat him into the concrete.

He couldn't wait for that to happen. From the corner of his eye, Chase caught sight of a plastic drum in bright fire-truck red. Black stenciled letters and hazmat labels on the side of the container warned about the volatility of whatever it was full of, but Chase didn't have the time to double-check. He threw himself at the cylinder, hearing cries of alarm as some of the captive workers scattered before him.

Chase put his weight onto the top of the drum and used that to rock it on the wooden pallet where it stood. It was half-full, and thick liquid sloshed around inside. He directed a kick at the base of the wobbling drum and that was enough to push it off the pallet. Gravity took over. The plastic container tipped on its side and the impact blew out the safety cap, vomiting the contents across the concrete floor. A noxious gush of industrial-strength iodine solution washed over the boots of the bikers, the spill lighting a surge of panic through the workers. They bolted for the doors, chaos erupting around the echoing concrete chamber.

• • •

There was a dizzying moment when Jack was actually flying through the air; then he collided with one of the water containers, bouncing off it with a hollow, echoing clank. He tried to get to his feet, but the big man was already there, already hauling him up again by the straps on the vest. Jack kicked and punched, but his blows didn't seem to have any effect. The giant biker threw him to the right and the left, back and forth, slamming him into the drying racks over and over again. Showers of meth rocks exploded around him, raining down, trays full of freshly cooked crystal tipping over and grinding to powder beneath the boots of the man trying to bludgeon him to death.

Perhaps the guy Jack had killed with the knife had been a blood brother of this towering biker, or perhaps he was just deep in his rage and out for murder. Whatever the reason, the big man seemed ignorant of all the property damage he was doing and product he was destroying. He just wanted to beat Jack to death.

Jack tasted blood in his mouth as he struck the racks again, feeling the rebandaged bullet wound beneath his shirt rip open afresh. He was on the edge of a concussion, losing his grip on the fight, suddenly caught by the undertow of fatigue that he had been fighting off since he left New York City. If he lost his grip now, that would be the end of it.

No. Jack arched his back and threw up his hands. Before the big man could react, he brought them both down in hard chopping motions on either side of his thick neck. The double blow was enough to jar the biker out of his rhythm, and Jack followed it up by jerking forward again. He brought his forehead down as hard as he could on the bridge of the man's nose and was rewarded by the crunch of breaking cartilage. Abruptly, he was out of his assailant's powerful grip and falling to the floor as the biker snarled and clutched at his face. Jack landed badly and cursed, scrambling back to his feet as quickly as he could, ignoring the cascades of pain rolling up along his torso.

Streaked with blood, the long-haired biker gave a wordless bellow of fury and reached for Jack again, hands out before him in grasping talons.

Jack grabbed the first thing that would serve as a weapon—a glass chemical bottle—and hurled it at the other man. It broke against his chest and instantly an acrid, sickly sweet stench filled Jack's nostrils. Where the liquid in the bottle had struck, the biker's shirt, his jacket, his bare skin were burning ghost-white with a vicious acidic reaction. The big man's eyes widened and he forgot all about Jack, instead clawing at the spreading patch of hissing, melting material. He screamed and staggered backward as the concentrated hydrochloric acid ate into him. Before Jack could get clear, the wounded man's flailing motions sent the man pitching into another workbench, where an unshielded gas burner was alight with yellow flames. Fire caught the biker's trailing hair and it instantly became a torch. He knocked the burner on its side and Jack saw the flames escape across the span of the bench, greedily devouring everything they touched.

There was a hot surge of smoldering air, and for the second time that night Jack turned away as an infernal heat beat at his back.

• • •

The belch of fire from across the meth factory was so bright, so sudden, that it made Chase hesitate—and that was the moment his attackers had been looking for. The closest man went for him with the cattle prod, leading with a jabbing motion. Chase tried to parry the blow, making the block through pure reflex action, but it was ill-timed and missed the motion. Instead the metal tines of the prod glanced off the flesh just above his wrist, in the meat of his forearm muscle.

It hit him like a hammer. Fireworks detonated behind Chase's eyes and a shuddering shock went through his entire body as every sinew in him seemed to go taut at once. But Chase fought back, he chewed down the pain and forced it away. The sharp, quick bolt of agony was not new to him. He had felt the same kind of brutal burn through his damaged flesh more than once, and it did not lay him out as that Taser shot had, all those years ago in training. Maybe it was the wound, the places where the nerves in his severed and reattached hand had never truly healed. Maybe that kind of pain was something he had become insensate to. It didn't matter.

Chase struck out with his good hand and grabbed the cattle prod before his first attacker could reel back and away. He deflected the sparking tip of the weapon away from his midriff and forced it back into the chest of his assailant. Chase slammed the deadened palm of his bad hand into the base of the prod where the trigger button was located, and before he could stop himself, the biker was forced to discharge his own weapon into his torso. A buzzing crackle cut through the Night Ranger's shirt and he went into a twitching spasm, crying out as his legs turned to water.

Disarming him as he fell away to the chemical-slicked floor, Chase spun around to meet the attack he knew was coming from the other biker. He batted the other man's cattle prod away with the one he had taken, and triggered it into the face of the second assailant. The electro-conductive tines didn't make contact with flesh, but the searing burst of discharge was enough to flash blind the other man at such close range. While he was clawing at his eyes, Chase rocked forward and clubbed him hard about the head, putting down the third of them.

Panting and shaking, he turned to hear the *snap-clack* of a round being racked into the breech of a shotgun.

• • •

With the drug factory now alight, the last Night Ranger guard decided to ignore Jack's warning about uncontrolled gunplay inside the garage bunker and opened fire with a pump-action Winchester M12, blasting away with heavy-gauge buckshot that blew ragged holes in water tanks and shredded debris across the workbenches.

Jack dove for cover as a glass carboy full of chemicals blew apart behind him, spilling more poisonous liquids into the growing slick across the concrete floor. Streamers of orange flame crawled up the nearby walls and gathered along the ceiling. His throat stung with the cut of toxic gasses that were building up inside the enclosed space. Every worker had broken and run, leaving whatever they had been doing to boil over, catch fire or otherwise turn lethal.

He moved, hunched low, as more shotgun blasts peppered the workbench to his side. The biker with the gun was yelling something, but Jack didn't listen. This fool was standing between him and the exit.

He drew the M1911 pistol from his jacket pocket and in a smooth, continuous motion, Jack burst out of his cover and into the open, the gun rising into a Modified Weaver stance as the sights came level with his eyeline. The shotgunner was already aiming in Jack's direction—to hesitate would mean it was *game over*.

Jack fired a single .45 ACP round that caught the biker center-mass, striking his chest just below the sternum. The man went down, the ragged cavern the penetrating bullet tore through his lungs filling with blood.

He kicked the shotgun away from the dying man's grip and cast around. It was getting hard to breathe now, and the noxious smoke filling the chamber made his eyes sting. Jack saw movement, and a figure lurched out of the haze toward him.

"Chase . . ."

The other man nodded, handing him the MP5/10 he had lost in his earlier fight. "Thought you'd want this back."

Jack nodded and holstered the pistol, breaking into a jog as he checked the SMG and brought it to the ready. "Let's go!"

"Right behind you . . ."

Acrid, sour vapor billowed out of the open bunker door, and Jack and Chase stumbled blindly through it—and into a storm of gunfire.

The Night Rangers gathered outside had witnessed the sudden, mass exodus of the workers from the old tank garage, and their reaction had been a predictable one. Weapons came out, and they opened fire on their captives, shouting at them to go back. Caught between a building inferno and a rain of bullets, they had scattered. Many had been cut down or badly wounded as the bikers reacted with violent reprisal.

Jack switched his Heckler & Koch to burst-fire and shot back into the ranks of the Night Rangers, and they reacted with shock, never expecting to take withering salvos of 10mm bullets from what they had thought were unarmed targets. Chase did the same, spraying three-round jolts across the open parade ground. Shooters caught unawares were hit and went down hard, but it only took a few seconds for the rest of them to locate the source of the incoming fire.

Finding temporary cover behind a stack of wooden forklift pallets, Jack unloaded the rest of his rounds with a blind burst and reloaded. Behind them, the open doors of the bunker were like the mouth of hell, the hot breath of the fire searing and poisonous. He glanced at Chase as the other man picked off his targets. "The bus," said Jack, inclining his head toward the battered old Greyhound. "Can you drive it?"

"Sure, if there wasn't ten guys between me and it." Chase flinched as bullets chewed splinters out of the pile of pallets.

"Get the captives on board and get them the hell out of here. Don't stop for anything."

Chase gave him a level look. "And you're gonna be doing what, exactly?"

"I'll draw them off." Chase opened his mouth to say

something, perhaps to suggest that was a damned stupid idea that could get him killed, but Jack didn't wait around to hear it.

He burst out from behind his cover with a shout on his lips, running as fast as he could in a diagonal path across the open ground, firing the MP5/10 from the hip in chattering bursts of fire.

Shots from the Night Rangers sliced through the air around him, heavy-caliber rounds spanking off the ground near his feet as he sprinted toward a cluster of tumbledown buildings that had once been shower blocks. He heard the choking snarl of motorbike engines behind him and the white glow of a headlight washed across his path like a search beam. A too-close shot hummed past his ear, so near it made him flinch and almost stumble over the broken brickwork surrounding the fallen blockhouse. Jack ducked around the side of the building as guns boomed and more rounds lanced after him.

"Get that sucker!" Jack heard someone shouting, baying for his blood. "Get the bikes, run him into the dirt!"

More engines growled to life after the first, and he knew the hunt was on. He smiled. *Good.* The more of them after him, the better chance Chase had to do what they had come here for.

The white beam that had briefly silhouetted him as he pounded across the parade ground now swept over the sides of the blockhouse, and Jack knew that the leading rider would be upon him in moments. Slinging the MP5/10 over his shoulder, he grabbed a section of rusted rebar lying amid the ruins of the half-collapsed shower block and went flat against the wall.

The bike came thundering around the corner of the blockhouse, a matte black Harley-Davidson Iron 883, its engine emitting a nasal, big-cat snarl. The rider—a Night Ranger from the Dakotas charter—had only a fraction of a second to process the flash of movement from the corner of his vision before Jack struck out with the iron rod. The length of rebar hit him across the chest, instantly dislodging the biker from his saddle and pitching him back over the rear wheel. Ribs shattered by the impact, the Night Ranger could only lie there and fight for breath.

The riderless bike wobbled and fell over, slewing to a halt in a spray of gravel. Jack sprinted to it, pitching the Harley back onto its wheels with a grunt of effort. He slipped easily into the saddle and gunned the throttle, bringing the motorcycle around toward the direction it had come. With the MP5/10 in his hand, Jack accelerated away, back down the narrow alley between the shower blocks. He shot out in front of the rest of the Night Ranger pack, spraying bullets in their direction as he slewed the bike away from the tank garage and the motor pool hangar.

The night was torn by more howling engines as the bikers turned the pursuit into a hunt, hurtling after Jack on his stolen mount, following him as he wove a slalom course around abandoned vehicles and potholed sections of the old base's wide streets. Fort Blake's derelict buildings echoed with the noise. Jack dared to throw a look over his shoulder as he pulled the submachine gun's trigger again. The weapon's breech locked open with a metallic snap as the last round in the magazine was expended, but the shots fired had made a mark. One of the bikes snapping at his heels abruptly twisted into a sideways skid, veering into a mud-choked ditch. Jack let the spent weapon drop on its sling again and hunched forward over the Harley's gas tank, cutting the air resistance as it pulled at his jacket.

The roadway ahead terminated in a T-junction. The footprint of the army base's ghost town roads was just three or four blocks square, laid out in a wide grid that doubled back on itself. For a moment, Jack wondered about cutting the head off the junction and blazing a path out across the tall grasses beyond—but the heavy Harley was no cross-country scrambler, and if he hit a hidden gulley out there, it would all be over.

Instead, waiting until the last possible second, he pushed into a leaning turn that followed a sharp race-line curve to the left, powering the bike through as the rear tire left black streaks on the crumbling asphalt. Guns barked behind him. Some of the riders were trying to get off a lucky shot in hopes of knocking him out of the saddle. Jack worked the handlebars, putting the bike through a sidewinder slide to throw off their aim.

"*Jack! Jack?*" It took him a long second before he realized that the faint voice he could hear was issuing out of the tactical radio still clipped to his belt. "*We're on the move*," he heard Chase say. "*Rolling out. You copy? Jack, do you copy me?*"

He couldn't risk letting go of the handlebars to toggle the radio and respond. Jack could only hope that Chase would be able to get the bus and the press-ganged workers away from the base before the bikers realized they had been blindsided.

• • •

"Holy crap!" Fang cried out as the little business jet screamed low over his head and turned in a wide, sharp bank before lining itself up with the middle of the highway. He blinked and grinned as he realized what was going to happen. "Well, lookit. This is gonna be interestin'."

The jet dropped toward the white line running down the middle of the road, the running lights on the wings and the undercarriage dazzling as it came nose-on. Fang heard the squealing of the tires hitting the asphalt and then the rolling thunder of the engines as they went into reverse. Wheel brakes screeched as the aircraft frantically bled off speed, shaking and shuddering as it bounced over a surface never designed for the relatively smooth ride a jet plane required.

Sitting atop his bike, it didn't occur to Fang to get out of the way, unlike some of the other Night Rangers who had come out here with him, past the outer limits of Deadline. They backed off, but he kept waiting, grinning at the jet as the distance between the aircraft's nose cone and the handlebars of his panhead grew less and less. After all, Fang had once faced down a brown bear and lived to talk about it. That was how he had gotten his nickname. He didn't see this as any different.

The biker could see the faces of the pilot and copilot clearly by the time the plane rolled to a halt no more than twenty feet from his idling motorcycle. He gave them a jaunty salute, which neither man returned. Fang chuckled to himself and got off, wandering to the side of the plane as the cabin door dropped open.

An angry-looking guy in a suit filled the doorway. "You're not Rydell."

"Naw," Fang admitted. "I'm the welcoming committee. You gotta be Special Agent Hadley, yeah?" He nodded at the plane. "Any landing you can walk away from is a good one, huh?" He gave a low whistle.

"Where is he?"

Fang gestured back in the direction of the town. "He's puttin' something together for ya."

Another man, young and serious, appeared behind Hadley. "Where are we?"

Fang spread his hands. "Welcome to Deadline!" He pointed out a car—a dusty Ford Contour that the MC kept around for the times when they needed a cage—and tossed the keys to Hadley. "Got ya some wheels for while you're visitin'. Y'all can leave your bird here and follow us." He wandered back to his bike and revved the motor, turning it around, aiming it back down the highway.

Around him, the first drops of rain started to fall from the sky.

He heard the other FBI agent asking a question. "What have you done, Hadley? What's going on?"

"I'm making use of available resources," he snapped. "Get the others. We're on the move."

18

The Night Rangers were still on him as Jack veered the stolen Harley-Davidson off the cracked roadway and down a narrower side street that threaded between a line of low, wide hangars. Sheer sheet-metal walls reared up on either side of him, capturing the howl of the bikes and reflecting it back. Off to one side, Jack could see the growing pillar of smoke rising from the burning drug factory and he used it as a landmark, orienting himself. There was little light here, nothing but the glow from his Harley's headlamp, nothing to warn him of a sinkhole ahead or a lethally broken stretch of asphalt until it was too late. One of the bikes pursuing him had already fallen to such a hazard, and Jack didn't want to go out the same way.

To his right he saw that one of the hangar doors was partly open, a tall and thin gap wide enough for two men abreast. At the last second, Jack jerked the handlebars and veered off the road and into the echoing space. He thought he heard a bullet clank off the doors but then he was through and roaring across the empty, warehouse-sized area.

He hoped that there would be another open door on

the far side, but immediately he saw he had been mistaken. Nothing but walls were visible in the spill from his headlight, and Jack knew he would have to act quickly. His miscalculation could see him trapped in here, and then the bikers would have him.

The Harley bounced over something and he glimpsed the corroded length of discarded chains snaking across the dusty concrete. Jack pumped the brakes and slowed down, leaning out of the saddle so he could snatch up a fat steel link and pull it to his chest. The chain rattled as he accelerated away again, and Jack switched off the bike's headlamp, plunging the view ahead into darkness.

Other bikes had come charging into the hangar after him and they lit the space with their own shifting illumination. Jack aimed the stolen Harley at his pursuers and set off like a missile, feeling the chain tug and clatter across the ground as it came with him.

Too late, the other riders saw him racing back toward them and tried to veer off; but Jack spun the rusted chain up and over his head like a lasso, throwing it with all his might toward his pursuers. He sped past, aiming for the open door, hearing the catastrophic crash of metal meeting concrete at high speed as bikes and riders went down behind him.

• • •

The bus thundered down the roadway, bouncing over every patch of rough asphalt, the sound of the laboring diesel engine a heavy droning beneath the fearful muttering and crying of the passengers. Chase put them out of his mind as he concentrated on keeping the big coach astride the center line, hoping that they wouldn't meet something coming the other way.

It was hard to steer, and turning the huge wheel to get it around the corners was an effort that made his shoulders ache. His bad hand slipped now and then, and he cursed, fighting to keep the vehicle from getting away from him.

The big windshield was marked with spiderweb impacts where the bikers at the gates had tried and failed to stop them. Chase blew through the motorcycles acting as a roadblock without pause, and there had been an ugly crunching sound as one shooter—too slow to get out of the way—vanished under the old Greyhound's front axle. Reflected on the inside of the fractured glass, Chase could see the people behind him packed tightly into the bus's cabin, far more than the vehicle was supposed to carry. The overloaded bus translated that weight into a rumbling, shaking ride, threatening to give out at any second.

Then ahead, he saw the black, slab-sided shadow of the deserted mega-mart building. *Almost there.* If they could make it to safety inside, they could figure something out, find a way to get everyone away from the predations of the outlaw bikers.

"Hold on!" he called, applying the brakes as the bus bounced across the road and came to a juddering halt in the overgrown parking lot. Chase stood up, raising his hands as dozens of faces turned his way, questions and demands coming at him all at once. "We're clear of the base," he told them. "You understand that? You're free."

Confusion and fear reflected back at him. It had been hard enough to convince these people to board the bus, and now they were hearing him without really believing what he was saying. They had no reason to trust him. After the lies that had brought these people to Deadline, Chase couldn't blame them.

"Listen," he began again, opening the doors. "There's another vehicle inside that building, I could use another driver . . . We can all get out together—"

Chase was halfway down the stairway when a figure

loomed out of the rainy darkness and grabbed a fistful of his jacket, pitching him forward and out onto the ground. Before he could react, a heavy steel-toed boot crashed into his gut and he curled up, the pain making him choke.

He heard screaming and shouting, and suddenly there were bright lights all around. Chase shielded his eyes, blinking furiously.

The same man he had seen leaving the derelict base a short while ago, the one who seemed to be the bikers' pack leader, emerged from behind a line of parked motorcycles. Framed by headlamps all blazing with sodium-white light, he came over to where Chase was laying, pushing his men aside to get a better look. "Which one are you?" he demanded, then dismissed his own question. "Ah. Doesn't matter. You ain't from Chicago. You're messing with my program, and that don't get to happen."

"You . . . must be Rydell," Chase managed.

That got him a cold smile. "This here is my kingdom, pal. My soldiers, my subjects, you dig? And you don't come in and start screwing with that." He looked around. "You actually thought you'd be able to get gone with those bitches from the 'Case? And these chumps?" He pointed at the terrified faces of the people crammed onto the bus. "Stupid. That's gonna cost you."

Rydell nodded at his men, and they all came in around Chase to take a shot at him.

• • •

Jack saw the floods of smoke churning from the burning tank garage and realized he had completed a full circuit around the edge of Fort Blake. As he raced on, he dared to look back and fired off a shot from his pistol. Despite everything, there were still riders on him, and he wondered if he would ever be able to shake them.

But in the next second, it didn't matter. Jack was barely past the burning remnants of the Night Rangers' illegal manufactory when the fire inside touched off a detonation that resonated like a bomb blast. He had no way of knowing what it was—perhaps some chemical drum superheated to a temperature beyond criticality—but this massive explosion was enough to blow out the metal doors and vents along all the bunker's sides, and bring the thick concrete roof caving inward.

A pressure wave knocked Jack off his bike and sent him and the motorcycle spinning in different directions. He crashed back down to earth and rolled, landing hard against an overgrown sandbank, the air sucked out of his lungs.

Burning debris was raining down all around him, and as Jack spun over, he caught sight of another bike, rider and all, sheathed in flame as the fireball caught them directly in its path. If the other bikers had been in the plume of killing heat, then they had suffered the same fate.

He staggered back to his feet, his head pounding, and found his mount lying on its side a few feet away, wheels turning. The frame was bent, and some of the fairing was ripped away, but the Harley was a tough machine and still roadworthy.

Searing, murderous, infernal heat beat at Jack as he pushed the bike forward, walking it until the engine caught and he scrambled back into the saddle. The scene around him resembled a snapshot of some war-torn battleground. He turned his back on it and rode on, leaving the fire to consume everything.

• • •

Kilner took the wheel of the beaten-up Ford, and at Hadley's insistence, he followed the bikers back along the arrow-straight highway toward the town.

Dell remained behind at the impromptu landing site, but Markinson had come with them, and now she sat in the backseat, checking her weapon and eyeing their outlaw escorts warily. "These guys are going to take us to Bauer and Edmunds?" Her misgivings were evident. She read the biker club's name off the back of one of their jackets. "Night Rangers MC. . . . Who the hell are they?"

"A means to an end," Hadley said. "I'm handling this."

Kilner wanted to say that, *no, it doesn't look like you're handling it at all*. He was becoming more concerned by the moment that Special Agent Hadley had lost all perspective on this assignment. Still, he held his tongue. Kilner was honestly uncertain of how the man would react if he challenged him further.

He expected to be led straight into the center of the small town, but before they could clear the outskirts of Deadline, the bikers made a turn and veered off toward a cluster of darkened structures. As they came closer, Kilner saw what looked like an abandoned warehouse and a gathering of more Night Rangers outside.

"Is that . . . a bus?" Markinson peered out the window. "There's a Greyhound bus out there. What is this?"

She was correct. Off to one side, a passenger coach was parked with a couple of bikers standing guard around it, and Kilner saw faces pressed up against the windows. But then they were stopping, and the rider with the tattoos who had greeted them was beckoning them out of the car.

"Stay here," Hadley ordered, and climbed out.

Kilner shot Markinson a look. "You heard him."

"He meant both of us," she replied.

"I know what he meant. Get up front, be ready to light out of here if anything goes wrong." Kilner exited the car and went after Hadley, putting his hand on the butt of his holstered gun as he went.

Hadley glared at him. "I said wait." Behind him, a

hard-faced biker was approaching. "That's a direct order!"

"Bureau policy. I'm your backup."

Hadley was going to say something else, but then from out in the distance to the west there was a low, rolling roar of detonation. Everyone tensed, and Kilner turned to see a churn of red-orange fire roll up into the air a few miles away.

"*What the hell?*" The biker behind Hadley put hateful venom into the words. "Stupid mother. . . ." He trailed off, then sucked in a breath through gritted teeth and pointed at the lead agent. "You see that, Mr. FBI? That's my money burning up out there! All because I am surrounded by idiots!" He glared at his men, and some of them backed away.

"Benjamin Rydell, I presume?" Hadley kept his voice level.

"Your timing is either real bad or real good, Mr. Special Agent Hadley," Rydell spat. "I warn you now, if *that* was you . . ." He stabbed a finger at the distant tower of fire. "Judges will have to make up new words for the crimes I will do to you and yours."

Hadley folded his arms, unimpressed by the warning. "I'll tell you what's happening here, Rydell. *Jack Bauer.* He's a walking disaster area. And I'm guessing your nasty little enterprises in this town, whatever they happen to be, have gotten in his way."

Rydell snorted with harsh laughter. "Is that some kinda threat?"

"No. It's a fact. He's a very dangerous man, like I told you on the phone. Are you only now just getting that?"

The outlaw biker's wolfish smirk faded. "You talked about a deal."

"That's right."

"I've given it some thought." Rydell nodded toward the darkened building ahead of them, the shell of a derelict big-box store. "Come see." He started walking, his men trailing around him.

Hadley made to follow, but Kilner grabbed his arm. "Wait," he said in a low voice that wouldn't carry. "What *deal*? You're not authorized for that! What did you promise this scumbag?"

"Information on the stalled investigation that St. Louis is following on the Night Rangers MC. Details of what phones are being tapped. Names of confidential informants. Basically, enough for Rydell to go dark and slip out before his entire drug ring gets broken up."

Kilner couldn't believe what he was hearing. "All that in return for, what? Bauer's life? Are you crazy?"

"Two things." Hadley leaned close. "One: what I *told* Rydell I would give him is not what he will *get*," growled the agent. "Two: if you come between me and my target, I will shoot you."

• • •

Chase blinked, his right eye gummed shut with sticky blood, and rolled onto his haunches. The bikers had dragged him inside the gutted mega-mart and dumped him near the stolen van from the strip club. As he watched, unable to intervene, the biker called Sticks had taken Laurel, Trish and the other girls and made them stand in a line.

He saw Laurel looking his way, her face pale and full of dread. "I'm sorry," he said, at a loss for any other words.

"It's not your fault," she told him. "Should have known we'd never get out of this place alive."

"Still time," Chase insisted.

"Shut up," Sticks barked. "Both of you! Gonna answer for what you did to Sammy, punk!"

Rydell walked in through the broken doorway, and

with him were two new arrivals who were decidedly *not* motorcycle gangers. He knew federal agents when he saw them, just from the cut of their clothes and the way that they behaved. But the fact that they were here, now, only filled him with an even greater dread.

"So," the biker was saying. "This ain't your boy Bauer?"

The taller of the two agents shook his head, a dark-faced man with a cold cast to his gaze. "Chase Edmunds." He said the name as a statement of fact, not like he was actually speaking to him. "You should have stayed dead."

"He had this on him, boss." Sticks offered something to Rydell, and belatedly Chase realized that it was his tactical radio, stripped off him along with his vest and his guns when the bikers had beaten him down.

"Well, now." Rydell toyed with the handheld. "Let's cut to the chase, then." He grinned at his own joke and walked across to the line of women, grabbing Laurel by the wrist, pulling her aside. He put the radio in her hand. "Go ahead, sweet britches. Talk to Mr. Bauer. Find out where he's at. Hold that radio up now, so we can all hear."

Laurel glanced toward Chase, taking a step toward him, then hesitating. "I . . . I don't know . . ."

Rydell walked over to Chase and crouched next to him. He drew a big Desert Eagle pistol from under his jacket and waved it in the woman's direction. "You ought to encourage her, pal. 'Cause with the day I'm having, I might just blow her pretty head off if she wastes my time."

"She's not part of this," said Chase.

"Oh, but she *is*," Rydell insisted. "You and her and your pal, look at all the shit you brought to my door tonight." He nodded toward the two agents. "The feds now? You killing my brothers, burning up my goods ain't enough?"

The other agent, the younger man, started forward, but the senior agent blocked his path and said something Chase didn't hear.

"I will kill her," said Rydell. "For starters."

Chase glared at the dark-skinned man. "You're just gonna let him do this?"

"If I were you . . ." The agent made no move to intervene. "I would do as he tells you."

When Chase looked away, he found Laurel staring right at him. He gave a reluctant nod.

Laurel swallowed a sob and held the radio to her mouth, squeezing the "talk" switch. "Jack? C-can you hear me?"

• • •

He halted the motorcycle in the lee of a shallow rise by the roadway and recovered the gear bag he had stowed there. Jack was reloading his M1911 pistol when he heard the woman's voice on the open channel, over the low hiss of rainfall.

"Laurel?" He glanced around, looking for any visible threats out in the grassland, and saw nothing. "Where are you?"

"With Chase . . . I . . ." Panic overwhelmed her. "They're here, Jack! They found us!"

He called out her name again, but the next voice he heard was an unfamiliar one. "Jack Bauer. That's you, right?"

"Who is this?"

"You been looking for me, Jack? You come into my town from outta nowhere and you start messing with my operation, you think you can get away with that?"

"Rydell." He frowned. The Night Rangers had been smarter than he had expected. "I've got some bad news for you." Jack glanced over his shoulder in the direction of the old military base. "Your operation is now a smoking hole in the ground. Most of your men are scattered or else they're dead."

There was a pause. "*Lemme ask you somethin'. Did I piss you off somehow? I mean, did I screw your sister or steal your bankroll? Help me out here, Jack. Tell me why you're running around with a grudge.*"

Jack glanced down at his watch. "It's what I do." The freight train was less than an hour away now. He didn't have time for any complications. "If you're smart, you'll leave town right now. By dawn federal agents will be swarming all over this place, and you'll have no way out."

Rydell gave a dry chuckle. "*Feds, huh? That's a worry. I tell you what, though. I got a better plan. It goes like this. I'm going to shoot you dead, and then I dust off and get back to work like you were never here.*"

"So come and get me."

"*Naw,*" Rydell drawled. "*I reckon I'll just start by putting a bullet through little blondie here. Unless you want to stop me.*" In the background, he heard Laurel cry out.

Jack tensed. "You'd kill an unarmed woman? You're that much of a coward?"

• • •

Rydell gave an exaggerated shrug and looked around the interior of the derelict building. "Jack, buddy . . ." He pitched his voice so it would be heard by the radio, but he was really performing for his audience. "You really think I give a shit about some skank we scooped up outta the gutter? You think I give a shit about *anyone* not a brother?" He chuckled. "I guess you don't think I'm a man of my word. So let me correct that." He turned and brought up the Desert Eagle, thumbing back the hammer.

Laurel cringed and held up her hands, as if by doing

so she could stop the bullet that was going to end her life.

Chase pulled together all the energy he still had and propelled himself up from the dirt in a sudden, headlong surge. He grabbed at Rydell and the two men came together in an ugly collision of blows, spinning and stumbling.

Clutching at the biker's arm with his good hand, Chase forced it away and there was a flat bark of discharge as the heavy pistol went off. The muzzle forced aside, the wild shot keened from a metal gantry overhead. He was face-to-face with the other man, struggling with him, clawing and punching.

Sticks and the handful of other Night Rangers had their guns drawn in seconds, but none of them were willing to risk a shot. Chase and Rydell were on each other with barely a hand's span between them—and in truth, it was likely the charter president would be angry if any brother member robbed him of the chance to kill this man himself.

Chase felt blows landing in his chest, his gut, and he tried to ignore them. He butted Rydell in the face and dropped a swing that slammed hard into the biker's throat, making him spit blood. They went around and around in a staggering, violent pirouette, like a brutal parody of two dancers.

Trapped between them was the massive frame of the Desert Eagle, the wedge-shaped muzzle yawing back and forth as each tried to keep it pointed toward the other man. Rydell shouted and pulled the trigger again, letting another thunderous shot blast a hole in the ceiling. Chase was so close, he flinched as the brass casing flicked out of the ejector port and the sting of exhaust gas raked his face. He clawed at the barrel of the gun, and his palm burned where the metal was hot from the discharge.

Slowly, inexorably, Rydell began to take control of the duel between them. Little by little, the man was pushing the Desert Eagle's muzzle toward Chase's chest.

"Just . . . die . . ." Rydell ground out the words.

Chase swung his burned hand and hit the biker with a backward blow that made Rydell's ears ring. In the split-second opening that gave him, he reflexively clutched at the pistol and fought to tear it from the other man's hands.

But he couldn't do it. His bad arm was alight with threads of fire coursing down the length of his nerves. His fingers were dull, twitching pieces of meat. He couldn't reach around the pistol grip, the trigger, couldn't grab the weapon. The broken, half-dead hand that had cursed his life and cost him so much now failed once again, in the moment when Chase Edmunds needed it most.

Rydell's expression shifted, as if he saw something in Chase, like an apex predator sensing the shadow of death falling over a prey animal. The biker's arm was locked around Chase's, his dirt-smeared and dark with complex tattoos, Chase's marked with the white web of long-healed sutures and surgical cuts.

A horrible, chilling terror settled on Chase as he saw what he would never be able to stop. *This wasn't how it was supposed to be! This wasn't right!* He had fought hard for every victory his life had tried to snatch away, and survived every knock back, every single loss. Suddenly he was remembering Kim's face, her smile and her bright eyes. He was thinking of Angela, of how much he loved her and how sorry he was that he had never been the father she had needed him to be.

Slowly, the blunt maw of the Desert Eagle tipped back and back until it was pressing point-blank into Chase's chest.

"*Bang,*" said Rydell, and he pulled the trigger.

• • •

"*Damn it!*" Jack roared into the radio as he heard the hollow shout of the gunshot. "You son of a bitch!"

An icy surge of cold prickled his skin and his breath choked in his throat. Jack gripped the radio, falling silent as the open channel crackled.

"*Your . . . friend . . .*" The voice was Laurel's, and she was sobbing. "*Oh god. Chase . . .*"

"What?" Her words hit him like a punch in the gut.

There was a rattling, scuffling sound as someone snatched the handset away from Laurel, and then he heard Rydell breathing hard. "*Jack . . . Change of plan. The girl's still breathin'. Your buddy, though? Not so much.*"

And then, as if it wasn't enough to leave him with that terrible prospect, Jack heard a gasping wheeze and he felt his legs give out beneath him. He sank down on the side of the road and listened to Chase Edmunds breathing his last.

"*I'm sorry . . .*" The voice was so faint, he couldn't be sure he really heard it. After, there was only silence.

In that moment, Jack Bauer felt a hateful sensation wash over him. Emotion seemed to drain from his body. The burning fury at the core of him was struck out, the fire doused—and all he felt was hollow inside.

Another. He looked down at his smoke-blackened hands and thought about the blood on them. *Another friend gone.* The unseen scars, buried in his soul, one for each life that had been lost over the years gone by.

Jack took a shuddering breath, and at the edges of his perception he could feel pity and sorrow crowding in, countless ghosts at his shoulders threatening to drown him in a torrent of grief.

"No." He surged back to his feet, and the emptiness within went away as quickly as it had come. Beneath that emotion was something else, as old and familiar as anything Jack had ever known.

Anger. Hard-edged and diamond-sharp, it filled him anew.

Rydell's voice was issuing out of the radio. "*I know you're still listening! Enough of this shit. You got a butcher's bill to pay, man. You don't give yourself up in ten minutes, I shoot two of the women. Ten minutes after that, three more.*" He bellowed into the microphone. "*You hear that? Your boy was just the first! I will kill my way through every single one of these trailer trash fools until you come to me!*"

Jack let the radio drop and walked back in silence to the idling Harley.

19

"You know what the hell is going on?" Marshall glowered at Fang, his hands on his hips.

"Payback," said the other man. The two of them stood in front of the old Greyhound bus's door, splitting their attention between the shouting they could hear from inside the derelict mega-mart and the fearful passengers on the motor coach. Fang paused. For a moment, he thought he heard the sound of a bike engine on the wind.

"Sounds like Rydell is kicking off in there." Marshall was still talking, rubbing his chin. "Man, if this thing is all going south, maybe it's time to think about *options* . . ."

"What you mean by that?" Fang shot him a steely glare, then turned away. The dusty Ford parked across the way caught his eye, and he stared at the woman fed in the driver's seat. She looked steadily back, as if she were daring him to do something.

"I mean, who's the guy that's been out all over scaring up these chumps to work making the ice, huh?" Marshall nodded toward the bus. "*Me*. All of them know my face. I've been *seen*, Fang. I got a lot to lose if this whole scam goes wrong!"

The other biker prodded him in the chest with a thick finger. "You forget who you are, Marsh? You spend too long walking around without your cut on your shoulders, you start thinking like a civilian. The MC is the family, bro. Don't lose sight of that."

Marshall blew out a breath. "Yeah. Yeah, I know it. But, shit, first the 'Case got set alight and now the works too, I mean did we just wake up the ghost of all bad luck or what?"

"Something like that," said a voice.

From around the front end of the parked bus came the guy with the short hair and the craggy face that Fang had glimpsed in the strip club, the one that Sticks said had killed poor Sammy and set the fire.

Marshall spun, but his reflexes had become dull in his time out of the saddle, and the man came at him in a blur of motion. He had a pistol in one hand and he used the weapon like a cudgel to crack Marshall across the temple and send him sprawling down into the weeds.

Fang was faster, pulling a snub-nosed Colt .38 revolver from across his belly, but the weapon had barely cleared his belt loop before he found himself staring into the muzzle of an M1911 semiautomatic aimed squarely at his nose.

• • •

"Drop the piece," said Jack, and Fang reluctantly obeyed, letting the gun fall to the ground at his feet. Above him, the biker saw some of the captives on the bus daring to watch the unfolding fight from their windows.

But Marshall wasn't out for the count just yet. The other man shook off Jack's blow and swayed back to his feet, ignoring the deep gash across his head and the streamers of blood washing down his cheek. He went on the offensive, woodenly leading into an attack, his hands coming up like claws.

Glimpsing the motion from the corner of his eye, Jack spun to meet Marshall's clumsy assault, even as Fang went down, grabbing for the gun he had just dropped. Jack blocked Marshall midmotion and wrenched his arm around, acting on pure kill-or-be-killed instinct. Using Marshall's weight against him, Jack caught the man around the throat and twisted, snapping his neck with a sickening crack.

Marshall fell a second and final time. Turning, the heavy bag slung over his shoulder dragging on his back, Jack saw Fang's fingers close around the .38's trigger and again he reacted without conscious thought. Dropping into a deadfall, he landed on the biker before he could rise and pressed his knee across Fang's throat, choking the life from him. Fang took longer to die than Marshall had, but the result was the same. Both kills were nearly silent, meaning that Rydell and the rest of his men remained unaware of what had just happened.

Jack boarded the bus in three quick steps and found the passengers staring at him in shocked silence. To them, he had to resemble a blackened, bloody wraith. As one, they recoiled from him as he advanced. "Where are the others?" he demanded.

"In-inside!" said a florid-faced man. "Please, don't hurt us!"

"Stay out of sight," Jack ordered, and turned away, dropping back down to the ground.

"Bauer." A woman in a dark, severe pantsuit was waiting for him with a gun cocked and aimed at his head. She looked stern and the worse for wear, with the steely gaze of a career law officer. "Hands up."

He didn't comply, studying her instead. "I know you," he began. "I saw you in New York. With Hadley." Jack's lip twisted in a humorless smirk. "I was wondering when you'd show up."

"Agent Markinson, FBI," she explained, pulling out her handcuffs. "And you are under arrest."

Jack shot a look at the mega-mart. "I don't have time to waste with you." His gaze settled on the parked Ford Contour sitting nearby. "I'm gonna need that car."

"You're not walking away, Bauer!" she snapped.

"If you put those on me, you think I'll last more than ten seconds before Rydell blows my brains out?" He took a step toward her. "You heard the shots. He just killed my friend in cold blood! Did Hadley even try to stop him?"

The barrel of Markinson's gun drooped slightly, slipping along with her rigid expression. "I have my orders . . ."

"What do your orders say about a busload of innocent people forced to work as slave labor in a drug factory?" Jack jerked a thumb at the vehicle behind him. "You want to do some good? *Help them.* Get these people out of here. Because I'm betting that Agent Hadley doesn't give a damn about them, or you, or anything else but seeing me dead."

He saw the change in her face, the slow acceptance. "Hadley's gone off the reservation," Markinson admitted, lowering her weapon. "Way off."

"Don't make the same mistake," Jack told her, and made for the car, unlimbering his bag as he went.

• • •

Rydell shot Sticks a look. "How long is that?"

"Two minutes more and then he's up," said the other biker.

Rydell nodded. "Ain't looking good for you, Laurel, is it?" He leered at her, and then turned his attention to the older woman by her side. "You neither, Cherry. Better make peace with your lord. Tick tock."

His gaze met that of the younger FBI agent who had rolled up with Hadley. Rydell knew the look he got from the guy, he knew it well. Disgust and hatred, he'd seen it a hundred times on the faces of men who thought they were better than him. He opened his hands, challenging the agent to respond.

He did so. "This animal killed Edmunds right in front of us!" said the agent to Hadley. "Are we going to ignore that?"

"Edmunds was a murder suspect and a fugitive, Kilner." Hadley cocked his head. "And it looked like self-defense to me."

"And two innocent women?" The younger guy was reaching for his sidearm. "What's that going to be?"

"No, no." Rydell made a gesture, and suddenly the handful of other Night Rangers standing around were all lazily aiming their guns in Agent Kilner's general direction. He froze. "You don't want to get in the middle of this, son," Rydell went on "See, it's just like the bad old days out here in Deadline, yeah? *Rough justice,* of a sort. If your pal Bauer don't show his face, then it's his fault these ladies will be taking a dirt nap. All he's gotta do is surrender."

"He'll be here," said Hadley.

"Sixty seconds . . ." began Sticks, but then he trailed off as an engine growled outside the building, and tires squealed on cracked concrete. "The car . . . Rydell, it's moving . . ."

The Ford Contour that the MC had provided to Hadley's team came to life, and without warning it turned in a tight circle to lurch around and face the gaping, broken-down doors that led through to the derelict building's interior. Lights on high beam, the car shot forward at full throttle, making straight for the gap.

"What the hell is that woman doin'?" cried Sticks.

"It's Bauer, you moron!" Rydell shouted. "Shoot the son of a bitch!" The Night Rangers took aim and started to fire as the Ford bounded over the weed-strewn parking lot, closing with each passing second. Rydell jabbed a finger at Hadley and Kilner. "Stay the hell outta my way unless you wanna take a hit!" He left the FBI agents to take cover along with the women from the van, and took up a position where he could fire at the car as it approached.

Rydell's heavy handgun blasted fist-sized holes in the radiator grille and the windshield, but he couldn't see anything inside the oncoming vehicle. Plumes of thick white smoke rolled out of the Contour's open windows, as if the inside of the car was on fire—except there were no flames . . .

Gunshots sparked off the car's hood and a lucky hit blew out the right front tire, but it wasn't enough to stop it. Rydell threw himself aside as the vehicle crashed in through the open doors, ripping away part of the frame as it scraped the walls and skidded on the damp concrete floor.

Still belching smoke, the Contour came to a crashing halt as it struck an iron roof support with such force that the whole prefabricated building seemed to shake. The choking white haze rolled out through the car's broken windows, and Rydell knew that Jack Bauer had never been in the vehicle in the first place. He must have jammed it into drive, tossed a dozen smoke grenades into the back-seat and thrown it at them.

Which meant . . .

Rydell spun around, back toward the wrecked door-way as a bunch of slim black cylinders came skidding in across the floor. He didn't have time to warn anyone else; instead he buried his face in the crook of his elbow and turned away as the flashbangs went off in crackling succession, temporarily deafening and blinding anyone within range.

• • •

Gaining access to the derelict building had been easy enough. These were common criminals, after all, not the kind of trained, disciplined threats that the contractor was used to dealing with.

Arriving secretly in Deadline and finding the place in chaos had been a fortunate situation. It made the assignment all the more easy to execute. While these motorbike thugs had been distracted by the havoc that was being wrought on their nasty little empire, the contractor had simply walked through their lines. Two outrider guards were killed in the process, both shot at close range with a silenced Walther P99 semiautomatic. Their bodies were lying out in a culvert a few hundred meters from the shell of the mega-mart, and it was likely they would not be found until they started to rot.

Climbing up to the apex of the roof without drawing attention had been challenging. At first, there had only been the refugee women there with the van, but soon after, the arrival of a group of the bikers and their leader had complicated matters. However, the contractor was nothing if not adaptable, and after finding an adequate position for a firing nest, it was a small matter of unlimbering the component parts of a Nemesis Arms sniper rifle from a backpack and assembling the gun in place.

The skeletal weapon had a bulky thermal-optical sight that cut through the haze from the smoke grenades, making every human form below appear as a white phantom. Brighter blinks of light showed where guns were firing, muzzle flashes flaring in poorly controlled bursts.

The view through the sight moved back and forth, briefly passing over a lone figure that came in through the smashed doorway. A man, hunched low around the shape of a submachine gun.

. . .

Jack slipped into the derelict shopping mart with the MP5/10 rock-steady to his shoulder, and he proceeded to pick out his targets. He found a half dozen of the Night Ranger bikers still disoriented by the distraction grenades, firing blind or staggering toward cover. Methodically, he took them out of the equation.

Using calculated three-round bursts from the SMG, he aimed for headshots on his targets, putting them down before they could gather their wits and offer up any kind of adequate defense. Jack let his thoughts drop briefly into a feral, hunter's mind-set where there were only targets, only enemies to be dispatched with clinical, cold-eyed detachment. In this moment, he was a soldier again, and he knew this kind of war.

A biker with a heavy SPAS-12 shotgun dodged out of his arc of fire and tried to draw a bead on him, but Jack had his range and shot him as he rose up from behind a dust-caked display rack. He fell into cover behind a thick concrete stanchion and swept the space around him, finding more targets and ending them before they could combine their forces to engage en masse.

Jack's eyeline crossed the parked van and he met Laurel's gaze, the young woman down low near the wheel well. She was shocked and relieved all at once at the sight of him, but he could see she understood that the danger was still far from over. Then Laurel turned away, a flash of guilt on her face, and Jack followed her look.

Chase was nearby, sprawled on his back, his sightless eyes open and staring up into the dimness. An ugly red halo surrounded his head and neck, and Jack felt his moment of disconnection fall away as he saw his former partner's body lying where it had fallen. The anger that had powered Jack through so many confrontations surged again, the raw need for vengeance running through him like octane fuel.

"Rydell!" he snarled. "I'm coming for you!"

• • •

The biker heard Bauer shout his name and he snorted with laughter. If he was going to call him out like this was some Old West showdown, then Rydell was more than happy to oblige. It didn't cross his mind that his men were falling all around him, that perhaps Jack Bauer was a kind of opponent that he had never faced before. That wasn't important to him. Sticks was bleeding out his last where the man had gutshot him at close range, and Rydell didn't think to consider that. It was beyond him to wonder how many of the Night Rangers had fallen in the chaos of the past few hours. *He* was all the mattered, *he* was the club, the last of the original founders and the mind and will at the heart of it all.

In that moment, Rydell didn't care if it all came down around him, if every dirty cent, every bloodstained dollar the MC had made went up in smoke. All he wanted was Bauer dead, right here, *right now*.

Shouting his fury, Rydell walked out with the big Desert Eagle raised high and started firing, releasing shot after heavy-caliber shot toward the pillar where Bauer was hiding. Chunks of masonry blew away into fragments and dust, the thunder of the hand cannon booming back across the echoing interior of the derelict building.

Bauer broke away and sprinted, shooting from the hip as he powered toward a heap of junked chest freezers. Rydell felt the burning agony of a bullet as it creased the meat of his thigh, ripping open a long, bloody furrow, but he kept on firing, and one round finally found its mark.

A .50-caliber round hit Bauer square in the chest and blew him back off his legs with the shock of it. Rydell watched him go down in a crumpled heap.

But not dead. *Not yet.* Rydell advanced, limping on his injured leg, ignoring the blood soaking through the denim of his jeans. He was going to finish this.

• • •

The transition from running to being flat on his back seemed to happen instantly. Jack felt the impact in his torso like the kick from a bull, and now as he tried to right himself, pain erupted across his chest in a wash of fire. His lungs were filled with knives as he struggled to take a breath, tasting iron in his mouth. The MP5/10 was gone.

Digging deep, Jack found the energy to roll onto his side. He could smell the hot odor of burned plastic from the bulletproof vest under his jacket, where the kinetic energy of the big bullet had been translated into heat as it flattened itself against the armor.

Rydell was stalking toward him, leaving a trail of crimson as he crossed the floor. The biker's allies were either dead or dying. It was just the two of them now.

"Shoulda stayed out of my business, asshole!" shouted Rydell, raising the Desert Eagle.

Through the pain, Jack couldn't manage an answer. His fingers snaked around the grip of the semiautomatic in his belt and he let the gun speak for him instead. Before Rydell could react, Jack fired low from where he lay half-prone, and struck the other man with two shots that tore through his shin bones.

Rydell bellowed in pain and buckled, coming down hard against the concrete floor. He stopped himself from falling all the way, jamming the Desert Eagle into the ground as a prop to support his weight.

Another man might have given up and let himself drop, but the biker didn't have it in him to quit, even if there was no other option. Rydell spat hate at Jack and lurched back, swinging his arm up to let off the last round in his magazine.

Jack fired again before Rydell's finger could tighten on the trigger. The single shot went through the middle of the biker's jawbone and blasted a mess of dark fluids out across the blood-streaked floor. Rydell's body sagged under its own weight and fell forward.

• • •

It took an age for Jack to get back to his feet, and with every action aching, every move sending jolts of pain all through him, he reached up and pulled at the tabs holding the heavy armor across his chest. The constricting bulletproof vest fell from his shoulders and he felt like he could breathe again, even though it was still an effort to suck in air without flinching from the pain. He looked up, his gaze crossing the dark rafters overhead, then away.

"Jack . . ." called a voice. He ignored it.

Holstering his pistol, Jack limped toward the van, halting just short of it to drop into a crouch next to Chase's body. A turbulent mix of emotions swelled up inside him as he reached for the dead man. Gently, he brushed his fingers over his friend's face and closed his eyes.

"I'm sorry," he managed, the words coming out low and broken. *I never wanted this for him.* Jack's sorrow echoed in his thoughts. *I needed his help and he never questioned it.*

And look what it cost him. Nina's ghost was there once more, and if he closed his eyes, Jack knew he would see her standing there, silently accusing him. *More death, more revenge . . . Is it ever going to be enough?*

What happens when you have no one left, Jack?

"Jack, watch out!" Belatedly, he realized Laurel was calling out his name.

"Bauer!" A shadow fell over him and he looked up into Hadley's eyes. The FBI agent had his weapon drawn and aimed at his head.

• • •

With the melee over, the mess of the gunfight was no longer an issue, and the contractor could concentrate on the endgame. There had been a moment when it seemed as if the biker would make the assignment a moot issue, but Bauer had dealt with the criminal in short order. Even wounded, he was still a lethal adversary, and never one to take lightly.

The face behind the sniper scope split in a smile. Experience had proved that point on more than one occasion. Slowly, so as to move in total silence and ensure no one below was alerted, the contractor eased up the handle and opened the rifle's well-oiled bolt, revealing an empty chamber. Gloved fingers felt for and retrieved a single hand-loaded .308 Winchester cartridge from a vest pocket. Like every round the contractor fired, this one had been prepared individually—bullet head, powder, case and primer, all made ready to the exacting standards of a professional killer.

The cartridge dropped into the chamber and the bolt was locked. Leaning into the rifle, the contractor's index finger settled lightly on the knurled trigger. A breath was taken, half-released, held.

• • •

Jack rose slowly to his feet, holding his hands out to his sides. "You get what you came for?" he asked.

"How are you still breathing?" Hadley asked, his eyes narrowing. "What gives you the *right* to survive, Bauer? Good men perish all around you, but you sail on, untouched."

Jack's gaze dropped. "Not a day goes by that I don't ask myself that question."

"Did you kill Jason Pillar?" spat the agent. "Did you make it happen?" He didn't wait for a reply, and Jack knew that no matter what answer he gave, it would be the wrong one. "I know about you and what you did to Charles Logan! I know exactly what you are, Bauer! This country is on the verge of war because of what you have done! Men like you, you're not fit to walk the streets with normal people. You're a *weapon*. A menace." He shook his head. "Terrorists, criminals like these bottom-feeders . . ." Hadley indicated the corpses of the bikers. "You're more of a risk to this country than any of them!"

"He saved our lives . . ." managed Trish, hanging back with Laurel and the others. "He came back for us."

"Get out of here," Hadley warned them. "*Go!*" His shout was enough to make them run for the doors, but Laurel remained, frozen to the spot and unable to look away.

Jack held up his hands, wrist to wrist. "Are you going to arrest me, Agent Hadley? That is what you're here for, right?"

Hadley snarled and took aim, pointing the muzzle of his gun at Jack's forehead. "It's too late for that. Some-body has to put an end to you."

"Hadley, stop!" Behind him, Kilner drew his own weapon. "I can't let you do this. Stand down, now!"

"He won't," Jack told the other agent. "He can't go back with me alive to talk. Dead, he gets to make up whatever the hell story he wants. Isn't that right?" He let his hands drop. "So do it, then. Shoot me." Jack made a pistol-to-the-head gesture with his fingers. "Put me out of your misery."

• • •

What happened next was so fast, when he looked back on it over the days that followed, Kilner would find it hard to break it down into individual moments.

Bauer turned his back and took a step, as if he was going to gather up the body of his friend, Edmunds.

Hadley shouted for him to turn around, and the senior agent's last fraction of reserve broke.

Kilner surged forward and grabbed Hadley's arm, pulling him aside, struggling to stop the man before he could cross a line there would be no coming back from.

And then they all heard the crash of a single gunshot, from high up in the rafters of the tumbledown building. They saw Bauer twist sharply, jerked around like a marionette, and then collapse against the side of the van. A bloom of fresh, bright blood grew on his chest. The woman, Laurel, screamed.

Shocked rigid, Kilner watched the light go out in Bauer's eyes as he crashed to the ground. "Shooter!" he shouted, aiming out into the shadows. Had they missed one of the Night Rangers hiding in the darkness, waiting for the opportunity to open up on them all?

But a second shot did not follow the first, and then there was a hissing sound as a black cable descended from above them. Laurel ran to Jack's fallen body, and as Kilner watched, a figure in tactical gear came down the cable with almost balletic ease, the spindly form of a sniper rifle across their back.

He knew the shooter was a woman before the hood fell back from her head; the figure was too lithe and balanced for a male. Kilner saw a pale, hawkish face framed by short black hair. In one hand she held a silenced P99 pistol, and with the other she drew the sniper rifle around to aim it from the hip.

"Get away from him," she told Laurel. The accent was American, but Kilner couldn't be certain if it was learned or natural. The inflection seemed off. "You're not on my list, but that will change if you get in my way. Anyone moves, they die." Hadley shifted and she pointed the pistol at him. "Was I unclear?"

"Who are you?" Hadley spat. "You shot him . . ."

"Call me Mandy. That's as good a name as any. And yes, I did just kill Jack Bauer." She moved to the fallen man and gave him a once-over. "Isn't that what you wanted?"

Kilner hesitated, aware that the woman had the rifle trained on him. "You're not one of Rydell's people . . ."

She smiled thinly. "No. I'm a little out of their price range." She looked at Laurel. "You. Pick up his body and put it in the back of the van."

Warily, the woman did as she was told, dragging Bauer up. Tears streaked her face. "You bitch."

"I've heard that alias before," Hadley said quietly. "The Heller kidnapping. The Palmer assassination. You're wanted in connection with both those crimes. You're a contract killer."

"Still talking about those, huh?" Mandy pursed her lips. "It's just business, understand? Don't interfere and you won't get hurt."

And now it came to Kilner in a rush. "At the field office . . . there was chatter from the Secret Service about the Russians having their own beef with Jack . . . Did they send you?"

"Does it matter?" Mandy walked around to the front of the van and tossed the rifle inside. "You wanted Bauer gone . . . he's gone." She opened the driver's-side door. "My employers want proof, though. Don't do anything as stupid as trying to follow me." The van's engine rattled into life, and the vehicle slewed around before bouncing out through the wrecked doors and into the rainy night.

Hadley jogged after it, falling short as Kilner came up beside him. Markinson came running. "Is it over?" she asked. "I saw Bauer . . ."

"It's over now." Kilner's jaw hardened and he holstered his gun, reaching instead for his handcuffs. He grabbed Hadley's wrist before the other agent could react, and hooked the metal loop around it. "Thomas Hadley," he said, his tone firm. "I'm relieving you of operational command of this assignment. You're under arrest pending a full investigation into your actions tonight."

"You can't . . ." Hadley's denial seemed weak; it was as if all the man's energy had suddenly been drained from him. *He's lost,* Kilner thought, *and he knows it.*

"You're done," said Kilner. "Markinson, take his badge and his sidearm."

The woman nodded and disarmed Hadley. "Shit. What a mess."

Kilner looked back and saw Laurel and the other women gathered at the door of the bus. Their expressions were a mix of grief and elation, but there was hope there too, for the first time.

"Yeah," he agreed.

Out beyond the Deadline town limits, the railroad came off a wide, long curve into the beginning of a straight-away that fell like an arrow across the countryside. It vanished into the western horizon, lost in the low clouds and the sheeting rain that was now coming down hard and constant.

The rails dropped through a cutting, slicing their way through a low rise. A skinny metal bridge made of dull iron, big enough to carry a cluster of power cables over the line but little else, glittered wetly in the night as the van's headlights caught it.

Mandy brought the vehicle to a skidding halt on the dirt track road that paralleled the rails and turned to look over her shoulder. Bauer lay there in the back of the van, his face pale and lifeless, his shirt a wet, blood-sodden mess.

How many people wanted this man dead? The question played on her mind. Some said you could measure the caliber of a person by the number of enemies they had, and if that was true, then Jack Bauer's worth had to be high indeed. The Serbians, the Chinese, the Russians, the cartels in South America, who knew how many different radical extremist groups both here in the West and in the Middle East . . . They all prayed for his ending, for revenge on him. And now, she could give them exactly what they wanted.

Mandy pulled back the cuff of her glove and looked down at her wristwatch, seeing the glowing green numerals there. Miles distant but coming closer, the distant moan of a train horn sounded. She scrambled out of the van and recovered a large waterproof kit bag she had secreted earlier at the foot of the cable bridge's main support. The trail bike Mandy had used to get here was still where she had left it, hidden under a few loose branches.

She took the bag back to the van, hauled open the cargo door, and dumped it on the deck. Mandy fished a TerreStar satellite smartphone from among the gear inside and set about taking photographs of Bauer. She got shots of his face, his chest. The white blaze of the phone's camera flash lit up the darkness.

Selecting the best images, she tapped a number into the device and hit the "send" key. The phone gave a melodic chime, and with that, it was done. Mandy looked at her watch again. Ten minutes, give or take, and her fee would materialize in the Cayman Islands trust account.

She took a small black plastic case from the bag and opened the lid. Puffs of dry-ice vapor billowed out. Inside, a preloaded jet syringe sat on a cooler cradle, and she picked up the device, feeling the chill of it through her leather gloves. Mandy weighed the injector in her hand, considering the import of what it represented.

It would be easy to *wait*. Time had almost run out. She could just stand here and do nothing.

The reduced-velocity bullet Mandy shot into Bauer's chest had penetrated the upper layers of his flesh, but did not enter his body cavity or do any serious organ damage. The tiny measure of synthetic tetrodotoxin that had been contained in the bullet head was just enough to simulate the appearance of death. Cultured from puffer fish venom, the TTX neurotoxin analogue could kill instantly with a large enough dose . . . but even a small amount would be fatal if it was left to work unchecked. The compound in the injector was capable of neutralizing the compound. If she *wanted* it to.

For the second time that night, Mandy held Jack Bauer's life in her hands. She liked the feel of it.

But then she smiled to herself, and pressed the syringe to his carotid artery. It hissed like a snake, discharging its drug load into his bloodstream.

For long seconds, Bauer didn't move, and Mandy wondered if her timing had been off, but then he was suddenly twitching, coughing, his arms and legs curling inward as pain wracked his body. He rolled over and vomited up thin, watery bile, gasping for air.

"Welcome back, Jack." Mandy replaced the injector back in the case and started gathering up her gear.

"Where . . . ?" he managed.

"Outside Deadline," she explained. "Exactly where you wanted."

"Good." Color began to return to his face, and Mandy watched him systematically check himself over. He came upon the shallow wound in his chest where the frangible bullet had struck and shot her a look.

Mandy handed him a small first-aid kit. "You said there would be two of you. What happened to the other man?"

Jack looked away, wincing as he cleaned the wound and patched the fresh injury. "Chase . . . He didn't make it."

She picked up her rifle and strapped it to side of the gear bag. "The fee remains the same."

"You'll get your money," he grated.

"I know I will." Mandy smiled. "Because you're a man of your word, Jack. That's why I'm here." She hefted the bag and stepped away. "I've got to say, though . . . you're the last person I ever thought would hire me for a job."

Bauer gave a weary nod. "I'm low on friends right now. You were the smart choice." He drew his gun and checked it. "But don't think that makes us allies. You're an assassin, a mercenary, and if I had my way, you'd be behind bars paying for your crimes."

She cocked her head. "You wouldn't have gotten to Habib Marwan if it wasn't for me. You haven't forgotten that, have you, Jack? I helped CTU stop a nuclear detonation." Mandy smirked. "The president pardoned me. I guess it's too much to expect that you could forgive me as well."

"You'd have let Marwan's plan go ahead if we hadn't caught you, if it was to your advantage. Don't pretend you gave him up out of any kind of conscience." Unsteadily, Jack got to his feet and climbed out of the van.

"True enough." She shrugged. "As much fun as it is to talk about old times, this is still a business transaction." Mandy offered him the smartphone. "I did what you asked. I killed you in front of a handful of witnesses, agents of the FBI, even. You're a dead man again, Jack, as requested. Now pay up."

He made no move. "The Russians gave you the same job, didn't they? When did the SVR contact you? Was it before or after I called you from the diner?"

Her smile returned. "Still as sharp as ever, aren't you?" Mandy nodded. "You're right. They knew I was on the East Coast. They knew you and I had history. I took the assignment. Their money is as good as yours . . ." She eyed him. "Although I'm guessing that whatever secret bug-out fund you're using doesn't go as deep as Moscow's cash reserves do. After all, you're just one guy."

"Is that your play?" He still had his pistol in his hand. "I pay you to pull me out from under, then you kill me anyway and take the bounty from the Russians as well."

When Mandy turned back she had her Walther drawn. "Jack." She said his name in a chiding tone. "I've *already* claimed the price they put on your head." She held up the phone, showing the photos of his "corpse." "So let's behave like professionals here. I already killed you once tonight. You want me to make it twice?"

Jack's gun didn't waver. "Why were you on the East Coast?"

The question caught her off guard. "What?"

He pulled back the hammer on the pistol. "Were you in New York?"

She saw where his reasoning was going and shook her head. "If you're asking if I had anything to do with the plot against Omar Hassan, the answer is *no*." She shook her head. "I turned down that particular job. Too many variables."

The train horn hooted again, much closer now.

At length, Jack lowered his weapon. "Our ride's here."

"*Our* ride?" she echoed.

He nodded, moving to a service ladder that ran up the side of the cable bridge. "You want your money? You'll get it when I'm on that train and not before."

• • •

The Union Pacific Blue Arrow high-speed freight run out of Chicago, bound for the Port of Los Angeles, had lost a little time. Forced to drop below its normal cruising pace as it entered the great turn that bisected the map of the county like an iron bow, the procession of cargo wagons, flatbeds and double-stacked car carriers was almost half a mile long from the dual engines at the head to the pair of pusher power units at the rear.

As the Blue Arrow's lead locomotive finally cleared the outer edge of the turn and settled onto the start of the long straightaway before it, automated systems began to apply more power to the bogies to make up the time. A slow, inexorable climb up to full speed began, and from here the train would be racing the sunrise at its back all the way to the West Coast.

The crewmen in the cab were paying attention to the computer-controlled dashboard, as the lead engine rumbled under the cable bridge that was all that marked the passage past the township of Deadline. They didn't see the two figures hunched low on the middle of the open-framed metal arch.

Blocky box cars full of freight streamed past beneath the bridge, followed by flatbeds where the massive iron drums of huge electrical motors had been lashed down. Beyond them, there were container wagons, more flatbeds but these were filled by the familiar steel bricks of rectangular cargo units. With their long, flat upper surfaces, they were the best place to board the moving train. Waiting too long would bring the automobile carriers at the rear under the bridge, and attempting to drop onto their irregularly shaped gantries would be too risky.

• • •

Jack took a last look over his shoulder to be certain of where he would land, then he leapt forward, off the cable bridge, throwing himself in the same direction as the moving train. He was still dizzy and nauseous from the effects of the tetrodotoxin dose in his system, but there was no time to wait for that to wear off.

He felt the air rushing around him, the thin rain against his face, and the drop seemed to take forever. The gap from the cable bridge to the top of the moving wagon was less than three feet, but it could have been a mile for all the time it took to cross it.

Then his feet hit the roof of the metal container and he stumbled forward, buffeted by wind, throwing out his hands. Jack went down and let it happen, spreading his weight so he wouldn't trip and roll over the side. If he fell, he would be dashed to the ground racing past below, or worse, dragged under the bogies and crushed.

He heard a pair of clattering impacts behind him; first, as Mandy tossed her gear bag in his wake, and then as she followed it down. The mercenary made it look easy, dropping into a cat-fall without ever losing her balance.

Jack rose into a crouch and looked forward along the length of the train. In the distance, he could see the lights of the twin locomotives, but there was no sign that anyone up there had detected the arrival of the stowaways. He waited a moment to be sure, then started back down along the car. The rocking motion of the train took some getting used to, and Jack advanced in a zigzag pattern, letting the roll and shift of the container beneath his feet govern the speed of his advance.

Mandy pulled her gear bag to her as he approached, keeping her head down. "What now?" she shouted, fighting to be heard over the howl of the wind.

He pointed forward, indicating the nearest of the automobile carriers. "That way."

Slow and sure-footed, they advanced along the moving train until they came to the end of the container car, and one by one Jack and Mandy dropped to the floor of the flatbed. The thin rain and the wind noise lessened in the lee of the container, and Jack paused to take a breath. He looked out across the landscape flashing past beside them. It was a featureless blur that seemed to go on into infinity. *Dark territory,* he thought to himself.

The vehicles on the lower deck of the closest car carrier were all well-appointed Volkswagen MPV minivans, and Mandy made short work of the lock on the nearest one, hauling open the sliding side door to gain entry. Jack followed her inside and closed it behind him.

"Not exactly a private cabin, but close enough," she

muttered. The gear bag dropped to the floor between the seats and she worked at her windblown hair, pushing it into some semblance of order. "Level with me, Jack," Mandy asked, leaning back. "Do you actually have a plan of action, or are you just going to keep on running until you hit a brick wall?"

"It's not your concern," he retorted.

"I beg to differ. When there are people like you out in the world, I like to know where they're at. So I can be somewhere else. Did you really believe anyone would think you're heading to Hong Kong?"

"When I called you, why did you answer?" He held her gaze. "Why not just give me up, then and there? It would have been an easy payday."

"Call it nostalgia. I'm not all about the money," she demurred. Then that cunning smile came back. "Actually, that's a lie." Mandy drew out her smartphone and worked at the keypad. "And speaking of which . . . I need the code to get the balance of your payment from escrow. So let's finish this, yes?"

He gave a nod. "I got a password: *lifesucks,* one word."

Her smile grew into a grin as she entered the text string. "That's so *you.*" After a few moments, the phone gave off a chime and Mandy nodded. "Transfer complete. A pleasure doing business with you."

"Can't say the same," Jack replied, helping himself to a bottle of water from her bag. He guzzled it down in one long pull, and then took a shuddering breath. When he looked up, he saw that Mandy's sly expression had hardened into something else: annoyance. She stabbed at the phone's tiny keypad, eyes narrowing. "What's wrong?"

"The money," Mandy said quietly. "It's not here."

Jack's hand dropped to his gun. "I paid you. We're done."

"Not *you,*" she hissed. "The Russians. They canceled

the transfer to my offshore accounts. They reneged on the deal . . ."

He found it hard to summon up any sympathy for the woman. She was a murderer-for-hire, after all. "I guess they don't trust you either—"

Out of nowhere, the satellite phone rang, and the abrupt rattle of the digital tone set them both to silence. Mandy reached to tap the "accept call" button, but Jack caught her wrist.

"Don't worry," she said, shaking him off, "I'll put it on speaker." She pressed the tab and the line connected. "Arkady. I was just thinking about you. Where's my payment?"

• • •

Dimitri Yolkin pressed two fingers to the side of his headset and spoke carefully into the microphone. "Bazin is not available," he told the woman. "He is on his way to another location. You will speak to me. There are questions."

Across the dimly lit cabin of the Super Puma cargo helicopter, Yolkin's SVR compatriot Mager was peering at the screen of a laptop computer. He nodded without looking up and pointed toward the ground below them. Behind Mager, there were two other operatives each in the process of making ready their weapons. In the shadows at the back of the compartment, the bodies of the Super Puma's crew were barely visible, stacked like cordwood. They'd refused Yolkin's demands to take off into the bad weather when he had arrived at the airstrip, even after he showed them his fake police ID. In the end, it had been the more expedient alternative to kill them and have one of his own men pilot the aircraft.

In fact, Yolkin was not completely certain where Bazin, Ziminova and the other helicopter were headed. That was not important. He and his hunter team had their orders, and they would execute them.

"*What questions?*" demanded the contractor. "*You got the pictures? You saw? It's over. Bazin told me to proceed how I thought best. I've done that. Suvarov has gotten what he wanted.*"

"Yes," Yolkin agreed, feeling the helicopter start a descent through the buffeting winds and persistent rain. "But he will not be satisfied with only pictures. Where is the body? Physical proof is required."

"*That wasn't part of the deal.*" The momentary pause before she went on told Yolkin that she was lying to him. "*It's gone. I burned it.*"

"I am not convinced." Ahead, through the cockpit windows, he could see a long strip of lights shimmering as it moved across the barren landscape below.

"*Not my problem.*"

"You will see that it is." He cut the call and pulled the headphone jack from his handset, switching it back to the helicopter's onboard intercom.

"Location is confirmed," Mager said. "She's on the train."

"She is attempting to deceive us," Yolkin told Mager and the others. "Find her. Kill her."

• • •

"Shit." Mandy glared at the silent phone in her hand. "Bazin must have . . . inserted a code worm into the intel data he sent. They *tracked* me." She dropped the device to the floor and stamped on it.

Jack went to the window of the minivan as a distant flash of lightning lit up the sky. "Little late for that now." He glimpsed a flickering shape overhead and realized it was the sweep of a spinning rotor disc. "They're coming."

He turned back and found the muzzle of Mandy's Walther P99 aimed directly at his right eye. "I knew I should have really killed you," she snapped.

"Do it," he said. "And that'll get you, what? An extra thirty seconds before the Russians decide to shoot you anyway? You know how the SVR works. They don't like loose ends."

Jack heard the thrumming rotors as the helicopter made a low pass over the top of the train, the pilot lining up and matching speed.

Mandy swore again and let the gun drop. "Just know this. Get in my way and I won't hold fire."

"I was going to say the same thing." Jack pulled the Nemesis sniper rifle from the Velcro straps holding it to the gear bag and pocketed a spare ammunition magazine. "If the train crew are alerted, we're blown. We've gotta deal with this quickly." He grabbed the handle on the minivan's door and yanked it open. "Get their attention."

Windblown rain spattered his face as he dropped out of the vehicle and onto the bottom of the car carrier. Jack held the spindly rifle close to his chest and moved low toward the rear of the wagon.

Above, the gray form of the helicopter's belly was visible, and as he watched a hatch slid back. A head peeked out over the side, then vanished back within. The aircraft shifted, dropping closer to the top of the car carrier. Jack had no angle, and he kept moving, letting the shadows conceal him.

A figure—a stocky man clutching a silenced short-frame AKS-74U—emerged from the open hatch and hesitated on the threshold, looking for a place to put down. His delay cost him his life.

Mandy had ditched the Walther's suppressor and so Jack saw the flash and heard the *crack-crack* of shots as she fired straight up from below. Both rounds hit the Russian operative and he dropped from the helicopter's open hatchway, crashing hard into the roof of a town car on the wagon's upper deck. The dead man's body slid down, off the rain-slick hood, before falling over the side. The rushing blackness swallowed up the corpse and it was gone.

Guns opened up from inside the helicopter's cargo bay and Jack ducked as bullets shredded metal and shattered glass. The gray aircraft drifted forward, turning to present its flank. The pilot put the helicopter into a sideways attitude perpendicular to the line of the train cars, and the men inside kept firing, shooting wild to keep Jack and Mandy in cover.

Two more figures dropped out of the open hatch and landed on the roof of the containers one car back. They started forward, but with only the ghostly, random illumination of distant lightning, it was hard to see anything of them except vague shadows.

The bulky Super Puma helicopter was a different story. Even though the pilot had switched off the navigation indicators, the cockpit was still aglow through the greenhouse-like canopy, and dull illumination spilled from the still-open hatch.

Moving quickly, Jack snapped open the bipod legs on either side of the sniper rifle's barrel and laid it across the hood of a Jetta chained to the deck of the car carrier. He put his eye to the thermal-optic sight just as the helicopter pivoted, pointing its nose back toward the rear of the train. His first shot was a little wide, something to be expected with an unfamiliar weapon, and he saw the bright flare of the bullet as it ricocheted off the hull of the aircraft, narrowly missing the hazy figure of another gunman in the rear compartment.

He worked the bolt, ejecting the round and chambering another in one smooth motion, and now the prow of the helo was turning directly toward him, presenting a perfect target. Through the canopy the thermal scope showed him the white phantom of the pilot's upper torso. The sight picture was a mess of motion. Every element in the shot was shifting. Jack fired again and put a round into the cockpit, but missed anything vital. He saw the pilot twitch in shock and hesitate.

It was enough. A split second after Jack had worked the rifle's action once more, he ranged his third shot right into the helicopter pilot's sternum.

• • •

Slumping forward, the pilot's hands went loose on the controls and the Super Puma's engines revved. As if it had been jerked on an invisible line, the cargo helicopter lurched away, describing a terminal arc that sent it up into a stall and then back down again, slipping sideways into a plowed cornfield a few hundred yards from the rail line.

Rotors chopped at the dirt, buckled and snapped off. The fuselage rolled onto its side, crumpled and broke. In seconds, fires started in the overstressed engine compartment.

The train was long gone by the time the flames reached the fuel tank and turned the crashed aircraft into a blazing torch, the crash of the explosion and the flash of light blending into the thunder of the storm high above.

• • •

The men that dropped from the helicopter came to the far end of the cargo container, leading with their guns, firing bursts of suppressive fire down toward the car carrier beneath then. Bullets chewed up the hood of the minivan and punched through metal, forcing Mandy to give up her position and break into a run. She sprinted back down the length of the wagon, shoving her way past Jack, and she leapt the gap to the next carrier along.

Jack saw her go and frowned. Falling back wasn't going to cut it. They would run out of train long before the SVR hunters ran out of ammunition. He crouched, his thoughts turning. Every second the Russians were still breathing was a second they could be calling for reinforcements. With the chopper out of the picture, Jack had the edge, but hard experience had taught him never to count on the odds.

• • •

Ahead, the two men scrambled down from the wagon and began moving forward. Yolkin tapped Mager on the shoulder and pointed toward the carrier's upper deck. Mager nodded his understanding and slung his Kalashnikov, reaching for the rungs of a metal ladder.

Yolkin snapped on a tactical light under the barrel of his weapon and advanced, panning the beam left and right across the flanks of the cars rattling and pulling against the tethers holding them in place. He glimpsed a flicker of movement in the next wagon along and smiled. The woman—the contractor—had nowhere to go, and if, as he was certain, she had Bauer with her, the two of them would soon be dead. Yolkin allowed himself a smirk, and wondered if he would be personally rewarded by President Suvarov for ending the life of the troublesome American.

He moved slowly past a silver sedan, ignoring the increasing force of the downpour as the train drove deeper into the storm line. A lightning flash gave him a moment of stark, white-lit visibility, and it betrayed the woman. He saw her pressed against the wheel of a people-carrier, her gun held high.

Yolkin raised his weapon and thumbed the fire selector to full auto.

• • •

Jack waited until the Russian's outline was in the right spot, and then with all the force he could muster, he kicked out with both feet against the inside of the Jetta's passenger door. Laying low across the back seats, the gunman had missed Jack there in the shadows, and now he would pay for it.

The door hinged open like a pinball flipper and knocked the Russian off his feet, slamming him into the frame of the wagon. Jack slid out of the car and hit him again with the sniper rifle. The weapon was too long for him to use in such close quarters, so he repurposed it as a club, cracking the gunman across the side of the skull as he tried to recover. The whipcord-thin Russian fumbled at his weapon and Jack kept on hitting him, keeping him off-balance.

The other man swore in his native language and fought back, grabbing the stock of the rifle as Jack brought it across his head once again. Despite the gunman's tall, thin build, he was strong enough to be a match for Jack. They fell into a savage push-pull battle, back and forth across the wet metal deck of the wagon, bouncing off the flanks of the rain-slick cars. The Russian forced the frame of the sniper rifle back at Jack's throat, putting all his power into the motion, trying to choke him with it.

Jack slipped against the trunk of the sedan and used the motion to his advantage, pushing himself about, abruptly spinning the Russian back around to face him in the opposite direction.

Pistol shots rang out in the damp air and the gunman jerked, his eyes going wide with agony. His legs bent and he staggered. Jack glimpsed ugly entry wounds across his back and saw Mandy, half in cover from where she had shot him. The Russian collapsed to the deck and was still.

In the next second, Mandy was shouting into the wind. "Above you!"

Jack twisted away as automatic fire blazed down at him from the car carrier's upper deck, losing the rifle. He felt the burning line of a bullet crease his arm as he vaulted out of the line of fire, and almost overbalanced. For one unpleasant moment, Jack lurched out into the rush of the wind whipping past the train, and he clutched at a dangling chain to stop himself from falling into the darkness.

Swinging back around, he used the chain to haul himself up onto the roof of the dented VW, and from there he scrambled to the upper level.

The second shooter was still looking down on the wrong side of the wagon, aiming into the shadows where he mistakenly thought Jack had fallen.

Jack planted his feet against the deck plates, drawing and aiming his M1911. "Who sent you?" he shouted.

The other Russian jerked in surprise, then slowly he turned to face Jack. His hands were still on his assault rifle, but the muzzle was aimed away. Plain-faced and ordinary, the second shooter glared at Jack and said nothing.

"Suvarov?" Jack prompted, and that got him a slow, sullen nod in return.

He wondered if the Russian could fully understand him. He could see the thoughts unwinding behind the gunman's eyes, the calculations of survival versus termination. If either one of them moved, death would be the result.

"How many of you did he send?" Jack demanded.

The Russian smiled. "*Enough*. There is no path open

to you, Bauer. No place for you to hide. No one you can go to. We will be there."

A signal pole flashed past the train, a bright crimson light glowing atop it, and the motion made Jack reflexively look away, just for a fraction of a second. The gunman had seen it coming, had been waiting for the moment, and now he flipped up his weapon, turning it toward his target.

But Jack's aim never wavered. He fired three times in quick succession, putting the shots into a line up the Russian's chest. The man toppled off the side of the gantry and was gone.

Jack turned as the ladder behind him rattled. Dragging her gear bag over her shoulder, Mandy emerged on the upper deck and glowered at him.

"Always a party when you're around," she called out over the rushing wind. She pulled a spool of nylon line from the bag and connected one end to a fastener on her belt. "But if it's all the same, this is where we part ways."

Ahead, Jack could see a blurry arch over the track speeding closer, another cable bridge like the one they had used outside Deadline. Mandy pushed past him and positioned herself at the end of the wagon.

"Where are you going?"

"This is my stop," she said, unfurling a metal claw at the other end of the nylon line. "Next time you're in trouble? Do me a favor and *lose* my number."

Jack ducked as the cable bridge passed over his head, and Mandy tossed the claw up to snag it as it went by. The line twanged and pulled her up and away from the train, jerking her backward. Dangling from the steel arch as the train rolled on, the assassin shrank into the haze. Jack watched her go, and then turned away to find some shelter.

Los Angeles was still hours away, and he ached all over.

He dropped back down to the lower deck and sank into the shadows, looking out along the railroad ahead and the miles yet to be covered.

The gunman's words nagged at him. *We will be there.* Jack grimaced and turned away.

"I'll see you soon, Kim," he said to the air. "I promise."

21

He awoke as the train shunted onto the tracks threading out across Terminal Island and the docks of the Port of Los Angeles. Sleep had taken Jack down, hard and quick, even as the storm had clattered all around him—and now, waking to see shafts of sunlight peeking through the gaps in the frame of the cargo wagon, he felt as if he had come to in another world. Jack moved fast, ignoring the aches and pains that ran though him as he got back to his feet. In moments he was at the hatch.

Timing it carefully, Jack leapt from the slow-moving train and landed as if he was dropping in from a parachute fall, knees bent, letting the momentum bleed off into a forward tumble across the trackside shingle. Gathering himself, he slipped between the buffers of two tanker wagons on the next siding over. The big Union Pacific rolled on, and he saw the car carriers flash past. The police would be called when the dock inspectors came across the bloodstains and bullet holes in the vehicles, and he needed to be somewhere else when that happened.

Keeping out of sight, he moved from cover to cover until he could see a highway on the far side of a rusting metal fence. Jack looked left and right to make sure he wasn't being observed, and then stepped out, walking calmly in parallel to the barrier until it came to a break, the mouth of a service road that spilled out onto the street. There was nothing approximating security, not even razor wire or a drop-gate, nothing but a caution sign warning about the hazards of moving trains. But then there was little here for the attention of thieves, and across the four lanes of the highway there were only endless lines of scrapyards and parking lots for big rigs. Human traffic was nonexistent.

Jack pulled his jacket closed and started walking east, in the general direction of Long Beach, waiting to find a place to cross the highway. Los Angeles welcomed him home with the same dusty, dry and fume-laden air that had become so familiar to him since the days of his youth growing up in Santa Monica. Despite his grave circumstances, there was something reassuring about being back in a city that he knew well, like a greeting from an old friend. It was home ground, he realized. Jack had fought and bled on the streets of this city, and held it back from the brink of chaos on more than one occasion. He felt a sting of regret as a nagging voice in the back of his mind reminded him that he would soon have to leave it again, perhaps never to return.

No time to dwell on that, Jack told himself. He was close now, close to his objective, and he couldn't lose sight of that even for a moment.

It didn't take him long to find an auto yard off East Anaheim Street and a beaten-up Hyundai Accent hatchback that he could hot-wire in short order. Jack slipped into the sparse traffic and headed northward, following the line of the Los Angeles River toward the 405 freeway. He checked his watch. His son-in-law Stephen was an oncologist at the Cedars-Sinai Medical Center up in West Hollywood, and finding him there would be Jack's best option for getting to Kim without alerting anyone of his presence in the city. Or so he hoped.

Jack willed himself to keep his driving casual, to do nothing that might draw attention even though every- thing in him wanted to mash the accelerator to the floor and dash across the city. He reached out and snapped on the dashboard radio, tuning to a news-only station, and caught the middle of a report coming live from the nation's capital.

The ripples from Allison Taylor's shocking announce- ment less than a day ago were still echoing across the country. Having first walked out of the historic United Nations peace conference with the Islamic Republic of Kamistan, Taylor had gone on to resign her presidency only hours later. She had offered a confession of sorts about her knowledge of a plot against the IRK and its leader Omar Hassan. Killed on American soil as the re- sult of a conspiracy by his own people, right now there were very few people who knew exactly what had happened—and Jack Bauer was one of them. He listened to the reporter asking the question that everyone else had to be asking: *What happens now?*

Taylor's honesty, the promise she had made to Jack and then kept, meant that she was liable to bear the full weight of any criminal charges that might be brought against her. No matter how things played out, her politi- cal career was in ruins, and she could face a lengthy prison sentence. Jack had not found it easy to trust the woman, and he still felt conflicted about the choices she had made . . . but Allison Taylor had kept her word, and that was something that was all too rare in the clandes- tine world where Jack moved.

The discussion went on, first with a cursory mention of Charles Logan. Against all odds, the scheming polit- ico was still alive. Jack's hands tightened on the steering wheel as he listened. There was no justice there, he mused.

Pushed to the point of committing a suicidal act by the revelation of his misdeeds, it was now slowly coming out that Logan had apparently botched an attempt to shoot himself, and that he might also be responsible for the death of his assistant Jason Pillar. Jack wondered if Agent Hadley was hearing this story too. How would the driven young FBI agent react to that revelation?

If the world had been a fair one, then Logan would be dead, or he would be paying for his crimes. But instead, doctors at Walter Reed Army Medical Center had announced that Logan was in a deep coma. If he *was* ever to regain consciousness, it was likely that severe brain damage would have destroyed whatever of the man he had once been.

Too easy, Jack reflected. It was too lenient a punishment for someone who deserved to forfeit the full price for his treachery and greed.

But it was not just the United States of America that was reacting to the fallout from what the media were now calling "the Hassan incident." In the hours since Jack had fled New York, as he and Chase had found themselves caught up in the situation in Deadline, the murder of Omar Hassan continued to resonate around the world. From Russia there were fragmentary reports and rumors that President Yuri Suvarov had returned home to an icy reception, having raced back to Moscow ahead of suggestions that he had played a key role in Hassan's murder.

Jack carried a very particular kind of hatred for the Russian official, as it had been on Suvarov's personal orders that Renee Walker was fatally wounded. Rationally, Jack knew that someone like Suvarov would forever be beyond his reach, but in his heart he wanted to see the man destroyed. Now he wondered if the ministers in Russia's own government would be the ones to do that for him. According to the news report, some members of the Duma—the Russian state assembly, their equivalent to the US House of Representatives—were agitating for Suvarov to follow in Taylor's footsteps and turn himself over for arrest. Suvarov's involvement in the Hassan assassination was as certain to Jack as his part in Renee's death, and it seemed that Russian fears over the reaction from the IRK might now accomplish what Jack could not. But even if Yuri Suvarov's career ended in disgrace, even if he were to rot in some gulag for the rest of his days, it would not be *enough*. As with Logan, the price Suvarov paid would be a pale shadow of the true bloody cost he owed.

And then there were the Kamistani people themselves. Adversaries to America for so long, the peace treaty their leader had come to New York to sign had meant much. Even someone who considered himself as apolitical as Jack did could not deny that making peace with the IRK was the right thing to do, a first step toward bringing stability to the troubled Middle East and a way to build bridges. But all those good intentions were dust now.

Omar Hassan's wife, Dalia, had taken up his role as president, and now the IRK's leader was a widow whose husband was dead because of a conspiracy involving the very nation-states that had sued for peace. As the report came to an end, no one said the words, but Jack could hear the echo of another, more pressing uncertainty beneath it all. There would be many out there who would use the events of the past days as a spur toward hostility . . . perhaps even *war*.

His jaw hardened. Once, that might have preyed upon him, but here and now Jack found it hard to connect with the thunder of global events happening elsewhere in the world. He had spent most of his life as a soldier of one sort or another, sacrificing much of himself to make sure his homeland remained safe and secure. He had trusted in the men and women who issued his orders, believing that they were honest and true. Jack had always believed that he was doing the right thing, no matter how hard that road was.

It was different now. So much of that certainty had been burned away from him. He had been asked to do questionable things, time and time again. Betrayal and loss took their toll. Now, Jack understood that he was *still* that soldier, still ready to sacrifice and bleed red for what he believed in; what had changed was the nature of the things he fought for. Not for nations or for flags, not for a uniform or a badge, but for what was *right*. For that ideal and for those that he loved dearly.

He blinked and swallowed a lump in his throat, for a moment recalling the faces of Renee Walker, of Audrey Raines, his wife Teri and his daughter Kim, his trusted friends Chloe O'Brian, Chase Edmunds and all the others. These were the people that he fought for, they were the weight that he carried and the strength that he drew from. Nothing else mattered to him.

• • •

Ditching the car in a side street off the Beverly Center, Jack turned up the collar of his jacket and kept his head down as he set off toward Cedars-Sinai. The hospital complex towered high over the neighboring buildings, sprawling across several city blocks, and Jack ran through his memory of everything Kim had told him about her doctor husband, thinking about how he would find him in there.

Admittedly, he didn't know Stephen Wesley that well, but Jack had always been a man who relied on his gut instinct to measure a person. Stephen made Kim happy, and that was the most important thing. Jack had only to see the two of them together to know that they loved one another, and he wanted that for his daughter. Kim deserved a good life, a normal life, and Stephen had helped her find it.

Halting at an intersection, Jack scanned the street around him, the act coming to the former federal agent like second nature. His eyes flicked over faces, measuring and discarding them as potential threats or possible observers. He did it almost without conscious thought, a part of his mind looking for patterns and shapes that seemed out of place.

He found something.

A pale-colored Chevrolet Suburban was parked in the shadow of a sun-bleached palm tree, the hood pointing toward the hospital entrance. The windows of the SUV were tinted black, but the most obvious tell was the way the vehicle sat low on its shocks. The SUV was far heavier than a normal model, and that could only be from the addition of bulletproofed windows, body armor and a more powerful engine. Jack knew this kind of vehicle intimately. He had undergone tactical driving training in the same model.

Which meant only one thing. The Suburban was a mobile from the LA division of the Counter Terrorist Unit.

The lights changed and Jack crossed the road, keeping the SUV in sight, gauging his next move. *Why would CTU be here?* Then he remembered the last words he had spoken to Chloe back in New York, a conversation that seemed like a lifetime ago.

My daughter . . . Her family . . . They're going to try and use her to get to me.

Chloe hadn't hesitated. *I'll make sure they're protected. I promise.*

She had been as good as her word, as she always was. Chloe must have used her last moments at CTU to deploy a team to keep Jack's family safe, even as the hammer was falling.

But now the protection detail posed a problem. Odds were, everyone in that SUV knew Jack Bauer's face. They might even be agents that he had worked with or trained in the past. He couldn't chance being recognized by any of them, not after he had risked so much to get away from his pursuers. All it would take was one person reporting in, and Los Angeles would be on lockdown and the hunt would begin all over again.

The lights changed again and Jack suddenly saw the solution to his problem. An ambulance on its way back to the hospital rolled to a halt at the intersection, engine idling. No lights or sirens were running, indicating that whatever emergency call the vehicle was returning from was not a time-critical one.

Jack walked past the side of the ambulance, noting the two paramedics in the cab chatting about their plans for lunch. At the last possible second, he stepped aside as he reached the back of the vehicle and twisted the handle of the rear door. It came open easily, revealing the empty compartment within. Jack heard the engine rev as the lights shifted back to green, and he was inside, the door closing quietly behind him as the ambulance moved off. Keeping his head low, Jack peered out of the rear window as the ambulance passed the parked SUV on its way to the dispatch bay. He saw no movement from the inside of the CTU vehicle and let out a breath. *In the clear*, he told himself.

Acting quickly, he ditched his dark coat and stole an EMT's visibility jacket and baseball cap from a rack in the back of the ambulance. The vehicle had barely rolled to a halt as he slipped back out, his disguise in place.

He didn't run. Witnesses noticed when people moved in haste. Instead, Jack walked calmly across the ambulance bay, following a group leading a stretcher into the interior of the hospital. Keeping the bill of his cap down low across his nose, Jack's searching gaze found a sign directing him deeper into the building, toward the oncology wards.

He shot a look at his watch. *I still have time.*

• • •

"This is an infirmary?" Bazin's tone bordered on the incredulous as he looked around the private room. "I have been to whorehouses that were less extravagant." He curled his lip at the well-appointed bedroom.

Ziminova did not doubt that her commander's estimation was correct. She moved to the window and looked down at the street below. With her back to Bazin, she stifled a yawn and blinked away a moment of fatigue. She had not slept on the flight to Los Angeles, and it was beginning to wear on her. "This is a gamble," she offered. "We do not know if Bauer will come here."

Bazin snorted and nodded to the blond-haired man who had met them at the airstrip. "Keep watch." The man nodded and stepped out into the corridor.

His name was Lenkov. All she knew was that he was one of the SVR's local operatives on the American West Coast, and it was his duty to help Bazin, Ekel and her find and terminate their target.

"Bauer's daughter is on her way here," Bazin explained. "Her husband treats those with cancers . . . Such a worthy profession, eh?" As if in mockery, Bazin produced a lighter and a cigarette, raising it to his mouth.

Ziminova took two quick steps to his side and snatched the cigarette from his fingers. Off her commander's furious glare, she nodded at a pale green cylinder near the unoccupied hospital bed. "Oxygen," she said by way of explanation.

Bazin scowled and pocketed the lighter again. "He will come. And if he does not? We use his family as leverage to draw him out."

"You have placed much faith in the words of a dying coward." Ziminova looked around. The room they had secured was hardly an ideal base of operations, but they were operating well beyond their mission remit now. Bazin had not made contact with the consulate in New York for hours, and she was starting to wonder about Yolkin and Mager, who were similarly silent.

"Of course," he replied. "Precisely *because* Matlow was dying, *because* he was a coward. At such moments, the ability to lie flees from men of that kind."

She folded her arms. "What about the images your contractor sent us?"

Bazin's craggy face turned to granite. "Staged, I imagine," he growled. "I am very disappointed in her. I would like to think that Dimitri made my displeasure over those lies plain to her."

"Is that what you think happened?"

He eyed her. "No," said Bazin at length. "Yolkin would not hesitate to break protocol and contact me if he had ended Bauer or the assassin. He would want to show off."

"The fact that he has not—" she began.

"The fact that he has not means Bauer killed him," Bazin snapped irritably. "Mager and the others too, I imagine. All the more reason for us to succeed here."

Ziminova fell silent, unable to frame her thoughts in a way that would not annoy her commander more if she voiced them.

He saw it in her eyes, though. "Galina, your silence is insulting."

She sighed. "Does it not concern you that we have heard nothing from the consulate in New York or headquarters in Moscow? It has been several hours since President Suvarov touched down at Sheremetyevo. If Bauer's capture is of such importance to him, why has there been only silence?"

Bazin looked away. "Suvarov has more to deal with than just the balance of this account."

"My point exactly," said Ziminova. "He may not even be in office anymore. In which case, our orders will be in question."

He eyed her. "You think I am exceeding my remit? Bauer killed Russian citizens. That's reason enough."

"We are now well beyond the mission parameters given to us at the start of the operation, sir."

"I expect better from you." Bazin sniffed. "I did not recruit you to my command because you *question* orders, but because you *obey* them."

"I serve the Motherland," she replied after a moment, "not one man's need for belligerence."

Bazin was about to chastise her, but before he could draw breath there was a chime from his jacket pocket. He pulled a cellular telephone from the depths of his coat and spoke into it. "Report."

Ziminova heard the faint mutter of Ekel's voice on the other end of the line. "*I have located the watchers.*"

• • •

"*Deal with them,*" said Bazin, and he cut the call short.

Ekel nodded as if the commander were there with him, and continued walking up the shady sidewalk toward the parked Suburban. He made a point of looking carefully at the vehicle, even though he had already observed it from the front entrance of the hospital for several minutes. The American security agents had chosen a good viewpoint for themselves, but at the cost of making their presence highly visible to anyone with even the most basic understanding of surveillance techniques. Perhaps that had been part of their mission brief, to make sure they stood out in order to deter anyone who might come looking for their principals. If so, then the Americans had seriously misunderstood the adversaries they were facing.

But then again, Ekel thought, *they so often did.* He guessed that these men felt secure and in control here, on the streets of a city that belonged to them. That over-confidence would work to the Russians' advantage.

He approached the passenger side door and came up close, tapping on the opaque black glass of the window. After a moment, it dropped open a few inches, revealing the face of a Latino man wearing dark sunglasses. "Yeah?" he asked.

Ekel produced a gold detective's shield with one hand and held it in his palm. He had exchanged a fake NYPD badge for a fake LAPD one on the way in from the airstrip. "You can't be parked here." He nodded toward a sign on a nearby light pole that said the same, warning drivers not to block a road used frequently by emergency vehicles.

"It's not a problem."

"What?" Ekel gestured at the window, motioning for the man to open it a little more. "You got to move this thing." He mimicked an accent he heard on American cop shows.

The opening widened, revealing a shield of a different design dangling from a chain around the other man's neck. "Federal agents," he explained. "That doesn't apply to us."

Ekel took in another man in the driver's seat and a third behind him. The Russian's free hand dropped out of sight, snaking into the folds of his jacket.

"Show me your badge again," said the Latino man, his tone flat and hard.

"Okay, sure." Ekel nodded, offering it up for scrutiny. As the agent leaned forward to get a better look, Ekel's other hand came back gripping a Makarov P6 pistol. The modified gun had an integral silencer capable of reducing the sound of a shot to a loud cough, and Ekel fired it into the agent's face at close range. He kept on shooting, putting bullets into the driver and the other CTU operative until the magazine was empty, unloading the weapon in less than three seconds. He didn't worry about through-and-through shots penetrating the walls or the windows of the SUV. The vehicle's armor worked both ways.

When it was done, Ekel hid the P6 away and leaned briefly into the SUV to tap the automatic window control, slipping back out as the glass rose up and concealed his kills.

He walked casually back toward the hospital, watching an ambulance blaze past in a skirl of sirens and flashing lights. "It's done," he said into his cell phone. "What next?"

"*The daughter has arrived,*" Bazin replied. "*Make sure the package is in place.*"

Ekel nodded and made for the underground car park. "Confirmed. And the primary?"

He heard the smile in Bazin's voice. "*Patience.*"

The elevator doors slid back and the first face Kim saw was her husband's. He looked no different from the first time she had seen him, a chance meeting at the hospital before a lunch date with her friend Sue. In the months that followed, Kim had learned that Sue—a college roommate who was now a senior nurse as Cedars-Sinai—had intended the two of them to cross paths all along.

That memory seemed like something from another life, as if it belonged to another Kim. She had been single for a long time, drifting though a handful of relationships after she and Chase Edmunds had suffered their fractious breakup, but never finding someone she could really connect with. Sue later admitted that on meeting Dr. Stephen Wesley, she had known immediately that this was the person that Kim Bauer needed in her life. She'd been right.

Stephen was kind and he was patient, and most of all he was always there for her. Right now, Kim needed that more than ever.

"Hey, pumpkin," she told her daughter, shifting the little girl's weight where she lay draped over her mother's shoulder. "Here's Daddy . . ."

"Okay." Teri blinked and yawned.

Stephen smiled ruefully as Kim approached. "She's still sleepy?"

Kim nodded. "The flight back from New York wiped her out, I think."

"I know the feeling," said her husband, and he stifled a yawn of his own.

The trip home hadn't been a smooth one. The sudden, unexplained addition of extra security measures at JFK delayed everything, and that alone would have been stressful enough, but being forced to fly home without her father had made Kim irritable and worried. A day ago, she hugged him when he promised that he would be coming back to California with them, to finally stick to his retirement from government service and find some low-key private security job. But that had not happened. Events overtook Jack Bauer, as they seemed fated to do, and now Kim was in the same place she had been time and time again over the past few years. She couldn't be certain if her father was alive or dead, and she hated that this hollow feeling in her chest was so familiar, so well-known to her.

Stephen came close, and without words, he drew his wife and daughter into an embrace. Kim saw the understanding in his eyes, and she blinked away tears before they could form.

"Thanks for coming to see me," he said. "How are you doing?"

"I don't know."

She put Teri down and all of a sudden the little girl came alive with a spurt of new energy, dashing ahead to lead the way down the corridor toward Stephen's office. Other nurses and staff smiled and waved at the child. She was well-liked by her husband's work colleagues, and a regular visitor. Kim tried to make sure mother, father and daughter spent a lunchtime together at least once a week.

When Teri was out of earshot, Kim leaned close to her husband. "No one is saying anything. All the news coming out of New York is frightening, this assassination, the president's resignation . . . And nobody knows where my dad is."

He frowned. "You used to work with these people once, right? The Counter Terrorist Unit? Isn't there anyone you could call?"

She shook her head. "I already tried. But Chloe isn't answering her phone, and the numbers I had for CTU Los Angeles are coming up dead." Kim swallowed hard, fighting down a sob. "Oh god, Stephen, it's happening just like last time. I think . . . I think I'm going to lose him." She looked away. "I can't go through all that again."

Stephen squeezed her hand. "You don't know that he got caught up in all that trouble."

"*I do!*" She halted. Teri was fixated on a conversation with Sue, but still she turned so the little girl wouldn't see the anguish on her mother's face. "I know my dad," Kim went on. "I know he could never stand by and let bad things happen to good people, it's who he is!" She wiped at her eyes. "And . . . and I told him it was okay. I told him he could stay at CTU and come back with us later . . ." The next words made her blood run cold. "What if something terrible happened to him because he stayed in New York?"

He pulled her close again. "Kim, no. That's not on you. Don't blame yourself."

"I told him to be careful," she said in a small voice.

Stephen nodded. "Come on, honey. Come into my office. We'll see if we can't find somebody with some answers."

Kim nodded and walked with him to the door. Teri dashed ahead to get there first and rushed in, running through the anteroom outside the office proper, dragging her plush toy bear along with her.

She heard her daughter call out in surprise as Stephen closed the door behind her.

"*Jack!*" piped Teri. "I mean, *Grandpa!*"

Kim pushed past her husband and into the inner room. There, crouched on his haunches so he could look his grandchild in the eyes, was her father. A smile, behind it a mix of joy and fatigue, relief and fear, split his face. "Hey, sweetheart. How's Bear?"

Teri held up the toy. "He's good. He was sad that you weren't coming with us but now he's happy."

"Me too." He stood up. "Hello, Kim. Stephen. Sorry to surprise you like this."

"*Dad.*" Kim went to her father and hugged him. She felt him tense, and immediately she knew he had been hurt. He smelled of sweat, cordite and smoke, as if he had come from a battleground. "You're here."

"Yeah."

Stephen came forward, casting a practiced eye over his father-in-law. "Jack . . . you look like you could use some help." He nodded toward an examination alcove across the room. "Take what you need."

A silent communication passed between the two men, and Kim's father nodded. "Thank you." He smiled down at Teri. "Sweetheart, Grandpa and Mommy need to talk about something. Why don't you and Daddy go play with Bear, huh?"

"Okay . . ." Teri's tone was a little sullen, but the girl didn't question him. Jack had that way with her, Kim noted. She trusted him implicitly.

Stephen shot Kim a questioning look, and she responded with a nod. "We'll be right outside," he said, taking his daughter by the hand to lead her back out into the corridor.

As the door closed, Kim's father slumped against the examination bed. "Hey. I know this isn't what you had in mind when you asked me to come."

"You're in trouble." It wasn't a question.

A rueful smile crossed his face. "It's complicated." He shrugged out of his jacket. "Can you help me get this shirt off?"

Kim nodded, and winced as bruising and blood-caked wounds were revealed beneath. Her hand went to her mouth. "Dad . . . Good grief, what happened to you?"

"It's not as bad as it looks."

"You're the worst liar." Kim forced aside her worries and set to work helping him redress his injuries with fresh bandages, finding clean clothes in Stephen's work closet.

When he finally met her gaze, there was so much sorrow in it, Kim's breath caught in her throat. The last time she had seen that look in her father's eyes, it had been on the day he had come to tell her that her mother was dead. *What have they taken from you this time?*

"I'm sorry," he told her.

"For what?"

"I'm not going to be able to keep the promise I made."

• • •

"Is Grandpa going to stay with us?"

Stephen couldn't keep a frown from his face as he took his daughter out to the waiting area beyond the doctors' offices. "I don't know, pumpkin. That's up to him. He's got a very important job."

Teri nodded with the kind of seriousness that only a child of her age could muster. "I remember. You said he has some work to do." She studied the face of her toy bear, as if it would provide some input as well.

"That's right." He glanced up and his eyes fell on a television screen mounted on the wall. The sound was muted on the feed from CNB, still showing the same endless round of footage of ambulances racing down New York streets from the day before, mixed in with shots of police helicopters hovering in the gaps between skyscrapers and news anchors with grave expressions.

Stephen sighed. Kim had never spoken in great detail about her father's job, but he knew enough to guess at the shape of it. He knew that Jack Bauer had been a high-level federal agent and part of the Counter Terrorist Unit, and from his wife's reticence on certain things, he was certain that the man had been involved in working against threats to the USA for several years. Kim's pain at the loss of her mother, the woman they had named their daughter after, was all caught up in that, but Stephen had never pressured Kim to tell him more than she wanted to. He loved her dearly, but he had learned there were things in the Bauer family history that they wanted to stay buried . . . and that was fine. When the day came that Kim wanted to tell him, he would be there, and it wouldn't change a thing about how he felt about his family.

"Dr. Wesley?" He turned as a nurse he didn't recognize came toward him. She had blond hair tied back in a tight, severe bun, accenting an attractive if austere face. "Pardon me. I know you're on break . . ."

"Is there a problem?" He noticed that she wasn't wearing an ID tag.

The nurse held up a medical chart. "Dr. Lund has an issue that requires a second opinion . . . It will just be a minute."

He took the chart and scanned it. "All right . . ." Stephen beckoned Sue over. "Hey. Can you watch Teri for me? I've got to deal with something." He bent down and kissed his daughter on the top of the head. "Be right back."

"Okay." Teri didn't look up, still engrossed in her staring contest with the stuffed toy.

Sue smiled. "Sure, Doctor." Her smile faded as she glanced at the nurse. "I'm sorry, you are . . . ?"

"I'm new here," came the reply. "Nice to meet you."

The nurse walked on toward the elevator and Stephen fell in behind her, still poring over the chart. The patient was one of Lund's problem cases, but Stephen was sure that he'd heard the other doctor saying the person in question was showing improvement. As he read on, he could find nothing that would require the insight of another oncologist.

He looked up as the elevator doors shut. "You're sure this is the right chart?"

The nurse ignored him and punched a button. Instead of descending to the floor below where Lund did his rounds, it began to rise to the upper wards.

"Hey," he began, reaching out to tap her on the shoulder.

She moved like a striking cobra. The woman spun in place, grabbing his outstretched arm and twisting it hard enough to force him down toward the deck of the elevator car. Her other hand pulled a serrated push-dagger from a lanyard hidden in the collar of her scrubs and pressed the tip into his throat. "Do not call for help. Do not speak." The nurse's accent had abruptly shifted to a Middle-European inflection that he didn't recognize. "Do not try to escape. Nod if you understand."

He did so, slowly and careful to avoid the tip of the dagger pressing into his flesh.

The elevator came to a halt and the doors opened to reveal two men in nondescript clothes. One of them, a large man with a tanned complexion, gestured for him to get back up on his feet. The nurse—although he doubted now that was what she was—drew back and allowed it to happen, pushing him out into the corridor.

This floor of Cedars-Sinai was empty at the moment, cleared for refurbishment work that was due to start in a day or so. Stephen looked around, and realized he was very alone. "What do you want?"

The big man smiled without warmth. "You are an intelligent man, Dr. Wesley. Why not take a guess?"

• • •

Kim blinked back tears, but she didn't look away from him. "Dad. No, please, don't do this." She shook her head.

With each word, it felt like Jack's heart was being torn out of him. "I came here because I had to see you, Kim. I owed you that. I couldn't just drop off the face of the world and let you go on wondering, never knowing . . ." He remembered the aftermath of the thwarted reactor meltdown attacks a few years earlier and the circumstances that had forced him to stage his own demise. That act still haunted him for how much it had hurt his daughter. "I hated myself for doing that once before. I never want to put you through that again."

"But you have. You will!" She shied away from him as he reached for her, anger in her eyes. "I lost Mom. I lost Chase. I lost you, but I got you back . . ."

Jack frowned. Part of him wanted to tell Kim the truth about Chase Edmunds, that he hadn't died in the Valencia bombing, and of the bravery and loyalty he had shown right up to the end . . . But the other man's death was still raw, and Jack could see no reason to heap more pain and anguish on his daughter.

He opted for the one truth that he knew was certain. "Your mother loved you. Chase cared about you. And I will always love you too, Kim. That's why I have to do this."

She sat quietly and absorbed his terse recounting of the incident in New York, only breaking her silence with a muffled sob as Jack told her of Renee Walker's death.

Kim guessed how much Renee meant to her father, and the fact that she shared his pain in that moment cut him like knives. He told her of the men and women hunting him, and his headlong race across the country. And now it was coming to an end, now that he had reached her, he couldn't find the words to express how he felt. Everything he said was a pale shadow, a ghost of his real sentiments.

He took a breath. "As long as I am here, you are in the crosshairs. And not just you. Stephen and Teri too. There are people out there who will use you to get to me, ruthless people. You were part of CTU once, you know what kind of world that is. There's so much darkness, and I don't want it to touch your life anymore." He came close and took her hand, and this time Kim let him. Jack gave a shaky smile. "Your mother would be so proud of you, to see the woman you have become. And I know one thing for sure, Kim. *You are the very best thing I ever did.* You're the one bright light at the center of my life, and for all the bleak places I've ever been to, all the things I've had to suffer . . . You make that worth it."

Without words, she drew him into a hug, and he felt his daughter's warm tears on his chest.

"You're all I have left," he told her, emotion choking his voice, "and I can't put that in harm's way. Even if it means I have to leave you behind. I will not let anyone hurt my family. You deserve a good life. I want you to live it."

"That's not fair!" Kim blurted out the words. "Damn it, Dad . . . You don't have to be alone anymore. You don't have to shoulder this by yourself. We can find a way . . . We could . . ." She trailed off as she finally came to the same understanding that he had. "It's not fair," she repeated.

"This is how it has to be," Jack told her. "It's the only road that's open."

They held each other in silence for long moments. Finally, Kim found her voice once more. "Where will you go?"

"Someplace off the clock," he said. "I'll go dark, I'll slip away . . . and you'll be safe."

• • •

Lenkov pushed the American into an empty chair and took up a position too close to the other man, towering over him with obvious menace. Bazin leaned indolently against the wall across the room from the young doctor, his eyes flicking to Ziminova. He didn't need to order her to keep watch. She just nodded and waited by the door, scanning the corridor.

Bazin didn't expect to be interrupted, though. He gauged the man in the chair and guessed that this wouldn't take long. "Well?" he prompted. "Tell me why I am here, Dr. Wesley."

"How do you know who I am?"

"We have a file," Bazin explained, making an airy gesture. "Information is so freely available in this country, honestly . . ." He chuckled. "It's embarrassing. It's not even difficult to find." He told the man about how he had used a common Internet search engine to not only track down details of the doctor's position at the hospital, but also of how he had been able to find social networking sites in short order that had pictures of charity baseball games and picnics, where Wesley's wife and daughter were caught on camera. "A sweet child," he concluded. "I have two myself."

The doctor licked his lips. "This is about Kim's father."

"Where is he?" The doctor didn't speak, but Bazin saw the answer in his eyes. He nodded to himself. "A few hours ago, I repeatedly brought a man to the point of drowning in the waters of a river. Over and over again, until he stopped hiding the truth from me. This I did in order to find Jack Bauer. And I am capable of far worse."

The young man glanced up at Lenkov, who remained stone-faced. "I . . . I can't help you."

Bazin continued as if he had never spoken. "It is not a simple thing to betray someone. It goes against the grain. You are a good man, Dr. Wesley. I saw that about you, so I understand your reluctance to commit an act of disloyalty. You wonder how you would live with yourself afterward? I can tell you this: It is easier than you think."

"Bauer is here," Lenkov spoke for the first time.

Caught by surprise, the doctor flinched, and Bazin knew that Lenkov's guess was correct. Ekel was already performing a sweep of the hospital in case Bauer had slipped into the building, but this was the first confirmation of it.

"I am going to make it easy for you, Doctor." Bazin pushed off the wall and came closer. Wesley fought down his fear, admirably so for a man in his position, still clinging to a shred of defiance. Bazin cocked his head. "You have made life-or-death choices many times in your work, yes? This is no different. And there is no need to blame yourself. This is not your fault, my friend. I am giving you no choice."

"I . . . I don't—"

Bazin silenced him with a look. "Do you really want to consider what will be done if you refuse?" The words came to him effortlessly, with all the rote smoothness of a polished performance. "Unless you do exactly as I tell you, or if you try to disobey me, I will have your wife and your daughter killed."

Color drained from the doctor's face. "Please," he managed. "No."

"It will only take one word from me," Bazin explained. "And I can assure you, it will be quite horrific."

That defiance returned for one final flash of anger. "You son of a bitch!"

"Oh, yes." He nodded, accepting the insult like a gift. "The lives of your family mean nothing to me. But Jack Bauer's life does hold value. And so that is the trade we will make, Dr. Wesley. You will give up your father-in-law, and in return you, Kim and little Teri will go on living."

"You'll kill us all!" he blurted. "I know how this goes . . . I've seen your faces . . ."

Lenkov gave a rough chuckle. "You watch too many movies."

"Let me explain it to you," Bazin went on. "I have no interest in you, the woman, the child. I only care who you are in this moment because you have a connection to Jack Bauer. When that goes away, you will be beneath my notice. That is why we are making this arrangement." He talked about the odious deal as if Wesley had already agreed to it, because on some level the man already had. "You will never speak to anyone of this conversation or of who you met, because that would mean your wife would learn about what you did. You don't want that. You want Bauer to simply go away and for your very pleasant life to carry on as before."

When the doctor hung his head, Bazin knew he had him. "What do I have to do?" he whispered, beaten down by his circumstances.

Bazin nodded to himself. He felt no pity for the man, no guilt for what he had just done. It was a transaction, nothing more. "A simple thing. I want you to help him," he explained.

• • •

Jack trailed Kim out into the corridor and watched her bend down to sweep his granddaughter up into an embrace. She nodded a grateful smile to one of the nurses and turned back to him.

"Hey, Grandpa," said the girl. "Do you have to go to work now?"

"I do," he told her, forcing a smile. He took the paw of the plush toy she was holding. "Listen, sweetheart. Your friend Bear here is going to look after you while I'm not around, okay? You keep him close, and you make sure you listen to your mom and dad."

"Okay," Teri replied. "*Be safe.* That's what Mommy always tells Daddy when he goes to work in the morning."

"I will." Jack turned to see Kim's husband walking quickly toward him from the elevators. The man looked pale and sweaty, and Jack knew instinctively that something was awry.

Time to go, Jack, said a silky voice in the depths of his thoughts.

Kim saw it too. "Stephen, what's wrong?"

He took a breath, meeting his wife's look before he tore himself away to glance at Jack. "Someone is, uh, here. I just talked to one of the security guys and they told me they removed a man with a Russian accent who was loitering down by the reception. Said he looked like a soldier."

"The SVR." Jack's blood ran cold. "If there's one, there'll be more. They're here for me." He turned to Kim and gave her hand a squeeze. "This is it. I have to go."

She nodded, eyes shining, and let him pull away. Jack headed down the corridor toward a service elevator, and Stephen fell into step with him. "Jack . . . Look, I can't pretend to know what's going on with you, but I have . . . I have to protect my family."

"I know." He nodded. "That's all I ask of you."

Stephen sighed. "Okay." He swallowed hard and then pressed a key fob into Jack's palm. "Take my car. The black Audi R8, in the staff parking lot. Ride the elevator down to the basement, cut through the first storage room on the right. That'll lead you into the parking garage."

"Thanks."

Stephen looked away without meeting his gaze. "Good luck," he said, as the elevator doors slid closed.

Jack went down to the basement with no stops, using the time to check his pistol. *Only one mag left.* He scowled. A stand-up engagement was not an optimal choice. *I've got to draw them away . . .*

The sublevel corridor was empty and Jack ducked out of the elevator, breaking into a run. As he went, he spun out multiple plans in his thoughts, weighing up his tactical options.

But until he entered the storeroom, it did not occur to Jack that he might have been betrayed.

He was barely through the door when they came at him.

23

"Daddy, what's the matter?" Kim heard the panic bubbling up under the words as her daughter asked the question. Teri was a highly empathetic child, forever picking up on the emotions of others around her. Right now, she was feeling their fear.

"It's okay," Stephen insisted. "It's all fine, pumpkin." He carried Teri up close to his chest, arms wrapped around her as if she were the most precious cargo.

And she is, Kim told herself. She kept pace with her husband as they exited the elevator and made their way quickly toward the public parking lot where she had left the family sedan. "Stephen," she insisted. "Did he tell you something?" When he didn't answer, Kim pulled on his arm. "*Stephen!* Talk to me!"

He whirled around and she saw an expression on his face she didn't recognize. Fear, yes, that was there. But something else. *Anguish. Guilt.* Kim's stomach flipped over and she felt sick with a sudden, nameless dread.

"You have to get out of here," he told her. "Take Teri and get away. Go to my mom's place in Pasadena, stay there until you hear from me, don't open the door to anyone else . . ."

Kim shook her head. "Not until you tell me what he said to you!"

"Damn it, Kim! For once will you just do what I ask?" Stephen shouted at her and she recoiled, taken aback by his unexpected reaction. In his arms, Teri immediately started to cry. As quickly as it had come, the moment of anger faded again. "I'm sorry. *I'm sorry,*" he told them both. "Please. Just do this for me. Don't ask why."

They were at the car now, and Kim took her daughter, putting her into the booster seat. She strapped Teri in with her toy bear and then rounded on Stephen. "You know I'm not going to do that. That's not who I am, it's not how my father raised me."

"Oh god, your father . . ." Stephen looked away. "Kim, we're all in danger."

"What did he say?" she repeated.

Stephen shook his head. "I didn't have a choice." He took a shuddering breath. "He didn't say anything. It's what Jack did, it's the people who want him . . ."

A chill ran down Kim's spine. "What happened?"

He looked back toward the hospital. "I'm going to make it right. But you have to get away from here, don't you get it? The ones hunting him, they were already here! They know who we are, they know where I work . . . They could be watching the house, or looking for us right now. I can't let them hurt us. I can't lose you two."

"Did . . ." She could barely form the words. "Did you give him up?"

"They said they would kill you. And Teri." The words fell from him in a rush. "I had no choice! I had to stall them . . ."

Kim backed away. "No . . ."

"I'll make it right!" he said. "But you have to leave. Please."

For a moment, all Kim wanted to do was push past Stephen and run headlong back into the hospital to search for her father, but then she saw Teri in the back-seat watching her with questioning eyes.

"Mommy?" said the little girl. "Are we gonna go?"

She seemed so small, so fragile, and suddenly Kim felt a powerful surge of protectiveness toward her child, enough that she found herself understanding the crippling choice her husband had made. "Yes," said Kim, the words like ashes in her mouth. "We're going."

All around them there were hundreds of windows looking down on the street, and any one of them could be hiding somebody with a weapon, some killer ready to do them harm. Stephen glanced up, thinking the same thing, and pushed Kim toward the driver's seat. "I won't let anything happen to our family," he vowed.

"I believe you," said Kim, and she meant it.

Two minutes later they were on the highway racing east, and Kim found it hard to stay focused on the road ahead as tears blurred her vision.

• • •

Ziminova paused to check the safety on her Makarov pistol and then returned the weapon to the paddle holster in the small of her back. The weapon was a bad fit with the disguise of the nurse's scrubs she was wearing, but now they were down on the lower levels of the hospital complex, it was less likely they would encounter someone who might recognize the SVR hunter team as interlopers. Ekel was waiting for them on the sublevel, that cocky grin he liked to wear plastered across his face. He talked about the American agents lying dead in plain sight up on the street, hidden inside their car, and made a passing mention of "other preparations" he had made. Bazin accepted this with a dismissive nod and did not explain any further. Ziminova wondered what Ekel was referring to, but she said nothing.

They found the storeroom and waited there, among the racks of medical supplies, old compressed air cylinders and stacked chairs. Lenkov bounced from foot to foot like a boxer limbering up before a bout, rolling a stubby baton around in one hand.

"You should have put a man on the doctor," insisted Ekel. "He might panic and run."

"No." Bazin shook his head. "He will not flee. A doting young father has little perspective on things when it comes to his wife and child. I know. I was once that man." He drew his Makarov and screwed a long silencer to the end of the muzzle.

Ekel raised an eyebrow. "Really? I find it hard to believe you are that attached to anything, sir."

"Some parents are capable of great sacrifice," he replied. "Others do not realize that their love for their offspring is a weakness they can never overcome."

"If you are wrong . . ." began Lenkov.

Out in the corridor, they all heard the clank of the service elevator arriving.

Bazin smiled. "I am not wrong." He nodded to the two men, his voice dropping to a whisper. "Remember. I want him alive."

Ziminova shrank back into the shadows cast around by the stark lightbulb dangling from the ceiling, as Ekel and Lenkov took up positions on either side of the door.

It opened a moment later and Jack Bauer came into the room in a rush. Ziminova recognized the face she had seen staring up at her from the file documents she had read in the consulate, now set in a determined cast.

She held back and watched as Lenkov and Ekel rushed him. The blond-haired SVR agent led the attack, disarming the American as Ekel came in for his own shot at the man. The metallic shape of Bauer's weapon skittered away across the concrete floor.

Their target shook off the moment of shock at the

surprise attack almost instantly, however. Ziminova was impressed with how fast he turned it around. In seconds, Ekel was reeling backward with broken bones while Bauer was engaging Lenkov in close-quarter hand-to-hand combat.

It wasn't an elegant engagement by any stretch of the imagination. Lenkov took a beating, coughing out specks of bright blood. Bauer's fighting style was all about violence and velocity, putting as much hurt as he could on his assailants as was possible in the smallest amount of time.

Ziminova was already gauging him, considering how she would approach this man if the fight came her way.

But then the question became moot. She saw the moment as it happened, when the ebb and flow of the fight suddenly turned against Bauer. *He is tired, yes*. All that pressure from running, hour after hour, fleeing across the country, battling every step of the way . . . it had exacted a toll. The American made a mistake, he hesitated, and it was enough to bring him down. Ekel struck him in the back of the knee and Bauer toppled.

"End this," snapped Bazin, gesturing sharply. "Now!"

The dark-haired man nodded wearily and pulled a boxy stun gun from his jacket pocket. He stepped up before Bauer could get to his feet, and pressed the contacts of the weapon into the man's chest. Ziminova winced as raw voltage ripped into the American and sent him crashing back down to the floor.

With his foot, Bazin nudged a threadbare office chair into the middle of the basement, directly beneath the stark white lightbulb. "Secure him," he ordered.

Lenkov and Ekel struggled with Bauer's dead weight, both men feeling the harsh effect of the blows their target had laid on them. It took a while to maneuver him into place.

Finally, Lenkov tuned his head and spat out a glob of

blood-laced spittle, producing two plastic cable ties that he used to tether Bauer's wrists to the arms of the chair.

The target—no, the *prisoner* now—lolled forward and blinked owlishly. Ziminova drew her cell phone from a pocket and raised it to her face. She selected the camera application and snapped a couple of shots of Bauer. He seemed to become aware of her, and peered in her direction. His gaze was feral and full of anger.

Bazin walked around the chair until he was looking Bauer in the eye. "It amazes me you are still alive. You should be dead a dozen times over."

"It's been said." Bauer's words were gruff.

"No longer." Bazin kept talking, amusing himself with the largely one-sided conversation, almost trying to goad the American into . . . *what?* Ziminova wondered what her commander's intention was. Did Bazin think this was some sort of game? Or was it that he liked to revel in the victory?

Bauer's death, when it came, would be a moment of import. The man was a renegade, and if his record was to be believed, he was a loose cannon in the black ops world. Killing the American would make a fine trophy for Bazin to carry home with him. That was why he had told the others to hold off from simply shooting Bauer the moment he entered the room. Bazin wanted to do the deed himself.

For her part, Ziminova found such attitudes distasteful. There were the needs of the mission and the orders at hand from the proper authorities to consider, nothing more. She disliked the way that Bazin played his operations out like they were games, to be scored and ranked upon completion.

"Your own people want you dead!" he was saying. "I do them a favor."

Bauer's answer was a weary, fatalistic snarl. "So do it, and be on your way."

His breaths rasping through his bruised throat, Lenkov held up his own cell phone and tapped a tab to begin recording a video file.

Bazin raised his gun and took aim. "Jack Bauer . . . your time is up." He turned and looked into the eye of the cell phone camera, switching to Russian for a moment to make the recording an official record of the act. "I am Major Arkady Bazin, field commander of Active Unit Green Six. Present with me to witness this lawful termination of a terrorist enemy combatant are operatives Lenkov, Ekel and Ziminova. Orders are authorized directly by the president." He continued on in English as he spoke of the men that the American had killed in New York during his one-man crusade to find those responsible for the death of his lover, the root of the hunt that had led them across the United States to this dark, subterranean room and this final moment. "You are guilty of the murders of Diplomatic Attaché Pavel Tokarev, Foreign Minister Mikhail Novakovich and the members of his protection detail, of conspiracy to assassinate President Yuri Suvarov and sundry other crimes against the people and the government of the Russian Federation. You are a threat to the security of our nation. For this, you have been declared an enemy of the state and sentenced to death. Do you have anything to say?"

The prisoner looked up and met their gazes, each one in turn. As he looked Ziminova in the eye, she was startled by a sudden vibration from the phone in her hand. She looked down, frowning. The display read INCOMING CALL: CONSULATE.

Bauer's reply came in pitch-perfect, unaccented Russian. "Maybe you should get that."

• • •

"Ignore it," snapped Bazin. "We'll talk to them when this is over."

But the woman, the one called Ziminova, shook her head and raised the phone to her ear, walking away across the room. She spoke Russian in low tones that Jack could barely register. Something about "the mission," and he guessed by her manner she was talking to someone in authority.

Bazin, clearly the SVR field commander, gave her an angry look for her disobedience. Jack assumed that this guy had already plotted out a neat little narrative in his head about how this confrontation would work, and now the flow of that was being interrupted and he wasn't happy.

He took the moment to test the flex in the two zip-ties holding him to the chair. They were tight, but his legs were still free, which meant he had a chance to exploit a weakness in the restraints.

Then the distraction he needed made itself available. Out in the corridor beyond the storeroom, the service elevator door slid open and they all heard the voice that called out a second later.

"Jack, where are you?" Stephen Wesley was shouting, desperate and terrified.

"*Stephen!*" Jack took a lungful of air and bellowed back at him. "Run! Don't—"

His words were cut off as his would-be executioner cracked him hard across the temple with the butt of his pistol. Pain lit pinwheels of light behind Jack's eyes, but he deliberately allowed the powerful impact to knock him over. The chair tilted under him and he went down to the floor on his side.

The blow rang through his skull like a bell, but it let Jack put the left arm of the office chair right beneath him. Out of sight beneath his body, he crushed the tiny block of plastic that acted as the zip-tie's lock between his weight and the hard concrete floor. He felt it fracture, and the binding on one wrist loosened, blood rushing back to his fingers with a sharp prickling sensation.

From the floor he saw Lenkov, the SVR operative with the blond hair, the one he had struck in the throat, draw a snub-nosed Smith & Wesson revolver and move toward the door as it opened.

Paying no heed to Jack's warning, Stephen rushed into the same trap that Jack had fallen into only moments ago. Lenkov caught Kim's husband by surprise as he entered, and used his free hand to punch him squarely in the face. A fan of blood spurted from Stephen's nose and he cried out in pain. Before he could react, Lenkov grabbed a handful of the doctor's overcoat and dragged him deeper into the basement room. He shoved him to one side and stepped back, aiming with the revolver.

Bazin made a disappointed noise. "Dr. Wesley. You are being very foolish." He walked toward the other man. "What is it about you Americans? You seem to think that you can be the hero of the story just because you wish it to be so? Did you think you would come in here and save him?" He pointed back toward where Jack lay. "*You?*" He released a bark of laughter, then shook his head. "No, no. You could have kept clear of this ugliness, Doctor. Now you will be a part of it."

From the corner of his eye, Jack could see that the woman had ended the call. She had become very still, watching events unfold. He considered her status as a combatant—no visible weapons deployed, out of range. She wouldn't be his primary threat vector. The others, Bazin and Lenkov, the ones with pistols in their hands, those were the enemies Jack had to deal with. The third one, Ekel, was still panting, nursing his broken rib.

Jack eased his hand around, getting ready. He would only have one shot at this.

"Sir," said Ziminova. "We have new orders. The situation has changed."

Bazin ignored her. "Put him up," he said, and Lenkov swaggered over, a smirk forming on his lips as he kneaded the grip of his revolver. He wanted some payback for the pain Jack had inflicted on him, and saw this as an opportunity. *That was good.* It would make him sloppy.

"*Sir,*" Ziminova repeated with more force. "Moscow wants us to abort."

"I will address their lack of will when this is over," Bazin snapped. "We have come too far to falter now."

The woman continued. "The kill order on Bauer has been suspended by the Duma. He is to be taken into custody instead. Pending an official trial into his crimes."

"This is his courtroom, right here," said Lenkov. "And the sentence has already been passed." He reached down with one hand and yanked hard on the arm of the cheap plastic chair, putting his strength into hauling Jack back to a sitting position.

What he didn't count on was Jack slipping his feet across the floor and pushing off against the concrete as he came up. Still tethered to the chair by his right wrist, Jack struck out violently with his off hand, grabbing at Lenkov's weapon before he could bring it to bear. In the same motion, he swept around with the other arm outstretched, and the chair came up and around. He broke it across the torso of his adversary and Jack felt the other zip-tie snap off with the force of the impact. The pieces of the chair clattered to the floor and the two men went into a frantic back-and-forth with the pistol between them.

"Stephen, get down!" Jack wrestled with the SVR agent, and the revolver discharged at the low ceiling over their heads. The bullet shrieked as it sparked off hanging pipes. Lenkov was strong, and he tried to push the gun back down and into Jack's face, but he twisted, wrestling the muzzle away. As they turned in place, Jack saw Ekel struggling to draw his own weapon.

He mashed the grip of the revolver and Lenkov could not stop his finger from contracting on the trigger. More shots rang out again and again, deafening in the tiny concrete space of the basement, rounds flashing brightly as they ricocheted from storage racks. Jack forced the gun to aim in the direction of a dozen medical oxygen canisters, and a bullet clanged into the side of one of the pressurized cylinders.

The shot didn't cause an explosion; that would have needed a naked flame, and in these close confines it would have been death for all of them. But the round was enough to pierce the steel tube and vent the gas inside, a jet of compressed oxygen abruptly turning it into an unguided missile. The cylinder leapt out of the rack in a wild, spinning trajectory that threw it straight at Ekel as he tried to duck away. The head of the canister struck him in the back of the neck with an ugly crack of breaking vertebrae. The man went down and did not move again.

Against the hissing, screeching chorus of escaping gas, Jack shouted with effort, digging deep to find the strength to wrench the revolver around. Dimly, he saw Bazin raising his pistol to shoot toward the two combatants, ignoring Stephen where he had dropped to the ground nearby.

Jack deliberately let himself go off-balance, pivoting into a half-turn that spun the blond Russian about just as his commander opened fire. Bullets from the silenced Makarov slammed into the back of the gunman with angry chugs and the man danced as they punched through his spine and his lungs.

Lenkov's death grip slackened and Jack let him go, still holding tight to the burning-hot metal frame of the Smith & Wesson. Stepping over the body, he pointed the revolver at Bazin's chest. In his haste to take Jack down, the big, craggy-faced Georgian had emptied his own firearm, and now the Makarov's slide was locked back, the magazine dry.

Weary with the effort of it all, Jack didn't offer any last words to the man. He pulled the revolver's trigger.

The hammer fell on a spent cartridge with a hollow, echoing click. Jack cursed inwardly.

Bazin grinned. "Lose count, did you?"

"Don't move!" Stephen scrambled toward something on the floor and in the next second he had shot to his feet. "Stay where you are!" Jack saw he had grabbed Ekel's gun from where it had fallen, and now he was brandishing it before him, moving the thickset pistol back and forth between the two remaining SVR agents.

Ziminova raised her hands slowly, but her commander only cocked his head, his grin widening.

"Stephen," said Jack. "Give me the weapon." He held out his hand.

"I wouldn't do that just yet!" Bazin barked. Tossing his useless pistol aside, he produced a small black rectangle from his jacket pocket, no larger than a pack of cigarettes. A short, flexible antenna extended from the top of the device, and on the face of it was an illuminated flip-switch. "Bauer knows what I have here, don't you? You've seen them before."

"Yes." All of Jack's rage, all his energy, drained from him in a brutal rush, as if it were water flowing out and soaking into the stony floor. Suddenly the dense, corditestinking air of the basement storeroom was stifling him, clogging his throat with dust and the odor of blood.

Bazin was holding a narrow-band, long-range radio detonator, the same kind that the Russian *Spetsnaz* special forces used in ambush attacks and denial missions.

"What is that?" Stephen asked, not understanding.

"I think your father-in-law sees where I am going with

this." Bazin shot a look toward the woman, who remained motionless, her face unreadable.

"Major, you must stand down," said Ziminova. "You cannot proceed. We have our orders."

"To hell with those vacillating fools!" Bazin snarled. "I will finish what I started. This is my contingency plan." He went on, gesturing with the detonator. "I only have to push this button and that spacious sedan you own, Dr. Wesley, will become a mass of torn metal and burning flesh spread out across some stretch of freeway."

"Bauer is the only target!" retorted the woman, appalled at her commander's words. "We are not here to murder innocents!"

Jack felt himself turning to stone, his mind unable to grasp the horror of that appalling image, knowing at once that it was no bluff. He remembered the words he had spoken to the assassin back on the freight train. *You know how the SVR works. They don't like loose ends.*

"I had Ekel place a charge on the vehicle just after your wife arrived at the hospital," added Bazin.

"No!" Stephen shouted, and he went pale, clutching at his stomach almost as if he were about to vomit. "Dear god, you can't be so callous . . ."

"I will give you this." Bazin wiggled the remote between his fingers. "Truly, I will. In return, all that I ask of you is that you take that gun you are holding, point it at your father-in-law there and shoot him dead." His tone shifted as he spoke, from casual and conversational to hard and unyielding. "A new agreement between us. Same as the old one, in point of fact. Bauer's life in trade for that of your wife and daughter."

"Jack . . ." Stephen's voice became a whisper. "I . . . I can't . . ."

"Why hesitate?" Bazin barked the question. "Only minutes ago, you were willing to agree to this trade, but

now you won't? You, who put your hands in other people's blood all the time, cannot get them dirty now, is that
it?" He was losing his patience, and he spat on the
ground. "Pitiful."

"No." Jack sneered. "You're the weak one in this room,
not him. He came down here to help me when he could
have just cut and run. That's not cowardice."

"You're right," Bazin retorted. "It is *sentiment*. And
you people are ripe with it." He glared at Stephen. "Kill
him. I won't tell you again."

Jack lowered his hands and turned to look his son-in-
law in the eye. The doctor's face was ashen. "It's all right,"
he said quietly. "Protect Kim and Teri. They're worth
more than I ever could be. I know you'll keep them safe.
Being here, now . . . That proves it."

The pistol trembled in Stephen's grip as he raised it.
"I'm so sorry."

"I forgive you." Jack turned away to save the man the
distress of having to see his face and pull the trigger.

Strangely, it didn't seem wrong to him that everything
would come down to a moment like this one. His life,
being put on the line for those he cared for. After all,
wasn't that the bargain that he had *always* made?

Time to pay up, Jack, said Nina's voice, out in the distance. He backed away a step, bracing for the shot he
knew would come.

But then another voice, another woman, spoke. "No,"
said Ziminova, stepping forward and drawing her
weapon. "This is not how we will proceed," she said
firmly.

Bazin's glare turned on the other agent. "Do not interfere!" he snapped.

And in that second, Jack was ready to embrace death.

"*No!*" The shout came from Stephen, and he pulled
the trigger twice. Jack flinched, his body instinctively

tensing in anticipation of the searing, brutal impact of the bullets, but instead the rounds whistled past his ear and he caught a strangled cry behind him.

Bazin took both shots in the chest and collapsed over a storage crate, wheezing as they pierced his lungs. Stephen cried out in horror at what he had done, repulsed by the act, staring down at the gun in his hand as if it were a poisonous snake.

Still alive but dying by seconds, Bazin clutched at his bloody torso. The radio detonator was on the floor, lost as the impacts knocked him back, and Jack saw a flash of brutal malice in the man's eyes as he came to the knowledge that he was already dead. Bazin lurched off the crate, clawing for the detonator.

Jack dove at him, landing hard atop the other man, fighting to get a grip. Coughing up spatters of crimson fluid, Bazin heaved himself toward the device, wanting nothing more than to commit one final act of hatred against a country, a people that he abhorred.

Hands grabbing at Bazin's throat, Jack fought to crush it, strangling the last breaths of air from him. Face-to-face, the two men battled to make their kill, each as determined as the other.

"No," Jack told him, inexorably tightening his grip. "*No*." At length, Bazin stopped struggling, stopped moving, stopped breathing.

Jack pushed off him and gingerly gathered up the fallen detonator, finding the disarming switch. The trigger button went dark, and he took a shaky breath.

When Jack looked up, the woman was standing over him. She held her gun in a loose but ready stance, not quite aiming it at him.

"What happens now?" he asked, for the moment unable to gather the strength to stand.

"The call," she explained. "It was a relay from Moscow. Yuri Suvarov has been forcibly removed from the office of president of the Russian Federation. He has been placed under arrest, pending an investigation into his involvement in a conspiracy to assassinate a foreign head of state." She paused to let that sink in. "As such, all personal executive orders issued by Suvarov have been temporarily suspended. This . . . hunt . . ." Ziminova glanced around the room. "It should never have gone this far. Bazin knew that. He proceeded anyway."

Jack watched her gather up anything from the dead men that could be used to identify them, stuffing wallets and fake IDs into a satchel. Stephen came to help him to his feet, and he winced at the pain as he got up. "Thanks," Jack managed. He took the Makarov from the other man's hands, and Stephen gave it up willingly.

Ziminova stood by the doorway, hesitating. She still had her gun drawn. Jack met her gaze, his finger touching the trigger of the pistol he held. "It's up to you how this goes from here," he told her.

Her eyes narrowed. "I follow my orders," she said. "But be clear, Bauer. This is only a stay of execution. A temporary reprieve. You have killed Russians. Important men. My people will want that blood cost to be paid in kind." Then, before he could find an answer, she slipped away into the basement corridor and was gone.

Stephen took a trembling breath and blew it out. "I think . . . I think this is the worst day of my life."

"You get used to them," said Jack, with a grim nod.

24

"Here." Laurel looked up to see the FBI agent offering her a steaming plastic cup of coffee.

She took it with a grateful smile. "Thanks. Agent Kilner, right?"

He nodded and sat down next to her on the low concrete wall outside the Apache Motel. "How are you doing?"

Laurel almost broke into laughter at the banality of the question. "I don't have anything to measure this against," she offered. "I thought I had it bad before, but . . ." Laurel gestured at the buildings around them, taking in the town. "Hell. Frying pan and fire, I reckon."

In the hours that followed the shoot-out at the old mega-mart building, a small army of lawmen had descended on the town of Deadline, largely on the summons of Kilner and his fellow agents. State troopers, officers from the US Marshal service and more people in FBI visibility jackets had arrived, and now it looked like they were in the process of dismantling the whole rotten place.

"You're safe," Kilner assured her. "It looks like whoever was left of the Night Rangers MC got on their bikes and fled south when things started falling apart. They had to know their little empire here was going to get blown open." He nodded in the direction of the former army base and the smoke still rising from its fire-damaged ruins. "Literally, in this case, thanks to Bauer."

Laurel sipped the coffee, thinking about the intense, steady gaze of the man who had saved her life just a short distance from where they now sat. "He took a powerful dislike to those scumbags. I know how he felt."

"Did you spend time with him?"

"Some." She nodded. "Chase too." Laurel felt a stab of grief at the thought of the younger man, who had taken a bullet meant for her. She looked away, wiping her eyes. "Why did they come here? I mean, they didn't have to. They could have stayed out of it."

Kilner shook his head. "Bauer . . . Edmunds . . . Neither were the kind of men to let injustice slip past them."

"What's gonna happen to Chase . . . His body, I mean?"

"It'll go back to his family, I guess. Our office in San Diego tracked them down . . . They didn't even know he was still alive."

Laurel nodded again. "When that happens, I'd like to talk to them. Tell them what he did for me."

"I'll see what I can do."

"What about Jack? That woman, do you know where she took him?"

He shook his head. "Truth is, there's a lot of people who wanted Jack Bauer dead."

"Like your boss?"

Kilner's lips thinned. "He's going to pay for his mistakes, you can count on it. Me, Dell and Markinson, we've all made statements about Hadley's actions. He'll never carry a badge again. He's looking at some serious jail time." Kilner fell silent for a moment. "Bauer deserved better than what he got. Edmunds too. They both put their lives on the line for this country a dozen times over."

"I don't know anything about that," Laurel ventured, "but I know they put them on the line for *me*. And all the other folks those bikers lied to."

"About that." Kilner looked at her. "Laurel, there's a lot of people here who are scared and they're reluctant to talk to law enforcement. But this is a big deal. We've stumbled on the hub of a major methamphetamine ring based in Deadline, along with all the crimes of fraud, kidnapping, human trafficking and everything else connected to it."

"Cherry has been around longest, I think," she said. "Talk to her."

"Maybe you could be there when I do that," he prompted. "Show her and the others they can trust the cops. Everyone in this town is a witness to what's been going on here, but we can't do anything unless they're willing to go on the record."

Laurel frowned. "With all due respect, I'm betting that no one hereabouts has ever had the law give a damn about them, Agent Kilner. No cops came looking before. And is this even your jurisdiction?"

"That's not important," he said. "What matters is that we help these people now."

For a long minute, Laurel said nothing, staring blankly ahead of her. In the light of day, Deadline looked every inch the worn-out, tumbledown ghetto. It was a vampire town, she realized, something that should have been dead a long time ago, kept alive by feeding off the lives of others. Somebody needed to put a stake through its heart.

Is that me? She wanted to run. That was the easiest thing to do, the most familiar of her choices. That was how she had dealt with bullies in high school, uncaring foster parents and abusive boyfriends. *Just run.* Because taking a stand required courage that Laurel had never dared to reach for, always afraid that she would look for it and find nothing there.

She thought about Jack and Chase. Both strangers to her, both people who owed her nothing, wanted nothing in return. And yet they had fought to keep her alive, stood up against the threats even though the price had been the highest of all.

Can I live with myself if I don't even try *to do the same?* The question echoed through her thoughts.

At length, Laurel drained the last of the coffee and tossed the cup away. "You should let me do the talking first," she told him. "Okay?"

"Okay," he said with a smile. "And thank you."

Laurel shook her head. "I'm just paying someone back, is all."

• • •

Hadley knew something was wrong when the helicopter that had been sent to take him back to division went off course, and the flight crew refused to answer any of his questions.

Now he was in a twenty-by-twenty room with bare concrete walls, looking at himself sitting in a metal chair before a metal table, his reflection staring back at him from a smoke-gray mirrored window. His expression was empty, his gaze hollow and defeated. Bright stainless steel handcuffs held his wrists to a ring bolted to the top of the table. There was no clock in the room, nothing to mark the passage of time. They had taken his watch, his belt and shoelaces, everything in his pockets. Thomas Hadley had never been a prisoner before, and he didn't like the feeling.

Across the room, a door opened and two people entered. One was a Hispanic woman with an unreadable expression, and the other was a taller man with tawny skin. Hadley pegged him as Middle Eastern but he couldn't be certain. Both were dressed in the same kind of nondescript jacket-trouser outfits that were practically a uniform for government operatives.

He ventured a guess. "You're not with the bureau."

The woman sat in another chair opposite Hadley and put a leather folder down in front of her. The man stood near the door, arms folded across his chest. "FBI Special Agent Thomas Hadley," said the woman. "Out of the New York field office. You've gone way off-book, Agent. There are going to be consequences."

"I want to talk to my supervisor," Hadley replied. "Mike Dwyer."

"No," offered the man. "You talk to us."

"About Jack Bauer," added the woman. "The way I understand it, you wrote yourself a blank check to tear up the place looking for him. An armed high-speed pursuit through Hell's Kitchen. Appropriation of a federal agency airplane. Interfering with investigations on a local and state level, collusion with known criminal elements, not to mention actions that caused reckless endangerment of other agents and civilians."

Hadley shifted in his seat, feeling his temper rise. "Who are you people? CIA? Homeland Security? NSA?" He shook his head. "I took the initiative. Bauer is a very dangerous man and an exceptional target. If I had to work outside the lines to bring him in and—"

"*Outside the lines,*" repeated the woman, with a sarcastic smirk. "That's cute."

"But you *didn't* bring him in, did you?" snapped the man. "According to eyewitness reports, both Bauer and his associate were shot dead. And it has to be said, your conduct didn't exactly square with the intent of making a live capture."

The woman eyed him. "Did you want payback for Jason Pillar's murder? You blame Bauer for everything that led up to that? Did you let yourself get fixated on him?"

Hadley realized they were deliberately trying to provoke him, and he looked away. "Bauer is dead. What does it matter now?"

"Where's the body?" said the man.

"I don't know. The shooter took it. The assassin." He gestured at the air. "She uses the alias 'Mandy.'"

"We know her." The woman glanced at her partner. "We also know that without a corpse, we don't have proof-positive that Jack Bauer was actually killed."

"He's been dead before," offered the man. "Doesn't seem to stick with him, though."

"I know what I saw."

"Uh-huh." The woman opened the folder to reveal a tablet computer inside, and used it to bring up a picture. It was a shot of the face of a male corpse, lying on a mortuary table. "Tell me about this."

Hadley studied the image. "Powder burns and an entry wound on the throat. Looks like the guy put a gun under his chin and shot himself. Don't know him."

"That's Arthur Nemec. Senior technical manager for Atlantic Cellular Systems, Incorporated. He blew his own head off at dawn today. Left a suicide note explaining that he had been coerced into working as an asset for agents of the Russian government. Forced to run covert cell traces through the telephone network. You want to guess who they asked him to find?"

Hadley licked his lips. "Like I said, I don't know him."

She tapped the tablet's screen, flicking past more pictures. These were shots of a crime scene, in a basement somewhere. Three more dead men, each starkly illuminated by the light of a camera flash, scrolled past. "These are a little fresher," she noted. "Killed in the basement of

Cedars-Sinai hospital out in LA earlier today. Initial analysis IDs them all as ex-Russian special forces."

"We also have unconfirmed reports that a CTU mobile unit was taken out at the same location," said the man. "And apparently one of their bomb-disposal teams was deployed on the one-ten freeway shortly after. Know anything about that?"

"CTU's been shut down since yesterday," Hadley insisted.

"Well, they're *supposed* to be," corrected the woman. "They're not exactly being cooperative right now."

"I've got no connection to this!" said the agent. "You people tell me who you are, right now! You have no right to hold me here!"

She showed him two more images, ignoring his angry tone. Side by side, both shots appeared to have been pulled from grainy security camera footage. The first framed a woman Hadley had never seen before, who clearly knew where the camera was placed and was trying to avoid its gaze. When he didn't respond, she presented the other image for his attention. In it was a man in an EMT jacket with a cap pulled down over his eyes and his collar raised. He couldn't be certain, but it could have been Bauer.

"Well?" prompted the man.

Hadley's jaw set and he glared across the room, past the two interrogators toward the mirrored window. "I'm not saying another word. Charge me if you want to, or let me out of this place!"

The woman studied him for a moment, then abruptly gathered up the tablet. "This is a waste of time. He can't tell us anything. We're done here."

He watched them both exit the room, and the magnetic bolts of the door locked shut as they left him alone.

In the silence that followed, Hadley could only hear the thudding of the blood in his ears, a sound like his life slowly collapsing around him.

• • •

The two interrogators walked into the observation room where their supervisor had been watching on the other side of the one-way glass, turning to see three armed men enter the holding space and gather up Hadley for transport. The man's face vanished beneath a sense-deadening hood and he struggled as they walked him out.

The woman turned her back on the window. "Useless," she explained.

Her supervisor, a balding man with gray at his temples, gave a curt nod. "It was worth a try. Toss him back to the bureau, let them clean up their mess. But keep a watch on what they're doing, just in case."

"There was an update from New York," said the other man. "An FBI team arrested one of Jack Bauer's known associates this morning. A senior CTU technician named Chloe O'Brian. Did it right in front of her kid."

"Classy," offered the woman. "I'll get eyes on her questioning."

"Do that," said the supervisor. "In the meantime, wheels are going to start turning. All of this proves that Jack Bauer is too big a risk to this country to be allowed to roam free. You both saw his file. He's been exposed to too much. He has knowledge that could have devastating effects if it got into the hands of a foreign power. I'll have a multi-agency warrant issued for his arrest and detention, and put every station we have around the world on notice. If he's dead, we need to be one hundred percent certain of it. If not . . . we need to find him and isolate him. No matter where he goes."

"Those are the orders?" said the woman.

She got a nod in return. "From the very top. The FBI clearly couldn't handle a target of Bauer's abilities . . . But we trained him. We helped make him what he is."

The supervisor walked away. "He's the CIA's problem now."

• • •

"Hey," said the crewman, walking across the deck toward him. "You Barrett?"

"John Barrett," he lied. "That's me."

"You work your passage on ships before?"

He nodded. "Couple of times."

"Good. We could use some experienced hands on this voyage." The crewman looked up at the sky overhead. "Looks like it's gonna be smooth sailing. We're all squared away right now, so I guess I'll show you your rack, if you want."

"It's okay," he said, shaking his head. "I'll be down in a while."

"Your call, man." The crewman shrugged and walked away.

Jack turned toward the stern rail and watched the Port of Los Angeles recede behind him, the flat and calm waters of the Pacific Ocean drawing the *Veracruz* toward the distant horizon.

The MV *Veracruz* was a container ship flying a Dutch flag, and she was an aging boat, a Panamax just over nine hundred feet long, heavy with rust and the smell of engine oil. But she was also the kind of ship that didn't draw attention, a plodder that made the run between Port Botany in Sydney across to LA and back, sketching the same course from California to New South Wales month after month, all year round.

Jack didn't want to look away from the sight across the ship's churning white wake. He didn't want to waste one second of this view of his country, because on some level, he was telling himself that it could quite possibly be the last time he would see it.

Much of Jack's turbulent life, from rebellious teenager to federal agent to international fugitive, had orbited around this stretch of the California coastline, and it seemed cruelly fitting that if he were to leave the land of his birth forever, it should be by this path.

It would take days for them to reach Australia, and once he was there Jack would not be able to rest. Sydney was just the first port of call for him, the start of a new existence that would happen under the radar, away from prying eyes. He wasn't sure where he would go next, but there were plenty of possibilities.

Not for the first time, Jack thought about returning to West Africa, back to the school in Sangala that his old friend Carl Benton had built. He wondered how that beleaguered country had fared in the years since the attempted military coup. *Would they come looking for me there?* he wondered. He frowned. That was a chance he didn't want to take, and a danger he didn't want to bring to their door.

Instead, Jack considered all the places where he had the *most* enemies. South America, packed with drug cartels and militias fighting for power and control. Eastern Europe, where unsettled scores from past wars were still festering. As much as there were people out there who hated him, there were also people who owed him favors. And no sane person would think to look for him in those places, because to go there was to put his head back in the lion's mouth. *But then I've never played a safe bet in my life.*

He had the whole voyage to think it through. No one had seen him slip out of the city, and thanks to some help from Stephen, he had made it to the port unchallenged.

Jack watched the coast grow distant and thought about Kim and her family. He had meant what he said in the basement storeroom. He held no malice toward his son-in-law for putting his wife and daughter's welfare before Jack's, and if the roles had been reversed, he would have done the same. The fact that the young doctor had endangered his own life to save Kim's father, that despite himself he had pulled that trigger, these things spoke volumes about Stephen Wesley. Kim had chosen a good man in him, someone who had a different kind of strength to Jack's, but a strength nonetheless. Jack had no fears for his daughter's safety—she was resilient, just as her mother had been—and with someone like Stephen at her side, they would survive.

The threat of the bomb had been very real, but Stephen had gotten to his wife in short order and after an anonymous call to CTU the device had been found and disarmed. That Kim and little Teri had come so close to death chilled Jack's blood, and he knew that if he ever needed to remind himself why he had to stay away to keep them secure, he would recall that feeling.

Still, it wounded him to know that he might never be able to watch his grandchild grow up, perhaps to have a family of her own. The peaceful life, the retirement that Jack had been ready to embrace only a day or so earlier, now seemed like a fantasy.

You don't get to have that, said a voice in the back of his mind. *Not after all you have done, Jack. Not after all the blood on your hands.*

He looked down at his palms, and for a moment he felt an irrational stab of dread, that if he turned around Jack would find Nina Myers standing there behind him, that predatory smile playing on her lips.

He shook off the thought, banishing the ghost of memory, knowing that it was just the fatigue talking, playing games with his mind.

As he watched the land finally slip beneath the horizon and vanish, he nodded to himself. The truth was, there were many ghosts following Jack Bauer, friends and lovers, enemies and victims alike.

A long time ago, he had made his peace with that, and Jack knew that somewhere out there a final deadline for his life was inching closer, a clock ticking down toward zero. He knew that one day his ghosts would catch up with him.

But today was not that day.

ABOUT THE AUTHOR

JAMES SWALLOW is the *New York Times* bestselling author of more than thirty-five books, including fiction from the worlds of Star Trek, Doctor Who, and more. His other credits feature scripts for video games and radio dramas, including *Deus Ex: Human Revolution, Fable: The Journey, Battlestar Galactica*, and *Killzone 2*. A BAFTA nominee, James lives in London and is currently at work on his next novel.

Turn the page for a preview of

24™

ROGUE

DAVID MACK

Coming Soon

FORGE®

A FORGE BOOK

Copyright © 2015 by Twentieth Century Fox Film Corporation

01

The Gulf of Aden—11°01'23.8" N, 44°57'04.4" E
Approximately 40 Miles North of Berbera, Somalia

The skiff's prow cleaved through black waves. Salt water sprayed Osman Xasan Muhamad's face as the narrow boat slammed into a trench between crests, kicking cold froth over its gunwales. At his back were two more skiffs loaded with armed and desperate men. Behind them hovered the waxing half disk of the moon, low and languid in its descent toward the western shore. Far ahead, lightning danced between the sea and the edge of a storm cloud.

He looked back toward Sadiq Khalif Fárah, his second-in-command, who manned the lead skiff's outboard engine. "Faster! We're going to miss them!"

"This is as fast as it goes." Sadiq held the boat's rudder in one hand and a digital compass in the other. He hollered back over the spluttering of the engine, "We should be close!"

As Osman peered into a darkness with no horizon, the fear of a missed deadline set his guts churning. "I don't see them. They must be running dark." Another spurt of water doused his face and left him spitting brine. "If we miss the rendezvous—"

"We won't."

Osman wondered if Sadiq would be so calm if he were the one who would have to answer for their failure should the freighter slip away. He tightened his grip on his AK-47 and strained to pierce the deepening gloom of night ahead of the speeding skiff.

Nothing but shadows pitching and rolling against other shadows.

All that Osman had, and all he hoped to have, depended on this mission. Raiding the freighter was a once-in-a-lifetime opportunity. Beyond the outrageous ransom he and his men had been promised for delivering its most valuable cargo, they each stood to earn a fortune from selling the rest of the ship's freight on the black market—not to mention the vast sums the ship itself would command from the right buyers. This score would free Osman from his life of piracy and fund his escape from Somalia—a journey for which he had longed his entire life.

Unfortunately, Sadiq appeared not to care about any of that. A sadist, he seemed born to live under the black flag. He needed money as badly as Osman and all the rest of their tribesmen, but that wasn't what drove him. Osman knew from the predatory gleam in Sadiq's eyes that he enjoyed being a pirate. An outlaw. A killer.

By tomorrow we'll be done, Osman promised himself. *After that, I will never have to see him again. He will be free to walk his path, and I will walk mine—far from here.*

He squinted against a stinging spray over the prow, wiped his eyes, and struggled to see anything ahead except darkness. Then he found what he sought—a pale red dot of light. Staccato blinks in Morse code, the prearranged signal from their contact on the freighter.

"I see them! Shift heading, north-northeast."

The skiff rolled and bobbed with nauseating swiftness as Sadiq adjusted its course toward the signal light. Osman fought back the urge to retch—he had always hated water travel—and watched the blinking crimson dot until he was sure he had seen the entire message.

"Their course is steady. Speed, ten knots. We're clear for an aft approach."

"Got it." Sadiq plowed the skiff through another frothy crest of water, right on target. Osman relayed the information to the other skiffs with his own red signal light. Then he tucked the miniature beacon back into a deep pocket on the leg of his cargo pants and faced the rest of the men in his and Sadiq's skiff. "As soon as we reach the main deck, you all know what to do?"

"I lead the search belowdecks," said Ashkir.

Osman pointed at another man. "Dubad? Where do you go?"

"My men and I help you secure the pilothouse and radio room."

"Good." Osman trained his keen eyes on the group's hothead, Feysal. "You?"

Sullen and brimming with half-muzzled violence, the youth muttered, "I hold the prisoners on the forecastle."

"*Prisoners,* Feysal. *Not* corpses. Remember that." He looked at his last henchman, Yusuf. "You need to clear the engine room as fast as possible."

Yusuf ejected the magazine of his AK-47, blew a speck of beach sand off it, then slapped it back into his rifle. "I know what to do."

"Everyone remember the plan, and by dawn we'll all be rich men." It was not an empty promise. Osman had every reason to believe that this mission would prove as lucrative for his men as it would for him and Sadiq. That had been a key factor in his decision to accept such a dangerous operation against so infamous an adversary. He had come to pay the ransom on his freedom and take back control over his own life.

Another series of red flashes from the target. The way was ready, the approach clear. Despite the cover of night,

Osman began to discern the shape of the freighter slicing across the gulf ahead of him and his men. He swallowed his fears, mustered a brave smile, and looked back at Sadiq. "It's time. Take us in, and stay out of their wake."

• • •

Unarmed, his back to the *Barataria*'s forecastle bulwark, Jack Bauer suppressed years of well-honed combat reflexes and let Callum Trent seize the collar of his shirt, when all he wanted to do was break the man's neck and dump his limp body overboard.

"I can't figure you out, Conway," the gunrunner said. Trent knew Jack only by his alias, Tom Conway, a name Jack had dredged up from an old mission profile and adopted as his own.

It took all of Jack's vast experience at deception to project an air of innocent alarm, and even more concentration to fake a Belfast accent. "What do you mean, Mr. Trent?"

"I mean, I don't get what you're doing here. You had a good thing going as a fixer for the IRA. So what're you doing on this rust bucket, pushing lead from port to port?"

Jack knew enough about the real Conway's troubles to pass them off as his own. "Times change. So do the people in charge. When my friends dropped out, I knew it was time to go."

"The way I hear it, McPherson didn't give you much choice."

"As I said—it was time to go."

It seemed Trent's misgivings had been set to rest. He let go of Jack's shirt and stroked his bushy horseshoe mustache. Then he shook his head. "Here's what bothers me, Conway. You were Belfast's bogeyman for years. Nobody agreed what you looked like. There were no photos of you, no arrest records, no fingerprints. You were a ghost. Now you're swabbing decks for Karl Rask. Why come out of the shadows for scut work?"

"You really need me to say it? I lost everything when things went bad in Paris."

Trent nodded. "Yes, the death of Seamus must have been quite a setback."

"You can't imagine." Jack was gambling his life on the fact that only a handful of people in the entire world knew the real Tom Conway had been assassinated after an undercover agent took out one of the Irish Republican Army's senior leaders, a merciless terrorist named Seamus O'Rourke. Both killings had been part of a clandestine mission Jack secretly set in motion several months earlier. As far as he could tell, no one yet realized he had been the source of the intelligence that led to O'Rourke's and Conway's respective downfalls. Fortunately, there were enough similarities between Conway's story and Jack's that he found it easy to steal.

"I can't go home. Not for a while, at any rate. For now, I need to make new friends."

"You want friends, you've come to the wrong place."

Jack sensed Trent would never respect anyone who didn't come at him from a position of strength. He changed his rhetorical tactics to keep the man off balance. "You're right. I never had much use for friends, either. What I need are new business relationships. New connections."

"A fixer without connections isn't much use to anyone."

"Seamus wasn't my only ally. I'm lying low—not down for the count."

"Meaning what? You think you have something I want?"

"You? I couldn't say. But your employer? Aye. Maybe I do."

Trent's eyes narrowed. "I doubt you have anything Mr. Rask needs."

"Maybe that should be for him to decide."

Derision put a smug smile on Trent's face. "You don't talk to Rask unless I say so. If you think you have something he wants, you have to convince *me* first."

There it was—the opportunity for which Jack had wrangled his way aboard this massive ark of arms and ammunition. The chance to put himself within striking distance of the inner circle of Karl Rask, one of the world's most elusive and notorious smugglers and dealers of arms great and small. The man could procure seemingly anything for anyone, anywhere. He had his hands in everything from small arms to field artillery, from fighter jets to cluster bombs.

"What if I told you I could get my hands on undocumented MIRV warheads?"

"Rask already has half a dozen waiting for buyers."

Jack masked his frustration with a grin. "Or the new MI6 ciphers?"

"We get weekly updates from our own source at Vauxhall Cross."

It was like trying to bluff someone holding four aces. "How about six vials of Russian smallpox virus, weaponized and ready for deployment?"

That cocked Trent's eyebrow. "Interesting. Where, when, and how much?"

"Odessa, four weeks from now. Twenty million, American."

"Tempting. Tell me again—why would we need *you*?"

"Introductions. And directions—Odessa's a big city."

Trent seemed almost amenable to the idea. Then his stare hardened. "I guess what really bothers me is that I've heard more than one person tell me Conway's dead." He shot an accusatory look at Jack. "Got his brains painted across the back of an elevator in Madrid."

Jack chuckled, as if at an old joke. "Good. That means the money I spent spreading that rumor wasn't wasted."

A faux-humble shrug. "As the saying goes, 'The greatest trick the devil ever pulled was convincing the world he didn't exist.'"

"You have an answer for everything, don't you?"

"No. You just keep asking questions I can answer with the truth."

Trent relaxed his guard—not by much, just enough that Jack sensed his interrogation was either over or at least on hold. The lean, thirtyish gunrunner looked out over the bulwark into the darkness ahead of the freighter, which plowed on a steady course toward its next port of call in Mumbai, India. "I don't want you to think your experience and your connections aren't valued or respected, Conway. But we have to be cautious."

"I understand. Hell, that's what led to Seamus's undoing. He let himself get too close to what was happening on the ground. It got him a bullet in the head."

"Precisely." The ghost of a sly notion animated Trent's weathered features. "Think you can talk your Odessa contact down to fifteen million for the smallpox?"

"Maybe. But they'll need to know I have the cash on hand when I arrive."

"That can be arranged, but I'll have to go with you to the meeting."

"Naturally."

Trent took a pack of Gauloises from his pants pocket, shook one cigarette loose, tucked it into his mouth, and lit it with a stainless steel Zippo. After a long drag that flared the tip of the cancer stick cherry red, he extended the pack toward Jack, who refused with a casual wave. Shrugging, Trent tucked the blue box of pungent French lung darts back into his pocket. "I thought Gauloises were your favorites."

"I quit after I went underground. Changed my habits to stay off the radar."

"Very smart." Trent put away his lighter—and came up

with a loaded Beretta, which he pointed at Jack's face. "Conway *never* smoked. He was born with asthma." He backed up a few steps to keep his pistol out of Jack's reach. "Now, then. Why don't you put your hands on your head, kneel on the deck, and tell me who you really are?"

With his lie unraveled, Jack folded his hands atop his head and sank to his knees. "It's a long story."

Trent leaned against the forecastle bulwark and steadied his aim. "That's all right. We have plenty of time to sort out the details. So let's start with your name."

What did he have left to lose? He dropped the accent. "My name is Jack Bauer."

• • •

A mouthful of harsh chemical aftertaste told Simon Dedrick, the ship's third mate, that he had smoked his cigarette down to the filter. He tapped its last crown of ash over the aft bulwark, then flicked the smoldering filter into the night, condemning it to oblivion in the sea.

Two quick, dim red flashes from astern. The pirates were close and ready to board.

He released the accommodation ladder on the *Barataria*'s aft starboard quarter. It fell with a shriek of rusted metal, loud and piercing enough to rouse the dead. Dedrick cursed under his breath and fought to ease the ladder toward the froth surging against the freighter's waterline.

It had been hard enough getting out of the pilothouse and off the superstructure without drawing attention. Then he'd had to risk being spotted by anyone who might be on deck, in order to signal the pirates in the skiffs. He still couldn't see them, but he had glimpsed their Morse code response, and whether he was ready or not, it was time to do what needed to be done.

Another red flash from below. The pirates were approaching the ladder.

Dedrick lifted the radio from his belt and pressed the talk button. "Conn, this is Dedrick! Man overboard, port side! Cut the engines! All stop!"

The second mate, Johan Schupp, answered without delay. "*All stop!*"

Alarms sounded throughout the freighter, on the main deck and through the labyrinth of compartments below. The great thrumming of its engines slowed and went quiet.

Another barked order into the radio: "Give me lights and a rescue party at the port bow."

Members of the crew scrambled up from belowdecks and sprinted forward. From high atop the superstructure, the *Barataria*'s spotlights snapped on. Blinding beams sliced through the darkness and swept the water ahead of the ship and along its port side.

Dedrick leaned over the aft starboard bulwark and looked down the accommodation ladder. The men of the first skiff were already piling out and climbing toward him, assault rifles in hand. As the last man left their skiff, he set it adrift to make way for the next one.

Osman, the Somalis' leader, was the first to reach the main deck. He greeted Dedrick with a condescending light slap on his face. "Good boy. Just like we told you."

The other pirates skulked past them, stooped like old men as they hurried in different directions—some forward, some toward the superstructure's aft staircase. Dedrick struggled to keep his attention on Osman. "I did what you wanted. Now let my family go."

"They go free when we control the ship." He pointed a Glock semiautomatic pistol at Dedrick's gut. "Take us up to the radio room."

"Not until I know my family is safe." It had been forty-eight hours since accomplices of Osman broke into

Dedrick's home in Pretoria, South Africa, and taken hostage his wife, Elaine, and his daughter, Karla. At the time, he'd known he had no leverage for bargaining. Now that the last group of pirates was climbing the ladder and their skiff was floating away, they were committed—which meant they needed his cooperation or else they were all going to die. "Let them go now, and show me proof, or you won't get anywhere near the radio room."

Osman's eyes burned with resentment. He summoned one of his men with a whistle. "Sadiq. Show him his women."

It surprised Dedrick to see the young Somali thug pull a large smartphone from inside his vest. He couldn't imagine how impoverished Somalis could acquire such a device, much less get a service plan for it, but he put aside his questions when Elaine and Karla's faces appeared on the screen. They looked haggard, with eyes red from weeping, but they were undeniably alive.

"Simon? Is that you?"

"It's me, *liefling*. Don't worry, everything's going to be all right."

Osman covered the screen with his palm. "Enough."

"They walk. *Now*. Or we all die."

An angry sigh. Osman took the smartphone from his man and grumbled into its microphone, "Bassar, we're done with them. Let them go."

He turned the screen toward Dedrick, who watched, unable to breathe, as a masked man cut Elaine and Karla's bonds, then shooed them out their house's back door. Osman switched off the phone and tucked it into his pocket. "My man can still chase them down. Take us to the radio room, and he won't have to."

"This way."

Dedrick led Osman and six bedraggled pirates up the superstructure's rear stairs, to the aft entrance of the command suite. Below them, a dozen of their compatriots split into teams of three and prowled forward on the starboard side, all but unnoticed by the *Barataria*'s crew, who were gathered on the port side searching for a non-existent man overboard.

Standing at the keypad beside the aft door, a small inner voice of courage urged Dedrick to enter the alarm code, to make at least an attempt at stopping the pirates. Then he pictured the pirates putting a bullet in his head, and he clung to the irrational hope that he might live through this calamity if only he cooperated. He entered the access code and unlocked the door.

"Thank you, Mr. Dedrick." Osman shouldered past him and pulled the door open. He flashed him a grin of stained, crooked teeth. "You've been most helpful."

Behind his ear, Dedrick heard the hammer of a pistol being cocked, and he knew his hopes of survival had been in vain. The crack of a gunshot was the last thing he heard as his world went black and washed away, just another flick of ash in the sea.

• • •

"You're making a mistake," Jack said.

Callum Trent was certain he held every advantage. He had the Beretta. He was standing, and Jack Bauer was on his knees, hands clasped on top of his head. So why was Bauer acting as if he were still the one in charge?

"Give me one good reason not to put a bullet in your brain."

"Because I'm not bluffing about being able to hook you up with Russian smallpox."

Suspicion gnawed at Trent. "Why would you do that? You're CTU."

"Ex-CTU. If you know my name, you know I'm a wanted man." He moved his hands from his head, then froze as Trent cocked the hammer on his pistol. "Living on the run takes money. I can't hold a regular job with half the world hunting me. This is all I have left."

Trent lined up his sights on the space between Bauer's eyebrows. "A minute ago, you tried to pass yourself off as Tom Conway. You're a bit short on credibility."

"My credibility will be the money I can help you earn. I *had* to lie about my name. I can't walk around telling people who I really am. I have too many bounties on my head."

What he was saying was plausible, but Trent's doubts ran too deep to be overcome so easily. "Maybe we should just put you up for auction, see who makes the highest bid."

"Advertising you have me would just get you killed."

Bauer was right, and Trent knew it. Neither the Russians nor the Americans took kindly to being extorted. Trying to pick their pockets for a bounty would only put Trent, his men, and the rest of Karl Rask's operation in the crosshairs of competing special forces operators.

He lowered his weapon just enough to signal that he was reconsidering his options. "All right. What am I supposed to do with you?"

"Hire me."

"I'll give you credit for audacity if nothing else. And how will I—?"

Alarms whooped from loudspeakers mounted on the superstructure and the cargo derrick in the middle of the main deck. The steady rumbling of the engines ground to a sudden halt. Searchlights mounted above the pilothouse snapped on and swept down the port side of the ship as members of the crew scrambled up from belowdecks and hurried forward, toward Trent and Bauer. Careful not to let Bauer use the distraction against him, Trent stole furtive looks at the unfolding chaos. "What the hell is going on?"

The captain's voice blared from one of the loudspeakers: "*Man overboard, port side!*"

Bauer looked as confused as Trent. "What're they talking about? Who's overboard?"

"Maybe they spotted someone adrift."

"I don't like it." Bauer tried to stand, then dropped back to his knees as Trent refreshed his aim. "It feels off. Who the hell would be adrift here?"

"Stranger things have happened." Trent was torn between curiosity about what was happening on the other side of the ship, and the nagging concern that Bauer might be right. "Let's just stay put and let the crew do their job. If it turns out to be—"

A faint crack of gunfire from the aft end of the ship turned both their heads.

Trent took his aim off Bauer and dropped to a crouch. "Did you hear that?"

Bauer nodded. "I need to check something." He motioned for Trent to follow him to the bulwark. Moving in tandem, they leaned over the side and looked aft. Bauer pointed toward the waterline. "Damn it! The ladder's down. We've been boarded."

Out of the shadows, Trent saw the dark shapes of men carrying assault weapons, a dozen of them, moving single file up the port side of the main deck. He and Bauer were outnumbered and outgunned. "Fall back," he whispered. They darted to cover on the forecastle, behind the gearboxes for the ship's anchors. Trent lifted his radio. "Shattuck! We're being boarded! Send a team to protect the shipment and get the rest of our men out of their racks, now!"

"*Roger,*" replied his right-hand man. "*On our way.*"

Bauer peeked through a gap in the gear assembly. "They'll be here any second. Do you have a backup piece?"

"You don't really think I'm handing you a loaded weapon?"

Frustration sharpened Bauer's whisper. "There's no time to argue! When they come up that ladder, it's gonna take *both* of us to hold them off."

"Then I regret to inform you that, no, I don't have a backup weapon."

"Tell me you at least have a spare magazine."

Trent bit down on his growing anger with Bauer. "I didn't expect to need it."

Bauer shook his head. "Great. Could this *get* any worse?"

Bursts of automatic gunfire ripped through the air. Fiery flashes from the muzzles of rifles lit up the shadows in the center of the main deck, revealing a second team of pirates, who had sneaked into position behind the ship's crew on the port side.

Trent frowned. "The number of hostiles just doubled. I'd say that qualifies as *worse.*"

Six pirates moved toward the forecastle ladder. Bauer eyed the deck between himself and ship's bow; then he turned to Trent. "Do you trust me?"

"Not one bit."

"Too bad. On the count of three, make *them* duck for cover."

"Why? What are you going to do?"

"Everything I can to save your ass and your shipment." He crouched and tensed. "One. Two. Three!"

Bauer leaped into motion. Trent sprang to his feet and emptied his Beretta at the squad of pirates. When his weapon clacked empty, Trent dropped back to cover behind the gear assembly. He caught a fleeting glimpse of Bauer's feet as they disappeared over the starboard bow.

I'm sure as hell not taking that way out, Trent decided. He cast aside his empty pistol and reached for his phone. He keyed the speed-dial code for Rask, who answered on the second ring.

"*What is it, Cal?*"

"We've been boarded. Somalis, I think. Don't know how many. We—"

A rifle's warm muzzle nudged his temple. Callused hands plucked his phone from his grasp. A pirate whose facial scars looked like Hell's highway map flung the phone overboard. He and five of his cohorts surrounded Trent.

The man spoke in thickly accented English. "On your knees. Hands on your head."

Forced to adopt the stance he had imposed on Jack Bauer only minutes earlier, Trent couldn't help but admire the cruel whimsy of life's little ironies.

• • •

Several short bursts from Sadiq's assault rifle reduced the *Barataria*'s radio room to sparking junk. White-hot phosphors spit from mangled banks of electronics, stinging Osman's face as he marched past the smoking mess. He keyed in the access code he had seen Dedrick use on the outer door. The magnetic bolt lock on the door to the pilothouse released with a buzz. He pulled the door open and stood aside to let Sadiq and his men charge inside, rifles braced.

Sadiq blasted out a side window with a single burst. "Nobody move! On the deck!"

The ship's officers did as they were told. Within seconds, the captain and his two senior officers were on their bellies, hands on their heads. The pirates searched their pockets and relieved the men of radios, keys, and cell phones. Sadiq took a .45-caliber Colt semiautomatic from the captain and tucked the bulky pistol under his belt.

Osman was bewildered by the consoles covered in gauges and levers. Dials and knobs were crowded together, and despite his facility with spoken English, he found it difficult to make sense of the controls on large ships such as the *Barataria*.

Sadiq seemed to sense Osman's quiet dismay. "What's wrong?"

"Nothing. I just—" Gunfire from the main deck cut him off. He rushed forward and looked out the window. Half a dozen men armed with sophisticated assault weapons and body armor had emerged from belowdecks and were engaging the teams Osman had sent to secure the crew. He turned toward Sadiq and pointed aft, toward the door. "Make sure they don't come in behind us! And dump them overboard when you're done."

Moving in fast strides, Sadiq snapped orders on his way out the door. "Khaled! Samir! Stay here with Osman! Everyone else, with me!" He led the other gunmen from the lead skiff out of the pilothouse, out onto the superstructure.

Alone with the ship's senior officers and only two of his men, Osman decided not to take any chances. "Samir, bind them. Khaled, cover them while Samir ties their hands and feet."

His men worked quickly, trussing the white officers as if they were goats primed for the fire. As soon as Osman was sure the situation was under control, he returned to the window and crouched to look over its edge, careful not to make himself a target for any stray bursts that might come toward the superstructure.

Muzzle flashes blazed in the darkness as Sadiq and the rest of the first team rained bullets down on the gunrunners. Blood spattered across the main deck as the mercenaries fell. The metal decks and bulkheads of the superstructure rang with bright ricochets from the mercenaries' wild attempts to return fire at opponents they couldn't see.

From his vantage point in the pilothouse, Osman watched the mercs group themselves into a tight huddle between a ventilator block and the heavy-lift crane. It wasn't a bad position for a defensive stand, at least in the short term. It would protect them from getting snared in a cross fire, and it would bottleneck any incoming assaults.

But only if the people attacking them don't know any better.

Osman fished the radio from his pocket and thumbed the talk switch. "Ahmed? It's Osman. Do you hear me?"

The starboard-side team leader answered in a hoarse whisper. "*What do you want?*"

"Listen to me. The gunmen on the main deck. They took cover ahead of you, between the crane and the ventilator block. Do you still carry that stun grenade you found?"

"*I understand. Hang on.*"

A few seconds later, Osman watched Ahmed lean around a corner and lob the grenade toward the crane. Next came a blinding flash and a deep boom. In the seconds of smoky confusion that followed, Ahmed and his team charged from cover and descended on the cornered mercenaries, firing on full automatic until they were sure the last of the gunrunners was dead.

"Good job, Ahmed. Main deck looks secure. Round up the prisoners as planned."

"*Okay, Osman.*"

He turned toward Samir and Khaled and pointed at the captain. "Get him up." His men lifted the gaunt middle-aged white man off the deck and propped him up in front of Osman, who studied him with contempt. "What is your name?"

His accent was unmistakably German. "Captain Markus Rohde."

Osman aimed his pistol at the head of one of the junior officers lying on the deck. "And who is in command of this ship, Mr. Rohde?"

The older man conceded Osman's point without argument. "You are."

"I am glad we understand each other." He kept his pistol trained on Rohde as he barked at his men, "Take them down to the main deck and put them with the others!"

Samir and Khaled ushered the ship's three officers out of the pilothouse at gunpoint and marched them down the outer stairs of the superstructure. Once they were gone, Osman looked out the windows and shuddered with anticipation of how rich he was going to be come daybreak.

By the time anyone knows this ship has been taken, I will be on the other side of the world, with a new name, a new life, and more money than I can ever spend.

• • •

Tightly wound bare copper wire bit into Trent's wrists. He resisted the urge to struggle against his bonds; doing so only forced the wire deeper into his flesh, and his palms were already sticky with his own half-dried blood. He and the crew of the *Barataria* sat in a tight cluster atop the forecastle, their backs to the bulwark. They all had been searched and stripped of weapons, radios, and phones. The pirates kept the weapons; the rest they'd pitched into the sea.

None of Trent's men, who had been separate from the ship's crew, survived the initial attack. Two pairs of pirates busied themselves heaving corpses overboard. Trent took a small measure of satisfaction from the fact that a few of the bodies being dumped were part of the pirates' contingent. *At least my men didn't go down without a fight.*

A lone pirate with an AK-47 slung behind his back climbed the port-side stairs from the main deck and joined the rest of his men. He shouted in Arabic at one of his comrades, who yelled curt answers in reply. Trent's Arabic was rusty, but he understood enough to realize the first man had asked whether the prisoners were secure, and the second man, the one with the dramatic facial scars, had assured him they were.

The one in command put himself in front of the ship's captain. "The ship is drifting."

Captain Rohde turned his weary gaze up at the pirate. "So?"

"Tell me which of your crew are qualified to drop the anchor."

Rohde let slip a derisive snort. "Are you stupid? You can't drop anchor here."

The second, scarred pirate reached for a pistol tucked into his waistband. "Why not?"

"Because anchors are meant to be used in water less than a hundred meters deep. We're in open ocean, you fools." He looked at the two pirates, who didn't seem to comprehend the simple words he was telling them. "There's nearly *fourteen hundred* meters of water beneath us. Drop an anchor here, and you'll just lose it to the sea."

They received his bad news with pained grimaces and rolling eyes. The pirate in charge struggled to rein in his temper. "How do we stop the boat from drifting?"

"Put me and my crew back at our posts. We can run the engines dead slow and set the rudder to hold our position against the current."

The leader refused with an adamant shake of his head. "No. You tell us how."

"I can't teach you twenty years of nautical experience in one chat at gunpoint."

Scarface pulled the pirate leader aside. The two Somalis traded angry whispers that Trent strained to hear. The leader didn't want to back down, but his second-in-command urged him to forget about the ship's drift. Scarface tapped the face of his battered wristwatch, the universal sign for *We're on a schedule*.

The leader frowned and breathed an angry sigh. He turned back toward Rohde. "These men around you. They are all of your crew, yes? Anyone missing?"

"No. All my men are accounted for."

An accusatory finger pointed at Trent. "Any more of *his* men?"

Rohde tried to play dumb. "What do you mean?"

"Rask's men."

Scarface tilted his head at the last of the bodies going over the side. "The gunrunners."

Sickening dread snaked through Trent's gut. There was no reason mere pirates should know Mr. Rask's name—and if they did, and knew who he was, they shouldn't have been brash enough to risk killing his employees or stealing his property. What was going on?

Scarface waved his gun at Trent as he told the leader, "We should kill this one, Osman."

"Not yet. We still need him." Osman squatted in front of Trent, drew the .45 from his belt, and pointed it between Trent's legs. "Now I ask you: Any more of *your* men aboard?"

"No. You just sent the last one down to Davy Jones's locker." Osman fixed his stare on Trent's eyes, as if searching for a glimmer of untruth. Trent kept his poker face slack and steady. *Technically, I told him the truth. Bauer's not one of my men—he only pretended to be.*

Apparently satisfied, Osman smirked and put away his pistol. "Tomorrow, I will be a rich man. Do what I tell you, and you will live to see my words come true. Cross me, and you will join the rest of your men."

Osman stood and issued a fast string of orders in Arabic. Trent caught that Scarface's name was Sadiq, and that he was to leave a team of six men to guard the prisoners and lead the rest of their team below to arm up from the ship's inventory. As soon as Osman finished giving orders, he descended the port stairs and stalked aft with a troop of four men close behind him.

Captain Rohde leaned a few inches closer to Trent and muttered while trying not to move his lips, "What are we going to do now?"

"Stay still, and be quiet," Trent whispered back, "until I tell you otherwise."

There was no reason for Trent to think that Bauer was his friend, but the renegade American agent was now the only hope he and the *Barataria*'s crew had of living through the night. Because regardless of Osman's promises, if these men conducted themselves the way most Somali pirates did, neither Trent nor the ship's crew could expect to see another dawn.

• • •

Jack swam below the surface, following the waterline of the *Barataria*. Every few strokes, he came up just enough to exhale and draw another breath, then submerged again and kept swimming. The ship had come to a near total halt in the water, but the current was pushing it backwards at a fraction of a knot. That had added some time and distance to the hundred-meter swim back to the accommodation ladder, which had been left down by the pirates.

He climbed onto the ladder's bottom platform, taking care to move as quietly as he could. There was a lot of commotion up on deck, more than enough noise to muffle the drizzling of water running off his clothes, but he knew not to take unnecessary risks. He squeezed the excess water from his hair, then took off his linen shirt and wrung it until it ceased to give water. Pressing his palms against his legs, he forced most of the moisture from his pants.

His first step up the ladder produced a squishing noise from his sneaker.

Damn it.

He knew of no way to wring out Nikes. Mumbling profanities, he kicked off his low-tops and set them adrift. He regretted the loss of foot protection, but he couldn't risk the damage the waterlogged shoes would have done to his ability to move stealthily with speed. He peeled off his socks and cast them into the gulf, then started back up the ladder.

Barefoot, unarmed, and soaking wet, Jack padded up the steel steps. He dropped to a crouch as he neared the top. Pirates moved about the main deck in pairs or groups of three. Most of them were armed with AK-47 assault rifles, but several also carried semiautomatic pistols, and a few wore bandoliers festooned with grenades.

To his relief, they had posted no guards near the accommodation ladder. He guessed they hadn't considered the possibility that anyone other than them might use it to reach the main deck. He watched the nearest pair of pirates until they turned away and moved forward. Then he slipped onto the main deck and darted into the shadows along the superstructure. He checked the starboard side hatch. It was unlocked. He nudged it open and listened.

From below came echoing footsteps, shouting voices, bursts of rifle fire.

The pirates must be rounding up the engine room crew, Jack realized. *I can't risk moving belowdecks until they bring the engineers topside.*

He slipped through the door and eased it shut at his back. Taking the stairs with slow, exaggerated care, he climbed to Level 01, where his shared cabin was located. He paused at the door and checked through its window to make sure no one was lurking on the other side. Confident the corridor was clear, he turned the door's latch by slow degrees, then opened it just wide enough to slip inside and guide it to a soft close behind him.

Now it was time to move quickly. He jogged to his cabin and went directly for his rack. He lifted the mattress and its platform to get at his clean clothes, making sure to pull the darkest items he could find—black jeans, a dark gray T-shirt, black socks and underwear. He tossed them on the bunk beneath his, then stripped off his wet clothes and hid them under his mattress. *Can't have one of the pirates finding my wet clothes and sounding an alarm.*

In less than a minute, he was dressed in dry clothes. Recalling that his cabinmate, an Israeli engineer named Yiram, wore the same size shoes that he did, Jack checked under the man's mattress platform and found a spare pair of rubber-soled black work boots. He sat down and put them on, knotting the laces as quickly as he could.

There were just a few more things Jack needed.

He went back to the space beneath his own mattress, shoved aside his dirty laundry, and uncovered what had been his best friend for the last nineteen months: a nine-millimeter SIG Sauer P229. He kept a full 13-round magazine in the weapon and three spares loaded and ready. He pulled back the slide, chambered a round, then tucked the SIG in its holster and secured it on his right hip. He took his shoulder duffel from atop the bed and loaded it with the spare magazines, four boxes of jacketed subsonic hollow-point rounds designed to inflict maximum damage on soft targets, and the pistol's suppressor.

For good measure, he grabbed a leather fold packed with lock-picking tools—torsion wrenches, rakes, hooks, and assorted other tools of the trade—and tucked it into his back pocket. Last but not least, he retrieved a flat-black KA-BAR knife with a partially serrated edge and secured it, in its sheath, on his left hip.

That would be enough, he hoped, to get him belowdecks, where more serious armaments were stored in shipping containers bound for Karl Rask's various international clients. He slung his duffel behind his back, drew his SIG, and slipped into the corridor. The pirates had rounded up the ship's entire crew on the main deck.

Time to call in the cavalry. He crept upstairs toward the command level.

Jack suspected it was no accident the pirates had targeted this ship for hijacking, but he was determined to make sure it proved to be a mistake—one they wouldn't live to regret.

Forge

Award-winning authors
Compelling stories

· ·

Please join us at the website
below for more information
about this author and other great
Forge selections, and to sign up for
our monthly newsletter!

· · · · **www.tor-forge.com** · · · ·